Praise for DOUBLE BLIND, the sequel to THE AURA by Carrie Bedford

"*Double Blind* is a cozy mystery with intense characters who struggle in a world of pharmaceutical intrigue with political twists. Author Carrie Bedford writes with a high suspenseful flair and creates an engaging protagonist, Kate Benedict. Paranormal elements mix with murders, kidnappings, and a dash of romance, all racing through an unusual and satisfying plot. A fast read, well-written, and thoroughly enjoyable." — *Paula Cappa, author of The Dazzling Darkness*

Praise for THE AURA, the first Kate Benedict Paranormal Mystery by Carrie Bedford

"Carrie Bedford is a real find... *The Aura* is an engaging paranormal suspense story whose heroine is smart, strong, and almost overwhelmed when she is suddenly able to see that someone— friend, family or stranger— is about to die. Bedford is a fine writer, an accomplished novelist, and a terrific storyteller whose characters ring true and pull us deep into the mystery." — *Shelley Singer, author of the Jake Samson-Rosie Vicente mystery series*

"... a terrific book with a likable protagonist, skilled plotting, and a supernatural spin. This gripping mystery had me hooked from the first chapter. " — *Janet Dawson, author of the Jeri Howard series*

THE SCOTTISH CONNECTION

A KATE BENEDICT PARANORMAL MYSTERY

CARRIE BEDFORD

booksBnimble Publishing
New Orleans, La.

The Scottish Connection

eBook ISBN: 978-0-9973630-8-1

Print ISBN-13: 978-0-9998131-1-9

www.booksbnimble.com

First booksBnimble electronic publication: January 2018

For James, Madeleine and Charlotte
With Love

1

The fog that delayed our flight into Glasgow airport swirled around the rental car, limiting visibility to only a few yards. After two hours of driving north on increasingly narrow and winding roads, my tense muscles relaxed when Josh pulled up to a set of massive wrought iron gates. He pressed a code into a keypad and the gates swung open, revealing a red gravel driveway that curved away into the mist. I caught glimpses of lawns, fountains and topiaries and then, suddenly, the castle loomed over us, grey and forbidding. Josh stopped the car at the base of a three-story crenellated tower, which was constructed of rough stone blocks, mottled with yellow lichen.

I got out of the car, shivering in my skinny cardigan while we gathered our bags from the boot. Josh took off his jacket and draped it over my shoulders, tactful enough not to mention he'd warned me that autumn in Scotland could feel like winter in London. We rolled the cases towards the entry, the sound of the wheels on the loose gravel muffled by the fog. As we climbed the short flight of limestone steps, I noticed that the black paint on the massive front door was peeling in places. Above the entry was a stone carving. Worn by rain and wind, the edges of the shield had crumbled. In the center, an image of a hand gripping a sword had become softened and indistinct.

Before we could ring the bell, the door opened, revealing a middle-aged woman in a sensible tweed skirt and heavy wool sweater.

Josh dropped his case and threw his arms around her. "Mrs. Dunsmore, it's good to see you."

"Master Josh, welcome back. It's been far too long since your last visit." She released him and smiled at me. "Ye must be Kate." She had a broad Scottish accent that I barely understood. "What a beauty ye are." I felt my cheeks flush, but she carried on. "Goodness, Josh, ye've grown another three inches, I swear. Come in, come in."

She waved us into an immense entry hall. Dark wood paneling covered the walls and a vaulted ceiling soared high above a black and white tiled floor. An oak bench, like an old church pew, ran along one wall, facing a marble fireplace on the opposite side. Above the mantel, several stag heads mounted on shields peered down at us with round, glassy eyes.

"I've put tea on and the chief is waiting for you." She leaned forward towards us. "Before you see him, I should warn you he's been a wee bit stressed recently." She lowered her voice to a whisper. "With everything that's happening."

"What's going on?" Josh asked.

"Och, he'll tell you himself. It's not my place."

Before Josh could respond, she went on. "Kate, I've put you in the blue bedroom in the tower." She smiled at me. "There are lovely views from the windows there, across the valley towards the loch. Josh will be right next door in the green room. I'll call for Lachlan to bring up your cases if you leave them here."

"We can take them up, Mrs. Dunsmore," Josh said. "There's no need to bother Lachlan. I know my way around. We'll freshen up and find some warmer clothes for Kate." He winked at me. "And then we'll come straight back for tea."

"I'll take the tray to your uncle's office then. You can join him there when you're ready."

She hurried away, and Josh picked up my case. "It's a bit of a trek," he said. "The quickest way is along the portrait gallery that connects the tower to the main house."

"Okay then. Lead on, Macduff."

He laughed. "You know that's not the correct version of the quote." He paused at the bottom of the wide staircase, where a faded red carpet softened the dark wooden treads. "It's actually 'Lay on, Macduff, and damned be him who first cries 'Hold! Enough!' ' "

"And then Macduff kills Macbeth."

"Yep, he cuts off his head."

"You're a bloodthirsty lot, you Scots," I teased, running my hand up the polished wood banister. The stairs brought us to a wide landing and, to the left, the gallery, aptly named for the scores of gilt-framed pictures hung along its walls.

"I won't bore you with the family history now," Josh said, "but many of these portraits are of ancestors of mine. This castle's been in our family for over three hundred years."

I glanced at the oil paintings as we walked, our steps muffled by the teal carpet that unfolded like a river in front of us. Old men with beards, bejeweled ladies in elaborate gowns, young men in uniform with rifles propped against their shoulders, little girls in pastel silks and boys in sailor suits; the array was stunning, like walking through a wing of London's National Portrait Gallery.

"What's all this?" I stopped in front of a glass case, filled with ornate swords displayed on racks. Some of the hilts were decorated with gold and silver and one gleamed with inlaid gems.

"My great-grandfather put that together. He was quite a collector of weapons, books, and paintings. Apparently, he had a good eye and made some canny purchases over the years. I'll show you his library later."

The carpeted picture gallery led to a square, travertine landing. To my right, a spiral staircase wound upwards. To the left, another stairway curved down. "The tower was redesigned internally in the eighteenth century," Josh said. "There are six bedrooms downstairs and six up. We're going up to the top floor, right below the ramparts."

I looked at the two stairways and then back to the gallery. "How on earth do you know where you are? This place is huge."

"Yes, but I spent a lot of time here when I was little. It was a kid's paradise, running around and hiding in these corridors. There are so many rooms that many are never used."

"You'd better let me carry my own bag," I offered, after watching his first attempt to juggle both cases up the tightly-spiraled stairs. Even with one, it was a challenge, and I was glad to reach the top and wide hallway with a red, tiled floor. Josh pushed open one of a half dozen dark wood doors. "Your room, ma'am," he said with an extravagant sweep of his hand.

Inside, a four-poster bed draped with dark blue curtains stood against one wall. Heavy wood dressers and a massive armoire provided far more storage than my one carry-on held, and a red Persian carpet covered most of the uneven oak plank flooring. Threadbare blue curtains hung on either side of limestone-framed windows with thin, wavy glass, hazy with old age. The view Mrs. Dunsmore had promised was currently lost in the mist.

Josh left to put his case in his room. I thought it was quaint that we were to be separated even though we shared an apartment in London. Knowing Josh, though, only his suitcase would spend the night next door.

I shivered, cold in spite of a cast-iron radiator hissing and clanking under the window. The chill of hundreds of years of fog, rain, wind and snow was enmeshed in the walls, seeping up through the floor. Despite the lingering damp, I was entranced. I was staying in a medieval tower where soldiers had fended off the armies of their enemies, where noblemen and ladies had lived and slept. History swirled like smoke through the wooden beams in the high ceiling. I was disappointed when Josh came back in and clicked on a table lamp— candles would have been the perfect way to illuminate this ancient room. I was so glad now that we'd decided to take two days off work for our trip. It was Thursday, and we didn't need to leave until Sunday, which meant I had plenty of time to explore the castle and the grounds.

"So, what's bothering your uncle?" I asked as I dug in my case for something more appropriate to the Scottish weather. All week, London had basked in the heat of a late Indian summer and, even at the crack of dawn this morning when we'd left Heathrow, there had been a hint of warmth in the air.

Josh's brow creased. "I'm not sure. He didn't mention anything when I talked to him last week. I hope he's not ill."

We were here for Fergus's sixty-fifth birthday celebration, a party to be held on Saturday night. Apparently, many friends and family members were coming. I'd never met Fergus, but I knew that Josh and his uncle had always been very close.

"Well, let's go find out," I suggested, shrugging on a long, grey cashmere cardigan and wrapping a matching silk scarf around my neck. Warm, but still presentable, I thought. We retraced our steps down to the travertine-paved landing and along the portrait gallery. After crossing the landing at the top of the grand staircase, we turned into another long corridor with deep green walls.

A man emerged through a door at the end and hurried towards us, his heavy leather brogues hammering on the floor. "Josh, my boy!" he yelled. "It's good to see you!"

I stopped in mid-stride, horrified.

I knew, from Josh's description of him, that this was Uncle Fergus. He was tall and wide-shouldered with cropped silver hair that stuck up in spikes.

But, above that hair, an aura hovered. The sight of it was like a kick to the stomach. Mrs. Dunsmore had intimated that something was wrong, but I hadn't expected it to be anything life-threatening.

I had no time to think before Fergus reached us and enveloped Josh in a bear hug. Although my boyfriend was tall, Fergus towered over him, and his hands on Josh's back were massive. He finally stepped away and shook my hand. "It's a pleasure to meet you, Kate." He had a faint Scottish accent, more like Josh's than Mrs. Dunsmore's. I remembered Josh saying his uncle had worked in Oxford until he inherited the estate ten years ago. I'd hoped for a kilt, but Fergus wore a heavy Shetland sweater and brown cord trousers tucked into thick woolen socks.

"Pleased to meet you, Mr. MacKenna," I said.

"Call me Fergus. That's what the boys call me. I've never been one for formalities and being called 'uncle' makes me feel old. Now, come with me. Mrs. Dunsmore has made her famous scones."

Soon we were settled in his office, which was in fact a comfortable den with wood paneling and tartan-covered sofas pulled up close to a log fire. What I first thought was a shaggy grey rug suddenly moved, and I realized it was a huge dog. Josh bent over and cupped its face in his hands, stroking the animal's white beard. "Arbroath, you old mutt," he murmured. "How are you doing, boy?"

"Arbroath is a Scottish deerhound," Fergus told me as I patted the dog's coarse slate-colored coat and tried to avoid its long pink tongue.

On the coffee table, a silver tray held fine china cups and platters of scones and smoked salmon sandwiches cut into delicate triangles. Fergus picked up the teapot. "I'll be mother, shall I?"

While Josh brought his uncle up to date on family news, I tuned out, contemplating that aura and what it meant. Nothing good, that was certain. When I saw that halo of moving air swirling over someone's head, it meant that death could come soon, within a week or two at the most, unless I did something to avert it. Josh would be devastated when I told him.

I focused again on the conversation, wondering if I could pick up any clues to the nature of the threat to Fergus's life. Bad health seemed the most likely, yet he appeared to be strong and hearty.

"I thought we'd give Kate a tour of the house once we've had our tea," Fergus said. He turned his blue eyes on me. "If you'd like that? Josh told me you're a history lover and a connoisseur of old buildings."

"I love looking at period architecture," I replied. "But I'm just an amateur admirer and certainly no expert."

"She's being modest," Josh said. "Her knowledge far surpasses mine."

The two of us worked for an architectural firm in London. We'd joined at the same time four years ago, but Josh had made junior partner already, and he deserved it. My own career, however, had nearly come off the rails a couple of times since I'd started seeing the auras. They had proved to be a major distraction. My attempts to save people consumed both time and energy, and I'd taken more time off work than I should. My dad thought that my efforts to thwart death had become something of an obsession. I thought of it as a responsibility. Still, so far, I'd managed to hang on to my job and I intended to keep it that way.

Mrs. Dunsmore's scones were delicious. I was on my second one when Fergus drained the last of his tea and stood. "Shall we go? I thought we'd start with the south wing and work our way back here."

"Before we head off, I have a question," Josh said. "Mrs. Dunsmore mentioned you've been worrying about something, but she wouldn't say what it is. What's going on?"

Fergus raised his thick white brows. "She said that, did she?" he asked with a grin. "Well, you know my housekeeper. She's easily agitated and quick to assume the worst. Now, let's go show Kate the place."

Josh flicked a glance at me and shrugged. I was sure Mrs. Dunsmore wasn't imagining things. Fergus's aura provided ample evidence that something was amiss. Perhaps we could coax more out of him as we toured the castle. I needed to tell Josh about the aura, but that would have to wait until later, when we were alone.

Away from the warmth of the fire, the corridor felt even colder than before, and I was glad of my cozy cardigan.

"Our ancestor bought the castle in the early 1700s," Fergus said. "He was a Scot by birth but he'd made his money as a sugar importer in Liverpool. He moved in here when he retired, first renovating the tower and the sixteenth-century hunting lodge and adding a mansion alongside. Subsequent generations expanded it further, so it's a bit of a dog's breakfast now, with its muddle of hallways and staircases. Still, it's a grand old building."

"It is," Josh agreed. "I love this place."

Fergus frowned, and I wondered what that meant, but he strode off, leading us along the green corridor, with the dog padding behind us. On the landing at the top of the grand staircase, he stopped and opened a set of double doors to reveal a room the size of a football pitch, with a high, vaulted ceiling and twenty-foot-tall arched windows.

"This is the Great Hall. When it's clear, you can see the gardens and Loch Awe in the distance."

Even though the mist still hung outside, the room was bright and cheerful, with creamy white walls rising to the ceiling where hand-sawn wood beams were decorated with painted medallions of red, blue and gold. Vases of yellow flowers sat on dressers and coffee tables, while comfortable chairs strewn with tartan throws hugged an imposing carved limestone fireplace. At the far end of the Hall, across a wide parquet floor with geometric inlays, was another matching fireplace and more seating. The symmetry of the room was perfect.

"It's stunning," I said, almost speechless with admiration. This was a marked contrast to the somber tones of the gallery and the tower bedrooms.

"It was the first room I refurbished," Fergus said. "When the sun shines, it's like heaven in here. My favorite place."

Mrs. Dunsmore appeared at the door just then. "I'm sorry to disturb you. If you don't mind vacating the Hall, sir, the volunteers are here to set up the tables and decorate for the party."

"No problem, Mrs. D.," he replied. He led us from the Hall, lengthening his stride so I had to almost trot to keep up. He slowed to a more sedate pace through the gallery, where he and Josh pointed out some of the characters in their family tree.

"That's Rannulph the Black," Fergus said. "A nasty piece of work, little more than a thug, although he called himself a warlord. He killed and pillaged for ten years before a rival clansman stabbed him to death." He glared at the portrait. "But here, this is my namesake." He jabbed a finger at a picture of a fierce man with a bristling mustache and a deep scar that ran from his left eye to his chin. "He fought and died for Bonnie Prince Charlie at the battle of Culloden in 1745." He sighed. "That was a terrible time for Scotland."

This review of his history seemed to be making Fergus so despondent that I thought we should move on. Josh had noticed too and suggested we take a look downstairs. "It's fun," he told me. "A rabbit warren of kitchens, sculleries, laundry rooms and wine cellars. The castle used to have a staff of fifty. Not any more, of course."

We descended to the grand entrance hall, crossing the black and white tile floor under the stags' fixed stare, to a narrow flight of stone stairs that wound down to the basement. Expecting a cramped, old-fashioned space with a spit turning in a fireplace, I was surprised to see an immense kitchen lined with stainless steel counters and state-of-the art cooktops and ovens. A young man in a chef's coat and blue trousers chopped vegetables on a massive butcher block island in the center.

Fergus introduced us and explained that Pierre was a classically-trained French chef.

Pierre wiped his hands on his jacket to shake hands with us. "*Enchanté*," he said.

"And where's Nick?" Fergus asked him.

"In the meat locker, arranging supplies for the party." The chef had a charming accent. "Shall I get him?"

"No, no. We don't want to disturb your preparations," Fergus replied. "We're having the trout for dinner tonight?"

Pierre nodded. "Fresh from the loch this morning."

Fergus rubbed his hands together. "Excellent. We'll get out of your way then." He took a step and then turned back. "How's it working out between you and Nick?"

Pierre gave an expressive Gallic shrug. "He does as I ask. He is polite. We get the job done."

"I see." Fergus hesitated as though intending to say more. Then he pressed his lips together and nodded.

"I didn't know you had a chef on staff," Josh said once we were out of earshot. "And who's Nick?"

"Nick's a local lad and a competent cook. He's been here for a year, so he wasn't happy when I brought in Pierre to run the kitchen. That was about four months ago. I thought things had settled but, obviously, I need to investigate further, to make sure Nick's doing all right. His father is a local farmer. Nice family, nice kid."

"So why do you need a French chef?" Josh asked.

"It's a money-making venture," Fergus said. "Gourmet dinners, cooking classes, that sort of thing. I'll tell you more about it later on."

"But—" Josh started, and Fergus held up his hand to stop him. "All in good time. Let's take a quick peek at the rest of the downstairs, and then you'll probably want to clean up before dinner?"

"I should take a shower and change," I agreed. It had been a long day since our early taxi ride to the airport— but what I really needed was time alone with Josh. I dreaded having to tell him about his uncle's aura.

"Then we'll meet in the living room for drinks in an hour or so," Fergus said.

"And perhaps then, you'll tell me what's worrying you," Josh said.

Fergus shook his head. "We'll enjoy dinner first. Your cousin Duncan is coming in late this evening. When he arrives, I need to talk to you both. There are serious matters to discuss, I'm afraid."

2

Back in my room, Josh sat and bounced on the four-poster bed. "Do you really need to shower? You look squeaky clean to me." He patted the mattress. "We've got time before drinks and dinner..." He wiggled his eyebrows, which made me smile, although only for a moment. I had to tell him about the aura.

"I don't need to shower. What I needed is some time to talk to you." Pulling at the sleeves of my cardigan, I lined up the cuffs to the exact same length. "I'm worried about Fergus. I don't know him, but he seems a little down. Is he usually like that?"

Josh leaned up against the pillows. "No. There's obviously a problem. If he'd just say what it is, I'm sure we'll be able to sort it out."

After kicking off my shoes, I sat on the bed, facing him. "There's something else." I said.

"What?" His eyes widened when he saw the expression on my face. "Please don't tell me—"

"Yes," I interrupted, wanting to get it over with as quickly as possible. "He has an aura."

Josh sat up straight and muttered a few expletives. I took his hand and squeezed it. "I'm sorry."

I was. Auras distressed me at any time, even more so now, with

Josh's beloved uncle as the victim. "What do you think?" I asked. "This serious talk he wants to have later— perhaps he's very ill? A health issue might be the reason for the aura."

"God, I hope not." Josh swung his legs over the edge of the bed and leaned his elbows on his knees, chin in hand. "This sucks."

I scooted over to sit close to him. "I know. But maybe we can make a difference."

For once, my boyfriend's habitual optimism seemed to have crumbled. "How? If he's ill, we can't make him better."

"We've saved people before," I reminded him. "We just have to identify the source of the danger, and then... who knows? I realize that if he is sick, we may not be able to do anything, but the threat may not be that. We have to try, at least."

I stood up and walked to the window, staring out at the grey fog that blanketed the landscape. It was like looking at an aura, inscrutable, revealing nothing. I pressed my forehead to the cold glass. I'd first started seeing auras three years ago and had learned that it was sometimes possible to change the fate of the victims. Occasionally, it was as simple as cancelling a trip or rushing to an Accident and Emergency. Once or twice I'd prevented a murder from taking place. With an intervention of some kind, the victim didn't die, and then the aura disappeared.

Of course, it didn't always work out that way. The muscles in my jaw clenched as I tried to suppress the memory of those I hadn't been able to save. But they were always there, lingering at the fringes of my consciousness, pale wraiths hiding in dark corners.

Behind me, Josh murmured to himself. I hurried over and wrapped my arm around his shoulders. When he turned his head to look at me, I put my fingers on his cheek and gazed into his troubled eyes, as light as blue-washed sea glass.

"You're sure?" he asked, but in a tone of resignation. He knew I was never wrong about auras. I'd never imagined seeing one that wasn't really there.

"I'm sorry, but yes."

"And how fast is it moving?"

I hesitated before answering, not wanting to make things worse than they already were. "Fast," I said finally.

"Damn." Josh buried his face in his hands. This thing I called an aura manifested as air swirling over someone's head, like air rippling over hot asphalt. The faster the air moved, the more imminent the danger. Fergus's aura was spiraling rapidly, which meant he might die within days.

We sat in silence. There wasn't much to say that would make Josh feel better. And I was wrestling with my own emotions. Anger, fear, anxiety— they all came bubbling up when I saw an aura over someone I knew. I'd learned through hard experience to ignore auras I saw over strangers on the street, on the Tube, in the supermarket. There's no way to walk up to a man you don't know and tell him he's going to die very soon. Even close friends and relatives often reacted badly to my revelations. My dad didn't want to discuss it at all. My friend, Anita, who was a doctor, had initially refused to listen to me, believing my visions were caused by a medical condition, probably in my brain. I'd even submitted to a battery of tests: MRIs, CT scans, bloodwork. Nothing unusual had showed up.

"See, I'm perfectly normal," I'd told her, with a laugh. She hadn't smiled back.

"I wish to God you couldn't see these wretched things," Josh said. It was unlike him to make that sort of negative comment, a sign of how worried he was for Fergus.

"Me too." I pulled one of his hands away from his face and gripped it firmly. "Believe me, if there was a way to stop them, I'd do it in a heartbeat. I wish I could roll back time. Things would be very different."

I wished almost every day for things to be different. I'd seen my first aura, as I called it, not long after my mother died, killed while crossing a road. I'd been texting her when it happened and I was convinced she would have seen the car coming if she hadn't been looking at her phone— at my message. Everyone told me it wasn't my fault, but I had a fast guilt trigger. My baby brother, Toby, had drowned in a pool where we were playing together. The burden of knowing I should have saved him had weighed heavily on me for the last twenty years.

Josh straightened his shoulders and looked at me. I could see that something had shifted inside him. "I'm sorry for reacting that way," he said. "The auras are a gift. We'll find out what we're up against and do whatever it takes to save Fergus."

I leaned into him, thankful as always for his steady strength and support. After a while, he gently pushed me away and stood. "Time to go find dinner. I'm hungry."

We ate in what Fergus called the breakfast room, where a table that seated ten was set for the three of us. Fergus kept the conversation light, talking about the way Pierre had prepared the trout, the Sancerre we drank with it, and plans for his birthday party. He told us that fifty guests were expected. "I haven't seen a few of them for years, not since I was working in Oxford, but most are locals. Josh will know some of them, like the Crays from over in Lochawe." He topped up my glass of wine. "I hope it won't be too boring for you, though. A bunch of old codgers reminiscing about better times, most likely. Half of them have at least a decade on me."

At that point, I caught sight of Josh staring at Fergus so intently I was sure his uncle would notice. Josh couldn't see the aura, of course. That privilege was mine alone, and I thought how unnerving it must be for him to have to take my word for it.

"We're bringing in some staff to help Pierre," Fergus said. "That will include waiters and some kitchen helpers. Pierre and I worked on the menu together, all based on local ingredients, trout, salmon and venison. Lachlan sourced the venison."

"You mean he shot a deer?" I asked.

Fergus smiled at my look of horror. "Aye, we have a deer stalking permit. We cull a few dozen roe deer each year."

"Do you shoot?" I asked.

"Naturally. I usually bring a few friends in, make it a party."

The thought of men running around the estate with guns gave me goosebumps. Was that the source of danger to Fergus? With the urgency of the aura on my mind, I touched Josh's leg under the table, nodding towards his uncle. This would be a good time to find out what was worrying him. Josh put his fork on his plate but, just as he opened his mouth to speak, lights flashed past the window and an engine revved.

Fergus raised an eyebrow. "That will be Duncan. Never walks if he can run and doesn't acknowledge that a car has any gear except fourth and up."

Car doors banged, and then I heard the rumble of suitcases being wheeled across the gravel driveway, the front door opening and a murmur of voices in the entry hall. A minute later, Josh's older cousin walked into the breakfast room.

In spite of their eight-year age gap, Duncan and Josh looked surprisingly alike, both tall and lean, with the same glossy brown hair. The only visible difference between the two was in the eyes. Duncan's were more grey than blue-green.

Josh jumped to his feet to embrace his cousin.

Duncan spoke with a lazy drawl that sounded put on. "It's been a long time. How are you, old man?"

Old man? Did anyone speak like that anymore? Duncan's turn of phrase matched his preppy outfit: tan suede loafers, khaki pants with a perfect crease, a striped shirt, and a navy blazer. "This is Lucy." He introduced the woman next to him. "We've been dating for what? Three months, Luce?"

Lucy nodded and gave us a shy smile. She was a little younger than Duncan, I guessed, maybe in her early thirties. Slim, with high cheekbones and perfectly-cut blonde hair that hung like silk to her shoulders, she wore a long skirt over leather boots. I didn't think Fergus had known that his nephew was bringing a girlfriend, but he kept smiling, made them both sit and poured them each a drink. They told him they'd eaten on the plane, which had been delayed for an hour. "It was almost too late to pick up our rental car," Duncan said. "We got a sports car, which was a waste of time. All that bloody fog slowed us down."

Lucy's wineglass shook when she lifted it to her mouth. I imagined a hair-raising ride, speeding along country lanes in the dark and the mist. No wonder she seemed anxious. At least Josh was a careful driver, and we'd arrived in daylight. While the three men chatted, I tried to make small talk with her. "Are you in finance as well?" I asked. I knew that Duncan worked in the City, doing something with hedge funds.

She shook her head. "No, I'm a professor at King's College, London, medieval history."

"Oh, how perfect," I exclaimed. "You'll love it here then. The castle tower was originally built in the 1200s. It's been repaired and expanded a few times, apparently, but it's mostly original."

Lucy nodded. "I can't wait to explore the place. Duncan hasn't told me much about it. He's always so busy. But I read up on it a bit before coming up here."

We chatted for a few minutes about our respective jobs. I kept my eyes on Lucy's face or on my glass, avoiding the sight of the aura moving over Fergus.

"I suggest we go to the library and sample my single malt collection," he said, getting to his feet. "We will be more comfortable there."

The library was upstairs, occupying a large space, with triple-arched windows at one end, and floor-to-ceiling shelves filled with leather-bound volumes. Two battered brown leather sofas, flanking a fireplace that glowed softly, faced each other across a coffee table strewn with more books.

"Let me introduce you to the drinks cupboard first," Fergus said. We followed him into a small room off to one side of the library. It was lined with mirrored shelves. On them stood scores of bottles in different shapes and sizes, many full and some half-empty. Their contents gleamed in myriad shades of amber, honey, and caramel. It was an impressive collection. My drinks cupboard at home consisted of a bottle of cooking sherry and a half-drunk bottle of Limoncello, stored in the back of the spice cabinet.

"Choose any one you want." Fergus passed each of us a crystal tumbler. I had no idea and selected the same Macallan as Josh.

Duncan opted for a thirty-seven-year-old Lagavulin, and Lucy nodded. "I'll have that too then."

Fergus laughed. "I'll have the same. You've got good taste, laddie. That's a three-thousand-pound bottle of scotch."

Lucy looked mortified. "Oh, no," she said. "Give me something generic. I can't tell the difference."

Fergus poured her a generous measure of the costly Lagavulin anyway. "My father bought this one. In fact, he acquired most of these bottles. He was quite the connoisseur."

Once we all had drinks, we settled on the sofas, sinking into the time-softened cushions. The fire cast ruddy shadows on our faces, and I was glad of the low light. It made it harder to see Fergus's aura.

"A toast," Duncan said. "To Uncle Fergus."

We raised our glasses, and I took a sip of my drink. It was smooth and smoky and felt warm in my throat.

"Thank you for coming," Fergus said. "We're going to enjoy my birthday party on Saturday, but first, I need to talk to you two about the estate." He pointed with his glass at Josh and Duncan.

Lucy and I looked at each other. "Do you want us to leave?" I asked Fergus. "We'd be happy to entertain ourselves for a while." Secretly, I hoped we could stay. I wanted to find out what might be threatening Fergus.

"Heavens, no. Stay right where you are. You may as well listen to it all."

Josh shifted, crossing and uncrossing his legs, looking anxious, obviously dreading what we might hear. I leaned forward, wondering if Fergus's revelation would cast light on the presence of that aura.

"I won't beat about the bush," Fergus began. "The estate is in trouble. It costs nearly a quarter of a million pounds a year to maintain the buildings, pay the utilities and taxes, and employ a bare-bones staff to keep the house and land under control. Last year alone, we had two major plumbing problems, which cost a small fortune to fix. Then we discovered that part of the roof on the main building is rotting away, so I took out a loan to repair it. Another loan, that is. I already have one outstanding. But we can't match the original roof tiles, so the historical society is insisting that we replace the whole damn thing."

"Why didn't you come to me?" Duncan asked, straightening up and staring at his uncle. "What kind of loan? What's the interest rate?"

Fergus held up his hand, palm out. "Let me finish." He swallowed a mouthful of whisky and leaned back against the sofa. "I'm trying out a few things to bring in extra income. I hired a chef to put on gourmet dinners on Saturday nights..."

"And is that working?" Duncan asked.

"It's helping. We rent out a few bedrooms on a B&B basis, and we're planning to turn the old Garden Cottage into a holiday rental. We're leasing out our grouse-shooting rights, and that does make good money. But not enough to repay the loans."

I thought about what Fergus was saying. The stress of running the estate might account for his aura. He might be ill, heading for a heart attack perhaps.

"I'll show you the books if you like," Fergus continued. "Duncan, you'll want to take a look as you're the heir to this sorry mess."

Duncan's expression was hard to read, but I guessed he was shocked. He sat rigid in his seat, gazing at Fergus without blinking.

"When your father died," Fergus said to him. "I told him I'd look after you, and I will."

When Duncan didn't respond, Josh leaned over to pat Fergus on the arm. "You're only sixty-five, minus a couple of days. It's far too soon to be thinking of passing on the estate. You've got plenty of years to go yet." He flicked a glance at me, and I bent my head over my glass. I didn't want Fergus to see the tears in my eyes.

"That's the thing," Fergus said. "There will be no property to pass on. I'm going to sell it."

3

When Fergus stopped talking, no one spoke. In the silence, the fire crackled and spat. Lucy looked from Fergus to Duncan and back. Josh gazed at me, his eyebrows raised.

"Sell the estate to whom?" Duncan asked eventually.

"And what happens to you?" Josh asked. "Where will you go?"

Fergus settled deeper in the sofa and swirled the remainder of the scotch in his glass. "There's an interested buyer," he said. "An American entrepreneur who works in Silicon Valley. He started up a technology company making an app of some kind, and he's worth a fortune. His name's Stanton Knox." Fergus grunted. "He claims to be a descendant of John Knox, the Protestant reformer. He was a revolutionary and a misogynist if you take the dark view of him, but a courageous and enlightened founder of the Presbyterian church in Scotland if you don't. I dare say young Stanton prefers the more complimentary version of his ancestor." He sipped his whisky. "Anyway, I've done my research, and Knox definitely has the funds to buy the estate. He says he's looked at several other properties in Scotland, but is attracted to this one because of its location, the private loch, and access to the river."

"He's already seen the estate?" Duncan asked.

"Yes, he visited last month for a couple of days."

"What's he like?"

"Well, he's young and cocky. Apparently, he has quite a reputation. They say he's always right about everything."

"Is he going to move here permanently?"

"I doubt it. He owns property in Montana and Hawaii and has a sizeable estate near San Francisco. He'll probably just visit here once a year or so."

Duncan put his glass on the coffee table. Whether he intended to or not, he slapped it down hard and some of the precious single malt slopped over the side, spreading a circle of droplets that glowed red in the light from the fire.

"Has he made an offer?" he demanded.

"Duncan, give Fergus time to tell us the whole story," Josh remonstrated. "We'll get to the details in due course."

Fergus nodded. "You'll know everything I know before we're done here tonight. Knox will arrive tomorrow morning to discuss the contract—"

"Contract?" Duncan shot forward in his seat. "What contract? You haven't signed anything, have you?"

Fergus patted the air as though trying to calm his older nephew. "No, nothing yet. We've drawn up an agreement in principle but, as you can imagine, there are many, many issues to be considered. Beyond the physical property of the castle and the gardens, we own two farms on the estate, both leased under the 1991 Tenancy Act, which would preserve the tenants' rights to farm that land. We have another three tenants with sheep-grazing rights on the grouse moors. Knox's lawyer has indicated that his client wants to convert these leases to Limited Duration Tenancies, but I'm not happy about that. Knox should continue their leases. They're all very experienced farmers and they know how to take care of the land. So that will be a major issue on the agenda tomorrow. I've got a good solicitor, Robert Dunne. He specializes in estates and trusts, and I'm getting solid advice from him on how to structure the contract."

"And the income from the farms isn't enough to maintain the property?" Duncan asked.

"I wish it were. It goes some way to mitigating the costs, but there's still a gulf between those revenues and our outgoings. We had to pay significant death duties when your father died, which put us into debt we've never recovered from." Fergus pushed his white hair back from his forehead. "I want you to know I've tried everything possible to generate new income."

His eyes glittered with unshed tears. The combination of that ill-concealed emotion and the presence of the aura made my heart clench. We had to find a way to help him.

"As I said earlier," Fergus continued, "I started the gourmet dinner program, and began renting out a few rooms on weekend nights. I brought in a second manager to work with Lachlan on organizing fishing expeditions and hiking trips." Fergus trailed off and sighed deeply. "It brings in a little money, but not enough, especially now with the loans to pay off."

He finished his scotch and stood up. "Anyone else for more?"

Duncan held out his glass, and his uncle took it into the drinks cupboard. I contemplated the value of all those single malts and of the picture gallery upstairs, as well as the rooms full of furniture and antiques. From an outsider's perspective, the castle looked affluent enough, even though it was a little rundown and shabby in places.

I wondered if Duncan would ask about the contents of the castle. He was whispering with Lucy. I couldn't hear their words, but Duncan looked furious, and Lucy's cheeks were pink.

When Fergus came back with the replenished glasses, he must have noticed Duncan's expression. "I'm sure you must be distressed, and very probably angry," he said as he handed him his drink. "You're not the only one. As you'd expect, there are plenty of people here who are outraged over my decision to sell, especially to a wealthy American who won't run it the way it's been run in the past. There have been threats."

"What kind of threats?" I asked, pouncing on a possible lead to the source of the danger to him.

Fergus waved a hand around. "Nothing that bothers me. It's understandable that the staff and tenants feel insecure and uncertain about their future here. I won't be able to address their fears until I speak with Knox tomorrow. It's my belief that he will keep on Mrs. Dunsmore and Lachlan at the very least, and that's what I will recommend to him. He will need reliable, knowledgeable people here to care for the place in his absence."

"When will the sale go through?" Duncan asked.

"Soon, I hope. The repayment on the first loan is past due. Assuming we come to an agreement this weekend, Knox would present a formal offer in the next week or two, and the sale would close four to six weeks after that."

"Bloody hell," Duncan muttered and took a long swallow of his drink.

"Have you told my mum?" Josh asked. She was Fergus's younger sister and had been planning to join us for his birthday party this weekend, but had fractured a bone in her foot and wasn't able to travel. We'd promised to send her lots of photos of the festivities.

"Not yet," Fergus said. "I didn't want to bother her while she's recuperating from her fall."

Duncan got to his feet and stood with his back to the fire. It irritated me that he was blocking all the warmth. Lucy had shrunk into a corner of the pillowy sofa, gripping her glass but not drinking. She seemed to be very nervous around Duncan, and I didn't blame her. He seemed to be having trouble keeping his temper under control. I'd be nervous around him, too.

"What about the assets?" Duncan asked, as I'd expected he would. "The silverware, the china, the paintings? If you sold all of that, it must add up to something?"

Fergus nodded. "Yes, but not as much as you'd think. None of the pictures are masterpieces, much as I cherish them. We could sell everything, maybe make enough to pay off the loan. But there will always be more repairs on a structure this old. I don't want to strip this place of its history and live in a leaky, dilapidated building, and I'm sure you won't want that either."

"The library then." Duncan pointed to the bookshelves. "Most of the books are valuable, first editions and the like. Or there's the sword collection. You could sell that instead of letting it sit gathering dust. Are you quite sure you've thought of all the possibilities?"

"Sit down, Duncan," Josh said. "This isn't—"

He was interrupted by a cry from Lucy. "Oh, I'm sorry. I spilled my drink over your sofa." She jumped to her feet. "I'll go find a cloth and clean it up."

"Nonsense," Fergus said. "It'll do no harm. I couldn't tell you how many gallons of wine and whisky have rained down on the castle's furniture and rugs over the years, but I guarantee it's a lot. So don't fuss. I'll let Mrs. Dunsmore know and she'll take after it later on."

Duncan went back to the sofa, but he sat at the opposite end, leaning against the armrest, clearly not wanting his perfectly pressed clothes to be dampened with whisky. Lucy sat again and held on to her empty glass, looking rather pale. She was obviously very upset.

"So, can you tell us more about the plan for the sale?" Josh asked.

Fergus pulled at a loose thread on his jumper, tugging on it until it broke. "The intention is to sell the house and the land, including the outbuildings and cottages, as well as most of the furniture and fixtures." Fergus rolled the piece of yarn between his fingers. "First, I'll repay the loans. The rest of the money will be put into a trust and, when I pass, what's left will go to you, Duncan."

Duncan's eyes narrowed. "I see."

"I intend to live as frugally as possible," Fergus continued. "I've agreed with Knox that I'll rent one of the estate cottages for a nominal amount. Perhaps I'll finally have time to get to that book on Robert the Bruce that I've always wanted to write." He tried to smile, but it was a weak attempt. "I want both of you to look around the castle tomorrow. Choose whatever you want to keep as a memento. Josh, there are some things I know your mother would like. You could take them with you on Sunday. And I hope you can break the news to her. I don't have the heart to tell her myself." He rubbed his eyes so hard it must have hurt. "So that's it. That's what I had to tell you. I never dreamed the estate would fail under my stewardship. And I wasn't even meant to be here."

Josh stood and put a hand on Fergus's shoulder. "Don't distress yourself. This isn't your fault." He glanced at Duncan as though expecting his agreement, but his cousin was staring into the flames, apparently lost in thought.

A gilt clock on the mantel struck midnight and roused Duncan from his trance. He stood. "I'm heading to bed. Lots to cogitate on. Come along, Luce."

I finished my whisky and stood up to join Josh. When I leaned over to kiss Fergus's cheek, he took hold of my hand. "Thank you, my dear. I'm sorry for all the doom and gloom. You came for a party, and it will be a good one. We'll settle the deal with Knox tomorrow and then move on to the celebrations. Might as well go out in style, eh?"

Before I could answer, Mrs. Dunsmore appeared, as if conjured out of thin air or listening at the door. "I can take you to your rooms," she said. "Master Duncan, you're in the red room and Miss Cantrell is just down the corridor from you."

Leaving Fergus in front of the fire with his half-drunk glass, Josh and I followed the others out of the library. Mrs. Dunsmore chatted while we made the long walk to the tower and didn't seem to notice that no one was responding. She shepherded Lucy and Duncan into their rooms, which were on the same floor as ours. When she'd gone, Josh slipped into my room and kicked his shoes off before settling on the bed.

"That's rather a shock," he said. "Poor Fergus."

"Yes, but it's not unusual, is it, for an estate of this size to run out of money? In England, lots of country houses have been sold to the National Trust, which saves them from further damage, or even demolition."

"It's true. I assume Fergus will make more from a private sale than selling to the National Trust for Scotland, even assuming they were willing to buy it." He sighed. "I had no idea Fergus was in such difficulties. I've not been up here for a year, and he's bad at communicating by phone."

We were quiet for a moment until I realized I was freezing. I snuggled up against Josh and pulled a blanket up around us.

"What do we make of Fergus's aura now?" he asked. "It seems obvious that it's linked to the sale of the estate." He tucked the blanket more tightly around us. "Good God, is Fergus going to have a heart attack because of all this?"

"That's what I've been thinking too. He's very distressed." I paused. "Tell me more about Duncan? He seems... a little aggressive?"

"He's always been like that. He's not a bad person. But he does speak before he thinks sometimes."

"Rather like our boss," I chuckled, but then I realized that Josh had closed his eyes. Within seconds, his breathing slowed. He had an enviable ability to fall asleep quickly, anywhere, and under the most adverse circumstances.

I clicked off the lamp and lay, wide awake, in the dark, listening to the unfamiliar sounds of the castle in the night.

4

I woke up to a room filled with thin grey light. We'd forgotten to pull the curtains closed last night; both of us had been exhausted, tired from our early start in London, and wrung out by the appearance of the aura and the news on the estate. Josh had slept soundly. Me, not so much.

Josh was still asleep next to me, face down, one cheek mashed into a pillow. As I pulled the covers up around us and listened to the rumble of the radiator, he snoozed on peacefully. There was no rush to wake him, so I slipped from the bed and hurried across the cold floor to the bathroom, which was surprisingly warm and cozy. The shower, a modern rainfall type, emitted plenty of hot water, soothing the ache in my shoulders, where my muscles always tightened in knots whenever I was stressed. My spirits lifted. We'd find a way to protect Fergus, I told myself. I hummed 'The bonnie, bonnie banks of Loch Lomond' while I washed my hair.

While I was getting dressed, I heard footsteps and voices in the hallway. "Come down for breakfast," Duncan called through the door. "Stuff to talk about."

He was right, of course. There was a great deal to discuss, but his attitude was starting to get on my nerves. He seemed to think he could boss us all around. I went back to the bed to see that Josh had kicked off the covers while I was in the bathroom. For a few seconds, I contemplated his lean, fair-skinned body, and then ran my fingers along his arm. When I found a ticklish spot, he yelped and jumped as though pursued by hellhounds. Complaining that he was cold, he pulled on my purple dressing gown, which looked ridiculous on him, and rushed to his own room. He was soon back with an armful of clean clothes.

I found a hair dryer and ran it over my hair, which was thick and long and took forever to dry naturally. Enjoying the stream of hot air, I raised my voice to ask Josh a question that had struck me when I woke up.

"Why did Fergus say he wasn't meant to be here?"

Josh was rooting around under the bed, searching for something. He looked up and raised an eyebrow at me. "Last night," I reminded him. "Fergus said he wasn't even meant to be here. What did that mean?"

Josh had found a shoe and pulled it on before answering. "Fergus was the middle of the three siblings. My mum is the youngest. The older brother, Hamish, Duncan's father, inherited the estate, but he died only six months after my grandfather passed away. He never even moved in. In theory, Duncan should have inherited, but before he died, Uncle Hamish changed his will and named Fergus. He picked his brother over his own son. You can imagine how well that sat with Duncan."

So Duncan had a solid reason to resent Fergus and to feel betrayed by the decision to sell the estate. "Was there anything suspicious about Hamish's death?" I asked. "That was a coincidence, surely, for him to die so soon after inheriting?"

Josh was padding around, looking for his other shoe. "No. He died of cancer. He'd been ill for a few months before Grandpa died. We all hoped he'd recover, of course, and run the estate for a while but... that didn't work out. Duncan's mother had run off with another man when Duncan was only four, so his dad's death effectively left him an orphan."

"And why—"

"Can I tell you the rest after breakfast?" he asked. "We should join the others and find out what time Knox is arriving. I want you to check Fergus again, to see if the aura is still there."

"Of course." I turned off the dryer and threw on an oversized cream-colored jumper while Josh stood by the door, waiting. He appeared to be on edge, but he held my hand after stopping briefly in his room to rumple the covers on the bed. "We don't want to scandalize Mrs. Dunsmore," he said with a quick smile.

Downstairs, we found Duncan and Lucy already at the breakfast table with plates of eggs and bacon in front of them. Josh led me to the sideboard, which held pots of tea, and warming trays of food. "Oh good, kedgeree," he said, spooning a mound of rice and smoked haddock on to his plate. I couldn't face fish that early in the day, so I opted for a bowl of porridge and drizzled milk and honey over it.

"Don't let Mrs. Dunsmore see," Josh whispered. "She's a staunch proponent of putting salt and nothing else on your porridge."

"That sounds very appealing," I said, rolling my eyes at him. He grinned and added another spoonful of kedgeree to his plate. We sat opposite the others, angling our chairs to not disturb Arbroath who was sleeping under the table. Lucy's fair skin was pale, and dark circles made her eyes look bruised.

Duncan still seemed angry, stabbing at his bacon with his fork. "So, what do you make of all this?" he asked Josh. "Bloody disaster."

"I'm not thrilled about letting the property go," Josh said. "But selling it makes sense. I think Fergus has thought it through carefully. He loves the castle. He wouldn't sell if he didn't think it was the only viable solution. And it seems as though there will be money left for you when the time comes, whenever that will be." Josh glanced at me when he said that, and I took a big gulp of my tea.

"I intend to negotiate hard with this Knox fellow." Duncan jabbed at a tomato, which shot off his plate and onto the floor. Arbroath was on it in seconds. He licked his lips and looked up, expectant, before putting a huge paw on Duncan's knee.

"Get off me, you ugly thing." Duncan pushed the dog away.

"Leave him alone. He hasn't done anything wrong," Josh said.

"Nor anything right either," Duncan complained. "He smells and takes up too much space."

"How are you this morning, Lucy?" I asked in a feeble attempt to defuse the tension.

"I didn't sleep well," she said. "I think I'll go back up after breakfast and take a nap."

Duncan patted her hand in an unexpectedly tender gesture. "You do that while we talk to Knox, and then I'll take you out for lunch," he offered. That was an improvement over his behavior the night before. The quiet moment quickly passed however. "And what of Mrs. Dunsmore?" he demanded, as he spooned sugar into his tea. "She's been here since she was sixteen and her mother and grandmother worked here before her."

Josh didn't answer. Instead, he passed me a cut-glass pot filled with thick orange marmalade. "Homemade," he said. "Mrs. Dunsmore's speciality."

I spread some on my buttered toast. It was delicious.

"Josh." Duncan waved a fork at him to get his attention. "What if Knox doesn't keep Mrs. Dunsmore on? What happens to her then?"

"I canna tell ye," Mrs. Dunsmore said, coming in with a tray. "But I trust your uncle to look after us." She started piling up plates and cutlery, and I stood to help her, uncomfortable with the idea of having staff waiting on me. "Sit ye down," she said. "Finish your toast."

When she'd gone, we sat in an awkward silence, which was, to my relief, broken by the arrival of Fergus. I wasn't so thrilled though to see that his aura still swirled over his silver hair. I wouldn't have expected anything to change overnight, but I always lived in hope. Josh caught my eye and I gave him a slight shake of my head. He pushed his plate away.

"Stanton Knox has been delayed a couple of hours," Fergus was saying. "He'll arrive at noon, and we'll gather in the Great Hall when he gets here."

"Good, because I have something to say." Duncan pushed his

chair back and stood up. "Tell Knox to go away, that you changed your mind."

Fergus gestured to Duncan to sit back down, and he settled into a chair opposite him. "Why would I do that?" he asked.

"Because I want you to pass the estate on to me right now."

Fergus lifted an eyebrow. "What would—?"

"Hear me out," Duncan said. "I'll take over management of the place. I can convert the loans..." He seemed to be calculating numbers in his head. "I'd develop the tenancy programs and invest the income properly—"

"Where would Fergus go?" Josh interrupted.

"He can rent a cottage on the estate. I mean, that's the plan if this Knox chap buys it, right? So, no difference there. I'd turn the bulk of the castle into a hotel. There's a developer friend of mine who knows all about that sort of thing. You met him, Luce, do you remember? Gary Croft?"

I looked at Lucy, who was gazing at Duncan with an indecipherable expression.

"Gary? Yes," she murmured.

Duncan talked on about income streams and ROIs until I felt my eyelids droop.

"I think you're overlooking a few things," Josh said. "To start with—"

But Fergus seemed to have heard enough. "We'll talk about this some other time," he said. He stood up and walked out, Arbroath in tow.

"Let's go for a walk by the private loch," Josh said to me, getting to his feet. "It's quite beautiful."

"Strictly speaking, it's a lochan," Duncan said. "A baby loch. And it doesn't even have a name."

"Nevertheless, it's still very pretty," Josh said, tucking his hand under my elbow and helping me up. Still chewing my last piece of toast and marmalade, I was propelled from the room.

"Sorry," Josh muttered. "He's rubbing me the wrong way today."

"Is he always like this?"

"We haven't spent much time together, but I don't remember him being this bad. As kids, our age gap meant we didn't have a lot in common. When I was a teenager, we met up here once or twice, and he was always argumentative. I remember him having walloping great fights with his dad. Then, when he graduated, he got into finance, which appears to have exacerbated his confrontational tendencies. I suppose it's a very competitive environment, and he seems to thrive in it. But asking Fergus to sign the estate over to him... I don't know what he's thinking, to be honest. We'll talk about it later. For now, I want to show you some of the estate. It's really quite stunning."

When we reached the entry hall, Mrs. Dunsmore was there. She had a miraculous ability to simply appear wherever she was needed, it seemed. "Coats in that cupboard there," she said pointing to a door. "And wellingtons in that one. You should find what's necessary."

Within a few minutes, we were bundled up in padded jackets and with thick socks under our rubber boots, mine a cheerful red, and Josh's green. Appropriately dressed, I felt warm even when we walked outside, where I could see my breath. The mist had lifted, revealing a leaden sky that seemed so low I could touch it. The red gravel drive wound between the lawns towards the gate, beyond which stretched moorland, dotted with sheep. I noticed now that the lawns hadn't been cut for a while and several of the hedges were in need of trimming. Grounds of that size must require a huge amount of upkeep.

Instead of going along the driveway, we turned left around the side of the house. A flagstone path ran between the main building and a line of dense conifers, dark and shadowy in the wintry light. The part of the building we were passing was built of smooth, creamy limestone, very different from the rough granite blocks of the tower. Ahead, the path jogged sharply right to accommodate a square extension that was cocooned in ivy. Even the windows were obscured by the thick green growth, but I caught a glimpse of wood where glass should be. I stopped, staring upward. "Is this part of the castle?" I asked. "Why are the windows boarded up?"

"It's the east wing," Josh said. "From the inside, you'd get to it via a door at the end of the corridor near the library. But it's been closed off for decades now, ever since a German bombing raid in the spring of 1941. Although the bomb didn't explode, the roof was destroyed and the windows blown out. Several family members escaped injury, but my great-grandfather's sister died. She'd been sitting in the upstairs salon. After that happened, he closed the whole wing off."

"Have you ever been in there?"

"No. God knows what state it must be in now. My great-grandfather died a few months later, of a heart attack. From what I've heard, my great-grandmother never recovered from his death. She had no interest in repairing the bomb damage and besides, in the years following the war, there was no money and few materials for repairs. So the place grew more and more dilapidated. By the time my grandfather inherited, it would have cost a fortune to restore it all, and he never bothered."

Saddened by the story, I followed Josh to the end of the building. Beyond was a large garden, similar to the one that lay to the front of the castle. Straggly topiaries in the shape of deer guarded empty flower beds. Untrimmed, the deer looked as though they were wearing woolly jumpers. To one side was a long red brick wall. "That's the vegetable garden and fruit orchard," Josh said. "Lovely in August, but not so much at this time of year."

He pointed ahead, to where a ridge of craggy rock loomed over the gardens. "That's where we're going," he said with a grin.

I looked down at my wellingtons. "These aren't exactly made for climbing."

"Follow me." He headed towards an opening in a thick yew hedge and pointed to a narrow path that wound between two blocks of speckled brown granite. "We go through here. It's mostly flat with a little incline at the end." He set off, and I tramped along behind him. Above us, a hawk wheeled and screeched, a desolate sound that raised the hair on the back of my neck. My feet slid on loose pebbles on the trail, and I put my hands out to steady myself against the rocks. After fifty meters or so, the path angled upwards. The walls closed in on us as we ascended, but just when my claustrophobia threatened to stop me in my tracks, we reached the top, a flat expanse of granite, dappled with moss. Beyond, a gentle slope of boulders and shrubs fell to the shore of a small lake, a long, narrow body of water that lay calm and still.

"That's the lochan," Josh said, spreading his arms wide as though to embrace the view. The water was slate grey, reflecting the iron sky and, beyond, rose a series of low hills covered with heather and gorse. "We should come up to see the heather blooming next year," Josh said. "The colors are spectacular."

Maybe, but today the moors were dark and dull. Goosebumps prickled my skin. The vista of the vast empty space was somehow spectacular and disturbing at the same time.

He pointed to the far end of the loch where, at its narrowest point, rose a spire of black rock. "That's the Brynjarr Stone. They say it was once part of a small henge, and it's reputed to have magical properties, but that's just local superstition. Past that are miles of moorland with nowt but grouse and deer to keep ye company."

I smiled at the verbal reminder of his northern heritage. If he stayed long enough, he'd start sounding like Mrs. Dunsmore. He led the way down a winding path to the lochan, which lapped on a thin rim of beige sand. We found a flat rock at the edge of the water and settled there together. I was glad to feel the warmth and weight of his shoulder against mine and, for a while, we sat quietly, absorbing the scenery and the stillness. But when a breeze came up and ruffled the surface of the lochan, I thought of Fergus's aura.

"We need to talk about Fergus," I said.

Josh sighed. "I know, but I have no idea what to do. We believe he may have a medical condition, but how do I persuade him to make a doctor's appointment?"

"I'd say it's impossible, at least for now. That American, Knox, is arriving today and then there's the birthday party. There's no way your uncle will take time to visit a doctor he doesn't even know he needs."

We lapsed into silence again. A tenacious plant clung to the edge of the rock, and I leaned over to break off a tiny bell-shaped flower, running my finger over its soft, white petals.

"Why did your Uncle Hamish will the estate to Fergus instead of Duncan?" I asked the question I'd started earlier in the day.

Josh shifted, making himself comfortable. "Duncan studied law at Cambridge but, after he graduated, he changed his mind about his career and took a job with a trading firm in the City. Apparently, it had something of a dodgy reputation, and Uncle Hamish didn't approve. My mum tried to patch things up between them, but that didn't go anywhere. Duncan succeeded though, in his new profession, and made a lot of money, which I have to say infuriated Uncle Hamish even more. But what really got my uncle's goat was that Duncan developed some very expensive spending habits."

"Really? Like what?"

"I don't know all the details, but he bought a couple of flashy cars, started wearing custom-made suits and eating at ridiculously expensive restaurants. I heard he rented a private jet a few times too. It all added up quickly."

"So he didn't trust Duncan with the estate?"

"No. When Uncle Hamish found out he was dying, he changed his will to make his brother heir to the estate on condition that Fergus leaves it to Duncan after his death."

"Duncan must have been furious."

"He was. I thought he'd calmed down over the last few years, but now I'm not so sure. Not that he'd want to live in Scotland anyway. I don't understand what he was going on about over breakfast. There's no way he'd want to saddle himself with running a failing country estate. I don't see him as the laird of the manor type, do you?"

I smiled. "Not exactly. What about you? Aren't you in line to inherit?"

Josh laughed. "I suppose I am, after Duncan. He's only eight years older than I am, though, and unlikely to kick the bucket any time soon. I'd probably be an octogenarian, and much good would it do me then. Besides, there won't be an estate to inherit. The castle and land will be sold, Fergus will live on the proceeds and, if there's anything left over, Duncan will almost certainly spend every penny he can get his hands on."

"Unless..." I stopped.

Josh tilted his head to one side, his dark hair flopping into one eye. I reached out to smooth it away. "Unless what?" he prompted.

"Unless Duncan tries to prevent the sale from happening. What if Fergus dies before the contracts are signed?"

"You mean that Duncan is the threat to Fergus? That's ridiculous."

"Is it?"

"Kate, please. I hope you're joking."

"Well, yes, sort of. But we should consider the possibility that someone intends harm to Fergus. He said there had been threats, that people are unhappy."

Josh bit his bottom lip, a sign that he was thinking hard. "It's possible. We should ask Fergus for the names of anyone who's been making noise about the estate sale."

"Should we tell the police?" I asked. "That we're concerned for Fergus's safety?"

"But tell them what? That always gets tricky."

It was true. It was hard to enlist the help of law enforcement when I couldn't explain the real reason why I knew someone was in danger. In general, policemen and auras didn't mix well. A London inspector on a case two years ago had suspected me of murder because I had warned him there would soon be another victim. When I came clean about the auras, he changed his mind. I wasn't a killer, but I was insane.

"Should we tell Fergus?"

Josh pressed his fingers to his temples. "I don't know. He's quite open-minded, but he's also very practical, very down-to-earth. I'm not sure how he'd react to your ability to see auras. Let me think about it before we say anything to him?"

"Of course." I didn't relish the prospect of describing my bizarre gift, or of telling Fergus he might die in the very near future. I slid off the rock and went to the lochan's edge. The water was clear and, in the shallows, I saw large round pebbles of different colors. As I leaned forward to examine them, something moved. I saw a flash of amber as it glided past. When I screamed and leapt backwards, Josh came running. He began to laugh. "It's just a fish," he said. "A brown trout to be precise."

"Well, I knew it wasn't the Loch Ness monster," I said, irritated that I'd overreacted. "It made me jump, that's all."

Josh crouched down and dangled his fingers in the water. "When I was a kid, the groundskeeper, Lachlan, taught me to tickle the trout so we could catch them without a line and hook." He sighed and stood up straight. I was beginning to realize how important Castle Aiten was to him.

"Let's walk to the end of the loch," he said. "We can circle round to the house over the moors from there, without having to go back through the passage between the walls."

"Good idea," I said, linking my fingers with his. When we passed by the Brynjarr Stone, I ran my hand over the smooth, black rock. My palm tingled, but perhaps it was just from the cold. Beyond the spire, the land opened up, moors stretching into the distance as far as I could see. Paths barely as wide as a sheep cut through the heather, so Josh let go of my hand and walked in front. We'd gone a short distance when I heard an engine and then the distinctive whump-whump of a helicopter blade. Seconds later, the chopper came into view and passed over us, flying low before disappearing over the roof of the castle.

"That must be Knox," Josh said. "We should head back."

The path led us past the walled vegetable garden and, as we rounded the corner of the house, we saw the helicopter, a glossy black shape crouched on the wide stretch of lawn near the front gates. We hurried to the house and into the entry hall to find a gaggle of people already there, including Fergus and Duncan. There was no sign of Lucy, and I remembered she'd planned to take a nap. Fergus introduced us to Knox, who was probably in his early thirties. He was skinny and of medium height, with light brown hair cropped short. In spite of the chill, he wore shorts, a short-sleeved T-shirt with his company logo emblazoned across the front, and flip-flops.

"Call me Stanton, please," he said, with an American drawl. "This is Anthony, my personal assistant and Maya, my lawyer." The two people with him nodded at us.

"And this is Robert Dunne, my legal counsel," Fergus said. "He'll be assisting us with the negotiations."

Dunne was white-haired and red-cheeked, his ample figure straining every seam on his navy-blue suit. He smiled, shaking everyone's hand in turn.

After the introductions were completed, we heard the helicopter engine rumbling in the distance. "Carl will take the 'copter to the airfield in Oban, so he can do some sightseeing there," Knox said. "He'll come back when I need him. I guess we can get started, right?"

"I'll catch up with you later," Josh whispered to me, as he pulled off his wellingtons and coat. He put on his shoes and followed the group as they moved off to start the meeting. The aura still rotated over Fergus and, worse, it appeared to be moving more quickly. I wished I knew what threatened him. For now, I had nothing specific to do, and no one to do it with, so I decided to take another walk. Perhaps a little time alone in the fresh air would help me organize my thoughts and come up with a plan to save Josh's uncle.

5

I walked back past the walled garden and took the path that circled around to the moors. The fog had drifted in again, softening the edges of the granite outcrop to my left. I kept my eyes on the track in front of me, watching my feet to make sure I didn't trip over stones or roots in my cumbersome wellingtons.

Lost in thoughts of Fergus and the estate, I didn't see the man until he was an arm's length away. I jumped, scared out of my wits by his sudden appearance. Tall, wide, and clad in green tweed, he wore a deerstalker hat jammed down over his broad forehead, revealing thick black eyebrows. His skin was tanned, which surprised me, given that I didn't believe the sun ever shone in Scotland, and his chin was stubbled with grey hairs. More alarming than his stature and appearance was the rifle that he carried in one hand. The other held a dead rabbit by its feet.

He eyed me suspiciously. "And who might you be?" he asked. I thought I could ask him the same question. He looked like a poacher to me, but I answered politely. "Kate Benedict. I'm a guest at the castle."

"Oh aye," he said. "For the party."

He held out his hand as if to shake mine, but then remembered the rabbit. "Lachlan McDermott," he said. "I'm the groundskeeper here."

So this was the man who'd taught Josh how to tickle trout. "Josh says you've been with the estate for a long time?" I said.

He nodded. "Fifty years in December, or it would be if the place isn't sold by then." He drew his heavy brows together and glared at me as if the upcoming sale was my doing. "It's a terrible thing, it is."

"I'm sorry to hear that. I can imagine that it will be hard on some people here if the sale goes through."

He snorted. "Hard? That would be the understatement of the century, lassie."

"Fergus said some people are quite angry, that there have even been threats?"

"Nay," he said. "Only a few drunks getting their knickers in a twist. There's no one who'd harm the chief, except for..." He stopped. "Anyway, I have to get on."

"Except for whom?" I asked. I stepped closer to him. I knew it might be risky to talk to Lachlan about my concerns. He had to be on the list of potential threats, given his situation. But time was short, and I needed to gather information where I could. "If you're aware of anything, please tell me. I'm worried for Fergus."

Lachlan narrowed his eyes at me and shifted the rifle across his arm. I stepped back, wary. For at least thirty seconds, he gazed at me but his eyes were unfocused as though he was actually looking past me. I shifted, uncomfortable with his scrutiny.

"From London, aren't you?" he said finally. He managed to make it sound like an insult.

Feeling the need to establish my credentials, I responded tartly. "Yes. I'm Josh's girlfriend."

His features relaxed. "I've known Josh since he was a bairn. He's a good lad." He glanced upwards at a sky that was invisible in the mist. "Mind how ye go," he said. "And get to the house before the storm rolls in."

I looked up as well. How could he tell there'd be a storm?

With that, he stepped off the path, trampled through the heather to get past me and headed off. I turned to watch him stride away, thinking he was an odd duck, hard to read. He seemed angry about the sale, but he'd denied that anyone seriously meant Fergus harm.

Still mulling over our encounter, I trudged on through the drizzly fog, hands in my pockets to keep them warm. I'd walk for thirty minutes, I decided, and then head back and hope that lunch might be ready. The bracing air was making me hungry, and, besides, I wanted to tackle Mrs. Dunsmore next, to see if she could cast any light on potential troublemakers in the village.

A few hundred meters further on, I noticed a number of tan-colored stones scattered across a stretch of rough grass. Curious, I stopped to look around and noticed the remains of a wall, an uneven line of blocks, like a row of broken teeth. Crossing the weed-strewn ground, I saw more rubble, a trail of broken rock and crumbling mortar. I bent to pick up a fragment and ran my fingers over the beige sandstone. It was the same material that had been used to construct the castle's main building, unlike the ancient tower. That had been built centuries earlier with a different rock, a rough greenish-grey metamorphic stone.

Clutching the fragment, I followed the line of the ruins, tracing the outline of a rectangle about fifteen meters long and ten meters wide. I wondered if it had been a barn or a crofter's cottage, yet the quality of the stone made me think it was unlikely to have been a simple rustic structure. I'd have to ask Fergus whether there had ever been another house here.

Was it my imagination or had the mist thickened? Although there was no breeze, the vapors swirled, obliterating my view of the moors beyond the ruins. It felt colder here too, a cold that sank into my bones, jabbing gelid needles into my skin. As I dropped the fragment and turned in the direction of the path, something flickered in the corner of my eye. A shape, dark in the murky gloom. It moved towards me. Transfixed, I waited as the black form approached and then breathed out when a deer appeared, a doe with soft brown eyes and black-tipped ears. She looked at me and I looked back, admiring her smooth coat, the color of milky coffee. My heart rate settled as we gazed at each other in silence. And then her ears twitched, and she leapt away, galloping into the mist as though being pursued.

I squinted into the fog, wondering what had scared her. Perhaps it was nothing. Deer are notoriously skittish. Still, I shivered, feeling alone after the doe's sudden disappearance. Stamping my feet to warm them, I pulled the hood up on my jacket, preparing to return to the castle. But just then, another dark silhouette loomed in the mist. I stood still, expecting to see a second deer. As the shadow moved closer, though, it took shape as a human figure, an auburn-haired woman, wearing an ankle-length leaf-green dress with a high waist. Her hair was piled up on top of her head with curly tendrils hanging at her cheeks. I thought her fashion style was a little unusual, but I'd seen weirder outfits on the streets of London. Maybe she was from the village.

"Good morning," I said.

When she came closer, I saw that she was very pretty and quite young, probably no more than twenty. She was clutching a small book with a brown cover. I retreated, suddenly unsure. The air around her coiled and churned. My heart pounded against my ribs. With a glance behind her, she took another hurried step and, stretching out her arms, she thrust the book at me. As if of its own volition, my hand reached towards her, palm up, prepared to accept it.

Behind her, in the eddying brume, an arched door appeared, framing the figure of a man in a black robe. His hair was tonsured and an iron crucifix swayed across his chest. In his bony white fingers, he gripped a knife, long and brutal with a sharp point. I watched, horrified, as he rushed forward. His footsteps were muffled on the grass, and the young woman didn't seem to realize he was almost upon her. I shouted a warning that she made no sign of hearing. My knees turned to water when he arced the knife downward, thrusting the blade deep into the woman's back. Her eyes opened wide and she crumpled to the ground. Blood drenched her green dress and puddled on the soil around her. Her auburn hair quivered like curled autumn leaves. The book fell from her hand, and the killer bent over her to retrieve it.

I screamed, my whole body shaking. I wanted to run, but my legs wouldn't cooperate. I had frozen in place, and it was impossible to think clearly. Time seemed to stop.

A second passed, or a minute, or an hour, I couldn't tell. A flight of geese passed low overhead, their raucous calls bringing me to my senses. My eyes focused again. The woman still lay on the ground, the book inches from her fingers. The man continued to lean over her, reaching for it.

And then they were gone.

The shock forced me to my knees, and nausea cramped my stomach. Panicked, I struggled to regain control. It was an effort to clamber to my feet, to walk to the place where the woman had died. There was no evidence of the atrocity that had taken place there, no flattening of the heather, no blood on the soil. The arched door and stone wall had disappeared. It was as though the fog had absorbed them whole. As though they'd never been there.

Sinking to the ground, I tried to rationalize what had happened, but found no plausible explanation other than one I was reluctant to accept. Giving into my weakened limbs, I lay down on the heather, which was soft and bouncy under my body. I felt I was floating six inches above the earth.

My breathing gradually slowed, my heart stopped thudding, and some clarity returned to my brain. I'd seen a vision, obviously, but was it a reenactment of a murder already committed, or a premonition of a future crime? The man, I thought, must have been a monk. The woman's dress had been more ambiguous, but I realized now that it wasn't contemporary. My skin prickled from head to toe. I resisted the idea that I'd seen ghosts, spirits from the past, but the evidence was irrefutable. Or I was losing my mind and I had imagined the whole thing.

I shut my eyes, trying to blot out the sight of that knife and the violence of the blow. Through closed eyelids, I sensed the sky darken, felt the air quicken around me. The rain Lachlan had predicted fell in huge drops that splattered onto my rubber boots and waxed jacket.

Standing, I bent my head against the deluge and turned back the way I'd come. Within minutes, I was lost. Multiple tracks webbed the moorland, and fog and low cloud deleted any view of the castle or the rocky outcrops behind it. I had my mobile phone in my pocket, but a quick check confirmed that there was no service out here. There hadn't been inside the house either.

Flustered, I picked a path and hurried along it. Ten minutes later, I almost bumped right into the strange rock formation, the Brynjarr Stone. Whether it had magical properties or not, I was overjoyed to find it. From there, I could follow the trail that ran alongside the water until I came to the track between the two granite boulders. Although that narrow shortcut made me nervous, it would take me safely to the castle grounds. I was drenched and still rattled by the vision; the faster I reached the shelter of the house, the better.

Ten minutes later, I realized I must have missed the passageway that led through the rocks. I turned to retrace my steps towards the end of the loch just as thunder rolled overhead and a flash of lightning split the sky. The rain fell in torrents, stabbing deep pockmarks into the surface of the grey water.

Amidst the tumult, I heard another sound. A voice. Startled, I strained to listen. And then I realized it was Josh calling my name. I shouted back over the din and stumbled along the trail. Soon, Josh's arms enfolded me, and I felt the warmth of his chest against mine.

"There, it's all right," he said. "You're soaked through. Let's get you back to the house."

"How did you know to come and find me?" I asked through chattering teeth.

"We all took a break from the meeting. I wanted to talk with you, to bring you up to date, but I couldn't find you. Then I saw Lachlan in the entry hall, and he told me he'd met you out on the moor. He said he warned you of the incoming storm."

"He did warn me. But he didn't come out to look for me, did he?"

6

After changing into dry clothes, I felt considerably better, but the memory of what I'd seen on the moors still roiled my stomach. Josh paced the bedroom while I told him about the ghostly encounter and the violent murder. I knew it must be hard for him to listen, outlandish as the story was, but he didn't interrupt and he didn't question what I'd seen.

"Have you been out there? You've seen the ruins?" I asked.

He nodded. "I can't say I've ever really stopped to look, but I've passed by a few times. I seem to remember Lachlan saying it was a shepherd's cottage, but I don't know when it was abandoned."

"It didn't look like a cottage," I said, remembering my vision and the heavy wooden door half-opened in a carved archway. "Could there have been a church there once?"

"I don't know, but there should be records somewhere in the library, I'd think, or Fergus might know."

"That would be a good start. If we could pin down the likely dates of construction, I'd at least have an idea of when those people were living."

"You're going to try solve a centuries-old murder?" Josh asked.

"I'd like to know what happened. Why did the man in the black robe kill that woman, and what was the book she was holding?" The skin prickled on my arms when I recalled the expression of desperation on her face.

Josh stopped pacing and leaned against the windowsill. "Kate, one of the many things I love about you is that you can you care about people. But you can't help that woman, whoever she was. And more to the point, unraveling a past mystery won't save Fergus. We need to stay focused until we know what it is that threatens him, which, in my mind, is something to do with the sale of the estate."

I felt his eyes searching my face as I perched on the edge of the bed to pull on my boots. "You think I'm barmy, right?" I said.

"No."

"You know I'm grateful to you for putting up with my insanity," I said. "And I agree we should be working on saving Fergus. But I have no idea where to start. It's so frustrating."

"Yes, it is. I feel bloody useless." He took a look at his watch. "I should get back."

"Oh heavens, I'm sorry. I didn't even ask how the meeting is going?"

"It's not bad, under the circumstances. Stanton may be a small, skinny guy, but he has an incredibly outsized ego. Truly epic. He has the reputation of being a tyrant to his employees, and I think he forgets we don't work for him. But still, he seems intent on making the purchase happen, and his assistants are cooperative. But Duncan's not helping. He's being very argumentative, picking on every detail. At this rate, it'll take weeks to resolve all the issues."

"How's Fergus holding up?" I asked.

"More or less as you'd expect. When they ask questions about the state of the building, he flinches as though they're slapping him in the face. But he shouldn't feel so guilty about it all. The decline has been centuries in the making, and began long before he inherited the castle. Duncan doesn't seem to realize that his father, had he lived, would have faced the same dilemma."

The zip on my boot stuck, and I yanked on it hard, pinching my finger in the process. I examined the red mark on my skin. "I know I raised this earlier and you don't want to talk about it, but you have to recognize that Duncan has a motive. If anything were to happen to Fergus, Duncan would inherit the estate, right? And if he inherited it now, and sold it to Stanton or someone like him, he'd receive a large sum of money, which would be his to keep. Or he could do all that stuff he was talking about earlier, developing the estate and investing the income. It was easy to see Fergus didn't want to discuss it. So Duncan might decide to force the issue."

Josh pushed away from the window. "I'm not going to talk about this, Kate. Duncan is a hothead, but you can't seriously believe that he'd kill Fergus?"

"I know it's a stretch, but it's all we've got. I'm just pointing out that Duncan stands to benefit if Fergus dies. So far, we don't know who else would."

"But why now? Duncan has always been the beneficiary. He could have killed Fergus any time in the last ten years if that's what he intended to do."

"Because the sale has introduced an element of uncertainty. Before, it was accepted that Fergus would live here, maintain the estate and pass it on to Duncan, who could then decide what to do with it. He could keep it and develop it, or sell it and capitalize the assets. Either way, he'd have some control over his inheritance."

Josh nodded. "True, but still, it's a bit far-fetched to imagine Duncan committing murder." He looked at his watch. "I need to go. I'm doing my best to moderate the proceedings."

I stood up. "Come on then, I'll walk over there with you."

Before we left, I checked that my iPhone was still in my pocket. Josh noticed. "There's no phone service or Wi-Fi because the walls are so thick," he said.

"I know, but it has a camera. I'd like to take some photos of the building. How does Fergus manage without a smartphone or a computer? That would drive me crazy." I grinned at Josh. "Crazier than I already am, that is."

We walked out, closing the bedroom door behind us, and took the stairs down to the gallery.

"Actually, Fergus does have a PC and an ancient dial-up connection," Josh said. "It's in his office, and I've used it a few times. The computer's as old as the castle, but it works. If you want to use it, he won't mind at all. The password is 'bannockburn.' "

"Bannockburn?"

"Fergus is a great fan of Robert the Bruce. Hence the dog's name, Arbroath. The Declaration of Arbroath was the Scottish declaration of independence, written in 1320. And the Battle of Bannockburn, June 1314, was a great Scottish victory over the English."

"Thank you for the history lesson. Although, in spite of what you think about my English education, I knew most of that already."

"Sassenachs," he muttered. "Think they know everything." His smile faded and he grabbed my hand. "What will you do for the next few hours? Promise me you won't go back out on the moors by yourself."

I slowed down, thinking about how best to spend my time.

"I realize this isn't quite what we planned for this weekend," he said. "I thought we'd be out hiking or sitting in the village pub today. Once this meeting is over, we'll have some time together."

I gave him a quick hug. "Don't worry about me. You stay close to Fergus, and I'll keep pondering possible threats. I'll go to the library and dig around. Maybe something will jump out at me."

"Hopefully not. You've had one scare already today."

"Very funny."

When we reached the Great Hall, Josh went inside and closed the door. I set off, hoping I could find the library without getting lost. As Fergus had said during my introductory tour, the castle was huge, and the layout was rather eccentric. Corridors dead-ended unexpectedly, and there were at least two staircases. But I soon recognized the wide, green-carpeted hallway that led to the library. At the far end of the corridor was the door that Josh had told me led to the abandoned east wing. I looked more closely. It seemed that the door was ajar. Yet Josh had said it had been shut off for years.

I tiptoed up the hallway. The door was open a couple of inches. I listened but didn't hear anything, so I pushed it open slowly and peered inside. A bright beam from a torch illuminated the furthest wall of a pitch-dark room. Before I could step back, the light turned in my direction, blinding me. I shielded my eyes with one hand.

"Who's there?" I asked.

No one answered, and I asked again. "Who are you?" I positioned myself in the door frame, ready to run if I had to.

"It's Lucy."

"Lucy? What are you doing in here? How did you get in?"

When she lowered the torch, my eyes adjusted to the gloom. In fact, the darkness wasn't as profound as I'd first thought. Gaps in the roof and chinks in the boards at the windows let in slivers of grey light. The room was large and square. On one wall was a limestone fireplace that had once been handsome, but the chimney had crumbled, leaving a rockslide of sooty bricks on the hearth. At the end of the room was a painted door, sage green and decorated with pink and white flowers. In the middle of the floor was a hole six feet wide with jagged edges. I looked up. The high ceiling above us had collapsed, leaving only exposed beams and, above them, panels of plywood that filled the spaces where the roof tiles had shattered. That must have been where the bomb crashed through. Decades of Scottish rain and snow had wreaked havoc on the damaged building, filling the air with the stench of damp and mold.

Surprisingly, the furnishings were mostly intact; a tattered sofa faced the ruined fireplace, and several side tables held ornaments and a clock. An armoire and several chests filled another wall while a desk was located under one of the boarded-up windows. Lucy was standing next to the desk, her hand on the closed roll-top.

"How did you get in here?" I asked.

"It's incredible, isn't it? Like that ghost ship, the Marie Celeste." She walked slowly across the room, skirting the treacherous hole in the floor to reach the green door. Grasping the handle, she turned it, and the door creaked open.

"Lucy," I began, but she was on her way through. I went after her.

On the other side of the door was an oak plank landing, leaning at an unnatural angle towards a staircase that led downwards. Mounds of greying plaster littered the landing and the staircase.

"What a mess," I whispered.

"What happened here?" Lucy asked, but more to herself than to me. I answered anyway, relating the story Josh had told me about the bomb. It had crashed through the roof, down through the salon, and had come to rest on the ground floor. "It didn't explode," I said. "Josh said the army came in to defuse it and took it away. But the impact was substantial enough to wreck the entire east wing. And one person died."

"So this place has been closed off for more than seventy years," Lucy said. "Fascinating. Who died?"

"Josh said it was his great-grandfather's sister. That's one reason it was abandoned. Didn't Duncan tell you about it?"

"No, it never came up in conversation. Why would it?"

A splash of color caught my eye, and I ventured closer to find a child's toy, half buried in dust and plaster, a wooden train covered in flaking blue paint. I wondered if it had once belonged to Josh's grandfather, and thought of taking it back to show Josh. But when I straightened up, I saw that Lucy was moving again, picking her way down the stairs. The banister had been destroyed, leaving only a couple of spindles that rose like bony fingers from the rubble.

A loud crack made me jump. One of the stair treads had collapsed, the wood splintering beneath Lucy's feet. She yelped and scrabbled at the wall to stop herself from falling.

"Lucy, come back up," I said. "It's dangerous."

"It's okay," she said, edging down more slowly, one shoulder against the wall for support. I sighed and followed, curious to see the extent of the damage, and even more curious to find out how— and why— Lucy had opened the door.

On the ground floor, a spacious hall appeared relatively intact. Octagonal green and white tiles, chipped in places, covered the floor, while the domed ceiling was painted with a chocolate-box scene of cherubs cavorting amidst greenery and roses. Off the hall, we found six rooms, all of them still furnished as bedrooms, with rugs on the floor and curtains at the windows. I heard a rustling noise behind me and swung around to see a mouse scampering to the shelter of a chewed-up armchair. Startled, I brushed up against one of the silky drapes, and the yellow fabric fell apart, cascading to the floor in a shower of tarnished gold.

"Lucy, how did you get in, and why?" I asked again. My first impression of her had been that she was nervous, perhaps shy, but now I wondered. She seemed to have no fear of rotten floorboards. Or mice and spiders.

"The door was unlocked," she answered. "I couldn't resist taking a peek. But we should go back before we're missed. Oh, and we probably shouldn't mention this to anyone. Duncan would be cross if he knew I'd been here, with it being so dangerous, you know."

It seemed to me that Duncan was cross all the time, and it puzzled me that Lucy would put up with him. I didn't answer her though. I certainly intended to tell Josh about my visit to the east wing.

With another look around the destroyed accommodations, we started back up the stairs, both of us hugging the wall and stepping gingerly around the holes. When we reached the main salon again, I gazed up through the joists to the roughhewn planks that blocked the void created by the German bomb. Thank goodness it hadn't actually exploded. There would be nothing left. Knowing what I did about the precarious finances of the estate, I understood why repairing the wing had never risen to the top of the priority list, but it was sad to see the ruins of rooms where the family once lived and slept. If Stanton Knox didn't buy the castle, perhaps this is what it would all look like in ten years' time.

Lucy brushed a cobweb from her skirt. She looked at me, her blonde head tilted to one side. "And what were you doing here?" she asked. "Suffering from the same curiosity as me?"

"No, I was on my way to the library and saw the door ajar," I said.

"Anyway, where is everyone? Are they still in the meeting then?" she asked. "With what's his name, that Silicon Valley entrepreneur?"

"Stanton Knox. Yes, they're still discussing the contract and will be for some time."

"What are you looking for?" she asked.

"Looking for?" How could she know I was searching for clues that might reveal the danger to Fergus? Then I realized she couldn't know that. "Just a book to read," I said.

"Anything in particular?"

"No." I didn't feel I needed to tell her I was looking for something to explain my bizarre vision. I turned to walk up the hallway, and Lucy fell in step beside me. The interior of the castle felt warm and cozy compared to the chill in the damaged wing.

"Duncan said there are some wonderful collections in the library," Lucy said. "Including a whole section of books on the Wars of Scottish Independence. I'd like to take a look around as well if you don't mind the company."

"Of course," I said, leading the way into the library, where we separated, each doing a circuit of the shelves. I scanned the titles of an extensive collection of science and astronomy books, and moved on until I reached the history section, where Lucy was kneeling, examining books on the lower shelves. I wasn't even sure what I was looking for, but one volume, *A Short History of Castle Aiten*, caught my eye. I eased it off the shelf and carried it to an armchair. It turned out to be a description of the construction of the castle over the centuries. Perhaps it would provide some information on the building out on the moor. I flipped pages, looking for a mention of the estate's cottages and outbuildings. But then I stopped. Looking for an explanation of my strange vision wasn't going to help Fergus. I needed to focus, as Josh had said earlier. With the book open on my lap, I struggled to come up with a strategy. What I should do, I realized after a few minutes, was talk to people. If someone out there intended harm to Fergus, I needed to find him before he could act. Reading books was not the solution.

When I stood up, Lucy glanced over from her exploration of the history section. "Are you leaving already?" she asked.

"Yes. I remembered something I have to do. I'll come back to read this later." I put the slim volume on a side table next to my chair. "Are you going to stay here? Maybe I'll see you when I get back?"

She nodded. "I'll be here for a while. Fergus has some histories that I don't even have access to in the university library." She waved a thick tome at me. The gesture reminded me of the woman on the moor holding out a book, and I shuddered. Luckily, Lucy didn't seem to notice.

"Oh, and like I said, let's not mention our tour of the east wing to Duncan," she urged. "He's got enough on his mind right now without worrying about me breaking an ankle."

7

W

hen I reached the top of the grand staircase, I was glad to see Mrs. Dunsmore down in the entry hall. It seemed likely that she would be aware, if not of everything, but of much that happened in the castle and on the estate. She was talking to Lachlan, who gave me a faint nod of acknowledgement before turning to hurry out through the front door. At some point soon, I'd have to try engaging him in conversation, a joyless undertaking. He didn't seem like the chatty type.

Mrs. Dunsmore appeared to be upset. Her cheeks were pink and she was out of breath.

"Is everything all right?" I asked, my chest tightening with anxiety as I descended the last few stairs.

"Nick has gone," she said. "I was just on my way to tell the chief."

"Gone?" My mind flashed quickly to the feud Fergus had sensed was brewing in the kitchen.

"Pierre thinks he quit. He didn't come in this morning. Can you imagine? With guests for dinner and the party tomorrow night? I don't know what we'll do."

I patted her hand. "We'll all pitch in," I said. "I'm sure we can make it work. But perhaps you could tell Fergus later? The meeting is still going, and it may not be a good time to distract him."

She smiled and wiped her hands on her apron. "That's a thought. We want things to go as smoothly as possible, though I canna say I like that young American much. I took trays up to the Great Hall earlier, so they could eat while they talked. He didn't bother to say thank you. But maybe that's what they're all like in America, what do I know? How about you, dear? It's well past lunchtime and you haven't eaten yet. Why don't you come down with me to the kitchen and you can tell Pierre what you'd like?"

That sounded promising, so I accompanied Mrs. Dunsmore down the back stairs to the kitchens. The young chef was there alone, stirring a pan of something that smelled delicious.

"Can ye make something for Kate here to eat?" Mrs. Dunsmore asked.

Pierre bowed to me and smiled. "Of course. What would you like? I have potato and leek soup, or perhaps you'd prefer a salad?"

"Soup sounds perfect," I said.

"Pierre will bring it up for ye," Mrs. Dunsmore said. "Make yourself comfortable in the breakfast room."

"Oh, no, that's far too much trouble. I'd be happy to eat down here if Pierre doesn't mind? Will you eat too?" I was hoping she'd say yes, so that I could talk with her, but she shook her head vigorously. "No, I have that much to do. Beds to make up for the new guests. I must get on."

"Why don't I help you? I can eat later."

Mrs. Dunsmore actually rocked back on her heels, as if I'd suggested something improper. "Goodness, no. What would the master think? I have a girl who's helping me, and we'll get it all done soon enough." She looked at Pierre. "Will ye manage without young Nick to help you? There will be eight for dinner tonight."

"*Pas de probleme*, Mrs. D.," he replied.

The housekeeper hurried out. For now then, I'd settle for a chat with Pierre. He pulled a stool up to the butcher block counter and, with a flourish, gestured to me to sit. With quick, practiced movements, he produced silver cutlery, a starched white napkin, and a plate of crusty bread with a tiny bowl of chilled butter. Then he served my soup as though we were in a Michelin star restaurant.

"Thank you," I said. "I don't want to distract you. You'll be busy now, with the party tomorrow and the extra houseguests. It's too bad about Nick not coming into work."

Pierre's brown eyes darkened. "Yes. The timing is most unfortunate. He was supposed to be here at eight this morning but he failed to come in. I called his number several times with no success."

"What happened? Did you quarrel?"

"Quarrel? *Mais non.* But he hasn't been happy since I arrived four months ago. He resents me and I do not blame him for that. But what can I say? He wasn't capable of producing haute cuisine of the quality needed for the estate's dinners. It is a serious money-making venture."

My soup was ample proof that Pierre was more than qualified as a chef. It was delicious, smooth and creamy.

While I ate, he lined up three glistening knives next to a chopping board. "I will be just a minute," he said, heading towards a massive steel door on the far side of the kitchen. He flipped up the door lever and stepped into what was obviously a meat locker. When he came out, he was carrying a large plucked bird. It resembled a chicken, but not quite.

"Pheasant," he said as he set it on the chopping board. With the largest of the knives, he expertly sliced wings, legs and breasts into neat pieces. The blade slid through the flesh easily, and I swallowed hard, remembering the knife attack I'd seen that morning. My stomach flipped, and I put my spoon down.

"The soup is not good?" he asked, his dark brows drawn together in a frown.

"It's wonderful," I assured him, picking up my spoon again. "So, do you think that Nick will come back? Has he walked out before?"

"He's left a few times and returned, often a little drunk," Pierre replied, selecting a smaller knife to chop up an onion. "Perhaps he will realize that leaving is not a sensible solution."

"I hope so," I said. "We all want Fergus's birthday party to be a success."

I settled back to admire Pierre's knife skills while I ate my soup. Josh and I enjoyed cooking and often spent our evenings experimenting with new recipes. We were reasonably accomplished home cooks, but my diced onions never looked as perfect as Pierre's did. He went on to make quick work of several bunches of fresh sage and oregano. The aroma of the herbs drifted across the counter towards me.

"Where did you learn to be a chef?" I asked him.

"I went to culinary school in Lyon and then I worked in several exclusive restaurants in Paris," he replied.

"How did you come to be here in Scotland then? Did Fergus advertise?"

Pierre's cheeks flushed red as he scraped the finely chopped sage leaves into a copper bowl. "Not exactly. It was a matter of chance. I was looking for a new challenge and Fergus needed a chef."

I looked at him with one eyebrow raised, waiting for him to elucidate, which, after a pause, he did. "I came for a little holiday," he said. "At the inn in the village, I met a young man who told me he was also a chef and that he worked here, preparing dinners for a few guests and for private events. I visited the castle and ate here one evening." He pulled a face as though smelling something unpleasant. "I realized there was an opportunity, and made a proposal to develop the menu in both range and quality to attract more diners. And that is how I came to be here."

"I bet poor Nick regrets talking to you at the inn," I said.

"Perhaps so. Nick is a competent cook, but..." He shrugged. "We have attracted many more patrons since I came."

Pierre was very French, handsome, and undoubtedly talented, but modesty clearly wasn't one of his greatest assets.

"And you don't miss the glamor of haute cuisine in Paris?" I asked.

He either didn't hear me, or pretended not to, because he turned away to fill a large pot with water and banged it down on the stove. I assumed our little chat was over and wondered about his real reason for leaving Paris. The castle was picturesque, and I guessed that Fergus was a good boss, but it was a far cry from working in a culinary epicenter of Europe. Maybe he'd been fired. That would explain his reaction to my question. Or maybe he just needed a job. Although my faith in human nature had taken a beating over the last couple of years, I still tried to see the best in people.

As Pierre continued to make a racket with his pots and pans, I finished my soup. "Thank you," I said loudly enough for him to hear me. "The food was scrumptious."

"*Merci, mademoiselle.*"

He centered the pot over the flame and turned back to look at me, flashing a wide smile. As he seemed to be back to his charming self, I ventured another question.

"Is Nick angry with Fergus for bringing you in over his head? Has he said anything that could be construed as a threat?"

Pierre shot me a puzzled look. "Threat? Not that I recall." He reached for a sack of potatoes and began to peel them. "Although, now I think about it, he did once complain that he felt Fergus had let him down. But then, many people are feeling that way at this time, because of the situation with the estate."

"You know about it then?" I asked. "About the potential sale?"

"Of course. Mr. MacKenna has been very open with all of the staff and he has explained the reasons for needing to sell. One or two of the tenants are unhappy. I saw them in the pub with Nick one evening, whispering in a corner."

"How about you? Are you unhappy too?"

Pierre slid the potatoes into a pan of water. "No. Why should I be? Fergus assures me that the new owner will keep me on. And if he does not, well, then it will be time for me to go elsewhere. I am content to take whatever path opens up to me."

"What about the other staff?" I asked. "Lachlan and Mrs. Dunsmore?"

"How can they be happy?" he said. "This place has been home to them for many, many years. But things change, and you have to look out for yourself." He returned to the chopping board and picked up another knife. "No one else will look out for you."

"That's sad but..." I began and stopped when I heard footsteps on the stone staircase. I wondered if it was Nick returning. A tall man in a black wool coat appeared in the arched entrance to the kitchen.

"*Bonjour* Pierre," he said.

The chef swung around, knife still in hand, a frown creasing his brow. He and the visitor talked in rapid French, both of them appearing agitated. When Pierre flung his hands up in the air in a gesture of frustration, the blade glinted under the halogen lights in the ceiling. I wished he'd put it down.

The men calmed down and carried on talking, more quietly now so I couldn't hear anything they said. Not that I'd understand it anyway. I spoke Italian fluently but my French was minimal, a rusty leftover from a couple of years in school.

The visitor's sharp chin and high cheekbones made him appear intense, even a little menacing. His skin was pale against his black coat. I wondered if he and Pierre were related. If they were, it didn't seem that they had the warmest of relationships. After a few minutes of earnest conversation, the stranger turned and left. I heard his hard-soled shoes tapping on the stone steps.

Pierre muttered something under his breath and came back to resume his chopping. Carrots were now the object of his impeccable knife skills.

"Who was that?" I asked, when it seemed likely he wasn't going to explain.

"Just a friend. He will help me at the party tomorrow night."

"I hope he's nicer to the guests than he was to you," I joked. "He seemed a little fierce."

Pierre shot me a glance, and I thought my attempt at humor was lost on him, but then he smiled. "Yes, I will make sure he is both pleasant and polite."

"Is he local?" It seemed unlikely that there'd be two Frenchmen living in a tiny community in rural Scotland.

"No. He is staying at the hotel in Dalmally for a few nights. We knew each other in France, and he stopped by on his way up to the Hebrides for a holiday. He offered to assist me with cooking for the party tomorrow. And he speaks very good English, so he can assist with the serving if needed."

When Pierre turned away to adjust one of the burners on the range, I hopped down from my stool. I'd enjoyed my late lunch, and had learned a little from Pierre about the unhappy tenants. For himself, though, he seemed resigned to moving on elsewhere if the sale went through. He didn't appear to be harboring any ill will against Fergus.

"Thanks again for the soup. I hope Nick turns up soon so he can help with the party too."

"Perhaps. He can only be helpful if he is sober."

8

I left the kitchen and climbed the narrow staircase, noticing the plain and functional banisters and spindles. Its stone stair treads were scarred and worn from centuries of use as servants hurried up and down, catering to the needs of the people upstairs. Although bustling and noisy once, today it was quiet and a little gloomy.

When I reached the entry hall, I stopped, gazing up at the mounted stag heads on the walls. They reminded me of the doe I'd seen earlier. Had she been real or was she too part of my strange vision? I thought about the young woman. Her style of dress suggested she'd been well-to-do, possibly a member of the family who lived in the castle. In spite of Josh's recommendation to stay focused on Fergus, my mind kept wandering back to her, wondering who she might be. Why was she out by herself, and what was the book she'd been carrying? The man in the black robe had been intent on taking it from her. Was that why he'd killed her? Still staring at the stag heads, I became lost in my vision, seeing it again like a slow-motion video.

Time to concentrate, I told myself. I needed to uncover more information on the house and its occupants, as well as the tenants. Pierre had indicated that some were angry with Fergus, and that Nick had been seen in conversation with them. He'd implied that Nick was also upset, resentful of the decision to sell, which wasn't too surprising. From what Pierre had said, it didn't seem likely that the young man would keep his job at the castle once Fergus left. I needed to talk to Nick, to find out how he was feeling. With any luck, he'd identify which of the tenants were so unhappy. When Josh was free later, we could go into the village to find him.

For now, though, I had no one to talk to, so I decided to go back to the library to read the history book I'd set aside. It had looked like a fast read, good for a basic background on the estate. I retraced my steps up the grand stairway, past the double doors to the Great Hall, which were closed. Beyond them, voices murmured like the low hum of bees, and I hoped the sale negotiations were going well. Sad as it was that Fergus had to relinquish the castle, it had to be the best possible outcome for him, and Duncan would certainly ensure Stanton Knox paid a fair price for the estate.

I turned into the green-carpeted corridor that led to the library, thinking Lucy might still be there. The huge room was empty, however, and my footsteps echoed on the old oak floors as I walked to my armchair. But when I reached the side table where I'd left my *Short History of Castle Aiten*, it was empty. Had Lucy picked up my book? Thinking perhaps Mrs. Dunsmore had been in to clean and had put it away, I went over to check the shelf. There was no sign, though, only a thin gap proclaiming its absence.

Certain there must be other histories I could read instead, I scanned the shelves. For a few minutes, I was happily distracted, pacing slowly along the walls of books, running my fingers along cracked bindings and peeling gold letters. Red, blue, green and brown, the books offered vast accumulations of knowledge and whispered messages from the past. But I didn't know which one might give me a lead to follow. Finally, I gave up. I'd go talk to Mrs. Dunsmore, ask her if she'd seen my book, and try to engage her in conversation about the estate sale. I needed further clues on the danger to Fergus.

Before I left the library, I found a pen and notepad next to the phone. A few minutes later, I'd completed a sketch of the woman I'd seen on the moor. It wasn't perfect, but it captured her slender figure, her pretty features and luxuriant curls. I'd show it to Fergus later to see if he'd recognize her from a portrait or a book.

Remembering that Mrs. Dunsmore had said she was going to make up beds for the guests who were staying overnight for the party, I set off for the tower. Traversing the picture gallery, I was conscious of dozens of eyes watching me from the gilt frames. Did these old ancestors see me as an outsider, poking my nose in where it didn't belong? If they could talk, would they tell me how to save Fergus?

The spiral tower stairway took me down to the ground floor where I walked along the hall past several open bedroom doors. I glanced in each one until I found Mrs. Dunsmore smoothing out a dusky rose coverlet on a bed.

"Can I help you?" I asked her.

"Thank you, but everything is in hand," she replied. "Only two more rooms to do. Then I'll tidy the dining room ready for the dinner this evening. I hope Pierre's managing on his own."

"He seemed to be doing fine. Of course, he should be, with all that Paris training and experience. He's an interesting character, isn't he?" I paused, giving her a moment, hoping she might offer some observation on the young chef, but she nodded distractedly while centering a small vase of heather on the dressing table.

"Oh, I wondered if you'd cleaned up in the library?" I asked. "I left a book on a table, but it's gone missing."

"No, dear. I haven't been in the library today." She glanced over at me. "It probably fell on the floor or slid down the back of the sofa. I often find books tucked away behind the cushions or throws." She hurried over to smooth the folds of the curtains into place.

It obviously wasn't a good time for a chat. "I'll get out of your way," I said and wandered back into the corridor, where I paused, uncertain what to do next. Maybe I'd ask Lucy if she'd taken my book. Thinking that she might have returned to her room, I trudged up the spiral staircase to the second floor where I heard the distant hum of a vacuum cleaner. The door to my room hung open and, inside, a young woman pushed the vacuum to and fro across the rug. She gave me a wave when she saw me. "Just a few minutes," she shouted over the noise.

"No rush." I continued along the hallway towards Lucy's room. Her door also stood open. I knocked on the frame and called out, but there was no answer.

Taking a step inside, I called Lucy's name again, loud enough that she could hear me from the bathroom. An open suitcase sat on the floor at the foot of the bed, spilling clothes out onto the Persian rug. Amidst the pile of silk and wool was a book. With its blue and white cover, it looked like my *Short History of Castle Aiten*. Had Lucy taken it? Without stopping to consider what I was doing, I hurried over and picked it up. Immediately, I saw that it wasn't the *History* after all, but a paperback text book on medieval architecture, the kind of thing I would like to read myself. As I turned it over to look at the back cover, a piece of paper slipped from between the pages. I caught it before it fluttered to the floor and saw that it was a press clipping, a short article in French, with the word *Fabergé* in the headline. Accompanying the text was a photo of a decorative egg covered in jewels and set on a stand. My French wasn't very good, but I knew enough to decipher the date, March 25, six months ago.

Suddenly acutely aware that I was trespassing and looking through someone else's things, I slid the clipping back into the book, almost certainly between the wrong pages. I had just put the book in its place on the rug when I heard floorboards creaking in the corridor. Three fast strides got me to the door where I took a breath, ready to explain to Lucy that I'd stopped by to see if she wanted to take a walk with me. It was Mrs. Dunsmore, however, not Lucy, and she was carrying a stack of bedding so high she could hardly see around it. I slipped into the hallway.

"Let me help you," I offered.

"Och, thank ye. We're almost done, but Fiona's very slow with the vacuuming." She glanced at Lucy's door. "Did Fiona leave that door open? I tell her to leave everything as she finds it, but her mind's on other things. Boys mostly."

9

After depositing the linens in one of the guest rooms under the direction of Mrs. Dunsmore, I wandered through the picture gallery, wondering how long it would be before Josh and Fergus returned. As I passed the top of the main staircase, I saw Lachlan down in the entry hall. Although reluctant to approach him, I knew I needed to talk to him. He'd been on the estate even longer than the housekeeper, and would have good reason to nurse a grievance against Fergus because of the sale. I took a step down as he opened the front door. I didn't know him well enough to call out to him, so I hurried to catch his attention. He'd gone, though, by the time I got to the bottom step, and had pulled the door closed behind him. I wondered if he was deliberately avoiding me as I hauled it back open, marveling at how heavy it was.

The storm had passed, leaving behind a blustery wind that bent the bare tree branches and roared around the eaves above my head. I could go after Lachlan, who was marching down the driveway with intent, his rifle resting on his arm, or I could delay that unpleasant interaction, avoid the bad weather and do some more research on the priory. It wasn't a hard decision to make. Instead, I retraced my steps to the library and my armchair. Thinking of what Mrs. Dunsmore had said, I slid my hand between the cushion and the armrest. Sure enough, my history book was there. I was certain I'd left it on the table, but I must have been wrong.

Settling into the chair, I opened the book. The title was accurate; the book was short, only fifty pages long. I skim-read the history, which confirmed much of what Josh had told me on the drive up from the airport. The first building on the site had been a wooden motte and bailey construction intended to provide both a residence and a defense against marauders. Built in the twelfth century as a stronghold of the MacArthurs, it had survived for two hundred years before being replaced with a three-story tower castle. I had seen drawings of these structures. Castle Aiten's was square, about twenty meters in width and length, with stone walls two meters thick and a crenellated battlement. Over the next four centuries, the tower stood, changing hands as land was lost and won in a never-ending succession of battles against the Norsemen, the English, and a range of Scottish clans, including the Campbells. My mind wandered, imagining the clash of swords as armies met on blood-soaked fields to battle over territory, power and religion. We were still fighting over the same issues today, I thought. Only the weapons had changed.

The tower had endured all those centuries of assault and yet it still survived. As an architect, I often wondered about the lifespan of the buildings we worked on. Would our descendants be admiring a five-hundred-year-old skyscraper or a glass-encased office block? It seemed unlikely somehow.

Concentrating again, I carried on reading the dry history. The residence attached to the tower had been expanded in the late fourteen hundreds, with further developments made until the mid-1700s, when it was abandoned in the aftermath of the Jacobite uprisings. After standing empty for fifteen years, it had been purchased by Robert MacKenna, a wealthy merchant who'd made his fortune importing sugar. He had repaired the crumbling castle and built two new wings to create a large and elegant country house, completing his estate with the purchase of an additional hundred acres of the surrounding land. His great-grandson had made further improvements in the 1840s, tacking on the east wing to provide more space for the extravagant parties he enjoyed.

My heart rate accelerated when I came to page twenty-two. The author described a priory, built in 1500 on the grounds of the original castle to house a small community of Benedictine monks. The building was abandoned in the mid-sixteenth century and later restored sufficiently to serve as a shelter for shepherds. At the time of writing, the author said, only a few scattered ruins survived as evidence of the early religious settlement.

It had to be the place where I'd seen the murder. The man had been wearing black robes and I vaguely recalled that the Bene-dictines wore black. So that suggested the murder had taken place during the period when the monks were living on the estate, from 1500 to the mid-century. Knowing a rough timeframe for the murder might help me discover more about the woman.

A voice in my head was telling me that this had nothing to do with Fergus's aura and that I was wasting time. I leaned back against the chair cushion and closed my eyes, forcing myself to concentrate. What or who was the threat to Fergus? After a few minutes of fruit-less thinking, I closed the book and left it on the side table. Josh had mentioned a computer. Perhaps some online research about the estate would yield some clues.

After a long climb up the stairs to Fergus's wood-paneled office, I found an old IBM PC on a table tucked away in a corner under the slope of the ceiling. I hadn't even noticed it on my first visit here. A prehistoric modem was attached to a phone outlet on one end and the back of the computer on the other. The PC's plastic casing had yellowed with age, and the keyboard was dusty, which made me wonder how often Fergus used it or if it would even work. The tiny monitor lit up as soon as I turned it on, though, and I entered the password that Josh had given me earlier. Sitting on the upright chair that had been tucked under the table, I squinted at the low-resolu-tion screen for a few seconds, listening to the primitive shrieks and squeals of the modem. To my surprise, a telephone icon appeared, confirming I'd connected to the internet.

Unsure of where to start, I entered the name of the castle into the browser. After a long delay, in which I was sure I could hear the cogs turning in the machine, a screenful of entries came up: a history of the castle, a mention in an environmental survey, confirmation of building permits for the new roof, and a marketing website describing the castle's Gourmet Dinner and Bed and Breakfast offerings.

I found no mention of a priory but I soon found a listing of once-extant monasteries going back to the tenth century. A Benedictine monastery about thirty miles from the castle had been founded in the early eleventh century and appeared to have closed in 1500. I searched more closely on those dates and finally found a mention of a small religious community being given shelter on the grounds of the castle in the years 1500 to 1545.

I sat back and drummed my fingers on the table. The man in the black robes had to have been a monk, with that hood and crucifix. But why did he kill that young woman? Did he retrieve the book she'd been holding? It seemed likely that he had, although I didn't see it happen. Like a damaged movie reel, the vision had stopped in mid-flow. I only saw the frames to the point where the film broke. Fueled by the desire to know what had happened there, I carried on searching, but found nothing useful, with no results for the book, and no reference to a murder. Of course, why would there be? Huge swathes of British history were well-documented on the Web, but a killing on a remote Scottish moor sometime in the sixteenth century was unlikely to have been recorded, leaving nothing to find its way onto the Web centuries later.

Disappointed not to find anything to explain my strange vision, I quickly checked my email. There were a few terse messages from my boss, which I ignored. He was a little hazy on the concept of time off. Because he rarely took any holiday time himself, he didn't expect the rest of us to either.

About to turn off the computer, I remembered the press clipping that had fallen out of Lucy's text book. I keyed in 'Fabergé' and the date, March 25. A dozen news sites popped up, reporting the recent discovery of a Fabergé egg, missing since the execution of the Russian royal family in 1918. Apparently, a number of the fifty bejeweled Fabergé eggs commissioned by the Romanovs had been seized by the Bolsheviks and hidden in the Kremlin Armory, together with a vast hoard of the Tsar's jewels, books, paintings, and icons. As the Revolution heated up, Romanov family members had managed to smuggle other treasures to safety. A cache of jewels had been sent by Nicholas II's aunt to the Swedish Embassy in St. Petersburg, where they lay forgotten in a storage room until they were rediscovered in 2009. Another treasure trove was rumored to be buried in Mongolia. Much of the Kremlin hoard had been sold off during the 1920s and '30s to raise money for Stalin's Treasures into Tractors program, with many of the artifacts being acquired by wealthy Americans and Europeans for private collections or museums. Many items went missing, lost forever in dusty vaults, or lying unrecognized on the shelves of antique shops.

In 2014, a Fabergé egg had been purchased for a song in a junk shop in the USA by a scrap metal dealer. And then a collector had discovered an egg in an antique shop in Paris six months ago. He'd paid just a thousand pounds for an item worth millions. The discovery unleashed a flood of articles speculating where other lost Romanov treasures might be.

I pushed the keyboard away and flexed my wrists to get the blood moving again. While my little jaunt into the rarefied world of priceless artifacts was fascinating, it was also feeling like a waste of time. Whatever Lucy's interest in Russian eggs, it had nothing to do with Fergus's aura or my vision of the killing on the moor. That gory scene kept replaying itself in my head, but it too was a distraction I could do without. I needed to focus on discovering what threatened Fergus. Time was slipping by, and I had no clues yet. A twinge of anxiety sent a pain through my temple. Josh and I couldn't leave the castle until we were sure Fergus was safe, but I'd used up most of my holiday time already. My boss, Alan, would be extremely unhappy if I didn't turn up on Monday. But there was no point in worrying about that yet. We still had two more days to save Fergus.

A glance at my watch told me it was already four-thirty. I looked towards the window and realized that I'd been concentrating so closely on the computer that I'd missed the fact that it had grown dark outside. This far north, the days were short, and sunset came early. Apart from the glow of the computer screen, the room was dim, draped in shadows that hung in the corners. Wind rattled the window and whistled down the chimney. I shivered. Suddenly, the old castle seemed far less romantic and intriguing, far more menacing and bleak. I was overcome by melancholy and a strange sense of being watched. I peered into the shadows. Was someone hiding there? Telling myself not to be ridiculous, I stood and crossed the room to switch on a lamp. I heard a creak, felt a brush of air as though someone had rushed past me. I stopped, feeling my blood chill in my veins. Forcing myself to move again, I fumbled with the lamp switch. The bulb glowed through the yellow shade, banishing the shadows. The tartan sofas looked cheery and inviting. Fergus's desktop was empty apart from a blotter and a pen. Everything was as it should be. But the door stood half-open. I was sure I'd pushed it almost shut when I came in.

I hurried to the door and looked up and down the darkened corridor. I felt as though I was standing in a tunnel, black and impenetrable, with a single lamp shining yellow at the far end. I stared at the light for a minute, but saw no sign of movement.

Convinced I'd imagined the whole thing, I stepped back into the office. My walk across the moor had unnerved me, I decided. First the strange vision, and then getting lost and soaking wet. No wonder I felt jumpy and a little discombobulated, which wasn't like me. I needed to calm down, focus on practicalities.

I took a slow tour of the room, picking up ornaments and knick-knacks, putting them back in their places, but I didn't know what I was looking for. Still shaky, I went out to check the hall again. Certain that no one loitered there, I closed the door and returned to the desk where I started opening the drawers one by one. I felt guilty about ransacking Fergus's office, but convinced myself that my slightly unscrupulous behavior was justified when a life was at stake. The drawers held a typical collection of pens, pencils and sticky notes, and piles of papers that looked like bills and receipts. No bottles of poison, knives or guns, no threatening letters or warning notes, nothing that would give me a hint as to what threatened Fergus.

The gilt carriage clock on the mantel struck five, reminding me that the meeting with the Americans would probably soon be over for the day. I hoped it was going well. Making sure the computer and the lamp were turned off, I left the office and hurried towards the main staircase where bright lights illuminated the glossy woodwork and carpeted treads. Descending, I arrived in the entry hall just as Lucy came in through the front door.

"I wondered where you were," I said. "Have you been exploring again?"

She smiled. "I planned to, but I found a book I wanted to read and lost track of time." She rubbed her arms. "God, it's cold out there. I went to get something from the car and never thought to put a coat on."

Through the open door, I saw the lights of Knox's helicopter blinking red and white down on the lawn.

"Why is the helicopter here?" I asked.

"I don't know. It landed a few minutes ago. Perhaps that means the meeting is over?"

As she spoke, we heard voices at the top of the stairs. Fergus led Knox and his team downstairs towards us. They looked cheerful enough, I thought, hoping that indicated the negotiations had gone well. Josh followed, but there was no sign of Duncan. "I'll leave you to listen to the boring business details," Lucy whispered. "See you later." She slipped away into the drawing room.

Knox and Fergus were chatting, so I joined Josh. "How did it go?"

"Good. I think it's going to turn out okay." He paused. "Aura still there?"

"Sadly, yes."

"See you around lunchtime tomorrow," Knox was saying, shaking hands with Fergus. As his two associates put on their coats and gathered their bags, Fergus opened the door, letting in a blast of cold air.

We stood on the front step to watch the visitors go. Their modern wheeled suitcases kept getting caught up on the graveled driveway. In the old days, the servants would have carried their travel chests to the waiting horse and carriage. Now, the helicopter's engine throbbed in sync with the pulsing of its lights.

"They aren't spending the night here?" I asked Josh.

"Knox wanted to go to Edinburgh, so they're flying over there. Something came up at work, apparently."

"Pierre's cooking for a crowd," I said. "He might not be thrilled to have a smaller audience for his pheasant cacciatore."

"Pierre?"

"The chef. Very French and very charming. He made lunch for me."

Fergus touched Josh on the arm. "Where's your cousin?"

They both looked around the entry hall. "Wasn't he with you?" I asked.

"He was until about twenty minutes ago," Fergus said. "He needed to use the head, but he didn't come back to the Great Hall. I hope he's not ill."

"I'll go find him," Josh offered.

Fergus nodded. "Thanks. Me, I need a drink. My head is swimming."

"I'll have one with you," I said to Fergus. I wanted to keep an eye on him.

"I'm going to my room to take off this wretched jacket and tie. You catch a minute alone with Josh. And then join me in the library, and we'll launch another attack on the single malts."

Thwarted in my attempt to stay close to Fergus, I followed Josh upstairs and past the entrance to the Great Hall. Halfway along the corridor, we stopped at a white door, and Josh banged on the paneled wood. "Duncan? You okay?"

When there was no answer, Josh turned the knob and opened the door to an empty loo. "He must have given up on us," Josh said. "The last half-hour was mostly small talk anyway, and we didn't cover anything useful." He closed the door and then pushed it open again.

"Actually, as I'm here... We did drink a lot of tea this afternoon. I'll see you in the library. Tell Fergus I'll have the Macallan again."

When I got to the library, most of the lights were off, and Fergus wasn't there. Duncan was, however, and he seemed to be searching for something in the semi-darkness. Not a book, I thought, because he wasn't looking at titles. Instead he was sweeping his hand along the gap behind the serried ranks of hardbacks. I knew I should say hello or cough, do something so he knew I was there, but his behavior was so odd that I couldn't help wanting to know what he was searching for. He moved on to a different shelf and repeated the sweeping motion. I stepped back into the hall when he moved from the shelves to a chest of drawers near the fireplace. There, he opened each drawer and felt around inside before closing it again. Clearly not finding what he was looking for, he expressed his frustration by slamming his fist down on the walnut surface.

Deciding I'd seen enough, I stepped into the room. "Hi Duncan," I said brightly. "Josh is looking for you. Are you all right?"

"Of course I'm all right. Is the meeting over?"

"Yes. Josh and Fergus are on their way up to have a drink. I don't know where Lucy is."

I groped around on the wall next to me and switched on the lights, filling the library with a soft golden glow. Duncan glared at me, red spots of color on his cheeks.

He smiled suddenly, a patently fake attempt that moved his lips up a fraction. "A drink sounds good." The red blotches gradually faded. "Come on, we'll go review our options while we wait for Fergus."

I followed him into the drinks cupboard where we examined the labels on the bottles until Josh arrived, with Fergus not far behind him. Lucy came in as Fergus was pouring our selections. He seemed to be in good humor. "To Stanton Knox," he said, raising his glass. "He's offering even more than we first discussed, although he wants me to throw in the collection of single malts, and I'm not so sure about that."

"He's only saying that to wind you up," Josh laughed. "But with what he's prepared to pay for the place, I say give him the whisky. You'll be able to afford to buy some more."

"Is Knox buying everything?" I asked. "Including the furniture and paintings?"

"That remains under discussion," Fergus said, leading us to the sofas in front of the fire. "I've drawn up lists of items that won't be included in the sale. I'll keep most of the family portraits, for example, and enough furniture for my new home. And I'm not prepared to include the entire contents of the library, although he's very keen to keep it all."

I stole a surreptitious glance at Duncan. What had he been looking for on the bookshelves and in the chest of drawers? He glanced at me and looked away. Perhaps he guessed I'd seen him searching.

"We'll have to come to an agreement on how to handle the books," Fergus continued. "I'll create a list of what I want to keep. When I inherited the estate, I was given a stack of binders containing inventory registers of the books, pictures and furniture. So the book register will be a good starting point. I'll go look for it after dinner."

"I'd be happy to help you," Lucy said.

Fergus patted her arm. "Thank you my dear. I'd appreciate the assistance."

"Not at all," she said. "I love books."

Duncan glared at her. What was that all about? Then I realized that he was probably angry at her offer to help Fergus with something related to the estate sale, but Lucy seemed either oblivious or deliberately ignoring his obvious disapproval. I thought about his search of the library shelves. He was up to something, that was clear. Was he the threat to Fergus? Josh had completely discounted that idea, but I wasn't so sure. I'd have to keep a closer eye on him.

10

"Wake up, Kate." It was Josh, pulling the covers back and shaking me harder than seemed necessary.

"I'm awake."

"There's something weird outside. You need to take a look."

I stumbled out of bed, woozy with sleep, and blinked when Josh opened the curtains, flooding the room with bright light. The window revealed a perfect view of azure sky, laced with threads of gossamer clouds. The rising sun set the moors alight in shades of amber and copper. I glanced back at Josh, eyebrows raised.

"It's a rare phenomenon," he said. "They call it the sun, and it rarely visits this northern wilderness."

"Can I go back to bed now? It's Saturday, and it's only nine o'clock."

He cocked his head. "And miss all that?" He waved his arm dramatically towards the window.

"It is beautiful," I conceded.

He ruffled my hair. "So are you, but get dressed. I'm starving."

Twenty minutes later, we found Fergus in the breakfast room, drinking tea and reading a newspaper. He looked up with a smile when he heard us come in. "Lovely morning," he said. "I'm glad you will finally see Castle Aiten in the sunshine, Kate. And as we have the morning free, I think we should go for a ride. Rob Bryant runs the estate stables. I called him earlier, and they're all ready and waiting for us."

I glanced at Josh. Riding sounded dangerous, and Fergus's aura still swirled. "Perhaps we should all stay here and help you with your book list," I said.

Fergus shook his head. "No need. Lucy and I started it this morning at the crack of dawn, but we need some exercise and a break from staring at letters and numbers. Grab some breakfast and then we'll go. Lucy and Duncan are getting ready. Duncan didn't want to come, but I managed to persuade him."

It didn't surprise me that Duncan would rather stay behind. It would give him a few hours to poke around the house in peace. But if he didn't come, then I'd stay as well. I needed to find out what he was up to.

Fergus went back to reading his paper while Josh piled scrambled eggs on to his plate, to which he added a slice of ham and a mound of sautéed mushrooms. But the continued evidence of the threat to Fergus had dulled my appetite. I poured myself a cup of tea and spread butter and homemade marmalade on a piece of toast. By the time I'd finished, Fergus and Josh were on their feet and waiting to go. In the entry hall, I held back as they put on their jackets, contemplating how best to excuse myself from the ride.

Just then Lucy called from the top of the stairs. "We're coming. Mrs. Dunsmore found some proper shoes that Duncan can ride in. He doesn't want to wreck his fancy loafers."

So Duncan would come after all. There went my excuse to avoid the ride.

Unlike some of my friends, I was never horse-crazy growing up. I'd taken a few lessons at the local riding school— on a pony appropriately named Placid. I thought, looking back on it, that my parents must have bribed the teacher to only let me ride the smallest and fattest pony in the school.

Hoping my horse today would be equally serene, I squeezed in with the others in the back of Fergus's dilapidated green Land Rover for the short drive to the stables. No one discussed Knox or the sale. In the front, Fergus and Josh chatted about Josh's job and what it was like living in London. Duncan and Lucy chatted quietly, making no effort to include me. But the drive was short, and we soon arrived at a neat stable block that held a dozen stalls and a small office where the manager greeted us. The smell of hay, manure and horse sweat filled the air.

A stable boy brought out our horses, one by one, starting with a handsome black stallion for Fergus. Duncan didn't seem happy with his smaller white horse, although I thought she was charming. While Duncan pouted, Lucy happily mounted her pretty black and white piebald, and Josh helped me onto a sleek brown mare called Missy.

"Have you ridden before?" I asked Lucy as I concentrated on stopping Missy from backing into Josh.

"I grew up with horses and was on an equestrian team at school," she said. "After I graduated and was living in Kent, I rode on weekends. But I haven't been able to do much since I moved to London, so I'm excited to get out for a while. Here," she added, leaning over. "Thread the reins through your fingers like this and relax your hands."

Lucy was full of surprises. For some reason, my first impression of her had been of a quiet, retiring, professorial type. But now it seemed obvious I'd misjudged her. There was something of a female Indiana Jones about her, with her secretive explorations of the castle and her horsemanship.

Once everyone was ready, we followed Fergus at a sedate pace out of the stable yard and along a dirt road, which quickly dwindled to a sheep track. I soon got used to the gentle sway of Missy's back under the saddle and remembered how to use the reins to move her in the right direction— not that she needed much help from me. She trotted along with determination as though she'd done this ride many times before.

As we wound our way through the heather, the sun transformed the moors into fields of molten gold, and the air smelled of warm vegetation, which reminded me of my dad's garden in the summer, with its scent of sun-kissed tomato plants. For a blissful hour or so, I pushed away thoughts of the vision and of Fergus's aura. It seemed impossible for anything bad to happen on a day as gorgeous as this one.

Catching sight of water glinting under the translucent sky, I saw that we'd circled all the way to the lochan that Josh and I had visited the day before. Gone were the ominous grey waves. Today, the surface was like glass, reflecting the lemony light. We rode to the water's edge to let the horses drink in the shadow of the Brynjarr Stone. The sounds of lapping and gentle nickering were peaceful and soothing. Even Duncan looked relaxed and content.

When Fergus turned his horse to start the ride back, the others followed, but Missy refused to budge. I tugged on the reins, trying to raise her head. She carried on drinking. Unconcerned, knowing I could catch up, I sat and patted her neck, enjoying the moment of solitude. Her coat was warm against the palm of my hand, and the sun felt like a heat lamp on my back.

A bird squawked overhead, loud enough for Missy to look up. Black and white, the bird flew over us and landed on a low boulder a hundred meters away. A few seconds later, another bird settled next to it. While I was trying to make out what kind of birds they were, I noticed something gleaming on the sand. It was very close to the rock, which sat half in and half out of the water. They were magpies, I realized, scavengers attracted to shiny things. Curious to see what the glistening object was, I tugged on the reins until Missy paid attention. We ambled slowly towards the birds. Even as we came closer, they didn't move, staring at us with the arrogance they were known for. In spite of their attractive plumage, they had a reputation as bearers of evil omens. Even my down-to-earth grandmother always crossed herself when a magpie flew past.

The object I'd seen from a distance was glass, probably a bottle of some kind. Certain that Josh or I would have noticed it yesterday from where we'd been sitting, I wondered who'd left it there and when. I pulled Missy to a halt and dismounted. She stood quietly, gazing at the birds out of the corner of her eye as though she didn't trust them.

It was only after I'd walked a few steps closer that I understood that there was no boulder. The magpies were sitting on the back of a man's body. His legs were in the sand and his head in the water. My stomach churned, but I moved forward. It didn't seem possible he was alive, but I had to be sure. Shooing the stubborn birds away, I knelt at the edge of the shallows and, screwing up my courage, rolled the man over. It was obvious at once he was dead. His face was a mess, grey and puffy, dreadful enough to make me look away quickly. His fair hair was darkened with water and I couldn't guess his age, but the Mumford & Sons T-shirt he wore suggested he was young. One of his hands stretched out towards what I now saw was a whisky bottle, with a few centimeters of brown liquid in the bottom. I forced myself to look at his face again and saw an abrasion on his cheek and a deep and jagged gash in his left temple.

Bile rose in my mouth. I jumped up and rushed to a bush where I threw up. Still shaking, I returned to Missy and tried to scramble into the saddle, but my muscles weren't working properly, and I couldn't pull myself up. Clutching her bridle, I leaned against Missy's neck, feeling her coarse mane rough against my cheek. I took a few deep breaths and straightened up. On my next attempt, I swung up onto the saddle, and turned the horse away from the man's body. Abandoning my earlier caution, I dug my heels into her flanks and coaxed her into a fast trot, guiding her along the lochan towards the Brynjarr Stone and the path that Fergus had taken.

At the black spire, I stopped when I saw Josh riding towards me. He waved me forward. "Come on," he called. "We thought we'd lost you."

My voice caught in my throat. I could hardly speak, let alone shout, so I waited until he rode closer. "We need to call the police," I gasped. "A dead body." I twisted in the saddle to point.

Josh's face paled. "Show me," he said.

Reluctantly, I turned Missy around and led Josh back along the shore. The magpies had already returned and now perched on the man's chest. I yelled at them to no avail while Josh slid from his horse and handed me the reins. After a moment of hesitation, he strode towards the water, flapping his arms until the birds flew off.

He knelt down beside the body for a moment and then stood and dusted sand from his jeans. He looked as shaken as I felt.

"Do you know who it is?" I asked.

"I only met him once a year ago, but if I had to take a guess, it's Nick."

11

A rush of activity followed. Leading Josh's horse, I rode after Fergus and the others to tell them what had happened; Josh took the footpath through the rocks to reach the house and a phone. Fergus insisted on seeing the body and refused to wait until the police arrived, which left me with a dilemma. I couldn't leave him alone, so I had to go with him, much as I dreaded seeing the corpse again. Duncan and Lucy said they'd ride to the stables and bring the Land Rover back to the house.

Fergus cantered fast enough along the lochan to make me nervous that his horse might stumble, but we soon arrived safely at the water's edge. I pulled Missy to a halt and stayed in the saddle while Fergus dismounted and strode towards the body.

"Is it Nick?" I asked.

"It is." Fergus knelt down, his head bowed for a minute before he straightened up. His aura swirled, a constant reminder of the threat to him. I was sure Nick would have had an aura too, but I hadn't seen him when he was alive. And, I knew from past experience that, at the moment of death, the aura disappeared.

Fergus remained next to Nick, keeping watch over him, until two police officers arrived, led by Josh along the pathway through the granite boulders.

"We'll take it from here, sir," the senior officer said. "We need to secure the scene so if you'd step back and get the horses out of the way, we'd appreciate it."

With nothing left to do, the three of us rode to the stables, where we were greeted by the grim-faced manager, who offered his condolences and a ride home in his Range Rover. We drove in silence back towards the castle.

The ambulance and a second police car arrived just as we turned into the castle driveway. One of the officers told us that Nick's father had been notified and was on his way. My stomach did flips as I thought of how awful it must have been to receive that call. Fergus was shaken, his face white and drawn. Of all of us, only he had known Nick well. Taking charge, Josh guided him inside and insisted that he sit down in the drawing room. Duncan, who must have heard us come in, joined us and said Lucy was resting in her room.

"What do you think happened?" he asked once we were all seated.

Josh shook his head. "It looked as though maybe he'd been drinking and he fell."

"Damn silly behavior," Duncan commented, apparently unmoved by the death. Josh rolled his eyes and we sat in silence until Mrs. Dunsmore came with tea. She poured it without talking, and the clink of china and silver was strangely soothing.

Half an hour later, a policeman came to tell Fergus that Mr. Jameson had confirmed the dead man was his son. The senior investigating officer was due to arrive shortly, he said.

It turned out that the middle-aged inspector, who introduced himself as DCI McMahon, knew Fergus through a prior case, something to do with sheep rustling. They greeted each other somberly and talked quietly for a few minutes before McMahon asked if he could interview me, as the person who'd discovered the body. Fergus suggested we use the breakfast room. I followed the inspector there, and we drank tea while McMahon filled out his interview sheet.

"This is purely routine," he said in a soft Scottish accent. "We only need the details of how and when you found the body."

His slate-grey eyes flicked between me and the notes on the paper in front of him as I talked. He had big hands, I noticed, which stuck out from the sleeves of his dark blue suit.

When he'd finished with me, he stood and straightened his tie, a muted green tartan that didn't really go with his navy jacket. "I'm sorry you had to go through this," he said. "Finding a body is always a shock. If you feel you need to talk to someone about it, I can make a recommendation for a counsellor."

I thanked him and said I was fine. It didn't seem like the right time to say that I was fairly used to stumbling across dead bodies.

"You're free to join the others," he said. "I plan to have a word with the chef, Pierre, while I wait for my team to finish up at the lochan."

When I wandered into the drawing room, Fergus, Josh and Duncan were talking quietly.

"Should we cancel the birthday party?" Fergus asked once I was seated next to Josh.

"I don't think so," Duncan replied. "It's too late. We can't possibly contact every guest in time. It is unfortunate timing, but we should go ahead as planned. Most of the guests don't even know the Jameson family."

Josh nodded his agreement. "Knox is coming back especially for the party, and the overnight guests will arrive at any minute. It's tough, but I don't see a way around it."

"You're right. It seems inappropriate though."

A heavy silence hung in the air, seemingly pushing the oxygen out of the room. I was finding it difficult to breathe, recollecting the sight of Nick's ruined body by the water. A little later, McMahon appeared in the doorway and, although Fergus invited him to sit, the inspector remained standing. Without preamble, he told us that their initial findings indicated an accidental death. "The whisky bottle was almost empty," he said. "We'll have to wait for results of toxicology tests, but it seems likely the victim was intoxicated. He fell and hit his head hard enough to knock him unconscious into the shallow water where he drowned. Or the fall itself may have been fatal. The medical examiner will be able to tell us whether he died from the head injury or drowning, but we won't probably hear anything until tomorrow or Monday."

I remembered Pierre saying Nick had walked out on the job a couple of times previously and had come back drunk. It was sad that he'd turned to alcohol. The young man had obviously been stressed by his work situation, and I imagined it must be hard to find employment up here. His options had probably been very limited.

The inspector went to his car after that, to follow the ambulance that carried Nick's body and his grieving father. Fergus paced around the drawing room. He'd rubbed his eyes until they were red and kept tugging at his beard. "It's my fault," he said. "I should have intervened. There was plenty of work here for both Nick and Pierre. I should have done more to make sure Nick was kept busy and happy."

I thought about Pierre. He hadn't shown much concern for the young man he'd replaced. Perhaps he should have mentored him, given him the benefit of his talent and experience. But maybe he'd tried, and Nick had resisted. It wasn't fair to judge without knowing the whole story.

As Josh tried to calm Fergus, we heard the helicopter flying overhead. Ten minutes later, Knox and his two colleagues came in, accompanied by Mrs. Dunsmore.

"What happened?" Knox asked. "There were police cars outside when we landed."

When Fergus explained what had happened, Knox shrugged. "Never drink alone by a body of water," he said. "Bad idea."

That was helpful, I thought, disturbed by his casual and rather callous reaction. He had other things on his mind, apparently, as he asked Fergus if he could borrow Lachlan to help him unload boxes from the helicopter. The four boxes turned out to be cases of Dom Pérignon champagne, Knox's contribution to the party that evening.

"Maybe chill them in the meat locker," Mrs. Dunsmore suggested, "as there isn't any space left in the wine refrigerator."

While Lachlan lugged the champagne downstairs, Mrs.

Dunsmore took Knox and his team back to their rooms where, they said, they planned to work on the draft of an agreement for the rest of the afternoon. That seemed to leave Fergus unsettled and unfocused.

"I should go talk to Nick's father," he said suddenly. "Offer him any help I can."

"Isn't it a bit soon?" Josh suggested. "Give it a day or two?"

"No. Nick died on my property and he worked for me. I have a responsibility. The least I can do is offer my condolences to Mr. Jameson."

"Then I'll drive you to the village if you like," Josh said.

Fergus climbed to his feet, looking as though he was in pain. I went with them to the front door, where Josh kissed me on the cheek before going down the steps.

"We won't be long," Fergus promised.

After watching them go, I returned to the drawing room, but Duncan had left. That was too bad. I wanted to ask him what he'd been looking for in the library. Perhaps he'd gone back there to resume his search. I set off to find him but the only person in evidence was Lucy. She sat at the small writing desk in the corner, pen in hand.

"What are you working on?" I asked, walking over to stand next to her.

"The list of books that Fergus plans to keep." She bowed her head over a sheet of lined paper, clearly not planning on talking to me.

"Is this the original catalogue of all the books that Fergus owns?" I picked up a leather binder filled with yellowed papers.

She looked at it. "Yes."

"So, what's the plan? How will Fergus decide what to keep and what to sell?"

"He's already decided what he wants to keep, more or less." Lucy put her pen down with a sigh. "Once he's made his final choices, they will be marked in the catalogue, and those books pulled out and crated up. An appraiser will value the remainder of the collection, which Knox will pay for."

"I doubt he'll know what he's getting," I said. "But having books on shelves will impress his friends."

"Actually, I've heard he's very well-read," Lucy said. "Apparently, he's one of those people who can absorb huge amounts of information almost instantly."

I raised an eyebrow, surprised that she knew anything about Knox. "I didn't mean to judge him," I said. "It's just that this is so distressing for Fergus, having to part with the house and its contents. I hope he finds some peace when it's all over."

At that moment, I decided to tell Lucy about Fergus's aura. I needed all the help I could get, and she was working with him now. At the very least, she could keep an eye on him when Josh or I couldn't.

"There's something I'd like to talk to you about. Shall we sit over by the fireplace? It'll be more comfortable."

Lucy settled at one end of the sofa, smoothed her blond hair into place and twitched her long skirt into neat folds. I took a seat in an armchair opposite her. "What I'm going to tell you will sound outlandish, perhaps a little insane," I said. "But I'm sharing it with you because Fergus's life is in danger, and it's possible you know something— even if you don't realize you do— that might help save him."

Ignoring her expression of incredulity, I hurried on, telling her about my ability to see auras that predicted death. "Fergus has an aura, and he only has a few days to live, unless we do something to help him," I said. "There's a chance he has a medical condition, but I'm beginning to believe the danger is somehow wrapped up in the sale of the estate."

"An aura?" Lucy's tone gave me hope that she'd hear me out. She sounded more curious than skeptical. I recalled her excursion to the east wing. She clearly had an inquisitive mind, and I would take advantage of that.

"That's what I call it," I said. "Air spins in circles over the victim's head. The faster the spin, the more imminent the danger."

"So Fergus is going to die?" Lucy's eyes widened.

"Yes, probably, unless I can do something to change his... fate." I hated that word, *fate*. It sounded so final, so inescapable. Yet I had managed to save people in the past. And I was determined to save Josh's uncle.

"You can make the aura go away?"

"I can sometimes alter circumstances just enough to save the victim. Then the aura disappears."

"That's quite a responsibility," she said, twisting a gold bracelet around her wrist. "But I'm not aware of a single thing that might affect Fergus's safety. What makes you imagine I can help?"

I shook my head. "I don't know, really. But perhaps you will come across something when you're working on these inventories. Maybe Fergus will mention something that might indicate what the source of the threat could be."

She tilted her head. "I'm happy to do what I can. But honestly..." She let the sentence trail off. "I like Fergus," she continued. "I hope nothing bad happens to him."

"I intend to make sure it doesn't." I spoke with far more confidence than I felt.

Lucy leaned forward towards me. "Do you see other things? Other supernatural phenomena?"

As she appeared to be open to the idea of auras, I decided I might as well tell her everything. "Yesterday, out on the moor near the ruins of the old building, I saw a vision." I described how the man in the black robes had plunged a knife into the back of the woman holding a book.

Lucy went very pale and put her put her hand on the armrest to steady herself. "How terrible," she said. "Do you think it was something that really happened?"

"I don't know, to be honest. It felt real." I shivered. "It's sad. The girl was so young."

"I'd love to learn more about it," Lucy said, with the color coming back into her cheeks. She seemed to accept my bizarre story at face value. "I've never had any encounters myself with, you know, ghosts or anything, but I find it all fascinating. In medieval times, people were very superstitious, and, with the rise of the Catholic Church and its threats of Hell, the living were quick to believe that spirits wandered the earth, looking for help to escape Purgatory. I've read hundreds of stories about hauntings, many of which can be rationally explained away, of course. But sometimes not."

The gilt clock on the mantelpiece chimed six. I got to my feet. "We'd better get ready for dinner. Will you keep an eye open this evening? With all these guests in the castle, it will be hard to protect Fergus."

"Do you think your vision has something to do with the threat to Fergus?" Lucy asked as she stood up to join me.

"How can a five-hundred-year-old murder have any connection to him?" Mine was a rhetorical question that Lucy didn't answer.

She walked with me to the door and gave my arm a squeeze. "Try not to worry. We'll look after him."

12

By the time I reached my room, I realized I didn't have long to get ready for the party. Fergus had asked us to be there early to help greet the guests. I was tired and distracted, still unsettled by the discovery of the body earlier, but I found my make-up bag, and put on eyeliner and mascara. My thick, wavy hair always looked more elegant tied up, so I wound it into a chignon and tried to secure it with a pin. But my fingers were shaking, and the pin didn't hold. I was on my second attempt when Josh came back. I let my hair fall down around my shoulders and gave him a hug.

"How did it go?" I asked.

"As you'd expect. Not well. Nick's father refused to open the door. He just shouted at us to go away and said he never wanted to talk to Fergus again." Josh sank onto the bed and took off his shoes. "I'm sure he'll come around. We probably shouldn't have gone over there so soon, but Fergus thought it would help if he expressed his sympathies in person. It was hard though. Jameson obviously holds him responsible."

I sat down next to him and wrapped my arm around his shoulders. "I'm sorry. But I suppose it's understandable that Nick's father will look for someone to blame for the loss of his child."

I closed my eyes, suddenly light-headed. I'd only been a child myself when my little brother died. Now I remembered the raw grief of my parents as though it had happened yesterday. My father had been the most changed by the tragedy, perhaps because, after an initial outburst of anguish, he'd done that British stiff upper lip thing. He rarely spoke of Toby and had thrown himself into his work, leaving at dawn each day to take the train into the City. He was a barrister and had always worked hard. But, after Toby's death, he took on double the caseload and seemed determined to bury himself in legal files and documents. They filled his home office and bulged from his briefcase. Quite often, he'd come home after I was already asleep in bed.

Josh, clearly sensing my distress, pulled me closer to him.

The years after Toby died had been painful. I'd felt so guilty that I'd been in the pool when Toby drowned that I had withdrawn into myself, choosing not to spend time with my friends. My grades had suffered, and I dreaded going to school. With my mum still grieving and my father at work so much of the time, my big brother Leo had been my savior. Once he realized what was happening to me, he waited every morning at my bedroom door until I'd dressed and then he walked with me to school. He made sure I did my homework and he dragged me with him to tennis lessons. I proved to be useless at tennis, but my grades improved, and I gradually rejoined my friends in the school playground. Years later, when my dad retired, he let down his guard, and went through another period of mourning. This time, though, Leo and I were old enough to be able to help, talking with him when he wanted to, distracting him when he didn't. I certainly understood the agony Nick's father must be feeling.

"Could Mr. Jameson be the threat to Fergus?" I asked finally.

"Possibly. But I find it hard to imagine. The idea of being furious enough to kill someone seems a bit unreal."

I leaned my head against Josh's chest and felt the strong pulse of his heart against my cheek. I knew what he meant, but there was nothing unreal about death. It could change our perceived reality in a moment. Not for the first time, I wished I didn't see auras. I really struggled with the uncertainty and fear they brought with them.

Josh stroked my hair as though he'd guessed what I was thinking. After a couple of minutes, he pushed me away gently. "I'm going to my room to get dressed. Tonight, we have to be vigilant, but we should join in the celebrations. I want Fergus to enjoy himself."

While he was gone, I slipped my dress from its hanger in the wardrobe. A deep midnight blue, with spaghetti straps, it was my favorite dress-up dress. The softness of the silky fabric against my skin made me feel pampered and special. I was putting on my high-heeled sandals when Josh returned. In a Stewart tartan kilt, with high socks to his knees, a white shirt and black jacket, he was breathtaking. I stood up, taller in my heels, but still shorter than him, and pressed my lips against his before straightening his bow tie.

"I have to ask," I said when the tie was perfectly aligned.

For a second, he looked confused and then he laughed. He grabbed the hem of his kilt and flipped it upwards. "Check for yourself."

I reached under the heavy wool fabric and slid my hands up his thighs.

After a moment or two, I let the kilt fall and took a step back. "Boxers? Really?"

"At least they match the kilt. I intend to do a lot of dancing tonight and I wouldn't want to embarrass anyone with an accidental flashing."

I shook my head in mock dismay. "So are you a true Scot or are you a Sassenach?"

He held his hand over his heart. "You know how to wound a man." He pulled me close. "You look delicious, and I won't be crass enough to enquire what you're wearing underneath."

We stood for a minute, holding each other, and I was able to imagine that we were going to a lovely party and would have a wonderful time. No auras, no imminent death. It was a pleasant fantasy.

"We should go," he said, smoothing my hair back into place.

Holding hands, we began the walk to the Great Hall. In our traditional evening clothes, instead of jeans and wellingtons, I felt an elemental link to the castle and its history. As we passed through the gallery, I was sure the eyes of Josh's ancestors were on us, beaming their approval of my dashing young Scotsman.

When we reached the top of the main staircase, we saw the entry hall was filled with arriving guests. Their excited chatter floated up the stairs as they divested themselves of coats and jackets, assisted by several young people in black pants and white shirts. Mrs. Dunsmore had told me that, although Pierre could handle all the cooking, she'd hired a team of wait staff from a catering company in Inveraray. We hurried on, anxious now to check on Fergus before too many people arrived.

The Hall was beautiful, with vases of yellow flowers on every flat surface. A dozen tables draped with white linen were grouped around one fireplace where flames leapt with a welcoming glow. At the other end, the floor had been cleared for dancing. A three-piece band would play later on the raised dais, but for now a piper stood alone, filling the room with music that sent tingles through my fingers and toes. I had no Scottish roots, and didn't recognize the tune, but I was captivated by the unfamiliar harmonics, accompanied by the wheezy exhalations of the pipes. Behind the piper hung a banner wishing Fergus a Happy Birthday.

The room gradually filled with a colorful array of tartans in red, green, yellow and black, as the guests greeted each other with smiles and handshakes— old clan rivalries forgotten or buried, at least for tonight. I doubted there'd be any fighting or swordplay to mar the evening's festivities, which was a comforting thought. The women mostly wore evening gowns, although one or two wore ankle-length tartan skirts, white-frilled shirts and tartan sashes. Jewels sparkled, and wine glasses gleamed under the warm light of the massive chandeliers. As I gazed around the splendid room, I felt sad. Although I'd normally enjoy the pageantry of such a formal gathering, tonight I could think only of Fergus. The elegant clothes, polished manners, and the rituals involved in serving and eating an elaborate dinner would be wasted on me.

Stanton Knox nodded a greeting at me when he arrived, dressed in tan jeans and a black sports coat. Boat shoes with no socks were a step up from his usual flip-flops at least. His personal assistant wore a dinner jacket, however, and his lawyer, Maya, looked gorgeous in a long cream dress that perfectly complemented her coffee-colored skin. Fergus, splendid in his dark green kilt and sash, guided them off to introduce them to some local dignitaries. I noticed that Robert Dunne, Fergus's solicitor, stood with them too. He'd changed his tight blue suit for a jacket and kilt.

"One of us needs to stay close to Fergus at all times," Josh said. "I'll join him now, and you keep your eyes open for any sign of trouble."

I nodded, grabbed a flute of champagne from a passing waiter and took up my position near the door, where I could observe everyone who entered. Not that it would do much good, I thought. They were all strangers to me. How could I tell if one of them was a potential assassin? When Lucy came in, I waved her over, hoping to enlist her help in protecting Fergus. She was lovely in a rose-colored dress, her blonde hair pinned up with a silver comb.

"Where's Duncan?" I asked.

"He's on his way. He said he had to make a phone call first. Something to do with work."

After waiting until she had a glass of wine in her hand, I explained that we needed to watch out for Fergus. "If you notice anyone doing anything suspicious, please tell me or Josh as soon as you can."

Lucy frowned. "Do you really think something could happen here? With all these people around?" She gazed around the room, scrutinizing the guests.

I was grateful she seemed to be taking me seriously. "I know it's hard to imagine, but we have to be on guard," I said.

"But how do we know what to look for?" She pointed at a huge man with legs the size of tree trunks. A pale scar ran down his cheek. "He looks like a killer, but he probably isn't."

"No, it's usually the quiet ones; the ones you don't suspect," I agreed. "We'll just have to do our best. Josh will stay at Fergus's side all night."

"Duncan can help when he gets here," Lucy said.

I wasn't convinced that Duncan would help at all. It bothered Josh that I thought of Duncan as a suspect, but he had a motive, and, so far, I'd been unimpressed with his personal characteristics. His reaction to the sale had exposed a basic lack of sensitivity, and his almost permanent bad humor was enervating. And then there was that surreptitious search in the library. He was up to something, for sure.

"How did you and Duncan meet?" I asked Lucy.

She blushed. "At a bar in the City. A friend introduced us. Why do you ask?"

"Oh, no reason. Just curious. He's rather intense, isn't he?"

She laughed. "That's an understatement. But he's fun and interesting. Never a dull moment, as they say."

"He's not very happy with the proposed sale of the castle, I gather."

Lucy held her hand over her glass as a waiter offered to top it up. "I don't blame him," she said. "He's always talked about the castle as his family home and of course he assumed he'd inherit it one day. He was ranting yesterday about finding some legal loophole that would stop Fergus from selling. But I doubt there is one. Besides he'll get over it. There's more than enough to keep him busy in London."

I thought about his odd behavior in the library. Perhaps he was searching for something that would provide him with a reason to halt the sale. I couldn't imagine what it might be. "Is he looking for something?" I asked. "I saw him going through the shelves in the library. Perhaps a book? Or a document that might affect the purchase of the estate?"

Lucy raised her glass and took a big swallow of wine. "I don't know. He hasn't said anything to me."

We were interrupted just then by a blast from a trumpet. Fergus picked up a knife and clinked it against his glass until the room fell silent. He gave a short speech, thanking everyone for coming, and making no mention of the imminent sale of the estate. Another half dozen speeches followed, as old friends of Fergus recounted stories of past experiences and escapades. It seemed that Fergus had been quite an adventurer in his youth, and a serious academic before he'd retired.

With the speeches over, the young attendants we'd seen in the entry hall directed us to our seats. I was glad to see that Josh was seated next to Fergus. An empty chair on Fergus's other side was presumably meant for Duncan, and Lucy's place was next to it. I sat between Josh and a large, florid-faced man in a green kilt and jacket. His wife and several older couples made up the rest of the head table. Stanton Knox and his team were sitting together. Lachlan sat at their table, and I hoped he'd use the opportunity to argue for his continued employment.

The bagpiper gave way to the members of the band, who played quiet jazz, obviously saving their energy for later. Fergus had told us they were famous for their traditional Celtic music, and would have everyone on the dance floor after dinner. Waiters arrived with the first course.

The young girl who'd been wielding the vacuum yesterday now carried plates of food to our table. I remembered Mrs. Dunsmore mentioning that her name was Fiona. She smiled when she saw me. "Hello, miss. Lovely evening, isn't it?" She sighed with a wistfulness worthy of Cinderella wishing she could attend the ball. Pretty and vivacious, she quickly attracted the attentions of the man in the green jacket. After subtly extricating her arm out from under his meaty hand, she told us that the salmon had been caught and cured locally in Inverawe. It looked delicious. Translucent slices of the smoked fish were artfully arranged on our plates, decorated with lemons and sprigs of sorrel. I noticed that Pierre's earnest French friend was serving the table next to us. He described the food in almost perfect English, but the smile on his face looked a bit false.

I saw Josh looking over at me. He nodded towards Duncan's

empty chair, one eyebrow raised. I was too far away from Lucy to ask her what she thought Duncan was doing, but she appeared unconcerned, engaged in conversation with the woman next to her. We'd just picked up our knives and forks when I heard footsteps and glanced up to see Duncan arrive. No kilt for him, but he did look handsome in his dinner jacket and bow tie.

Less attractive, however, was the aura that swirled over his dark hair.

Duncan with an aura? I felt the room tilt and dropped my fork with a resounding clang. Gripping the sides of my chair until the floor came to level again, I stared at Duncan to be sure I wasn't imagining it. But it was clearly there and moving fast.

Two auras? That wasn't good. Our theory that Fergus might have a medical issue dissolved like tissue paper in the rain. Something dreadful had to happen for two men to die at once.

13

I pushed my smoked salmon around on my plate, unable to take a bite, however appetizing it looked. Josh noticed and leaned over. "What's wrong?"

"Duncan has an aura."

Josh carefully laid down his fork. "Are you sure? Never mind, I know you are."

Watching Duncan cross the Hall, I wondered what could have happened to change his status from safe to endangered so quickly. I was positive that, when I'd last seen him, he had no aura. His cheeks were red as though he'd been running. When he took his seat next to Lucy, I noticed a mark on the lapel of his jacket; it glistened in the candlelight. Following my look, he glanced down and brushed at the offending spot. Not a stain, I realized, but a thread of spider's web, which stuck to his finger when he pulled it off his jacket. The castle was old, and there were many places where spiders could lurk, but my thoughts rushed to the east wing and the large webs I'd seen there. Had Duncan been poking around the abandoned rooms as well? Did he know Lucy had been there already? For him to be exploring the east wing now, with the party underway, was decidedly odd, unless he was merely taking advantage of the crowds to disappear for a while. Or had something happened to provoke him into an urgent investigation? Clearly, he was prepared to take a risk for whatever it was.

"What do you suppose it means?" Josh whispered as a waiter refilled his wine glass.

"Nothing good. Maybe that someone here tonight means harm to both Duncan and Fergus."

But why Duncan suddenly? He'd been fine up to this point. We both gazed around the tables filled with Fergus's guests. As Lucy had pointed out earlier, it was impossible to identify any possible assassins in the crowd. There were nearly sixty people in the room and any one of them could be the culprit. But it seemed highly unlikely that someone planned to pull out a gun and start firing. We were in Scotland after all. I knew knives could do a lot of damage, but it was hard to imagine one of these guests running amok with one.

The staff appeared to clear away the old plates and, shortly afterwards, Fiona set down our main course of venison and wild mushrooms, making sure to give the florid-faced man a wide berth. The food kept coming, and I picked at my plate enough to be polite and inconspicuous, but my stomach churned as I ran through possible scenarios. At one point, I asked Josh quietly if we should tell Fergus about the auras. "Maybe we should warn him. At least, he'll know to be on guard."

Josh shook his head. "It's too late now. We can't explain it properly here, and I doubt we can get him to leave the Hall and all his guests. I'll stay very close to him. You keep an eye on Duncan. And if we need reinforcements, use that phone over there." He pointed to a polished side table bearing a black phone. "We can call the police any time."

While I wasn't happy with any of it, I couldn't work out what else to do, short of barricading Fergus in his bedroom. As the feast wound down, the band warmed up, and the guests gravitated towards the dance floor at the other end of the Hall. Josh clung like a limpet to Fergus, and I stayed with Duncan, who didn't even notice my presence. A group of the younger guests gathered around him, listening to his stories of high finance in the capital. He seemed to be enjoying his moment in the spotlight; the dashing young heir from the City.

Although she'd promised to help me, Lucy had wandered off, and I caught sight of her talking to Stanton Knox in a corner. When she noticed me looking in her direction, she waved her glass at me and smiled. Knox was probably better company than Duncan.

The evening dragged on. The band played boisterous highland flings, and guests filled the dance floor. On any other occasion, I'd have joined in the dancing. Now, I couldn't wait for it to be over. All the time, I scanned the huge Hall, looking for any hint of something unusual, anyone who was behaving oddly. As the wine and champagne flowed, the decibel level rose. Every shout made my nerves jangle, and a slammed door made the hairs on the back of my neck stand upright. I kept forgetting to breathe, and my chest was tight with anxiety.

Duncan was drinking too much. His face was red, and he talked more and more loudly, but his coterie kept pace with him, all of them raising their voices to be heard. A young woman hung on his arm, and he appeared quite content to have her there. I wondered if I could persuade him to stop drinking, but he hardly even seemed aware I was standing close to him.

"We need more champagne," he said to his group of companions. "I know where the good stuff is. I'll be back."

I put my hand on his sleeve. "One of the waiters will bring it up," I said. "Stay here. I'll send someone."

He shook my hand off his arm. "Quicker to go myself. Although you could make yourself useful and help me carry it up."

Catching Josh's eye, I signaled that I was going with Duncan. He was standing with Fergus, talking with a group of kilt-clad men. When he nodded his acknowledgement, I followed Duncan as he weaved his way towards the kitchens.

"The Dom Pérignon is in the meat locker," he explained as we clattered down the back stairs to a kitchen full of people washing plates and drying pans, putting knives and tools away in drawers. Pierre was over by the sink, talking to his friend, the other Frenchman. The young chef looked surprised when he saw me, but gave a friendly wave and returned to his conversation.

Duncan collected six bottles of Dom Pérignon from the meat locker and gave me two of them. As he gripped two in each hand, he leaned his weight against the heavy steel door to close it, and a bottle slipped through his fingers. I was flinching in anticipation of the impending crash when a passing waiter thrust out his hand and grabbed it just before it shattered on the flagstone floor.

"Good catch," Duncan said, taking the bottle back. The waiter nodded. For a few seconds, he stood still, staring at Duncan, his dark eyes narrowed, his mouth turned down in contempt. When he turned away, I watched him go and wondered if he was a potential threat or if he was simply expressing disdain for a drunken rich guy from the City. Most likely the latter, but I thought I should check him out.

"Give me a minute," I said, but Duncan didn't seem to hear me, his gaze fixed on Fiona, the young Cinderella, who was chatting with another girl while they sorted cutlery on the butcher block counter. I walked over to Pierre. He and his companion were deep in conversation, talking French, so I didn't understand what they were saying, but I guessed they weren't chatting about the weather or the food. There was an urgency, it seemed, an intensity in the way the other Frenchman gestured. They fell silent when I approached.

"Mademoiselle Kate!" Pierre gave me a little bow. "How nice to see you. Did you enjoy the dinner?"

"Yes, very much," I lied. The food had been superb, but I'd barely touched it. "I was wondering who that man is? He saved a bottle of expensive champagne." I turned to point out the waiter who'd averted the broken bottle disaster but there was no sign of him. Pierre raised his eyebrows.

"Never mind," I shrugged. "I'm sorry to have disturbed you."

"Not at all. The party is going very well, *non*?"

"The party is perfect," I agreed. Aware of the two cold champagne bottles chilling my skin and dampening my dress, I said goodnight and walked over to join Duncan, who was now chatting up Fiona. Her dark curls bounced, and her cheeks glowed pink as she laughed at a joke he'd shared with her. Waiting for the little chat to be over, I leaned up against a counter, thinking we should just stay downstairs. The kitchen was smaller and easier to monitor than the Great Hall, but Duncan was ready to return to the party. I heard him say 'see you later' to Fiona, and then he jerked his head at me, which I took as an instruction to follow him. He set off, threading his way through the kitchen workers to reach the stairs.

The journey back took a while because Duncan walked with a particularly slow and steady gait meant to hide the fact that he was seriously drunk. A few people had congregated in the entry hall, where it was much cooler than upstairs. They sat on the oak bench or leaned against the walls, watched over by the bright glassy eyes of the mounted deer heads. Through the open front door, I saw a couple smoking on the front steps, giggling under a light drizzle. It all felt so safe. A joyful celebration of a birthday, the great house welcoming dozens of guests. My mind couldn't conjure a scene in which two men might die, but I had to stay alert. The fact remained that Duncan and Fergus were in imminent danger.

Duncan and I made stately, if somewhat wobbly, progress up the wide stairway. The hum of conversation in the entry hall receded, replaced by the strains of Celtic music, the beating of feet on the dance floor and loud laughter. I picked up the pace, hoping Duncan would follow suit. He lagged behind, though, and I slowed again. For a moment, I considered pulling him aside, telling him about the aura, and warning him to be careful. But it would be a pointless exercise. He'd hardly talked to me all evening, and even now, barely acknowledged my presence.

We finally regained the crowded warmth of the Hall, and Duncan dove through the melée to deposit his bottles on the bar. He turned to take my two. "Thanks," he muttered. "Want a glass?"

I shook my head. Staying next to him, I surveyed the room. Lucy was still talking with Knox, and she didn't seem to have noticed that Duncan had been missing for a while. Josh was with Fergus, chatting with several older couples. A half-dozen women had clustered around the fireplace, their tinkling laughs matching the chiming of glasses. Dancers thronged the floor, executing complicated moves accompanied by a lot of whooping.

It all seemed so normal that it was hard to imagine an assassin lurking amongst us. Perhaps I was wrong about there being a killer. Maybe something catastrophic was going to happen— a falling chandelier, a fire, a virulent case of food poisoning. But there were no other auras, not even over the heads of the most frail-looking guests. I didn't know what lay in their future, but it seemed death wasn't yet stalking them. So, a disaster that only killed Fergus and Duncan and spared everyone else? It was unlikely. I was sure they were both targets of a specific threat.

Lucy left Knox and made her way over to me. "Where were you?" she asked. I explained about the champagne run and gestured towards Duncan, who was filling champagne flutes.

"What's Knox like?" I asked.

She shrugged. "I don't know. Smart, obviously, egotistical— you'd think he'd personally invented the Internet, the way he talks about it, but he's nice enough."

"Did you talk about the sale? Is he going to close the deal with Fergus? No risk of him dropping out?"

She nodded. "Oh, he wants the purchase to go through. He was very enthusiastic, and said that he loves Scotland." She gazed around the room for a moment. "What's not to like? The castle is incredible." She fanned herself with her hand. "It's so hot in here. I need a bit of fresh air. You'll be okay watching Fergus?"

"There's something else..." I began, but Lucy was already walking away. I knew I should tell her about Duncan, but it was always hard to break that sort of news. Still, I thought she'd want to help, and I'd need her to watch out for him once the party was over. "Lucy," I called, and she turned back with a sigh. "I need to talk to you." I took her arm and led her away from the door towards a quiet corner. There was no point in prevaricating. "Duncan has an aura."

Her cheeks lost their pink glow, and her blue eyes widened. "That's a joke, right?"

"No. The aura only appeared this evening. I don't understand why. It means something has changed, that there is a threat to him now which wasn't there before."

"So, what now?"

"I need your help in protecting him."

"And how do we achieve that exactly?"

"The same way we're looking out for Fergus."

"It's impossible." She sounded almost panicked. "Think of all the ways someone could die, here, right under our noses. The only way to protect Fergus is to roll him in bubble wrap and lock him in his room with no food, where no one can get at him, he can't fall over and break his neck, and he can't choke on a piece of bread."

"When you put it like that..."

She put her hand on my arm. "I'm sorry. I'll do what I can to help." She turned to look at Duncan. "You're sure about the aura thing? He seems so... robust."

"I'm sure. Are you all right?" Lucy looked pale, which wasn't surprising after what I'd just told her. "Go get some fresh air," I said. "We can talk later."

I watched her go before hurrying to rejoin Duncan and the circle of young people gathered around him, where I loitered on the edges like a planet thrown out of its orbit.

When the grandfather clock against the wall struck midnight, there was a general movement towards the doors, as though the driveway would soon be filled with pumpkins and mice. The younger crowd lingered a little longer, but soon the band began packing up their instruments and the wait staff swept through the room like a swarm of locusts, gathering up every glass, plate and bottle. Josh and I collected Duncan and the three of us accompanied Fergus down to the front hall, where we found Lucy sitting on the bench with her sandals off. We gathered on the steps to say goodnight to each of the departing guests until finally the last of them had gone, whisked away in several minibuses that Fergus had hired to make sure no one drove home under the influence. Mrs. Dunsmore closed the door, bolting the lock and sliding the heavy bar into place. I was glad to see the door secured.

"Where's everyone else?" Fergus asked, looking around the empty hall.

"Mr. Knox and his team went up twenty minutes ago," Mrs. Dunsmore answered. "The Ballantines and the Coxes are already in their rooms too. They all have an early start in the morning. I'm going to check they have everything they need."

She hurried away up the staircase. The woman was indefatigable. It made me tired just thinking about the day she'd had.

Fergus sat down on the oak bench, sticking his legs out straight in front of him. "Remind me never to do this again," he said with a grin. "I'm too old for parties."

"It was a good one." Josh took a seat next to him. "A proper celebration."

"Let's have a nightcap," Fergus suggested. "I have a special bottle, a Springbank single malt from the Mull of Kintyre, which my father gave me when I graduated from Oxford. Might as well enjoy it now. Sixty-five isn't so old, but no one knows what's coming, do they? Follow me. It's in the drawing room."

He stood up, smoothed out his kilt and led the way. I was glad that Lucy and Duncan came with us without argument. We all needed to talk. As we filed in, I grabbed Josh's arm. "We have to tell them," I whispered.

Josh paused, half turned to look at me. "Tonight?"

"We might be running out of time."

"You're right. I'll leave it to you."

I waited until Fergus had poured us each a small dram and we'd all taken our first sip.

"I have something to say," I said.

Lucy's eyebrows shot up. Duncan grunted and took another swallow of his whisky.

"It's hard to tell you this," I began. I took another sip of my drink. "Fergus, you and Duncan are in mortal danger."

Duncan laughed and coughed at the same time. "What the hell does that mean?"

I explained about my ability to see auras and how their presence signified imminent death. "The good news is that because we know you're in danger, we can do something about it." I stopped, but no one spoke. "Usually," I continued, "the first appearance of an aura indicates that the victim might die within a week or two. But the way your auras are moving, very fast, it's more likely to be a matter of days, maybe hours. That's why I'm sharing this with you. You have to be hyper cautious while we work out where the threat lies."

Fergus's face creased into an expression of deep concern. He looked at Josh. "You believe all this?"

Josh nodded. "I do. Kate has a gift. She's been seeing these signals for three years now. Sometimes people die. But she's been able to save others. Actually, if not for Kate, our prime minister would be pushing up daisies."

"The prime minister?" Fergus asked me.

"It's a very long story."

"This is bloody ridiculous," sputtered Duncan, slurring his words. "Auras? Rippling air? Imminent death?" He waggled his hand in the air. "Oooh, scary stuff. Not. I can't believe you'd fall for this codswallop, Josh."

Fergus leaned forward in his chair. "Be quiet, Duncan. How do we discover the source of the danger, Kate? Do you know what it is?"

"No, not yet. It could be to do with the proposed sale. You two are the current owner and the heir to the estate, which suggests it is a factor."

"Someone wants to prevent the sale?" Fergus asked.

"Possibly. There are plenty of suspects. People who want things to stay as they are and will do whatever it takes to make that happen. We need time to find them, discover what they are planning— and stop them, of course."

Duncan glared at Lucy, who'd remained silent. "You already knew about this? This portent or whatever it is Kate thinks she can see?"

"Kate told me earlier, yes."

"But you agree with me that it's rubbish?"

Lucy declined to answer, instead bowing her head over her drink.

Duncan ran his finger round the rim of his glass, producing an eerie singing noise from the crystal. "Something just struck me. If someone kills off Fergus and me, the estate goes to Joshie." He pointed at his cousin. "You have a motive, old man. What are you planning? Sell it anyway and pocket the money? Or vacate London and enjoy the good life in bonnie Scotland?"

"Duncan!" Lucy admonished.

He burst out laughing. "I was only teasing. Good God. You're all so damn humorless." He slumped in his seat and swallowed the remainder of his whisky.

"Do we bring in the police?" Fergus asked, ignoring Duncan's outburst.

I glanced at Josh. We both knew how challenging that would be. "We could," I said, "but I know from experience that it's hard to convince a policeman to take any of this seriously."

Duncan laughed again. "I can't for the life of me see why."

I shifted in my chair and gazed at Fergus, as though the act of looking into his eyes would convince him of what I was saying. "I've never been wrong about an aura," I said. "I wish there were some doubt, some chance that I'm misjudging the situation, but I don't believe I am. So we need to do everything we can to keep you and Duncan safe, and we need to consider every possibility, however improbable it might seem. Can you think of anyone who means you harm? Or you, Duncan?"

Duncan snorted. "Only a couple of hundred people. Like every hedge fund manager I outperformed last year— and there were many. A few disgruntled investors who don't understand the way the markets work. I made them millions but that wasn't good enough, apparently."

"Oh, shut up, Duncan," Lucy snapped. "You think you're a goddamned master of the universe just because you gamble with other people's money and occasionally win."

Duncan's eyes widened and his mouth gaped open. He looked like the trout I'd seen in the lochan. "You can't speak to me like that..."

"Stop it," said Fergus. "I don't know what's going on between you two, but this isn't the time for you to be fighting."

"Let me get this straight." Duncan ignored Fergus and glared at me. "You see this swirly air, which you say predicts death, but you don't have the faintest clue what the danger is or when it will strike?"

"No." I wanted to slap him.

"Then what's the point? It's like my telling a client that he's going to lose a huge amount of money unless he invests in the right company. Well, of course he'll lose money if he bets on the wrong stock. That's where I come in. My experience and knowledge will shield him from financial disaster. I do my homework; I know the risks and the pitfalls. You, Kate, seem to know nothing. Why bother to predict this hypothetical doom when there's nothing you can do about it?"

"I don't choose to see the auras. Believe me. It's a gift I'd swap in a heartbeat. But once I see an aura, I try to help."

"And I bet that works out really well," he said, his voice laden with sarcasm.

"It is possible to change the outcome." I struggled to stay calm even though I was ready to strangle Duncan myself. "We simply need to pinpoint areas of potential danger."

Duncan threw himself back against the sofa cushion. "Unfreakingbelievable."

"It seems to me that we should have faith in Kate's prediction," Fergus said. "I trust Josh, and if he trusts Kate, that is sufficient for me. So, Duncan, I'd suggest you give this some thought. It might save your life."

He leaned over to pat my hand, as if I was the one in need of consolation. "As for me, my dear, my decision to sell has upset a number of people. Have I made them angry enough to want to kill me? I wouldn't have thought so, but who can tell what lurks in a man's heart? Or a woman's, come to that. Humans are messy and unpredictable." He poured himself another finger of the single malt.

Duncan stood up. "I've had enough of this tosh. I'm going to bed."

"I'm not sure you should go off by yourself," Fergus said. "Given what Kate's just told us." He smirked.

Duncan flapped his hand at him as though swatting a fly, but he looked at Lucy. "Coming, Luce?"

She paused, looking at each one of us in turn. I couldn't tell what she was thinking. Finally, though, she put her glass down and stood up to join Duncan.

When they'd gone, Josh spoke to Fergus. "What about you? I'm worried about you being alone all night."

"Well, you're not staying in my room, laddie," Fergus laughed. "I'll be fine. I've no intention of popping my clogs any time soon. The castle is all closed up, Arbroath will be with me, and I'll lock my door too. Lachlan's on call if I need him. Now, let's get to bed. Stanton Knox and his crowd are leaving as soon as it's light. I should be there to bid them goodbye." He got to his feet and patted Josh on the shoulder. "You did stellar work today. Knox told me after dinner that he has everything he needs and is ready to move ahead. We'll be able to hammer out the contract by fax and email over the next few days. For now, get some sleep. We'll reconvene in the morning to talk about... this aura thing."

14

When Josh and I reached the tower, Lucy's door was closed and so was Duncan's. We paused to listen, wondering if Lucy had managed to calm Duncan down, but heard nothing. Further along the corridor, the sound of laughter came from one of the other guest rooms where two of Fergus's friends were spending the night. Knox and his associates were on the ground floor.

In my room, I threw myself onto the bed, suddenly exhausted. Josh leaned over to unbuckle my sandals and then sat down to take off his own shoes. We undressed slowly, each lost in our thoughts. Josh was tense, his concern for his uncle visible in every taut muscle in his neck and shoulders. I rubbed his back, which felt like a block of iron.

"We should get some sleep," I suggested. "There's nothing we can do tonight." I unpinned my hair and ran my fingers through it to smooth it out. "You realize it's Sunday tomorrow and we're supposed to be flying home."

"We can't leave Fergus," Josh said. "I'll call Alan in the morning to let him know we'll be taking Monday off. Unless you want to go back? There's no need for us both to miss work."

"No way. I'm staying with you. And we're going to save Fergus."

"And Duncan."

"Duncan too," I agreed. "In spite of his shortcomings."

Although it was past one in the morning, Josh took the time to hang his kilt and jacket in the wardrobe. With a grin, he picked up my dress from the bed where I'd left it, and threaded the straps over a hanger. He got into bed, yawned widely and, within a minute of putting his head on the pillow, was asleep.

I lay awake, hearing the wind whistling in the chimney. The leaded windows, old-fashioned and single-paned, let in every sound from outside— the scratching of a tree branch on a wall, the patter of rain. I'd thought I was tired, but sleep wouldn't come. The wind swelled, sighing through the sashes. Then, as though a tap had been turned on, the rain intensified, a deluge that rattled the windows and hammered on the roof. A door banged somewhere, making me jump. I pulled the duvet up around me and snuggled closer to Josh, but the cold leaked in through the covers, and I couldn't get warm.

I thought I heard noises in the hallway, footsteps on the tiles. A late guest, perhaps, although I thought Josh and I had been the last ones to retire. I waited, straining to hear, but any sounds from outside the room were drowned out by the shriek of the wind and the pounding rain. I should check, I told myself, to make sure that no one was outside, but it was hard to force myself out of bed. When I did, my bare feet tingled on the cold floor. I moved quickly to the door and eased it open. Several red-shaded sconces lit the hall, which was empty. All the doors were closed. I stood for a minute, but heard nothing. It seemed that everyone was asleep.

My fears assuaged, I retreated back to bed, but the darkness felt like a heavy mass weighing down on me, compressing my lungs so that it was hard to breathe. Berating myself for being a baby, I got up, switched on the bathroom light and left the door open a crack so that a faint yellow glow alleviated the blackness.

Still I lay awake for hours, listening to the din of the storm. Sleep-starved, I could barely tell what was real and what I imagined. Voices in the hallway, a creak outside the door. I was sure I saw a bat hanging upside down from one of the wooden beams, but when I blinked, the sinister shape disappeared. Memories of Nick's water-logged body and of my vision on the moor swirled in my head.

When dawn finally came, the storm had abated, diminished to a melancholy drizzle. I sat up and looked around the room, benign now in the early morning light, stripped of its shadows and imagined terrors. Yet a lingering apprehension made my heart beat faster than it should. Josh had slept soundly all night, but now he woke as though from a nightmare, thrashing around in the bedclothes, throwing an arm out and narrowly missing my chin. I stroked his hair and murmured to him. "Wake up. It's okay."

While we were dressing, I heard the throb of an engine and crossed to the window to see Knox and his colleagues wheeling their cases through the mist towards their helicopter. I caught a glimpse of Fergus coming back inside. Relieved that he had got through the night safely, I told Josh that his uncle was up and about.

"Let's go down then," he said. "I want to make sure he's all right."

In the breakfast room, Fergus was working his way through a plateful of ham and eggs, orange juice and tea. His aura continued to spin fast over his grey hair, dashing my faint hope that the threat to him might have departed with Knox and his team. The race was still on, then, to locate the source of the danger before disaster struck.

Mrs. Dunsmore was in charge of the toaster and the teapot and served us scrambled eggs from a large warming dish. In spite of my anxiety, I tackled a slice of toast with enthusiasm. I'd eaten so little at dinner that my stomach was growling indignantly.

"Pierre hasn't come in yet," the housekeeper said. "I told him to take an extra hour or two after all he did last night, so it's a simple breakfast, but we'll have a sit-down lunch later on. You'll have time, won't you, to eat lunch before you leave?"

Josh glanced over at Fergus before answering. "We're going to stay another day or two."

"Oh, splendid," she said, smoothing out an imaginary crease in the tablecloth. "Then we can talk about what you'd like for dinner when Pierre arrives."

"Are Lucy and Duncan up?" I asked. "They're supposed to be leaving at midday." I was worried about Duncan. I'd try to convince him to stay, but doubted he would. He didn't believe in the auras.

"Not yet," Mrs. Dunsmore replied. "I'll leave the breakfast things out for when they come down, and, if you'll excuse me, I need to find Lachlan. The last two guests are on their way down and will need help with their bags."

Soon, we heard the sound of suitcases being wheeled across the entry hall, and Fergus left the breakfast room to say goodbye. When his visitors had gone, he came back and sat down with us. He poured himself another cup of tea and dropped two cubes of sugar into it before looking up at me. "I suppose we should talk about this aura situation," he said. "I assume that's why you're not planning on leaving yet? Is the aura still there?"

I nodded, feeling miserable.

"And it's moving fast?" Fergus passed his hand through the space over his head.

"Yes, I'm afraid it is. My recommendation is that you pass the day very quietly. Perhaps you could sit in the drawing room and read. You're not expecting any visitors today, are you?"

He set the teaspoon in the saucer. "Kate, I don't fully understand how this aura thing works, but I can't skulk around, trying to avoid whatever it is you think awaits me. There must be something more.... proactive I can do?"

I was desperate to help Fergus, and there was no guarantee that sitting on a sofa all day would save him. For all I knew, it would be better if he went out, left the castle, even traveled to London with us. That could be a solution we hadn't considered yet. Not knowing the source of the danger left every possibility open.

"You said you think that the estate sale is a possible reason for the threat," Fergus continued. "I've been giving that some thought. We need to talk to the tenants and staff, to assure them that nothing is going to change. From what I've discussed with Knox, no one is going to be evicted. He wants the place to keep going as it has been. He's got the money to do the repairs, and he understands that continuity is a good thing in this case. The Bryants will continue to run the stables, and the Donaldsons and the Gillespies will keep the trout farm and the sheep farm. Mrs. Dunsmore and Lachlan retain their positions and their accommodations. It's all agreed."

"Yes!" I jumped to my feet. "The sooner you can get the word out to everyone the better. That might be all that's needed to remove the threat."

Fergus rubbed his chin. "Much as I'll be happy to pass on the good news to my neighbors, I can't believe any of them wish me harm. People complain loudly sometimes but have no intention of following through with any real action. The bark is usually worse than the bite."

"Well, I think we should get on to it," Josh said. "I'll drive you. Once you've talked to everyone, maybe that aura will go away." His eyes shone, and he looked happy for the first time in three days.

A clock chimed on the sideboard. It was nine o'clock. "Some of them will be at church," Fergus said. "We should wait until after lunch."

"We'll go before lunch." Josh's voice was firm. "We'll catch them on their way home from church. And you should find Pierre and Lachlan, and talk to Mrs. Dunsmore now. Oh, I know they're not the threat," he said, holding his hands up when Fergus began to protest. "But they'll be delighted to know that their futures are secure here."

I stood up to make more toast while Josh and Fergus talked over other details of the contract. They were both in good spirits, buoyed by the prospect of erasing any bad feelings in the community. I'd remain vigilant, however. Until that aura disappeared, Fergus wasn't safe.

The toast was calming my stomach, and I'd taken an orange from a bowl in the center of the table when someone pounded on the front door, and then leaned on the bell.

"I'll go," Josh said.

I heard voices in the entry hall, a short exchange, and then a commotion at the breakfast room door. A middle-aged man in an anorak and dusty work boots burst into the room. "My son is dead!"

he yelled, pointing at Fergus. "And you have parties? Have you no shame? It's your fault that Nick died."

Josh, who'd followed in close behind him, grabbed his arm. "Mr. Jameson, that's an unfair accusation."

The man stopped in mid-stride, brushing off Josh's hand. He was shaking with emotion.

"Please sit down," Fergus said.

When Jameson remained standing, Fergus stood up and walked around the table. "I'm so sorry about Nick," he said. "He was a talented young man. He'll be missed here, very much."

Jameson ignored Fergus's outstretched hand. "He *was* talented," he said. "But not good enough for you, was he? You brought in that swanky French chef over his head. Sneered at Nick, he did, made him feel useless. And now he's dead. You did nothing. You didn't support him."

As Jameson swayed on his feet, Fergus took his arm and led him to a chair. I poured a cup of tea and added a couple of sugars before passing it to Nick's dad. His hand trembled when he took it from me. Although he sat quietly, not moving, his grief poured through the room like a river that had burst its banks, as cold and grey as the water that had lapped around his dead son's body. I was all too familiar with grief after the loss of my little brother and then my mother just three years ago. It was after she died that I first started seeing the death-predicting auras. I knew what Mr. Jameson was going to experience as he came to terms with the loss of his son. I'd quickly learned that in general, friends' tolerance for sadness had its limits, and strangers, unless they were exceptionally empathetic, didn't care at all. And so, after my mum died, I'd wandered around in my little bubble of grief, trying not to melt down in meetings, sob standing in line at supermarkets, or weep on the Tube. A fate that now awaited poor Mr. Jameson. And Josh too, if I didn't save Fergus.

Josh's fingers touched mine, warm and consoling. I felt the pulse of his love beating on my skin. Taking a deep breath, I struggled upwards, felt the cold draining away from me, dripping to the floor, absorbed by the blue and red Persian rug under my feet. I pulled my thoughts back to the room, noticing that Fergus's aura was swirling wildly. My heart thumping, I scanned Jameson for any sign of a weapon. If he intended to hurt Fergus, I wasn't confident that Josh and I could take him down.

My nightmare seemed about to come true when Jameson suddenly pushed his tea away and jumped up, pushing his chair back so hard that it tipped over with a crash. He rushed around the table towards Fergus, who scrambled to his feet and dropped his cup to the floor. Arbroath, who'd been sleeping under the table, shot up, ears flat against his head and teeth bared. Growling, he approached Jameson, who took a step backwards.

When he'd put some distance between himself and the dog, he pointed at Fergus. "Don't think I'm done with you."

"Ye'll not be threatening the master," came a voice from the door. Lachlan stepped in, with his rifle tucked under his arm.

15

The tense moment passed quickly. Jameson stalked out of the room, and we heard the front door slam. Lachlan walked to the window and confirmed that he'd driven off. "I'd like to stay close to the house today, sir. To make sure he doesn't come back."

Fergus rubbed his face with both hands. Lost for anything useful to say, I stood up and made more tea, using the electric kettle plugged in on the sideboard. When I offered a cup to Lachlan, he declined in his brusque way.

"Can't stand the stuff."

Wondering what he did drink, I lined up three cups and poured milk into each one while I waited for the tea to brew.

"I'll patrol the grounds closest to the house," Lachlan said to Fergus.

"If you think it's necessary."

"Aye, I do." Lachlan marched out, a man on a mission. I supposed I should be glad he was present and armed. He could probably do a great deal more to protect Fergus than Josh and I could.

I handed out cups of tea. "Shall we head to the church?" Josh asked his uncle after draining his. "It's almost time for the service to be over."

"Nick's father might be around. Is it safe to go out?" I asked.

Josh and Fergus looked at each other. Fergus drained his cup. "We'll bring Arbroath. Jameson seemed nervous around him." He patted the dog's big head. "Come along, Arbroath. Into the car with you." Excited, the dog bounded into the entry hall.

"Will you be all right here for a while?" Josh asked me.

"Yes. I've got some reading to do. Look after Fergus. And be careful."

Josh gave me a kiss. "Don't worry."

The clock struck ten as they drove away, reminding me that Lucy and Duncan hadn't come down yet. Maybe I should wake them up. I wasn't keen to see Duncan again. Although his reaction to my aura revelation wasn't unexpected, it had still hurt. But it was getting late, and a vague uneasiness gripped me. I made the long walk back to the tower and climbed the spiral staircase to the second floor. Both Lucy's and Duncan's doors were closed. I didn't know which room they would be in and decided to start with Lucy's. I knocked.

"Coming," Lucy called, and I felt the tension go out of my shoulders. I could handle Duncan's ill humor, I decided, although I imagined it would be in full force today. Lucy inched the door open and poked her head through the opening. "Kate. What's wrong?"

"Nothing. It's... just that it's a little late, and I thought you'd want breakfast before Mrs. Dunsmore clears it away. Fergus and Josh have already gone out."

"Oh, right. I don't usually sleep in. I probably had too much champagne at the party." She looked none the worse for wear, I thought. No dark circles, no wan skin. Even her hair had stayed in its neat shiny bob, unlike mine after a restless night, when it tangled into a snarled mass, making me resemble one of Shakespeare's three witches.

"Good, then. I'll wait for you downstairs, and let Mrs. Dunsmore know you're coming. Do you both want tea and toast?"

Lucy looked blank for a second. "Duncan's not here. Isn't he up yet? He usually rises at the crack of dawn. Let me get dressed. I'll be down soon."

She shut the door, leaving me standing in the corridor, feeling faintly embarrassed. In spite of their odd relationship, I'd assumed that she and Duncan would be sleeping together. I gathered myself, walked to Duncan's door and banged on it. No answer. At once, my vague unease blossomed into full-fledged fear. I knocked again and then tried the handle. The door was locked. In my head, a dozen different scenarios flashed past. He was lying dead on the floor stabbed, shot, or bludgeoned to death. He'd fallen and hit his head on the bathtub. He'd taken too many sleeping pills.

After another round of fruitless knocking, I hurried back to Lucy's room and hammered on the door. She yanked it open. "What's the matter now?"

"It's Duncan. He's not answering."

To my astonishment, Lucy threw back her head and laughed. "He's such a fleabag," she said. "I knew he was up to something. That little waitress girl is probably in there with him. Last night, he told me he was tired. Then he told me he needed time to digest what you'd told him about the aura. Then he said he was restless and he didn't want to disturb my beauty sleep. He was restless all right."

"Oh," I managed, lost for words. I remembered Duncan flirting with Fiona in the kitchens. He'd told her he'd see her later, but I hadn't given it any further thought. "I'm sorry," I said finally. "I didn't realize."

"Come in." Only half-dressed, she strode across the room to pick up her jeans from the bed. "Don't worry about me," she said as she pulled them on. "I knew what I was getting into when I met him."

I raised an eyebrow, thinking it would be rude to ask. "He has a roving eye," she said.

"He's done this before?"

She shrugged. "Yep. Come on. Let's go raise hell and wake him up, or at least disturb the peace enough for the pretty young thing to be shamed into leaving."

Back outside Duncan's room, I pounded on the door. My stomach churned. "Isn't it weird that he's not answering, even to shout at us to go away?" I said. "And why did he lock the door? I didn't even know these doors had locks. Mine doesn't lock."

"I don't know. Not sure I care, really." Lucy must have noticed my expression. "You're worried because of the aura, aren't you?"

"Of course I am. Aren't you?"

"I think it's too soon to panic. There must be a spare key. We'll ask Fergus." She turned to walk towards the stairs.

"I told you. Fergus is out. He's gone to talk to the tenants to reassure them that Knox won't be evicting anyone."

"Oh that's right. Well, Mrs. Dunsmore will have a key, won't she? Let's go down."

When we reached the breakfast room, Mrs. Dunsmore was piling up empty cups and plates. "What would you like for breakfast, Lucy?" she asked. "And master Duncan?"

"Actually, we need your help," I said. "Duncan locked his door. Do you have a spare key? We need to wake him up."

The housekeeper looked wary. "I'm not sure we should go barging into his room if he's still sleeping."

"It's an emergency," I said.

"Not quite," Lucy said to Mrs. Dunsmore. "But he needs to wake up and pack. We have to leave at noon if we're to make it to Glasgow in time for the train."

"Oh, that's right. Well, I expect master Duncan will forgive the intrusion." Mrs. Dunsmore dug into her apron pocket. "This is a skeleton key that fits the doors, or most of them anyway. We had the locks fitted on some rooms when we started taking paying guests a couple of years ago." She held the key out to me. "Please bring it straight back."

"I will," I promised. "Lucy? Will you come with me?"

Lucy hesitated and then, to my relief, followed as I hurried yet again towards the tower, dashing up the spiral stairs. If nothing else, I was getting plenty of exercise this weekend, nearly enough to make up for my missed daily run through Hyde Park.

We thumped on Duncan's door again before I put the key in the lock. It seemed to be stuck. After I'd fumbled with it for a few seconds, Lucy grabbed it from me and had a go. The lock clicked and she pushed it open. I took a deep breath to dispel a looming sense of dread. Inside, the curtains were drawn, but milky morning light poked its way around the edges of the fabric, revealing a neatly-made bed.

"Duncan?" I called before venturing in. A quick search showed that he wasn't in the bedroom or the adjoining bathroom.

"I'd take a bet he's with that girl at her place," Lucy said. "After he said goodnight to me, he could have sneaked out easily enough."

"The front door has a deadbolt," I pointed out. "If he went out that way, the bolt would have been unlocked this morning. We can ask Mrs. Dunsmore if she was the first one up, and if she noticed."

"I don't see what difference it makes. Besides, there are other ways out. There's the tradesman's entrance to the kitchen."

Lucy seemed resigned to his cheating and I felt sorry that Duncan treated her so badly. Still, at least he wasn't dead.

"He didn't even take his mobile with him," she said, picking up an iPhone from the top of the dresser and setting it down again.

"Well, when Josh and Fergus get back, we'll send them out to find him if he hasn't arrived by then." I was breathing more easily now. Duncan's behavior was reprehensible, but that was none of my business.

Lucy led the way out and pulled the door shut behind us. We walked in silence to the breakfast room, where the housekeeper had left places set for two, with a pot of tea and a rack of freshly made toast. Lucy sat and poured herself a cup of tea.

"I'll leave you to your breakfast," I said. "If you give me the key, I'll return it to Mrs. Dunsmore."

When I held out my hand, Lucy pressed the key into my palm. I walked into the entry hall before realizing I had no idea where the housekeeper would be. The kitchen seemed likely, so I went there first, but found it empty. A tray of dirty breakfast crockery sat next to the sink, but the counters were scrubbed clean and the stainless-steel range gleamed. Pierre and his crew had cleaned up well last night.

Still, the cavernous space had an abandoned feel to it this morning, so I turned quickly to go back upstairs. The skeleton key weighed heavy in my hand, and barely conscious of what I was doing, I soon found myself outside Duncan's room again.

I'd been puzzled by Duncan's odd behavior when he'd been searching the shelves in the library. That gave me an excuse for what I planned to do— that and a desperate need to find a clue as to what threatened him. I inserted the key and turned it before realizing the door was already unlocked. Lucy had forgotten to secure it. I pushed it open and slipped inside. I was struck again by how tidy the room was, but then it wasn't too surprising. Duncan's clothes were always pristine and well pressed.

His overnight bag sat on an armchair under the window. Telling myself this was all in a good cause, I unzipped it to check inside. It was empty. The wardrobe door creaked when I opened it, releasing the smell of old wood and cedar. Alongside an array of trousers and jackets were his evening shirt and dinner jacket. His black dress shoes were neatly lined up next to a pair of oxblood loafers on the wardrobe floor. So he'd definitely been back to his room to change after saying good night to Lucy.

A chest of drawers stood against the wall near the door, similar to the one in Lucy's room. Its dark, glossy surface held only a bottle of aftershave and Duncan's rental car keys. I hadn't thought to look outside earlier to check if he'd taken his car. Thank goodness he hadn't. He'd had far too much to drink to be out on the roads last night. I assumed that Fiona must have driven him, and wondered where they'd spent the night.

I made a quick decision. The top drawer slid out easily when I pulled on it. Feeling my cheeks burn, I pushed underwear and socks around, looking for... for what? Anything to help me determine the source of the threat. I may feel guilty, but my actions were justified, I told myself. My hand closed around a notebook of some kind. After a microsecond's hesitation, I took it out of the drawer and ran my finger over the luxurious black leather cover. I flipped it open, noting the thick, creamy paper with deckled edges. The first dozen pages were filled with writing, illegible scribbles, arrows, and question marks. Fully conscious of the fact I was violating Duncan's privacy, I felt my heart pounding against my ribs. I'd come too far, though, to give up. On the second page was a notation. "Fabergé egg, Rue des Rosiers, Paris." Did that refer to the egg that had been highlighted in Lucy's newspaper clipping? On the page opposite, was a single word, 'Helsinki' with a question mark next to it. I skimmed the rest of the pages. Most of them were half-empty, scrawled with annotations that made little sense to me. And then a list of names and dates: *Alexandra 1917. Anna Vyrubova 1939, Cyril Thorpe, 1940.*

I stared blankly at the page. Duncan seemed the least likely person in the world to have any interest in history. What could this mean? A noise in the hallway brought my musing to a crashing halt. My breath caught in my throat. What if Duncan had returned? How on earth could I explain my presence in his room? I shoved the book under some neatly rolled socks and slid the drawer shut quietly before inching closer to the door. I stared at the knob, waiting for it to turn. When it did, I remained where I was, petrified into inaction. I should have locked the door behind me, but it was too late for that. I dashed to the bathroom and pushed the door almost closed, leaving a two-inch gap so I could see what was happening.

The bedroom door opened, and Lucy stepped in. She looked around, glancing at the bathroom door. Glad it was Lucy, not Duncan, I wondered what she was up to. I watched as she did exactly what I'd done a few minutes earlier, opening the wardrobe, checking under the bed, peering into Duncan's overnight bag. Then she moved to the chest and opened the top drawer. Within seconds, she had the black journal in her hand and was skimming through the pages. She turned to lean against the chest while she read, her blond hair hanging straight like a silky curtain against her cheek. She smiled, as though she'd discovered something she expected to find. Putting the journal back in its place, she slid the drawer back in.

Then she eased out into the corridor. The door closed behind her with a soft click, and I began to breathe again.

16

I waited for as long as my nerves could stand the tension, torn between the fear of encountering Lucy in the hallway, and the risk of Duncan returning to find me in his room. After a minute, which felt like an hour, I opened the door. Certain the corridor was clear, I slipped out and walked straight to the breakfast room, assuming that Lucy might have hurried back there. But there was no sign of her— only the remnants of the toast and eggs she hadn't had time to eat. She must have left Duncan's door unlocked deliberately, I realized now, intending to go back there when she thought I'd be out of the way.

And where was she now? And what had she seen in Duncan's journal? How had she known it was there? I felt dizzy and bewildered, drowning in a deluge of inconclusive theories. I needed to gain control, put order into the chaos, if I were to have any hope of saving Fergus and Duncan.

Remembering there was a notepad and paper next to the phone, I hurried to the drawing room and jotted down the names and dates I'd seen in Duncan's notebook as well as his single word notation of 'Helsinki.' There had been the mention of a Fabergé egg and an address in Paris, but I couldn't recall all of the details. If I'd been thinking clearly, I'd have taken photos of the pages, but my forage through Duncan's belongings had made me so nervous that I wasn't functioning properly.

Sitting on the edge of the sofa, I gazed at my notes, thinking about Lucy and Duncan's odd relationship. Why would Lucy be looking at his journal? It struck me that she might have been searching for evidence of his cheating on her. A date or a note about another woman perhaps. Although she'd seemed unruffled by Duncan's dalliance with Fiona, she had to be upset or angry or both. I would be. Yet there was the mention of the Fabergé egg, a link to the press clipping in Lucy's room. Did one of them know something about the egg? Could Duncan be the collector who'd bought it in Paris? I thought back to the articles I'd read. None of them had mentioned the name of the buyer. I straightened up. Was that a possible reason for Duncan to be in danger? Because he owned something incredibly valuable? But then what was he searching for in the library?

An uneasy feeling coiled through my stomach, rising into my chest. Obviously, Lucy and Duncan were searching for something, possibly a Fabergé egg. But how could such an incredibly valuable item be here without Fergus being aware of it? What made Lucy or Duncan believe that it was hidden in the castle? Were they working together? That seemed unlikely. Their relationship was hard to fathom, but it didn't seem very collaborative. Just the opposite.

Then there was my mystifying vision of the killing in the ruins. Why had I seen it? The murder had taken place five hundred years before the manufacture of any Fabergé eggs. How could there be a link?

There probably wasn't one. Frustrated, I threw myself back against the cushions. Time was running out, and I'd made no progress on identifying the source of the threat. The estate sale still seemed the most obvious, but now that Knox had agreed to keep on all the staff and tenants, much of the tension had been defused. There was Nick's father, of course. He certainly represented a threat to Fergus. I couldn't imagine why he'd go after Duncan though.

But sometimes people got caught up in dangerous situations and were hurt or killed as innocent bystanders.

My imagination went into overdrive. Jameson going after Fergus with a gun. Duncan stepping in to protect his uncle. Both of them shot dead, blood on the floor. I sat up, rubbing my eyes and stretching my neck from one side to the other, telling myself to calm down. Where would Jameson get a gun? That wasn't so easy in Scotland. Then I thought of Lachlan's hunting rifle. Maybe Jameson owned one of those too.

Perhaps I should call Inspector McMahon to ask him to monitor Jameson. Could the police take someone into custody on the suspicion that they meant harm but hadn't yet committed a crime? That seemed unlikely but, if I told the inspector about the nasty threat Jameson had made to Fergus, he'd have to look into it. I didn't have McMahon's direct number memorized, however, and calling the emergency operator seemed a little over-dramatic. I'd have to ask Fergus for the number later.

Meanwhile, my sitting around conjuring a list of possible calamities was pointless. I needed to get moving. Tucking my scribbled note into my jeans pocket, I considered going to find Lucy. She had a vested interest in protecting Duncan, and she seemed to have grown fond of Fergus. Still, for now, I decided, it was best to work alone and ask Josh for advice when he wasn't too busy with the estate sale negotiations. He had good instincts, and Fergus's well-being was his highest priority.

As if knowing I was thinking about him, Josh walked in just then.

"Where's Fergus?" I asked.

"He's fine. He's outside, chatting with Lachlan."

"I'm glad you're back." I threw myself at him, relieved to feel his arms around me, a solid reassuring presence in the center of the chaos. "How did it go?"

"We talked to everyone. And they were all happy with the update on their future employment." He removed his jacket, which was soaking wet, and laid it over the back of a chair. "To be honest, I don't think any of them had any intention of doing harm to Fergus, but I feel better for being able to give them good news." He looked towards the door. "Maybe we neutralized any threats. Perhaps the danger is over?"

I hoped so, but as soon as Fergus came in, I saw that his aura still swirled. When I gave Josh a faint shake of my head, his shoulders sagged.

"Any sign of Duncan and Lucy yet?" Fergus asked. Water dripped from his coat, and flattened his hair. "It wasn't supposed to rain today," he grumbled.

"Lucy, yes," I said. "But Duncan is in the village and I haven't seen him this morning. We need to find him."

"His car's on the driveway," Fergus said. "Are you sure he went out?"

"Lucy thinks so. Apparently, he had a tryst with a young woman."

Fergus's expression would have made me laugh if I weren't so depressed about his situation. "A tryst?" he repeated. "But what about Lucy?"

"I don't know. She didn't seem too surprised. But I'd feel better if we saw him— to be sure he's all right."

"Do we know where he is?" Josh asked.

"It's only conjecture, but it's possible that he's with Fiona, the girl who's been helping Mrs. Dunsmore."

Fergus looked shocked. "Fiona? Ramsay's young daughter? Well, we can go take a look, I suppose. I've taken Arbroath over there a few times. The vet's office is attached to his house." He buttoned up his coat again. "I'm not sure we should be chasing after Duncan, though. He's a grown man, after all."

"I'll go myself if I have to," I said. "I don't care about Duncan's feelings. I just want to see him, to check he's okay."

"Ah, the aura things," Fergus said, as though he'd forgotten all about them. "You have a point. Come along then, Josh. We have a good reason to meddle. Besides, the young whippersnapper deserves to be embarrassed. He can't bring his girlfriend up for the weekend and then dump her for a dalliance with a younger woman. Most ungentlemanly behavior."

That made me smirk. I would never have associated the term 'gentlemanly' with Duncan. Josh picked up the jacket he'd just discarded. With Arbroath at their heels, the two men set off to the Land Rover once again, leaving me alone to fret over Fergus's aura, which spiraled ever faster.

Unable to face another trek around the castle in search of Lucy, I sat on the sofa and retrieved the scrap of paper with the list of names I'd copied from Duncan's journal. It was a bewildering line-up with no obvious relationships between them: *Alexandra 1917, Anna Vyrubova 1939, Cyril Thorpe, 1940.*

Alexandra must be the Tsarina, wife of Nicholas. She and her family were executed in 1918 by the Bolsheviks after the communist revolution. It was the Romanovs who'd commissioned the creation of the Fabergé eggs. I thought back to what I'd read online. Of the fifty eggs they had owned, some had been shipped to safety at the start of the Revolution, while a few had been seized by the Bolsheviks, and seven of them were unaccounted for. Each one was worth millions of pounds.

I had no idea who Anna Vyrubova was, nor Cyril Thorpe, which meant that Alexandra was the most promising lead to pursue. After a moment's reflection however, I tapped my finger on Alexandra's name, perplexed. Intriguing as the list was, what possible relationship did it have to Fergus? It might be a massive diversion, drawing my attention away from the real threat. I couldn't afford to run around after dubious clues. When Duncan got back, I'd confront him, confess to reading his notebook and attempt to enlist his help in the interests of saving Fergus, and maybe himself too. For now, with little else to do, I decided to go back and do some more research on the computer. The sprawling castle was starting to get on my nerves. Everything I wanted to do involved a mile-long walk. Still, I started towards the stairs. Apart from the ticking of a grandfather clock that stood against the wall, the entry hall was quiet. The first stair tread creaked underfoot, making me pause. As I took the next step, a shrill scream ripped through the silence, sending my heart pounding against my ribs. I stopped, gripping the handrail, and turned my head to work out where the sound had come from. Then again, a second scream. I realized it came from the direction of the kitchens. I jumped back to ground level and ran across the hall. Taking the stone stairs two at a time, I slipped and only saved myself from falling by grabbing the thin wood rail.

In the kitchen, with one hand on the counter, Mrs. Dunsmore was doubled over, clutching her stomach. She straightened up when I called her name.

"What's wrong?" I asked. "Are you ill?" I rushed to her, pulled up a stool and grasped her hand. "Sit down. Talk to me. Should I call for an ambulance?"

The housekeeper stared at me with eyes widened. Her cheeks were pale and a sheen of sweat glazed her brow. She had no aura, but she looked deathly ill. "It's..." she murmured. "I can't..."

"Please Mrs. D., tell me what's wrong." I let go of her hand, planning to reach the phone that hung on the wall near the sink, but she grabbed my wrist and held it tightly. "No, I'll be all right," she said. "You need to fetch the police."

Why the police? Still held captive, I glanced around the room. No one else was there. The kitchen was as clean and neat as when I'd visited it earlier this morning, with no signs of a break-in or damage. The clock on the wall showed that it was nearly noon. I assumed that Pierre would be in soon.

"I'll ring the police station," I said, gently extricating my wrist from by lifting her fingers up one by one. She didn't seem to notice. "But you have to tell me why. What do I say to them? What happened?"

She jutted her chin towards the other side of the kitchen and then lowered her head into her hands, her shoulders shaking. Frustrated that I wasn't able to make any sense of what was bothering her, I went for the phone. She was obviously in shock and certainly in need of a doctor.

"The meat locker," she whispered, stopping me in my tracks. I turned back. On the far wall, the heavy steel door of the meat locker gleamed. It hung ajar, I noticed as I got closer. Cold air escaped through the opening in wisps of white mist. My heart thundered so loudly that it drowned out the noise of the compressor. I put my hand on the lever, curled my fingers around it, and pulled the door open wide enough for me to look inside. The vapors obscured my view. Wary, I took a step in. Objects loomed at me through the fog. I brushed up against something soft and jumped back. It was only a pheasant hanging from a hook, but my pulse raced as I stepped forward. And then I saw something lying on the floor in a corner, a dark mass that took shape as I peered more closely, just as the monk had materialized through the mist in the ruins. It was a man, I saw, lying face down, in tan trousers and a blood-soaked blue shirt. The blood had come from a deep gash in his back, visible through the ripped fabric.

Without seeing his face, I knew it was Duncan. I knelt and touched his hand. It was as cold and unresponsive as the dead pheasant.

17

W hile we waited for the police to come, I made tea and then stood facing Mrs. Dunsmore, trying to coax her out of the kitchen to a more comfortable seat upstairs. She refused to move, though, and remained on the stool, shaking and crying. "It's Master Duncan, isn't it?" she asked me a few times. I told her yes and held her hand.

Two local police constables arrived within ten minutes, and they told us Inspector McMahon was on his way. The older of the two directed us to stay where we were while they investigated. A few minutes later, another group of people arrived, looking like a CSI team I'd seen on a television program. In blue paper suits and booties, they set up cameras and strung up yellow tape. Several of them were soon dusting for fingerprints, starting with the meat locker door. They all had serious expressions, and no one spoke to us until a man requested that we move to the other side of the big butcher-block island. We watched all the activity for a while, and I cringed when a team went inside the chilled room. Luckily, we couldn't see the interior from where we sat.

With my back aching from perching on a less than ergonomic stool, I stood up to stretch just as DCI McMahon arrived. He shot me a strange look when he saw me there, but didn't say anything until he'd consulted with the police team in the meat locker. When he came out, he was rubbing his hands to warm them. "I wouldn't mind a cup," he said, nodding at the steaming mug in front of Mrs. Dunsmore. While I poured milk into a clean mug, he pulled up a stool and sat down.

"Were you the one who found the body?" He directed the question to me. He must think my special talent was finding dead bodies.

"It was me," Mrs. Dunsmore said, with a tremor in her voice. "I found him."

McMahon took his notebook and pen from his pocket and put them on the counter. Unlike Duncan's elegant journal, McMahon's had a cardboard cover and its pages were littered with sticky notes, all yellow. I remembered from my interview following Nick's death that the wire spiral was bent out of shape from when he jammed his pen in there to store it.

"And what made you look in the meat locker?" he asked.

"Pierre is supposed to be making lunch for everyone," she answered. "He rang me to say he's running a little late. So I thought I'd get a start on things for him and went to bring out some smoked fish and a ham. I saw the body lying there and... I yelled, I suppose. It was such a shock I couldn't help it."

"And where were you at this time?" he asked me.

"In the entry hall. I heard a scream and ran down here. Mrs. Dunsmore was in a bit of a state." I patted her hand.

"And you saw the body yourself? Do you know who it is?"

"Yes, it's Duncan MacKenna, Fergus's nephew."

I shifted on my stool and wished that Josh and Fergus would get back. I glanced at the phone on the wall and thought of calling Josh, but I didn't think he'd taken his mobile phone with him. He and Fergus were out looking for Duncan and they wouldn't find him. I couldn't believe that he had been here, dead, all morning, perhaps all night. I had a hundred questions, but McMahon kept talking, mostly gathering basic information, it seemed, on the residents and guests. He grimaced when I reminded him of the party the previous evening.

It would make his job that much harder, I supposed, if he had to talk to everyone on the guest list. But he quickly recovered his equanimity and asked me who was still in the house. I told him Lucy was around somewhere, and that Josh and Fergus had gone to the village to find Duncan.

He looked surprised at that. "You already knew he was missing?"

"Well, we thought he was out with a friend. When he didn't come back for breakfast, we decided to go find him."

"Come back for breakfast," McMahon repeated. "When did he leave the house? Why do you think he was out with a friend?"

I looked at Mrs. Dunsmore, who shrugged. "I believed he'd gone out last night, after the party," I said. "That's what Lucy told me anyway."

"Lucy?"

"Lucy Cantrell. Duncan's girlfriend. She came up from London with him for the weekend."

"Oh, that poor dear girl," Mrs. Dunsmore's voice shook. "Lucy doesn't know that Duncan's dead. She'll be devastated." She put her cup on the butcher block counter and stood up. "I should go to her."

McMahon rested his hand lightly on her arm and gave her a reassuring smile. "All in good time. If you don't mind."

Around us, several officers were measuring distances from the meat locker to the bottom of the staircase and various other points around the kitchen. The kitchen was a hive of activity, but I felt disconnected, removed from it all as though watching it from afar. The bustle calmed briefly when a man clattered down the stairs and entered the kitchen. He waved a hand in greeting to McMahon and followed one of the officers into the meat locker.

"The medical examiner," McMahon said. "I need to consult with him. Perhaps you'd like to go upstairs, and I'll come to you when I'm finished here."

I jumped to my feet, glad to be released, and Mrs. Dunsmore followed me up the stairs. She moved slowly, one hand to her chest as though having trouble breathing. I paused, waiting for her to catch up. "Are you sure you don't want me to call for a doctor?"

"No, no. I'm right behind you."

As we emerged from the staircase into the entry hall, I saw Pierre coming in the front door. Like the rest of us, he'd had a late night, but he looked bright-eyed and well-groomed. "*Je suis désolé*, Mrs. Dunsmore. I am sorry to be late. I was delayed but I will catch up. We will serve lunch in one hour, yes?" He tipped his head towards the door. "There are many cars out there. There is something wrong?"

Mrs. Dunsmore didn't answer. Her face had paled, and she seemed to have trouble getting the words out. I jumped in. "Something happened. Duncan MacKenna is dead."

"Dead?" Pierre echoed. "I am sorry to hear that."

I waited for him to ask a question. In my experience, when apprised of a death, people expressed curiosity about the how and the when. Yet Pierre barely reacted. Was it a language issue or a cultural difference? Of course, he didn't know Duncan, other than that he was a member of the family.

"He was murdered," Mrs. Dunsmore added, looking a little better, with the color returning to her cheeks. "He was stabbed to death in the meat locker."

That statement finally elicited a gasp. "*Mon Dieu!*" he exclaimed. "In my kitchen?"

"The police are down there now," I told him. "I don't think you'll be cooking lunch for some time."

Pierre looked lost. "What should I do?"

"We'll get sandwiches from the pub," Mrs. Dunsmore said, suddenly in control again. "I'll send Lachlan, and we'll set everything up in the breakfast room. Pierre, check the rack in there for a couple of bottles of Beaujolais. Kate, dear, can you try to find Lucy?"

She must have seen the expression on my face because she patted me on the arm. "It will be hard, but she needs to know. I'll watch out for Fergus and Josh too." Her face paled. "Poor Fergus. This will come as a terrible shock."

We went our separate ways, each of us glad, I thought, that we had something specific to do. In the aftermath of a catastrophe, we were cast adrift, our normal roles and routines snatched away, leaving us lost and uncertain amidst the tumult. I climbed the stairs with intent, determined to find Lucy but, when I reached the landing, I paused. Where on earth could she be? The prospect of the trek to the tower was daunting, so I turned instead towards the library. And as I reached it, Lucy appeared at the end of the hallway, coming from the direction of the door to the east wing. So that's where she'd been. Again. But why? What was in there that interested her so much?

She gave me a little wave and came closer with a sheepish expression on her face, probably embarrassed that I'd caught her exploring again.

"I've been looking for you," I said.

"Well, here I am. Why were you looking for me?"

"I think we should go sit." I gestured towards the library, but she didn't move.

"Something's happened," I began. "Please, let's sit down." Still she didn't budge. There was no way out of it. "I've got some bad news. I'm afraid that Duncan is dead."

She didn't flinch or register any reaction at all. Shock can do that to people. "Dead?" she repeated.

"He was murdered. The police are here."

She put a hand on the wall then to steady herself. "Where was he killed? How?"

"Please, come with me. Inspector McMahon is downstairs. You know, the one who came after Nick drowned?"

Our eyes met, registering horror at the enormity of two deaths in one weekend. I took her arm. "Let's go."

Lucy walked with me, docile and silent, until we reached the breakfast room. Pierre had left wine and glasses on the table, and I poured us each a small glass.

"Where's Fergus?" she asked after she'd taken a big sip of wine.

"Out with Josh, trying to find Duncan. They— we— thought he was in the village. With Fiona, like you said."

Lucy put her glass down. "It was a reasonable assumption." She rubbed her eyes, smearing her mascara. "Tell me everything. What happened to him?"

I related what I knew, which wasn't much yet when it came down to it.

"Stabbed," she repeated, just as Inspector McMahon walked in.

"This is Lucy Cantrell," I told him.

She gazed up at him, her fingers clutching the stem of her glass. He took a seat across the table from us and flipped pages in his battered notebook until he reached a blank one. Then he paused and looked at me. "I'd like to talk to Miss Cantrell alone. A few minutes. I'll call you back in when I'm finished."

Unsure what to do with myself, I wandered into the entry hall and opened the front door. A car engine sounded in the distance, and soon Fergus's Land Rover turned in through the gates. I took a deep breath as the vehicle sped along the red gravel drive and skidded to a halt at a random angle on the lawn. The parking spots were filled with police cars and McMahon's old Renault.

Josh threw open his door and rushed across the wet grass towards me. "What's going on?" he demanded. "Did something happen? Did the police get more information on Nick's death?"

The words I needed to say stuck in my throat. I shook my head.

"Oh jeez," Josh murmured. He'd known about Duncan's aura and joined the dots at once. I turned to watch Fergus approach, with Arbroath panting alongside him. Fergus's aura was spinning so fast it made me nauseous. Two deaths already, and one imminent.

"What happened?" Fergus demanded. "Is this about Nick?"

"We'd better go inside," I offered, putting off the inevitable. Perhaps McMahon would rescue me. He could the one to break the news. But my suggestion seemed to glue Fergus's feet to the driveway. "What's going on?" he demanded.

All I could do was repeat what I'd told Lucy a few minutes ago. "I'm sorry, but Duncan is dead."

Fergus's face turned waxy. He reached out to put his hand on Arbroath's broad back, as though needing the support. Although Josh stepped forward to take him by the arm, Fergus remained bent over. I could hear his breath coming in short, sharp bursts. Finally, he straightened up. "Give me a minute."

In the ensuing silence, a bird called from the cypress trees that edged the drive. The rain had slowed, but a steady drip of water splattered to the ground under the water-laden branches. The sky was a slab of grey iron, threatening to unleash another deluge at any moment.

"Inspector McMahon is here," I said.

Fergus gathered himself, pushing back his shoulders and raising his chin. "Then let's go talk with him."

18

Once we were inside, Fergus went into the dining room to find the inspector, but he quickly returned to the entry hall, where Josh was hanging up his jacket. "McMahon's interviewing Lucy," he said. "He needs a few more minutes."

As he turned towards the kitchen stairs, Josh caught him by the arm. "There's no reason to go down there," he said. "We should let the police do their jobs."

"I'd like to see Duncan." Fergus's voice cracked. "I was supposed to look after him, you know, after his father died."

"Come and sit down for now," Josh said. "I'm sure they'll let you see him later, if you really want to."

Fergus stumbled after Josh into the drawing room and sat heavily on one of the green sofas that flanked the fireplace. His eyes were unfocused, and he kneaded his hands together, obviously in distress.

The fire wasn't lit today, and the inglenook loomed dark and chilly. Its decorative backplate featured an engraving of a bear. The animal gazed out at us, a snarl curling its lips, long claws extended from its raised paws. I shivered and sat facing Fergus.

"A drink, if you don't mind," he muttered to Josh, who walked to the sideboard, poured a generous measure of Glenmorangie into a crystal tumbler, and handed it to his uncle.

Fergus held the glass tightly but didn't drink. His face had turned white, and he looked dazed, as though recovering from a blow to the head. I wondered if we should call a doctor. Our first hypothesis could have been correct, that Fergus's health was the source of the threat to him. While I worried about heart attacks, Fergus straightened up as if he'd read my mind and took a swallow of his Glenmorangie. "Tell me what happened," he said.

After taking a deep breath, I explained how Mrs. Dunsmore had discovered Duncan's body. "When I heard her scream, I ran down to the kitchen. Duncan was in the meat locker, dead. It looked as though he'd been stabbed in the back."

"What on earth was he doing in there?" Fergus asked. His voice sounded steadier now and his pallor had faded. These Scots were hardy folk, I thought, tough and resilient.

"Maybe he was looking for another bottle of champagne," I suggested, thinking of our earlier foray in search of the Dom Pérignon.

"I thought Duncan had gone to the village? Isn't that what Lucy told you, Kate?"

"Yes, she did. But it's likely she was guessing and just assumed he'd gone off with Fiona."

"McMahon will get to the bottom of it," Fergus said. "Although I can't imagine who would want to kill Duncan."

I had a short debate in my head about how much to share with Fergus and decided I should tell him everything I knew. His life was still at stake, after all.

I leaned towards him. "There are some things you should know."

Fergus nodded. "I'm listening."

I decided to start with the easy stuff, the facts about Lucy and Duncan conducting clandestine searches for an unknown item. "On Friday, I saw Duncan in the library, looking on the shelves behind the books for something."

"And what would that be?" I heard Lucy's voice and felt my neck grow hot.

Fergus invited Lucy to sit down. "Where's Inspector McMahon?" he asked her.

"He's talking with the medical examiner. The ambulance is on its way to... take Duncan to the morgue."

At the word 'morgue,' a damp chill slid into the room, clinging to my clothes and hair, so that I shivered in spite of my overheated cheeks. Duncan was dead. I found it difficult to grasp that fact, but I did understand that I'd failed. I'd known he was in danger and I hadn't saved him. And his death was so close to home, to Josh and Fergus. I fought to subdue the panic rising in my chest.

"So, what are you looking for, Lucy?" Fergus asked, pulling my attention back to the conversation.

She shook her head. When she looked up, her blue eyes glistened with tears. I was about to ask her about the Fabergé egg when McMahon appeared at the door. He adjusted his tie and ran a finger under his white shirt collar as though it was too tight. "Sorry to intrude. May I have a word, Fergus?"

Fergus finished his drink, as though fortifying himself, and put the glass on a side table. He climbed to his feet and followed McMahon out, a lumbering bear trailing a little brown fox. I blinked to clear the image, aware of the awkward silence that had fallen over the three of us. After a few seconds, Lucy pulled out a tissue and dabbed at her eyes.

"Lucy, do you know anything about a Fabergé egg?" I asked.

Her eyebrows shot up. "An egg?"

I opened my mouth to speak and then closed it again. I only knew about the egg because I'd seen the clipping in Lucy's room and read the enigmatic sentence in Duncan's journal. Poking around other people's rooms wasn't exactly something I was proud to confess to.

"I have reason to believe that Duncan was linked in some way to a Fabergé egg discovered in Paris six months ago," I said, keeping it vague. "Maybe he bought it? And he's been searching for something in the castle. Do you know what it might be?"

Lucy clasped her hands together. "You're right," she said. "Duncan is searching for an egg."

I was so shocked that my conjecture was correct that I forgot to breathe for a few moments.

"The discovery of the two Fabergé eggs, one in the States in 2014 and one in Paris six months ago, led to a resurgence of interest in the missing Romanov treasures," Lucy said. "If two eggs could turn up, then there's a chance others might, too."

"But why on earth would Duncan be looking here, in the castle?" Josh looked bemused.

Lucy squeezed her hands together so tightly that her knuckles went white. "We were both looking," she said. "Not just Duncan. But I want you to know that if I had found it, I would have given it to Fergus. It would be worth millions of pounds. I'm not so sure Duncan would have given it up if he'd found it though. He needed the money."

"Duncan? Why would he need money?" Josh asked. "He makes a fortune in the City."

"And he spends— spent— a fortune." Lucy gave him a thin-lipped smile. "Duncan's famous for his lavish entertaining. He has a lot of friends, all eager to help him dispose of his money. Have you seen his apartment in Chelsea?"

Josh shook his head. He hadn't been particularly close to Duncan, and, as far as I knew, they never got together in London. I tapped my fingers on the armrest. So, Duncan had a money problem. That was interesting and worth following up on.

Josh looked closely at Lucy. "You said this egg would be worth millions? That's ridiculous."

When she didn't respond, I jumped in, remembering the research I'd done online. "Not really. Apart from the intrinsic value of the gold and gems, the Romanov eggs are rarities. Only fifty were ever made. And their history and association with the Romanov name makes them highly coveted by collectors. The last egg that was discovered is believed to be worth about ten million pounds."

Lucy looked up at me when I'd finished. "Goodness, Kate, you know as much as I do."

"Hardly. And I certainly don't know enough to see any connection to the castle."

She finally unlocked her hands and settled back into the sofa. "The egg we were seeking was purchased in Paris in late 1940 by an English collector and brought to London, where he sold it. And, yes, before you ask, my interest is both academic and financial. Even a finder's fee would make a big difference to the state of my bank account."

"How do you know about the English collector?"

Lucy raised one shoulder in a shrug. "I did some research and uncovered a copy of the receipt describing the sale. It sold for fifty pounds."

"I'm sure I'm being slow," Josh said. "But what is the relevance of any of this?"

"The buyer was a Mr. Gordon MacKenna," she replied. "Your great-grandfather."

While we all absorbed that piece of information, Josh stood up and poured himself a finger of Fergus's special scotch.

"So you believe Fergus's grandfather purchased the egg and brought it back here?" I asked. "But if he did, why did he hide it? Why wouldn't it be on display?"

"Maybe it was on display for a while," Lucy said. "Or perhaps he worried that it would be damaged or stolen, so he put it somewhere safe." She picked up a cushion, wrapped her arms around it, and hugged it to her chest. "Of course, I'm not completely certain that the buyer was the same Gordon MacKenna. And it's not clear that he didn't sell the egg on to someone else. It could be anywhere, to be honest."

"Did Duncan tell you about the egg?" I asked.

"He did. He thought we'd have a better chance of finding it if we worked together. And, of course, when we got here and heard of the pending estate sale, we realized we didn't have much time. Once the new owner took possession, Duncan wouldn't have access to the castle any longer. That's why Fergus's announcement came as such a shock and Duncan reacted so badly to it. He'd assumed he had years to find the thing— if indeed it's here."

Josh looked troubled. "I still can't get over the fact that Duncan was short of money. Did he gamble?"

"No, he didn't do that at least. But it's easy to spend more money than you earn if you want to live well in London. And Duncan did live well." She paused. "I'm sorry. I don't mean to criticize Duncan. He was fun to be with, and his friends enjoyed his company, regardless of the money." She reached out and touched the back of Josh's hand. "My apologies. He was your cousin, and I have no right to be negative."

In the quiet that followed there were voices in the hall. Fergus came back in, looking wrung out. Pallor made his cheeks look sunken, and his grey hair stuck up in every direction.

"It's your turn, Josh," he said. "The inspector is waiting for you. He has a list of suspects a mile long from what I can see, starting with everyone who was in the house last night."

"Including Stanton Knox and company?" I asked.

"Yes." He patted Josh on the shoulder as they passed each other and picked up the whisky bottle before sitting down. "Have I missed anything here?" he asked.

I looked at Lucy, but she remained silent, so I plunged in. "Do you know anything about a Fabergé egg? Purchased by your grandfather and brought here to the castle in late 1940?"

Looking rather dazed, Fergus took a big gulp of his drink. "That's a new one on me," he said. "Never heard a dickie bird about any Fabergé egg." He gazed around the room as though looking for it.

Lucy raised her head. "It's probably a wild goose chase. I'm only going on what Duncan told me."

"How did Duncan know about it?" I asked.

Lucy flicked a tassel on the cushion with a well-manicured nail. "I'm not sure he ever told me that. Of course, I was already aware of the general history of the Romanov treasures. I'd heard the rumors and knew of the speculations about the missing eggs and other artifacts, so I was happy to pitch in and help him." She sighed. "It seemed like a game really, running around the castle looking for a piece of treasure. I never dreamed... that he would end up dead."

"You think the egg has something to do with his death?" I asked.

A tear dripped down her cheek. "I don't know. But if not that, then what? Why would anyone kill him?"

If the missing egg was the reason for Duncan's murder, then it could also be the source of the threat to Fergus.

Someone was willing to kill, maybe more than once, to retrieve the treasure. I ran through a list of possible suspects in my head. The list was long, far longer than I had any hope of addressing; anyone at the party, guests or temporary staff, the estate tenants, Knox, Nick's father. And time was running out. Fergus's aura was spinning wildly. Tapping my fingers on my knee, I tried to put it all together, but it was like working on a jigsaw puzzle with no edge pieces and no picture of what the finished piece should look like.

"Do you think Duncan found it?" I asked. "And he didn't tell you because he knew you'd tell Fergus? But someone else knew about it and killed him to seize the egg?"

Lucy shook her head. "Duncan wouldn't do that to me. He..." She stopped. "He could have, I suppose. He was acting so strangely yesterday." She burst into tears.

19

The next couple of hours passed in a blur. We watched from the drawing room window as paramedics carried Duncan's body on a stretcher to a waiting ambulance. Long after the ambulance had disappeared through the gates, we remained, gazing out at the rain. The view was dismal, but no one seemed to have the energy to return to their seats.

Mrs. Dunsmore came in with a tray of sandwiches, egg and cress or ham and cheese, she'd told us, but they sat untouched, the edges drying out and curling up as the afternoon wore on. We drank tea, one pot after another, while McMahon talked to Josh and Pierre and then to Mrs. Dunsmore again before calling Fergus back for another private chat.

When McMahon summoned Lucy for a second time, she trailed out of the drawing room, looking tired and fragile. I wondered if she was at the top of McMahon's suspect list. Worryingly though, McMahon had also spent a great deal of time with Josh.

While Lucy was gone, Fergus told us the inspector seemed to think the murder weapon was a knife from the kitchen, an eight-inch carving knife now missing from the knife block. Pierre claimed it was there when he closed up the kitchen the night before. I remembered the chef's expertise with a knife, but I couldn't imagine why he'd want to murder Duncan. As far as I knew, they hadn't even met before.

When the clock struck three, I wandered over to the tray of sad-looking sandwiches and picked out the most appealing one. Egg and cress, not my favorite, but I was hungry enough that I felt a little faint. And a glance at Fergus's aura reminded me that I would need all the energy I could muster to get through the next day or two.

As I poured myself another cup of tea, voices were raised in the dining room next door, and then I heard Lucy shouting in the entry hall. As one, Josh, Fergus and I crowded into the doorway to see what was going on. Lucy was standing face to face with Inspector McMahon, stabbing her finger into his chest to make her point. "I didn't kill Duncan, and you can't keep me here. I have a job to go back to in London."

McMahon took a step back, out of reach of her finger. "Miss Cantrell. It would be helpful to me if you were to remain here within easy contact. However, if you really must return to London, then by all means do so. There's no problem as long as you keep us informed of your whereabouts."

"Good. Thank you."

She turned away and hurried up the staircase. I followed, calling her to wait for me. Finally, I caught up with her in the picture gallery where I grasped her arm and pulled her to a halt. We faced each other underneath a portrait of a man with a thick black mustache. His eyes glinted down at us from underneath a red plumed hat.

"I'm sorry about Duncan. I truly am," I said.

"I can't stay here," she said. "I don't know any of you. My only reason to be here was Duncan." She gulped in air, and tears trickled down her cheeks. "And he's dead. You understand that I just need to get away?"

"Yes. I suppose so. But there will be a funeral, most likely up here because Fergus is Duncan's closest relative. You'd want to be here for that, wouldn't you?"

Lucy sagged against the wall. "I'm not sure. Yes, probably, but I think I'll come back when the arrangements are made. That will take a few days, won't it?"

"Yes. Are you sure you can't stay? I need all the help I can get. If the Fabergé egg is at the bottom of all this, your knowledge would be invaluable. We could work together to save Fergus."

Lucy bowed her head. "I'm sorry. But this place... too many bad memories now. You're smart, Kate, and you have Josh. You can save Fergus."

She started walking again. I kept pace with her until we reached her room. A few steps further on, Duncan's door was festooned with yellow "Do Not Cross" tape. The police had been up and examined his room already.

"How are you getting back to London?" I asked. Our flight had left an hour previously, without Josh or me on board.

"I'll take the rental car back to Glasgow and catch a train from there." She glanced at her watch. "If I'm lucky, I'll be home around midnight. I have an early class tomorrow."

She opened her door and gestured for me to follow her in. I leaned against the chest of drawers while she dragged her case from the wardrobe and threw her things into it. After a brief trek into the bathroom, she returned with her toiletry bag and jammed it on top of the clothes. She was rushing, moving fast. When she came over to clear the chest of drawers, I moved to give her space. She swept her make-up from the wooden surface into a plastic bag, the kind you use at airport security. As she sealed the bag, I noticed the press clipping.

"That's what gave Duncan the idea to look for missing Fabergé eggs?" I asked, nodding towards the piece of paper.

Lucy glanced at the clipping. "Yes. His financial situation is— was — worse than I wanted to say in front of Josh. Duncan was grasping at straws, really. All that stuff he came up with to save the castle? Even if Fergus had agreed, Duncan couldn't have achieved it, I don't think. He'd burned a lot of contacts in London."

I thought about that for a moment but I couldn't see a connection between his financial state and his death, or any kind of link to

Fergus. I sighed, admitting to myself that I was no further forward than I'd been when we arrived three days ago.

"I should go," Lucy said, picking up her briefcase. "I'll see you again soon, though."

"Are you sure you don't want to stay? We could look for the egg together." Excited by the thought, I caught hold of her hand. "If we find it, we can save the castle."

Lucy's hand lay limp in mine. "For me, it's over," she said. "I don't care about the egg anymore. Duncan is dead, and Fergus is selling to Stanton Knox. If a treasure were hidden in the castle seventy-five years ago, it will most likely stay hidden for another seventy-five years."

I let go of her hand, feeling guilty. She was dealing with Duncan's death. They'd had a fraught relationship, it seemed to me, but that didn't mean Lucy hadn't loved him. "I'm sorry," I said. "That was insensitive."

"Don't be daft. It's not your fault. I know you want to help Fergus." She tilted her head to one side. "I don't know what to make of you, Kate Benedict, with your bizarre aura-sightings and your impulse to save people. Not, I would remind you, that you're doing a very good job of it." She smiled. "But that's beside the point. I think you're a good person and Josh is lucky to have you. I hope Fergus survives long enough to see you two get married."

I blushed. "Oh, that's not in the cards. Not yet, perhaps not for a long time. We're both focusing on our careers right now."

"Ah, the career thing." Lucy turned to zip her case closed. "A chimera, if you want my opinion. Like chasing a unicorn."

"But you have an amazing career going," I said, remembering what Duncan had told us over dinner on Friday evening. "You have tenure at a great university, and it seems as though you're studying and teaching something you love. Not everyone gets to do that."

"It's not all roses. But I have to run." She flung her arms around me in a quick hug. "Stay in touch. Keep me up to date on what's happening here, won't you?"

And then she was gone, flying out of the door and dashing along the corridor towards the spiral staircase. I perched on the edge of the bed, suddenly lonely and, if I had to be honest, rather lost. She was right. I wasn't doing a good job of helping anyone. Duncan was dead and Fergus was still in danger. Feeling sorry for myself wouldn't change anything, however, so I pushed myself up off the bed, determined to keep going. As I walked towards the door, I noticed a piece of paper on the floor under the chest of drawers. I reached under and picked it up. It was a business card. "Remy Delacroix, *Antiquaire*," I read. There was a phone number but no address.

I sat back on my heels, flicking the card with my finger. A French antiques dealer. Was this the man who'd sold the Fabergé egg to the collector in Paris six months ago? How would Lucy have his business card? Intrigued, I slid the card into my pocket and went to find Josh and Fergus.

They were in the drawing room, where DCI McMahon had joined them. Displaying old-fashioned manners, he stood up when I arrived, and then settled back in his seat. Fergus was reviving a dying fire, taking kindling and logs from a basket on the hearth and placing them in a stacked arrangement over the embers. The kindling caught, and flames sprang up, flickering blue and yellow. Fergus watched the fire for a minute and then sat on a sofa opposite the inspector. McMahon had been quiet until then, flipping through pages in his notebook and jotting a note or two.

"Miss Cantrell got away all right?" he asked me.

"Yes, she's trying to reach London tonight, in time for work tomorrow."

"And you? You don't have to be back at work?"

I glanced at Josh before answering. "We should be, but we're planning to stay on for a while. To keep Fergus company."

"Do you have any leads yet?" Fergus asked McMahon. He was nursing another glass of scotch, swirling the amber liquid around.

The detective didn't seem ready to commit to anything. "There were many people in the castle at the time of the murder. I have more work to do and will need the pathologist's report before I'm in a position to do more than conjecture."

A log shifted in the fireplace, sending up a volley of sparks. Fergus jumped up to prod the errant log back into place while Arbroath raised his head to see what was happening and then settled down again. The fire was throwing out heat now and filling the room with a welcome glow. The fearsome bear peeked out between the flames, his eyes glowing red.

"The most urgent question for me is motive," McMahon said. "Why was Duncan killed? If we could answer that, we'd be closer to finding our killer. Many people had the opportunity to kill Duncan, but how many had a reason to do so?"

"Josh and I have been talking," Fergus said. "We think it might be related to the estate sale. We're in the midst of drawing up contracts. Other than myself, Duncan had the most vested interest in the outcome of the negotiation. I feel as though there has to be a connection."

"You think Stanton Knox has something to do with it?" McMahon asked, his eyes glittering with interest.

Fergus leaned the poker against the blackened brick of the hearth and went back to his seat. "There's no logical reason to believe that, no."

Josh squeezed my hand, looked from me to McMahon and back again. Was he asking me to tell McMahon about Fergus's aura? My stomach clenched at the thought of it. McMahon had a calm and pleasant personality. He listened closely and didn't hector anyone. He was, it seemed, comfortable in his skin, assured that he could do his job well. But he was a middle-aged Scot, shrewd and down-to-earth. A discussion of my paranormal talents was unlikely to go over well.

Still, Fergus's aura was swirling, and Duncan was dead. "Inspector McMahon, there's something else…" I sat up straight and cleared my throat. "I believe that Fergus is in great danger. The killer may well strike again, and soon."

McMahon's expression didn't change. He watched me, his eyes the color of the rain-laden sky. "What makes you think that Fergus is a target?"

"I can see signs that predict death," I said. "Fergus has an aura.

That's what I call it anyway. It's air that swirls over his head and..." I stopped to lick my lips. My mouth had gone dry. Fergus had slumped back against the sofa cushions, as though distancing himself from what I was saying. Still, McMahon sat motionless, his expression inscrutable.

Hurtling on, I described how the auras worked and told McMahon that I feared Fergus had only a short time left unless we could defuse the threat to him. "We have to find the killer before he gets to Fergus."

When I'd finished, silence fell, broken by the crackle of logs and the soft snoring of Arbroath who lay on the rug at Fergus's feet. The inspector looked from Fergus to Josh. "You both know about this aura?"

When the two men nodded, McMahon seemed to sink into a trance, his eyes on the fire, his fingers tapping his notebook. After a minute or two, he stood and tugged his jacket back into place. "I'd like another chat with Josh, if that's okay. We'll use the dining room."

Josh blanched but got to his feet.

"Why?" Fergus demanded.

McMahon held up a hand. "Just a few minutes, if you don't mind." He gestured to Josh to lead the way.

Once they had gone, Fergus jumped to his feet and paced the room. "What the bloody hell—" he muttered. I was feeling nauseous. Had I implicated Josh by exposing the fact that Fergus was in danger? With Duncan dead, Josh was now the heir to the estate, or what would be left of it once the loans were paid off, and McMahon was clearly searching for a motive. While Fergus paced, I sat with my head in my hands.

Finally, Josh and McMahon returned. "I appreciate everything you've all shared with me," the inspector said. "You've been very cooperative. I'll leave you now and return as soon as I have more information."

We waited until we heard the front door close before asking Josh what McMahon had discussed with him.

Josh waved a hand dismissively. "He's simply being thorough.

Obviously, he realized that I will inherit now if anything happens to Fergus, but we can easily produce evidence to show that the estate is barely worth anything. Certainly not enough for me to wander around bumping off my relatives."

"I'll have a word with him," Fergus said. "It's utterly ridiculous."

Josh shook his head. "Just let it go. Things will work out."

"Maybe. Maybe not. What we have to do is identify the real killer," I said. "That's the best way to keep Fergus safe and to get you off the suspect list."

20

After McMahon had gone, the three of us sat in silence for a few minutes. The evening was drawing in, the gloom deepening, but no one moved to switch on a light. "It was brave of you to tell the inspector about your auras, Kate," Fergus said at last. "Even if it may have led him to the conclusion that Josh is after the estate."

I cringed. So far, all I'd done was make things worse. Or no better at least. Duncan had been murdered, Fergus was still at risk, and now Josh was a suspect. Not exactly a shining record of success. And, although it felt selfish to even worry about it, I was going to miss another day, or two or three, of work. Josh had called Alan earlier to let him know we wouldn't be at the office in the morning. According to Josh, Alan hadn't been particularly concerned, beyond griping about having to reschedule a client meeting. But Josh, in Alan's eyes, could do no wrong. I, on the other hand, was the object of a more critical gaze. I knew that my work was good, and that my clients and workmates liked me, but the amount of time I'd taken off over the last couple of years had caused some serious difficulties— delayed meetings, missed deadlines, frantic all-nighters to catch up. Sometimes, the burden would shift to a colleague, which made me feel like a horrible person or at least a bad co-worker. But I knew I'd feel far worse, and maybe the world would be a slightly worse place, if I walked away from an aura and did nothing to help.

Josh roused himself from his chair and stood up. "Let's take Arbroath out for a walk. I need to stretch my legs and breathe some fresh air."

Fergus was on his feet and heading for the door before I could respond. We were putting on our jackets in the entry hall when Mrs. Dunsmore came up to ask Fergus what he wanted to do about dinner. "Pierre's still here," she said. "And he's happy to cook whatever you want."

"Isn't the kitchen still off-limits?" Josh asked.

"Yes, it is, but he can use the small kitchen near the butler's pantry."

I remembered seeing that on our first tour of the house. Josh said that in the 'good old days,' the servants' meals would be prepared in there while the main kitchen was being used for the upstairs dinner.

"I'm not sure I can eat," Fergus said, to which Mrs. Dunsmore tutted and shook her head. "Rubbish. Ye need to keep up your strength. This isna the time to be starving yourself."

Fergus looked at Josh and me. "What do you two want to eat? Sandwiches or a proper dinner?"

I was hungry, and I guessed Josh would be too. It always amazed me that he ate as much as he did and had not an ounce of fat on him. "I could eat dinner," I said.

"Me too. I'm starving," Josh said.

Mrs. Dunsmore clapped her hands together. "Good. That will give Pierre something to do, to stop him brooding. He's worried. The police spent a long time questioning him, you know, because of the missing carving knife. It might well turn out to be the murder weapon. Poor man. As if he hadn't already been feeling bad enough about what happened to Nick."

Fergus patted Mrs. Dunsmore on the shoulder. "Don't be distressing yourself," he said. "The police have to do their work and they will find the killer. Why don't you let Pierre know that we'd all appreciate a nice dinner." He glanced at the clock. "It's six. Let's eat at eight so he's not too rushed."

While the housekeeper hurried off to give Pierre the good news, Josh and I followed Fergus outside. Arbroath galloped ahead, more like a small pony than a dog. It was drizzling, and I pulled up the hood on my coat. The patter of rain on the fabric was soothing. It reminded me of camping holidays with my parents. It always poured down, it seemed, but I'd loved the sound of raindrops on canvas. Josh and Fergus strode in front, talking quietly to each other. The lamps on the gateposts in the distance shone through the misty darkness that blanketed the grounds.

Walking slowly, I thought back over the events of the day. Duncan was dead, Lucy had gone. Lucy had confessed that they were both searching for a Fabergé egg that she believed had been purchased by Fergus's grandfather— although she had also insisted that she could be wrong. I wondered if Lucy had mentioned the egg to McMahon. I'd have to ask him next time I saw him. She'd said Duncan was short of money. Did that have something to do with it all? I should have mentioned it to McMahon too and would do so next time I saw him. Of course, my credibility with him was shot now that I'd confessed to seeing auras. I sighed, pulling my hood closer around my hair.

Arbroath started to bark, his deep-throated yowls breaking through my rain-accompanied meditation. Fergus called to him, but the dog ran off, hurtling himself into the trees that lined the drive.

"Come back, you big oaf," Fergus yelled, moving to the verge and whistling to the dog. I lowered my hood to listen more closely. Arbroath stopped barking suddenly and scurried around in the undergrowth, rustling the leaves on the shrubs and snapping twigs under his big paws. Something certainly had him excited. When Fergus stepped off the path to follow, Josh went with him. My heart pounded. What if someone were lurking among the trees? I edged closer, prepared to do my part if we had an intruder, but all I could hear was loud panting. Less than a minute later, Arbroath seemed to lose interest and padded back out onto the drive. Behind him, Josh and Fergus emerged from the bushes, soaked through.

"Barmy dog," Fergus muttered, extricating leaves from his hair. "It was probably a rabbit. When he was younger he'd have caught it, but nowadays he's too lazy."

My pulse slowed, but still I was happy that we were heading back to the shelter of the house. Arbroath stood in the center of the hall and shook himself, sending showers of water over the tiled floor. Fergus grabbed a towel from a hook in the boot cupboard. He rubbed the dog vigorously, leaving Arbroath's hair standing up in spikes and smelling like a wet carpet. I crossed the hall to put my jacket in the cupboard.

"Before dinner, I need to make some calls and send a few emails," Fergus said as he dried the dog's paws. "I promised Stanton Knox I'd let him have the painting and book inventories, and I still need to finish up the furniture." He straightened up and hung the wet towel over the oak bench. "I'm sorry. I'm sure you think I'm heartless to be thinking of business matters now, right after Duncan's death. And I need to make plans for his funeral, although I suppose we'll have to wait until the autopsy is done."

"You're not heartless," Josh said. "It's important to keep moving forward. Knox would be concerned if he stopped hearing from you. I'll help you, don't worry."

"I wonder if I should tell him about Duncan?"

"Yes, definitely. The police will almost certainly be in touch with him, as he was here the night of the murder, so advance warning might be a good idea."

Fergus nodded. "I'll do that."

The front door creaked open, making me jump, but it was Lachlan. He too began dripping water on the tiles. "Just checking in," he said. "I thought I heard the dog barking?"

"We think it was a rabbit," Josh said. "But he didn't catch it."

Lachlan grunted. "Very well. I'll carry on then."

"You don't have to be patrolling the place," Fergus said. "There's another storm rolling in. Come in and dry off. Mrs. Dunsmore will make you some supper."

The groundskeeper looked uncertain. "I told that inspector I'd keep watch," he said. "Until they catch the murderer." He rolled the word 'murderer' so that it sounded as though it had twice as many syllables as it really did. He shifted his rifle from one arm to the other and adjusted his cap. "I'll grab something to eat and then I'll get back out there," he said. "The rain doesn't bother me."

"There's no need to be outside," Fergus said. "But you do what you think is best."

"Aye, sir, I will, thank you." He strode across the hall towards the kitchen stairs, his heavy boots thumping on the tile floor.

"I'm going up to the office then," Fergus said. "If you want to join me."

"Perhaps I could use the computer once you're finished with it," I asked. "I'd like to take a look for more information on the Fabergé eggs, but there's no wi-fi or mobile signal so I can't use my phone." I tried not to sound whiny, but I did miss having easy access to the Internet.

"Be my guest," he said. "Off we go, then. Come on, Arbroath."

We all traipsed up the stairs and through the long hallway to the office where Fergus switched on the lights, banishing the shadows that had spooked me last time I was here. Josh and I sat together on one of the tartan sofas, while Fergus stood at the window, looking out at the rain, his reflection in the glass pale and ghostly. My stomach flipped. We had to stay focused. Someone or something still threatened Fergus's life. His aura rippled fast over his head although, in the reflection, it was invisible.

"Why don't you go ahead and use the computer first," he offered, without turning around. "I want to take another look at the purchase agreement."

We went to the table in the corner, where Josh pulled up two chairs. I turned on the PC, and we stared at the screen as though waiting for a celestial vision to appear. The dial-up modem screeched in the background as it struggled to connect. In spite of Fergus's intention to work on the contract, he remained by the window, apparently lost in thought. Arbroath, spread out on the rug in front of the unlit fireplace, whimpered in his sleep, his legs twitching as though he was dreaming of running.

"Chasing that rabbit," Fergus said, looking over at the dog with affection. He stretched his arms over his head as he moved towards his desk and sat down. We turned our attention back to the computer, which was still whirring and clicking its way to life.

A crash of glass followed by a boom and a blinding flash brought my heart to my mouth. Josh jumped up as I turned to see a jagged hole in the window and an eruption of flames in the middle of the room. Had the house been struck by lightning? I shot up, pushing back from the computer table, my chair crashing to the floor. Not lightning, my brain was telling me, but I couldn't understand what I was seeing.

"It's a firebomb," Josh yelled. "Get out, get out now."

Smoke, thick and oily, quickly filled the room. It was hard to see anything. Josh yelled at Fergus to get to the door while the dog howled. Wind poured through the broken window, fanning the flames higher. The varnished paneled walls caught fire instantly. My chest hurt as I struggled to breathe, with tears streaming down my face. Arbroath sprang from his place on the rug and backed away, barking at the fire that surged towards him. Ignoring Josh's pleas for him to stay back, Fergus weaved past the highest flames to reach the frantic dog, caught hold of Arbroath's collar and pulled on it. The dog refused to budge, and Fergus crouched down next to him, begging him to move.

"Kate. Get out, get help." Josh shouted. But like Arbroath, it seemed that my legs were glued to the carpet. I couldn't move, watching in horror as the flames swallowed Fergus's desk. The curtains at the broken window became cascades of fire, and the sofas blazed.

But then Arbroath's howls brought me to my senses. I calculated my path to the door, and ran. Just as I reached it, a figure filled the doorway. Through the miasma, I saw it was Lachlan. "Get out," he yelled over the din.

"Fergus won't leave without the dog," I gasped. "He's on the other side of the room."

Without a word, Lachlan plunged in, disappearing into the inferno. Doubled over, I held the door frame for support, struggling to breathe through the smothering fumes that billowed out into the corridor. Josh was in there. I couldn't leave him, but I had to get some air. I pushed away from the door and, as I staggered a few steps along the hall to where the smoke thinned, I became aware of a shrill ringing sound. A fire alarm, I realized, which must have alerted Lachlan. After inhaling deeply, I moved back towards the door. Someone was shouting above the roar of the fire, and suddenly Josh was rushing towards me through the haze, dragging the dog by its collar. I grabbed Josh, pulling him further along the hallway, away from the burning room. Freed from Josh's grasp, Arbroath fled up the hallway.

"Oh my God, are you all right?" I ran my hands over Josh's hair and face, across his shoulders, sweeping away several embers that had fallen on his jacket. I stamped on them until I was sure they were out. Josh leaned against the wall. "Fergus," he croaked.

My heart felt as though it had stopped. Was this it? Earlier, Fergus's aura had been moving so fast it was dizzying.

A crash like a clap of thunder made the floor vibrate under our feet. Josh's eyes widened. "What the hell?"

Seconds later Fergus and Lachlan burst through the open door, hurling themselves into the hallway. Using his jacket sleeve to protect his hand, Lachlan pulled the door closed. I ran to Fergus, patting him down as I'd done with Josh, extinguishing embers as I found them. The stench of burning hair and wool made me gag. Worse, Fergus's aura still swirled over his head. Lachlan staggered away from the door, his face blackened with smoke and soot, his clothes ruined.

"A book case collapsed near the door," Fergus coughed, answering our unasked question about the crash.

"We need to call the fire brigade," I wheezed, looking around for a fire extinguisher.

"They're already on their way," Lachlan said. "Mrs. Dunsmore called them when we heard the alarm going off." He pointed to the ceiling a few yards along the corridor, and I saw a smoke detector, its red light winking furiously, still emitting its high-pitched squeal. Mrs. Dunsmore appeared at the end of the corridor, brandishing an extinguisher, Pierre right behind her.

"That won't help at this point, I'm afraid," Fergus told her. "We need to get downstairs right now."

Another loud crack made me jump. The paint on the den door was bubbling and peeling, and the top panel splintered, releasing a blast of hot air and smoke. Together, we dashed along the hall and down the stairs to the entry hall, where we hurriedly took stock. Lachlan was nursing his hand, the skin from his fingers to his wrist red and blistered. Fortunately, at first glance anyway, neither Fergus nor Josh was hurt although their faces, like Lachlan's, were covered in black smudges and Josh's eyes were red.

Mrs. Dunsmore opened the front door and we emerged into the fresh, cold air as sirens sounded in the distance.

21

W e huddled out on the grass, watching in awe as the fire raged in the upstairs window. With the fresh air easing the pain in my chest, my panic subsided and my head started to clear. I leaned into Josh's arms, still trembling, but over-joyed that he was safe. We both reeked of smoke.

"Should we be thinking about saving anything from the down-stairs rooms?" Josh asked Fergus. "The fire might spread before the engines get here."

"I wouldn't know where to start," Fergus replied. "But the internal walls are all built of stone and the floors are thick, so that will slow the fire down. Hopefully, help will arrive before it can do more harm."

As if in answer, a siren wailed on the road nearby. A minute later, a fire engine roared up the driveway, lights flashing. A team of men in fluorescent jackets disgorged from the vehicle and sprinted past us, pausing just long enough to ask Fergus for directions to the location of the fire. A second team worked on fitting a hose to the fire hydrant half-hidden in the shrubs along the drive. Within a minute, four firemen were directing the hose at the window of the office upstairs, water puddling on the ground at their feet.

While we were watching, an ambulance arrived, and two paramedics jumped out. They insisted on examining each of us, and one began treating Lachlan's hand. Fergus fretted about Arbroath, who'd run far from the fire and hidden in the kitchens. Mrs. Dunsmore tried to convince Fergus that the dog had been scared, not hurt, but still, she hurried back inside to call the vet, who promised to come over immediately.

When another fire engine arrived, most of its crew hurried past us, but one man stopped and introduced himself as the fire chief. "What happened here?" he asked.

"Someone threw a firebomb through the office window. He might still be out here, in the gardens. Maybe a pyromaniac, enjoying watching the results of his work," Fergus said, with a wry smile.

"A firebomb?" The chief looked surprised for a split second and then he turned away, talking on his radio. When he'd finished his call, he told us we should sit inside in the entry hall. The police were on their way, he said, and planned to search the grounds for the firebomber. He didn't need to mention that being outside made us easy targets. I wished I'd thought of how exposed Fergus had been, standing at the window.

We straggled into the entry hall and huddled in a corner, out of the way of the firemen. In the light, I watched the air rotate over Fergus's head. For a few moments, upstairs in the hallway, I'd allowed myself to hope that the fire had been the threat to his life, and that he had survived it. But if that were the case, the aura would have disappeared. The danger would be over. Disheartened, I clung to Josh's arm, and we watched the comings and goings of the emergency crews.

Inspector McMahon's arrival soon afterwards induced a weird sensation of déja-vu. It was his third visit in as many days. He had a resolute, almost angry look on his face, as though this had gone too far, and he'd had enough.

"Good to see you, Inspector," Fergus said.

"The chief's saying it could have been a firebomb?" McMahon

already had his notebook out and appeared ready to start taking notes, but the arrival of the vet interrupted him.

"Dr. Ramsey," the man said, introducing himself. "And I think you know my daughter, Fiona? She often helps me on my calls."

Fiona, dressed in a green sweatshirt and spandex leggings, gave us a nervous wave. "I'm training to be a veterinary assistant," she said, explaining her presence. "Where's Arbroath? Is he all right?"

"I'll take you to him," Mrs. Dunsmore said. "Come along."

As Dr. Ramsey and Fiona followed her towards the kitchen stairs, Fergus made a move to join them, but McMahon raised his hand. "If you don't mind, sir, the sooner I learn what happened here, the sooner we'll catch the culprit."

"Don't worry," Fiona told Fergus. "I'll bring Arbroath up to you as soon as my dad's taken a look at him."

The paramedics had finished working on Lachlan's wrist. When they recommended he go to the hospital, he refused and stomped off towards the kitchens. In the suddenly quiet hall, McMahon asked if we were ready to talk or if we needed to clean up first.

"We're okay," Josh said.

McMahon nodded. "Let's move into the dining room," he suggested when a group of firemen clattered past us. We did, all the three of us sitting on one side of the table with McMahon facing us. "Can you tell me what happened?"

Josh explained everything, from when the projectile smashed the window to when Lachlan arrived and succeeded in dragging Arbroath to the door.

"You believe that someone deliberately attacked the room where you all happened to be gathered?" McMahon asked.

Josh hesitated, thinking. "I'm not sure it would have been apparent the three of us were in there, but Fergus obviously was. The lights were on, with him at the window looking outside. We'd just come in from a walk, and we hadn't turned lights on in any other rooms. So, on that side of the building, only one window was lit, and Fergus would have been clearly visible."

"You think, then, that the target was Fergus?"

Josh glanced at his uncle before answering. "Yes, I think I do. And Kate and I would have simply been collateral damage."

McMahon directed his iron-colored gaze at me for a few seconds, perhaps thinking of what I'd told him earlier about the aura. I wondered if he would mention it, but the fire chief poked his head around the door just then. "I have a quick update and a couple of questions if you don't mind. The fire is out. That room is a total loss, I'm afraid, but we can be thankful the fire didn't spread beyond it. You could have lost the entire castle. We're still working on establishing the cause of the fire, but we suspect a small incendiary device; a glass container containing an accelerant, kerosene most likely."

"Josh here says someone threw the container through the window," McMahon said. "Wouldn't that be hard to achieve?"

"Not really. Someone with a good throwing arm could manage it well enough, and those windows are single pane, very easy to break. I've got someone outside calculating the trajectory of the projectile to see if we can pin down the location of the thrower."

"Arbroath barked when we were out in the garden earlier," I said. "There may have been an intruder hiding in the bushes. We took a look around, but we didn't see anyone."

"Whoever it was has almost certainly gone by now, but we'll keep looking," McMahon said. "Don't worry. We'll catch them."

"I'll let my crew finish up and then we'll be on our way," the fire chief said. "And I'll send a full report to you as soon as I can, Inspector."

While the fire chief tramped out in his heavy gear, McMahon stared at us thoughtfully. I wondered what was going through his mind, but whatever it was, the noisy arrival of the dog disturbed his contemplation. Arbroath bounded up to Fergus and licked his face, leaving trail marks on his sooty skin.

Fiona followed close behind. "He's fine, my dad says. The poor thing got scared, and his eyes hurt from the smoke, so we put some drops in them. But his lungs and breathing are good. Dad's having a cup of tea with Mrs. Dunsmore. He's doing a good job of calming her down." She looked around the room as though at a loss on what to do next, and McMahon was quick to pounce.

"As you're here, I'd like to ask you a few questions," he said. "Take a seat."

"Me?" Fiona looked confused. "I wasn't here. I've been home with Dad all evening."

"My questions don't concern the fire," McMahon said. "I'm looking for information on your movements last night. Just a couple of details."

She sat down next to me, knotting the cord of her green sweatshirt around her fingers.

"There's no need to worry," McMahon assured her. "What time did you leave the castle?"

McMahon now had two concurrent investigations to run and had to be looking for connections between Duncan's death and this attack. It seemed like a daunting task, but he appeared calm, almost detached. When Fiona took her time answering, he didn't hurry her.

"Well, I left the kitchens once we'd finished the cleaning up," she said at last. "Around one a.m."

"Who was still there when you left?"

She pulled the knot in the cord tight. "Pierre, definitely, and his friend from France, and maybe half a dozen others, mostly blokes I didn't recognize who came in to help for the night."

"And you drove straight home?"

"No, I sat in my car for thirty minutes or so..."

"You were waiting for someone?"

Her face turned as red as a stop sign. "Uh huh," she mumbled.

"Who would that be?"

"Duncan." Fiona plucked at her spandex leggings. "We'd agreed to meet after the party. I'd parked around the back near the tradesman's entrance. He said he'd bring a bottle of champagne. But he never came. I waited until 1.30, gave up and drove home."

"You didn't come back into the kitchens to look for him?"

"No." She tossed her head. "I'm not, like, desperate you know. Half the boys in the village want to take me out. If Duncan had decided he didn't want to bother, I wasn't going to go chasing after him. He's not that good-looking, and he's, you know, old. His loss." Her eyes widened and her hand flew to her mouth. "I'm sorry. I don't mean to bad-mouth a dead person. But I never saw him, not after we talked in the kitchen around eleven o'clock."

I thought back to when I'd gone to the kitchen with Duncan to collect more champagne. It had been, as Fiona said, around eleven.

"And my dad knows what time I came in," Fiona continued. "Because he'd just got back from a call-out, a horse with colic over near Portsonachan. We had a cup of cocoa together."

"Thank you, Fiona," McMahon said. "You've been very helpful. Now, I've kept you all long enough. I'll be in touch as soon as I have anything to report."

Fergus stood up. "What do you think? Is tonight's attacker the same man who murdered Duncan?"

McMahon tapped his fingers against the stained and scratched cover of his notebook. "That's what I plan to find out. And until I do, I'm posting two officers here to keep an eye on the grounds and the house."

"That's not necessary—" Fergus started, but McMahon interrupted. "It's a sensible precaution until we know what we're dealing with. We have to assume that whoever threw that incendiary device intended for it to kill you, and that he'll try again."

Josh and I stood too, but McMahon remained seated. "Can you spare me a minute?" he asked me, gesturing me back into my chair. We waited while the others left the room. He had the ability to be perfectly still, I noticed. Not the stillness of lethargy or inattention, but of a contemplative calm I couldn't help envying.

"Tell me again about this threat to Fergus, this sign that you see," he said finally.

As I described the aura to him and related some of my previous experiences with it, his face remained inscrutable.

"You say it's possible to save people? How does that work?"

"When I see that someone is in danger, I try to identify the source of the threat. If I can determine that, then it's sometimes possible to alter the outcome."

"You fancy yourself as an investigator then?"

From his tone, I couldn't tell whether that he meant it as a sincere question or sarcasm. "Yes, in a way," I answered. "I find out as much as possible about the... victim and his or her current circumstances. I look for clues and for ways to avert the disaster. Of course, not every aura signifies death through foul play. Sometimes, it's far more straightforward, like a medical condition or an accident."

"Did young Nick have one of these aura thingies?"

"He must have done, but I didn't meet him. I only knew that he hadn't turned up for work. Mrs. Dunsmore told me, and Pierre was upset, because it meant more work for him."

"You're acquainted with Pierre?"

"I talked with him over lunch on Friday."

"Does he have a problem with Fergus? A reason to hate him?"

I stared, but McMahon's expression remained fixed. "You think Pierre is the killer?" I asked. "That he might go after Fergus?" I thought about the missing carving knife.

"I'm only asking your opinion."

"Well, he can't have thrown the firebomb through the window," I said. "He was in the kitchen with Mrs. Dunsmore and Lachlan when it happened. They both said so."

The inspector nodded. "Yes, that's right, of course. Any other ideas on who the perpetrator could be?"

"Well, it's not Josh," I said.

McMahon pressed his lips together. "Josh?"

"You seem to think he had a motive to kill Duncan," I said. The smell of smoke still filled my nostrils and my throat itched. "But he obviously had nothing to do with that firebomb, which means there's someone else out there who intends harm to Fergus. Besides, Josh loves his uncle. He's one of the most ethical, moral people I know. He'd never hurt anyone." Tears burned my eyes, and my chest hurt with the effort of convincing McMahon of Josh's innocence. My throat was scratchy, and I started coughing.

The inspector leaned forward and gave me a rare smile. "Please, try not to worry. It's my job to ask difficult questions, to try out various hypotheses in order to arrive at the truth."

"Will you take him off your suspect list?"

"Let's get back to you and your theories on the threat to Fergus. Do you have any ideas you want to share with me, something that I might not know?"

"I thought I knew what was going on, but now I'm not so sure." I slumped back in my chair, suddenly feeling weary. I wanted to lie down in my room.

"Please go on, Miss Benedict. Anything you say will be held in complete confidence."

"Can you call me Kate? It's less intimidating."

McMahon allowed himself another brief smile. "Kate it is."

"Lucy and Duncan were searching the castle for a valuable artifact, a Fabergé egg, to be exact. I don't know if it's relevant, but I thought you should know. In case it has something to do with Duncan's death."

"Tell me more about this egg. What makes it so valuable?"

I explained what Lucy had told me about the missing Fabergé treasure and the possible connection to the castle. "But it was all very vague," I said. "And even if the egg exists, why does it present any kind of danger to Fergus? He's never even heard of a missing egg. And he certainly doesn't know where it is."

For once, McMahon's normally composed features were creased in a frown. "This is very interesting," he said, as he jotted a note in his book.

"There's something else," I said. "Duncan had a journal in his drawer. There were some notes in it that I thought were unusual. I wrote them down." I dug around in my jeans pocket for the scrap of paper, spread it on the table and traced the writing with my finger. *Alexandra 1917. Anna Vyrubova 1939, Cyril Thorpe 1940.*

McMahon gazed at it. "Does that make any sense to you?"

"Not yet. I'm working on it."

McMahon copied the names and dates into his notebook and

then snapped it closed. "This number is my mobile," he said, passing me a business card. "I'll always answer it. If you think of anything at all, at any time, phone me."

I put the card and the list back in my pocket and pushed away from the table.

"One more thing," he said, as he got to his feet. "You say that you can change the fate of the victim, sometimes through a small action. Would you recommend that Fergus leave the castle, for a while at least? Perhaps he should come with you to London, or visit one of his friends in Oxford. Would that be enough to avert a disaster?"

"It might be. I'll talk to him. If I can convince him to leave, I'll let you know."

I wasn't optimistic though. From the little I knew of Fergus, he was stubborn and he loved his home. Nor would he go anywhere without Arbroath. I would do my best, but it seemed a foregone conclusion that I'd fail.

22

After Inspector McMahon had gone, I went to my room to get cleaned up. Josh was there, already showered and dressed. While I took off my delectably smoke-scented clothes, I told him what McMahon and I had discussed.

"That's good," Josh said. "He's not discounting your insights and he's listening to you."

"But he wouldn't commit to taking you off the suspect list. He told me not to worry, but that's no help. Oh, and he asked if we should persuade Fergus to leave the castle. Maybe a change of venue would be enough, you know, to alter the outcome. But I can't see him agreeing to leave, can you?"

"First of all, don't worry about me. And no, I doubt Fergus would leave, especially not right now with all the work to be done on preparing the estate for the sale. My view is that we have to stay and see this through. Besides, there's no guarantee that moving Fergus will eliminate the risk, is there?"

"No, not really. Which means we need to be focused, one hundred percent, on working out what threatens him. After dinner, let's review everything we know, however imprecise and fuzzy it is. If you and I collaborate, perhaps something will become obvious. We'll ask Fergus to help too."

In the bathroom, I examined my soot-marked face in the mirror and wondered how McMahon had conducted a serious conversation with me without being distracted by the black splotch on the end of my nose. My blue eyes, normally my favorite feature, were still red-rimmed and watery and my hair was sticky from the oily smoke. Once I was in the shower and standing under the cascade of hot water, though, I felt a little more optimistic. With a police presence on the grounds, help from Inspector McMahon, and some clear thinking on my part, we could save Fergus.

Dinner was a subdued affair. Pierre brought up plates of seafood risotto from the small kitchen and served us in the dining room, which loomed cavernous and cold with only the three of us there. I was happy, however, to see that Arbroath had survived the fire with nothing but a tuft or two of singed hair. He slept contentedly under the table, his chin resting on Fergus's shoe, but his master looked despondent, barely aware of Josh's valiant attempt to hold a conversation. Finally, Fergus pushed away his plate, the food half-eaten, and leaned back in his chair.

"I've got some work to do on the inventories. I never had time to finish them with everything that happened..." he trailed off, no doubt thinking of the chaos the weekend had brought. "And Knox is expecting me to email them to him tomorrow."

"We'll re-do them with you," I offered. "It'll go faster with three."

"I'm wondering if it's a sign." Fergus folded his napkin into a tiny square. "A sort of cosmic warning that I shouldn't sell the estate after all."

So that's what was on his mind. Josh laid down his knife and fork. "Cosmic warning? You don't believe in that sort of thing."

"I didn't think you did either, but you trust Kate and her aura sightings." Fergus sighed. "I don't know. Nick? Duncan? Would they be alive if I hadn't decided to sell the estate?"

"Nick's death wasn't related to the estate sale," Josh reasoned. "And there's no indication that Duncan's was either."

"Let's assume for a minute that there is a connection." My words drew a frown from Josh. "For one thing, there's the timing. Both of them died this weekend— after Stanton Knox arrived to negotiate the contract."

Fergus snorted. "You're saying Knox killed Duncan? And somehow convinced Nick to drown himself?"

"No, of course not. But bear with me for a minute. As DCI McMahon has repeated several times, what is the motive? Why was Duncan killed? Who stood to gain?"

We gazed at each other for a few moments, and then Fergus shrugged. "I have no idea, but I don't believe that Knox had a hand in it."

"No," I agreed. "Probably not, but that doesn't mean that the sale isn't in some way responsible for their deaths." Fergus grimaced, so I changed the subject. "Thinking of Knox, were you able to reach him?"

Fergus checked the gilt clock that ticked loudly on the sideboard. "Not yet. It's nine-fifteen. He'll still be in the air. His plane lands in San Francisco at four, California time. That'll be midnight here." He pushed back his chair. "I won't be able to sleep anyway, so I'll ring him later. Until then, I'm off to the library to finish my list of books. If you'd care to join me, I'll share my bottle of Lagavulin with you."

Ten minutes later, we sat in the battered old leather sofas, with our drinks in hand and Arbroath at our feet. "What do you want us to do?" I asked.

Fergus gave me a leather binder, the one I recognized that Lucy had been using when working on the book list. "Fortunately, this and the other original inventories were in here, not on my desk in the office," he said. "This one is the catalogue of all the books I own."

"Why the detailed lists?" I asked. I glanced at the shelves. "I suppose most of the books are valuable?"

Fergus nodded. "There are lots of rare books in here. My grandfather began the book register as a project when he inherited the estate. He was an avid collector and a mathematician. Apparently, he enjoyed combining his two passions by cataloguing his collections.

My father updated them all in the 1950s, but they haven't been touched since." He tapped the binder. "Lucy and I verified that the entries in here matched the physical books. If we couldn't find a book on the shelf, we wrote it on a "Missing" list. We just need to finish it. Then I'll put a check mark next to the books I want to keep, and that will be that."

"Seems straightforward enough." I wished we had a computer to work on. It would be much faster to enter everything into a spreadsheet, but the poor PC was a lump of molten plastic and metal now, so we'd have to do things the old-fashioned way.

There were around two hundred books left to match to the inventory document. I enjoyed handling the books, with their smell of leather and old paper, dust and a vague fragrance of vanilla. Duncan had been searching these shelves. Did he think the egg was hidden behind the books? I tilted a few of them forward and examined the space behind them. From the little I knew about the eggs, it was possible there was enough room for one to be stashed back there. I ran my eyes along the shelves that lined the room. It seemed as though there were miles of them. It would take forever to check every one.

"Remember Lucy said she and Duncan were looking for a Fabergé egg?" I said to Fergus. "Duncan was rummaging about in here, examining the shelves."

Fergus raised an eyebrow. "It's not a crime to look at a bookshelf."

"No, more than that," I said. "He was taking books down and searching the space behind them as though he was looking for something specific. He'd written some things in his journal too."

"Journal?"

"I found it in his room, had a quick look at it, and put back. The police have it now."

Fergus shook his head. "You're losing me."

I was losing me too. I needed to slow down and consider things more carefully.

"I'd be happy to stop talking about hidden treasures, Kate," Fergus said with a frown. "We have more important things to address than an egg with some jewels stuck on it. I can't tell you definitively that it's not in the house but I have my doubts. My father or my grandfather would have recorded it. Like I said, my grandfather was an expert collector and he was also very organized. Just about every teacup and saucer is accounted for, and he kept receipts for all his purchases. For now, we have to focus on getting these blasted inventories done so I can sell the old place and be done with it."

My neck flushing warm from the rebuke, I murmured an apology and continued checking the books in my section. But I was thinking about Fergus's grandfather, Gordon MacKenna. Lucy said he'd bought the egg from a dealer in 1940. Fergus said he kept all his receipts.

Although I knew I was risking Fergus's wrath, I had to ask. "Where did your grandfather store the receipts for his purchases?"

Josh coughed loudly as Fergus swung around to look at me. I knew he was stressed. Selling the estate was a heart-wrenching process. And then I'd told him he was about to die. "I just think it's possible the treasure is connected to the threat to you," I said. "It could be the reason Duncan was killed."

Fergus sighed, placed the book he was holding back on a shelf and walked over to the sofa. "The receipts were in a filing cabinet in my office, lass."

"Oh." So much for that line of inquiry.

"Can we take a break from the inventory?" I asked. "I think it's important that we follow any clues that might lead us to uncover the source of danger to you."

"I'd be glad to," Fergus replied. "We're close enough to done, although I still have the furniture list to prepare. Still, under the circumstances, Knox can wait for a few days. I have plenty of time."

That's not how I saw it. Gazing at his aura, I knew that time was not on our side.

"I need some paper and a pen," I said. "I always think more clearly when I write things down."

Fergus produced the items, and we huddled around the coffee table with the blank paper in front of us.

"Let's start with the main fact," I said. "Fergus, you're going to die unless we do something."

"Jeez, Kate." Josh looked shocked. "That's a bit direct."

"But it's true. It's what we have to focus on. All right, Fergus?"

He nodded. I picked up the pencil and dropped it a second later when the shrill tone of the phone tore through the room. Fergus jumped up and went to the desk to answer it. He had his back to us while he talked, and I couldn't hear his words, but the slump in his shoulders suggested that he'd just got bad news. He replaced the receiver and turned around. "That was Lachlan. He and those two police officers are pursuing someone in the grounds. They told us to stay away from the windows and turn the lights off."

Josh and I looked at each other and then at the window, a large black mirror reflecting the light from the table lamps.

"I say, no bloody way." Fergus headed to the door. "I'm not sitting here waiting for another bomb to be lobbed at me. I'm going to help Lachlan. You coming?"

"No, Fergus!" I yelled at his retreating back. Damn. Josh and I ran after him, calling to him to stop while Arbroath loped along behind us, panting with excitement.

Fergus rushed outside, approaching a shadowy figure on the lawn. My heart was like a piston trying to hammer its way out of my chest. The figure turned out to be Lachlan, who gave his rifle to Fergus. "You take this," he said. "I've got a knife. The officers went that way." He pointed towards the side of the house.

"Don't go over there," Josh pleaded. "They're professionals. Let them handle it."

Lachlan scoffed. "We've already had a murder and a firebomb. I'd say they've had their chance."

Fergus and Lachlan set off, sidling along the wall like a couple of aging commandos. At the corner, they stopped and peered around before setting off once more. Josh and I looked at each other. We had no choice but to follow them. Pitch dark, the night enveloped us, the only light bleeding from a couple of upstairs windows. Mist coiled around us, muffling sound. Still, I turned to stare into the shrubs along the driveway, sure I heard leaves rustling and twigs breaking. Someone was trampling through the undergrowth, moving in the direction of the road, away from the house.

Headlights lit up the driveway, sweeping wide yellow circles as a car sped in through the gate. It braked suddenly, and the tires skidded on the gravel. Silhouetted against the headlights, black figures spilled on to the driveway. Another vehicle arrived and pulled up beside the stationary car. Doors flew open, and several more people got out and ran up the drive. Then they turned sharply and disappeared amongst the cypress trees. Over the sounds of scuffling in the bushes, someone yelled. "We've got him."

In the darkness, a group of figures emerged from the trees. I couldn't see much, but it looked as though two officers held another man by both arms, pushing him into one of the police cars. Doors slammed, and the vehicle reversed out of the gate while the other sped towards the house.

Lachlan led us back to the front steps. I was shaking, not with fear, I realized, but fury. How could I protect Fergus if he threw himself in harm's way? Unable to help myself, I jabbed a finger at his shoulder. "That was irresponsible. You know you're in danger and you should be doing everything you can to look after yourself, not go running around in the dark like that."

Lachlan snorted when Fergus apologized. In the awkward silence that followed, Inspector McMahon got out of the car that had come to a halt right in front of the house. First, he hurried over to talk with the officers who'd been on duty in the grounds. Then he walked back to join us on the front steps.

"It was Jameson," he said.

"Nick's father?" Fergus looked dazed.

"He had another bottle of kerosene in his rucksack. And he was threatening you, screaming that he'd get you next time."

"That makes sense," Lachlan said. "I'd been thinking it might be him. He bowls for the cricket team. Took eight wickets in the last match of the season. He knows how to throw."

That was about the longest speech I'd heard Lachlan make.

McMahon nodded his agreement. "I haven't talked to Jameson myself yet, obviously, but we'll hold him for twenty-hours. The danger is over."

But the danger wasn't over. While everyone smiled at the news, Fergus's aura still swirled above his head.

23

The clock chimed eleven, but none of us were thinking of sleeping yet. Mrs. Dunsmore lit the fire in the drawing room, setting the backplate bear's eyes glowing. She insisted on bringing us mugs of hot chocolate to warm us up. Fergus barely moved or talked. He seemed stunned by McMahon's news. We all were. We'd all seen Nick's father, enraged by the death of his son, accusing Fergus of being responsible. I had put him on my list of possible threats, but the violence of his attack shocked me.

The problem was that nothing was resolved. The police had Jameson in custody, but Fergus remained in danger, which meant that the threat came from someone or something else. I whispered the bad tidings to Josh.

"We need to tell Fergus," he said. "He has to know. He has to remain on alert."

Fergus overheard our whispers. "It's still there then?" he asked.

I nodded.

"But who's left?" Josh asked. "Who could be after Fergus now, if not Jameson?"

"Whoever killed Duncan. Until the police find him, Fergus remains vulnerable."

"It could be medical," Josh said. "A heart attack or a stroke."

"We can't do much to stop that."

"Of course we can." Josh sat up straight. "We can take you to the hospital to have you checked out. If there's something wrong with your heart, they'll find it. We should go at once."

"I'm not traipsing off to Oban at this time of night. Besides, I feel absolutely fine. I had a check-up two months ago and the doc said my ticker's in perfect working order. Better than a Swiss watch, he told me."

"Then come with us to London. Maybe a change of venue is all that's needed."

As I expected, Fergus shook his head. "I appreciate the offer, but no. I've no intention of running away from my home, especially not now. For one thing, I have Duncan's funeral to sort out. That will have to be held here." He looked at me. "Would moving guarantee my safety?"

"No, not necessarily."

"That's what I thought. Let's not talk about that anymore then."

"So what next?" Josh asked.

"We should pick up where we left off," I suggested. "Going through our line-up of suspects."

"Isn't that the job of the police?" Fergus asked. "Inspector McMahon seems very competent."

"I think he is," I agreed. "But we have to do what we can to help him. We're running out of time. Let's start with the estate sale, as that appears to be a pivotal factor in terms of timing and the number of people it will affect."

"But we've told the tenants and the staff that their futures are secure," Fergus objected. "None of them have a good reason to hold a grudge."

"Lachlan?" I asked. "His job may be safe, but it won't be the same for him if you're not here. Perhaps he's unhappy about that. He doesn't want things to change."

"No way. He saved my life tonight, don't forget. If not for him, I'd have been trapped in the office and burned to a crisp. Besides, if I die, things would change here anyway. It wouldn't guarantee his job."

I stared at the fire, the leaping flames a haunting reminder of the terror we'd experienced that evening. "Not Lachlan, then."

"And not Mrs. Dunsmore, before you even think of putting her name on your checklist," Fergus added.

Josh stood up to poke the fire before picking up the Lagavulin and pouring three glasses.

"Then what about Pierre?" I suggested. "He told me how he came to be employed here and how he thinks he's succeeding in developing the gourmet dining business, but his story doesn't add up. He's a talented chef who worked in high-end restaurants in Paris. How did he end up working here?"

"I thought about that too. Maybe he upset his boss, maybe he got fired. But why would that make him want to kill me? Or Duncan, come to that?"

Could Pierre be involved? He handled sharp objects with ease, and one of his chef's knives had killed Duncan. Poor Duncan, stabbed in the back. Just like the woman out on the moor. Memories of the gruesome slaying flooded my brain. Why had I seen that vision?

I took the glass that Josh offered me ran my finger around the rim. "Fergus, have you ever heard anything about a murder here on the estate back in the sixteenth century? A monk who killed a young woman right in front of the priory that used to be there?"

Fergus tilted his head. "Yes, I'm aware of it, but I don't know the details. How did you hear about it?"

I looked down at my hands, thinking about stopping before blurting out a story that might convince Fergus I was crazy or unreliable or both. "I saw it happen. It was like watching a film, a short clip. The man wore a monk's habit, the woman wore a long green dress. And, in the background, I saw an arched doorway that could have been part of the priory building."

Fergus looked sad, as if I'd disappointed him. It took him a while, but eventually he spoke. "I don't see the connection. How is a five-hundred-year-old murder relevant to what's happening now?"

"I'm not sure. But it can't be random chance that I saw that vision and, given our lack of any other leads, I think it's worth pursuing."

"Perhaps there will be some information on the incident in the library?" Josh suggested.

"Maybe, but we'd have a hard time finding it," Fergus said. "I have a better idea. There's an old chap in the village who knows everything about this area. Name's Alistair Ross. If anything happened on the estate, he'll know about it." He glanced at his watch. "It's too late to ring him now, but I will first thing in the morning."

"Thank you," I said. "I mean, thank you for believing in me as well as for making the call tomorrow."

I was excited to meet Mr. Ross and to discover what he knew about the murder. If I learned what had happened at the priory, that would help me understand the significance of the vision.

Josh yawned loudly, but I felt as though I'd drunk ten cups of coffee. It seemed that Fergus had too, from the way he jiggled his leg and constantly checked his watch. "If you'd rather go to bed, you shouldn't wait up with me," he said. "I plan to keep myself busy for a while."

"I'll stay with you," I said. "I couldn't possibly sleep."

"I still owe Knox a list of the furniture I'm willing to leave with the house. If you fancy running around counting chairs, that would be very helpful."

"Definitely." I jumped up, glad to have something to do.

Fergus's face relaxed, some of the tension draining away. The lines around his eyes softened. He had to be going through his own version of hell right now: losing his nephew, nearly dying in a fire, and knowing that he remained in peril. Distraction was as good a tactic as any.

"What about you, Josh?" he asked. "You don't have to come, my boy, if you're tired."

"Oh, I'm fine." Josh pinched the bridge of his nose, which he often did when trying to solve a problem. "Mostly, I'm just feeling ineffectual. I desperately want to alter whatever is in store, but I can't work it out. It's driving me crazy."

I gave him a hug, sad to see him suffering. He loved his uncle and hated the idea of losing him. "We'll solve this," I said.

"Before we get started, I have a few words to say." Fergus stood up, his back to the fire. "Josh, you're now the heir to the estate. And with this aura indicating my imminent demise, you may inherit far sooner than anyone could have imagined. So, you get to decide what you think should happen to the castle. Should we still sell? Or does this..." He ran his hand over his head. "Does this, and Duncan's death, change everything? You've seen the accounts. You know what the financial situation is, but it's your choice. If you want to keep the house, then we simply tell Knox the deal is off."

Josh stood to face his uncle. "I'll pretend you didn't say any of that. You're not going to die. We won't let that happen. That means you should sign the contract with Knox and get out from under the debt and the stress of looking after this place. Enjoy your retirement."

After a few seconds' pause, Fergus nodded. A smile turned up the corners of his mouth. "I appreciate that," he said. "Now let's crack on, shall we?"

We followed Fergus to the library where he retrieved the leather binder that contained the furniture register. "My grandfather first drew this up just after World War One," Fergus told us. "Which means there will be many items on this document that are no longer here. We'll have to mark them on the inventory sheet, but it shouldn't take long."

By midnight, we'd been through most of the rooms in the tower, checking off all the beds, including several towering four posters, armoires in a range of woods from oak to walnut, side tables imported from Italy with marble tops and fancy carved legs. In one room, I fell in love with a pretty dressing table, painted white and decorated with green vines and leaves. The drawers were lined with green felt. The inventory described it as a nineteenth-century French pine dressing chest. Like a beautiful girl grown old, its bevel-edged mirror showed signs of age, with small black spots marring its surface, but it was still charming. We didn't go into Duncan's bedroom, even though the police had removed all the tape from the door. Fergus said he knew what furniture the room contained.

It was strangely exhilarating to be wandering the castle in the middle of the night, or perhaps I was just overwrought from the events of the day. My whole body felt wound up so tight it would be impossible to sleep, so, when Fergus asked if we were willing to continue, I agreed at once, and Josh nodded. We worked our way along the picture gallery, noting the hall tables that held antique lamps, while Fergus jotted numbers on the inventory list.

This part of the building reeked of smoke. The corridor leading to the burned-out office was closed off, with yellow tape crisscrossing the opening. We bypassed it and went downstairs. After checking off the dining room's table, chairs and sideboards, we arrived back in the drawing room, where we'd started. Josh threw himself onto a sofa. His eyes closed, and he leaned his head back against a cushion. I took a seat next to Fergus so that we could review the final list together. As with the books, there were quite a few missing items, as well as some new ones, including the sofas we were sitting on.

"What happened to this?" I asked, pointing to a listing of a Queen Anne tallboy dresser. "That will be a big piece of furniture. We can't have overlooked it. Or this." I put my finger on a description of a mahogany cylinder desk with satinwood inlays.

"They were probably in the east wing," Fergus said. "The damage occurred in 1941, and I don't think anything was retrieved after the bomb fell. My grandfather wanted nothing to do with it after his sister was killed, and then of course he himself died a few months later."

I thought back to my foray into the east wing with Lucy. I didn't recall seeing the tallboy, but there had been a desk.

"Shall we go over there to see if we can find some of these items?" I asked.

"There's no point. The furniture is probably damaged beyond repair, if not by the initial impact, then by the damp. No, we mark these off as missing. That way, Knox only pays for what he can actually use." Fergus ran his hands over his eyes. "I'll talk to the insurance company tomorrow and sort out how to get the fire damage repaired. Who knows, perhaps all this mayhem will change Knox's mind and he won't go through with the purchase after all."

"Not much chance of that," Josh said. "He seems fairly determined."

I felt my eyelids droop. When the clock struck two, I decided to go to bed.

24

J osh and I woke up late on Monday morning and scrambled to shower and dress, anxious to check on Fergus. Before we'd gone to bed, Lachlan had pulled a chair up outside Fergus's bedroom door and declared he'd remain there all night, which made me feel a bit better. I'd even managed to sleep for three or four hours. When we got downstairs, I gave Fergus a hug. He looked better than he had the night before, although still drawn and pale, and his aura continued to rotate rapidly over his head. He said he'd called the historian, Alistair Ross, who planned to arrive at ten, which would give us time to grab a quick breakfast.

"While he's here, I have things to do." Fergus sighed. "I should make arrangements for Duncan's funeral and also talk to the insurance company. I could do with Josh's help, if that's alright?"

I nodded, knowing Josh wouldn't be particularly interested in talking with the historian and would far rather be with Fergus. We ate in silence until the doorbell rang. I heard Mrs. Dunsmore's brogues clicking on the hall tile and then a short conversation before she brought in Mr. Ross. Thin and grey-haired, he wore a brown suit with leather patches on the elbow, and stood stick straight. He reminded me of my Latin teacher in school. Still, his eyes twinkled when Fergus introduced us. "Delighted to find someone who's interested in the history of the estate," he said, shaking my hand.

Fergus led us into the drawing room. "I'll leave you both to it. Stay for lunch, if you like, Alistair."

When he and Josh had gone, Mr. Ross sat down opposite me and launched into a story about the Campbells, once the most powerful clan in the region. "They built Kilchurn Castle in the fifteenth century. You've seen it?"

"Not yet." Josh and I had intended to visit the ruins of the castle up the road at Lochawe. But our plans for sightseeing this weekend had been dramatically curtailed from the moment we arrived and I saw Fergus's aura.

The historian described the genealogy of the Campbell clan, their rise to power, and their centuries-long feud with the MacDougalls, who were kinsmen of the MacDonalds. "The feud culminated in the Glencoe Massacre," he said. "They murdered their MacDonald hosts, a terrible act which has forever besmirched the Campbell name."

I nodded as he recited names and dates I would never remember. When Mrs. Dunsmore arrived with a tray of tea and scones, I took advantage of the momentary break in the monologue to ask him a question, hoping to direct him away from the Campbells and towards the specifics of the estate.

"I have a question about a priory on the castle grounds. I think it was occupied for about fifty years from 1500 on?"

"Ah yes. That is a fascinating story." Ross clapped his hands together. "The monastery at Ledaig was damaged by a fire, which claimed the lives of several monks and a few locals who were in the building at the time, probably being cared for in the infirmary. Anyway, the monastery was lost, and the monks were homeless. Some were taken into the abbey at Ardchattan, and others moved east. Thirty or so monks, including the abbot, were invited to move here to the estate, lodged in what had been a stable block, a short distance from a small chapel. Presumably helped by the laird, they rebuilt and expanded the stables, connecting them with the chapel to provide accommodations and a cloister. They ended up staying for, as you say, half a century or so. At that point, the community disbanded, its members moving to various other monasteries across Scotland."

"Did you ever hear anything about a murder at the priory during the period the monks were in residence?"

Ross blinked several times in quick succession as he extracted a handkerchief from his breast pocket and dabbed his forehead. "A murder, you say? What makes you ask?"

I fidgeted on the sofa, unsure what to tell him. Relating the tale of my bizarre vision might frighten him away before I could extract useful information from him. "Just a vague rumor I heard," I said.

His grey eyebrows drew together, and he patted his forehead again. "The story is public knowledge, but not many people are aware of it."

"You mean the murder really did happen? Please, Mr. Ross, tell me everything. Who was the woman? And why was she killed?"

"Do call me Alistair. Mr. Ross makes me feel old. Older than I am, that is." He folded the handkerchief and tucked it in his pocket. "The woman's name was Agnes Fenton, and she was the laird's niece. She came to live here at the castle after her parents died. Her beauty and intelligence were widely admired, and she wrote some remarkable poetry. I had the opportunity to read some of it in the National Library archives. What we know of her comes primarily from letters written by a nobleman from King James's court. He wooed her for several years and died of a broken heart after she was murdered in 1526."

He paused, lost in thought. His sad story had raised goosebumps on my arms.

"How did she come to be murdered?" I asked finally.

"The story goes that she took something valuable from the priory."

I thought back. She'd been holding a book. It had fallen to the ground, and the monk had leaned over to pick it up. I waited, and Alistair confirmed it. "It was a book. An extraordinary piece of work written and illustrated by a monk called Aethelwin. We know, because he signed the cover page. He started writing it when he lived in a Cistercian monastery in the north of England, where he was supposed to be working on a breviary— you know, a collection of hymns, psalms, and prayers. Instead, he filled the pages with hand-drawn images of machines and mechanisms, remarkable because of the book's age. It was written in Old English, and its vellum pages have been dated to the early eleventh century."

The historian paused to sip his tea. "Aethelwin drew a clock that predates the first geared clock by nearly a hundred years. The Arab engineer, Al-Muradi, working in Spain, developed a sophisticated gear train to drive the timepiece in the late eleventh century. And the book contains a drawing of a constellation not visible to the naked eye, although there were no telescopes yet invented that were powerful enough to view the heavens."

"How did the book get to Scotland?"

"It's believed that either Aethelwin was caught out, or feared he would be, so he arranged to transfer to a smaller monastery in Scotland. Sometime later, he died. The abbot found the book, realized what it was, and hid it in a secret place. Although it was a disturbing, perhaps even heretical, piece of work, it seems that the abbot recognized its unique nature and he didn't want to destroy it. Historians have conjectured that it was hidden for several hundred years."

"Historians? You mean this book is well-known?"

"Absolutely. It's called *The Aethelwin Codex*. I've done a great deal of research on it. There have been many documented sightings of the book, which is known to have traveled extensively, in the possession of kings, emperors and generals in England, France, and Russia. Over the centuries, it gained mythical status as an object of great value, reputed to bring good fortune and power to its owner."

"So that's why Agnes stole it?"

"No one thinks she stole it. It's generally believed she had attempted to rescue it. Although the codex remained under lock and key for centuries, rumors of its existence were rife. We may suppose monasteries to be secluded, introspective retreats from the outside world, but they maintained constant contact with the local community. The monks provided medical assistance to the villagers on occasion and purchased supplies of food and beer from merchants in the vicinity. The brothers had plenty of opportunity to gossip and speculate about the value of the supposedly secret book. Indeed, several attempts were made to steal it. Records show that two men were charged and hanged in 1510 for breaking into the priory. They claimed they were paid by an English aristocrat to acquire the codex for him. Therefore, the book's location was somewhat common knowledge at that point."

"Why did Agnes Fenton feel it needed rescuing?"

"Several theories have been proposed. One, she was attempting to save it from being destroyed. A number of monks deemed its contents to be the work of the devil. They claimed Aethelwin had been encouraged in his imaginings by conversations with Satan. They thought it should be burned."

"How awful. Book burning has always been used to censor information and silence opposition." I sat up straight. "Please don't tell me it was burned?"

"It wasn't. It appeared somewhat regularly over the next few centuries until it vanished in the early 1900s. So the other theory, more widely accepted, is that Agnes was trying to take the codex from a monk who'd already stolen it from its hiding place with the intention of selling it. He had newly arrived at the priory, and he disappeared, of course, right after the murder."

"The monk in the black robes. What else do you know about him?"

"His name was Hubert. He may have been French and he may well have not been a real monk. After he killed Agnes, he escaped with the book. It isn't known where he went or to whom he sold it. However, it made an appearance three years later, in the court of King Francis I of France. The king had a reputation as a generous patron of the arts; he sponsored several famous artists including Del Sarto and Da Vinci. During his reign, he established a substantial library and initiated the acquisition of many artworks, most of which are now in the Louvre."

"So, even though the French quasi-monk stole the codex, it fell into good hands, it seems. As a book lover and art aficionado, King Francis would have cared for it and kept it safe."

"That's true," Alistair agreed. "It did go on to cause its share of problems over the centuries. Apart from Agnes, others died in their attempts to secure it and hang on to it. In the 1700s, it became the subject of a duel between a grandee of Aragon and an ambassador from the court of Louis XV. Both men died, causing something of an international incident. No one knows where the codex went after that, until it reappeared in the house of an English duke, who shot himself after losing it in a card game."

Alistair took a swallow of tea. I tasted mine, but it had gone cold, forgotten as I listened to his account.

"Poor Agnes." I shivered as I remembered the violence on the moor. "The man, Hubert, looked so evil. She must have been terrified."

"What do you mean, he looked evil?"

"I saw him..." I stopped, but the words were out.

"Go on." Alistair took his hanky out again and patted his face where a sheen of perspiration glistened.

I couldn't take the words back. I didn't want to lie to him. I liked him, and he was being generous with his time and knowledge. But if I told him about my vision, our interview would probably be over.

"I walked out there to the priory, or the ruins of it at least, and I saw a vision, a sort of reenactment."

To my surprise, Alistair looked delighted. He stuffed the handkerchief in his pocket and stood up. "Miss Benedict, did you touch the Brynjarr Stone before you walked to the ruins?"

I recalled the morning when Josh and I had walked along the lochan and passed the ancient spire. I had brushed my fingers across the black rock. "Yes, I did. And, please, call me Kate."

He set off on a circuit of the drawing room, muttering to himself. And there I'd been worrying I was the crazy one. Finally, he came to a halt and sat down again. "Extraordinary," he said. He picked up his tea cup and, realizing it was empty, put it down again. "Very few are affected by the stone. Only myself and a couple of others that I'm aware of. Over the centuries, though, who knows how many people have been granted the ability to see the vision."

"You've seen it too? And you actually know others who have seen it?"

"I experienced it years ago, and have been researching the history of the place ever since. An old neighbor of mine saw it as well, but she died some time ago. Then there's Lachlan, Fergus's groundskeeper."

"Lachlan?" That was a surprise.

Alistair nodded. "I think he has the second sight, but he won't discuss it. The subject is firmly off-limits."

"Second sight?"

"A primarily Scottish phenomenon. It's the power to predict the future. My grandmother had it. In her case, she only saw good events, like the birth of a child, or an unexpected windfall. Some foresee terrible things like war and death. Once upon a time, it was considered a gift but, nowadays, people just think it's...."

"Weird," I finished. He nodded with a rueful smile.

"But Lachlan admitted he'd seen the young woman killed on the moor?" I asked.

"He did. He came to me to ask if I could explain it. We meet occasionally to talk about it, but honestly it's more an excuse to have a pint than conduct a serious scientific investigation."

"I'm confused though. Hundreds, even thousands of people, must have touched the Brynjarr Stone, yet, presumably, they don't all see the vision."

"That's true. I can only surmise that some souls are more susceptible, more open perhaps to paranormal experiences."

"Yes, I believe that too," I agreed.

He gazed at me. "Have you seen other visions, apart from the one you told me about?"

"Not here." I hesitated. The conversation had veered off in a direction I would never have envisaged, but I felt it best to tell him the whole truth. The more we shared, the better the chance we might uncover information that would help save Fergus. "I've had encounters with spirits, though, and I can see auras which predict death."

"Fascinating. Go on."

I described my meeting with my mother three months after her death, and my conversations with the dead nun who'd first explained my aura-sighting gift to me. When I described the aura over Fergus, which remained even though the police had arrested Nick's Dad, Alistair drew his brows together in concern. "Fergus is a good man."

"He is. I've been wrestling with the question of whether this vision has anything to do with the threat to him." I paused, feeling my shoulders slump. "But now I think not. If others have seen the murder in the ruins, it wasn't a sign intended specifically for me." I leaned my elbows on my knees, chin in hand, weighed down by frustration. I wasn't making any progress at all. And while it would otherwise be delightful to chat about visions and stone spires with special powers, I was acutely aware I was running out of time. "I'm back where I started, with no idea of how to save Fergus."

Alistair tapped his fingers on his knee. "Did young Duncan have an aura too?"

"Yes. But it appeared only hours before he died, which means something changed. Whatever it was, it put him in danger, but it all happened so fast. I couldn't do anything to keep him safe."

"I'm sorry, lassie. I'll do whatever I can to help you. Do you have any other information that might point to what threatens Fergus?"

I remembered the papers I had in my pocket and took out the sketch I'd drawn of the young woman who'd been murdered. I unfolded it and smoothed it out before giving it to him. "I drew this after I saw the vision."

"Agnes Fenton," he murmured. "That's how I remember her, but I don't have any artistic talent like you."

"And there's this." I unfolded the list of words I had found in Duncan's notebook and read it again before passing it over. *Alexandra 1917. Anna Vyrubova 1939, Cyril Thorpe 1940.* "Do you have any idea what this might mean?"

He pulled a pair of reading glasses from a case on the coffee table and perched them on his nose. It seemed to take him a long while to peruse the list. "Can you read my writing?" I asked. "I scrawled the words quickly before I forgot them."

He rested the paper on his lap and removed his glasses. "Extraordinary. Where did you find this?"

Reluctant to admit that most of my research so far had consisted of digging through other people's private property, I took a bite of my scone, and he carried on talking.

"Alexandra would be the wife of Tsar Nicholas," he said. "They were taken prisoner by the Bolsheviks in 1917."

"Yes, and they were executed in 1918." I struggled to conceal the impatience in my voice. "I learned that much in school at least."

"My apologies, Kate." Alistair smiled. "I was musing out loud. But here's the thing. The Tsarina was the last known owner of the codex."

"What?" My hand started to shake, and I put my plate down.

"Yes." Alistair's eyes gleamed with excitement. "The book was known to be in her possession following her marriage to Nicholas. After she and her family were executed, there were no further sightings of it. Many historians believe it was lost, destroyed perhaps by the revolutionaries."

"But maybe it wasn't destroyed. What about the other names on the list? Do you recognize them? Did they also possess the codex for a while?"

"Anna Vyrubova was Alexandra's lady-in-waiting, her favorite, according to many accounts. A staunch supporter of Rasputin, she encouraged the Tsarina's friendship with him. After his murder and the capture of the Romanov family, the Bolsheviks arrested Anna."

"That's impressive. How on earth did you learn all that?"

Alistair shrugged. "As I said, I've been pondering the meaning of the vision for years now. I've acquired all sorts of useless information about the priory, Agnes Fenton, and the codex, including its many owners, right up until it disappeared. But I haven't found any evidence that Anna Vyrubova ever owned it."

"What happened to her? Did she get executed too?"

"No. In spite of her very poor health, she somehow survived five months of imprisonment, after which she left Russia with the help of her family. She traveled to Finland, where she lived until her death in the late 1960s."

Mrs. Dunsmore appeared just then to offer us more refreshments. We gratefully accepted a pot of fresh tea and more lemon scones. The housekeeper set the tray down with a smile. "Pierre's using my scone recipe. They're very good, aren't they?"

We voiced our enthusiasm for the scones to Mrs. Dunsmore's retreating back. The woman was in constant motion.

There had been something I meant to say before Mrs. Dunsmore's appearance. I bit my lip, trying to remember.

"Oh yes, there's another thing," I said. "Duncan had written 'Helsinki' in his journal. A possible link to Anna living in Finland?"

"Duncan's journal?" Alistair's eyebrows marched upwards.

"It's complicated." I poured tea for both of us. "In a search for clues that might help me identify the source of the danger to Fergus, I've been digging around. I'm positive Duncan was searching for something before he died, but I thought it was a Fabergé egg."

Alistair leaned against his sofa cushion, still clutching the scrap of paper with the names on it and gazing at me intently. "I assure you I will keep in total confidence whatever you tell me," he said. "What gave you the impression Duncan was after an egg?"

"Several things, really. First, I found a news story about an imperial Fabergé egg discovered by a collector in Paris six months ago. Lucy— she's Duncan's girlfriend— had a press clipping about it in her room. When I asked her about it, she admitted to hunting for an egg, not the one in the press clipping obviously, but another of the seven that are still missing."

"I'm sorry, Kate. I don't know much about Romanov treasure or Fabergé eggs. Even if it is what Duncan wanted to find, how does it represent a danger to Fergus? Do you think that's why Duncan was killed? Because of his interest in it?"

I flexed my neck, trying to work out the kinks that had taken up residence there. "I don't know. What about Cyril Thorpe?" I asked, nodding towards the piece of paper in Alistair's hand. "Any thoughts on who he might be?"

"No, but I'd be happy to do more research. Can I copy this list down?"

"Of course." I jumped up to find a notepad and pen. "You'll contact me if you find anything? I want to know but, at the same time, I can't help feeling the egg and the vision are distractions from the real problem, which is finding out who means harm to Fergus."

Alistair frowned. "I heard about the arson attack last night. Even with Jameson in custody, you think Fergus is still at risk?"

"His aura's still there."

"Well, the word is that Inspector McMahon is one of the best. I'm sure he'll get to the bottom of it."

"Maybe. But I'm going to continue poking around myself as well. There's too much at stake to rely on a single police officer."

"You can count on my support," Alistair said as he stood up. "I'll make some enquiries and report back to you."

25

J ust as I waved goodbye to Alistair Ross, Josh and Fergus came downstairs, both looking somber. I guessed that the process of making the funeral arrangements for Duncan must be taking its toll.

"How did it go?" Josh asked.

I was still trying to make sense of everything Alistair and I had discussed. "Good, I think. Shall we sit down? There are tea and scones if you want them."

We were talking over the decisions that had to be made for Duncan's service when Inspector McMahon arrived. Mrs. Dunsmore showed him in and hurried away. I got the impression she was nervous around him.

Fergus invited the inspector to join us and offered him a cup of tea, which he accepted. "Are you here with news about Duncan?" Fergus asked. "A lead on who the killer is?"

"Not yet. I'm not here regarding Duncan, actually. Something important has come to light regarding Nick Jameson." He took a sip of tea and raised his head to look at us. "It appears his death wasn't an accident. It was deliberate."

The blood drained from Fergus's cheeks, and he gripped the arm of the sofa. "Deliberate?" he repeated.

"Nick suffered a blow to the head, which probably rendered him unconscious. His assailant then dragged his body a few feet to the water's edge and placed him face down so he would drown."

"But I thought he'd fallen and hit his head." Josh looked as stunned as Fergus did.

"It was the initial assessment, but the ME overruled that conclusion after examining the wound in more detail. The team went back to the lochan and identified drag marks on the ground close to the water. They'd been disturbed by horse hooves and footprints, but they were visible." He glanced at me when he spoke, and I stared back at him, refusing to feel guilty that I'd trampled across a crime scene that I hadn't known was a crime scene at the time.

"The ME puts the time of death somewhere between four and six on Friday afternoon," McMahon said. "And Kate found him at noon on Saturday."

"Which means you can eliminate almost everyone on the guest list for the birthday party," Fergus said. "Most of them didn't arrive until late Saturday afternoon or early evening."

"I tend to agree, although it's not necessarily an accurate assessment, as many of the guests were locals, with access to the lochan. Any of them could have been out there the day before the party."

"But why?" Fergus asked of no one in particular. "Why would anyone kill Nick?"

"It's possible that an outsider, a stranger, killed him for a reason we don't yet understand, but we found Nick's wallet in his jeans pocket and his watch was still on his wrist, which eliminates theft as a motive. And we don't believe robbery was the reason for Duncan's murder either. None of his personal effects were missing."

McMahon had a Scottish accent, but his tone was tightly modulated, with barely any inflection in it at all. He could be reading a shopping list out loud.

"Do you think Duncan's killer is the same person who murdered Nick?" I asked. The causes of death had been different, I thought, which either showed some flexibility on the killer's part, or presented the alarming possibility that two killers were running around the estate at the same time.

The inspector tapped a page with his pen. "I don't know, but it is an important question."

"You must have talked to Pierre." Fergus stood up and moved to the fireplace, where he leaned against the mantel. "We know he and Nick were quarreling over job responsibilities. And Duncan was murdered in the kitchens."

Only a faint nod acknowledged Fergus's question.

"Mr. Jameson attacked Fergus. Did he also kill Duncan?" Josh asked.

McMahon tilted his head slightly. "What would be his motive?"

Josh shrugged. "Same as it would be for trying to kill Fergus. He was just angry about Nick's job situation and blamed the family in general."

"I don't believe Mr. Jameson murdered anyone."

"Does he know now that Nick was killed deliberately?" I asked. "He can't believe Fergus had anything to do with it?"

"Yes, he is now aware of that fact, and no, he doesn't think Fergus is responsible." McMahon chewed on his lower lip. "Jameson is in great distress, as you can imagine. He deeply regrets his actions."

"You're holding him for arson?" Fergus asked.

"Yes. We have a full statement from him."

"The man has been through enough. I don't want to press charges against him for the fire."

The inspector didn't respond for a few seconds. "The prosecutor already has the case file, but I'll see what I can do." He finished his tea and put the cup on the coffee table.

"What happens now?" Josh asked. "It seems we have no idea what happened to Duncan."

"We keep going with our inquiries." McMahon examined his fingernails for a moment and then looked up at us. "Listen, I want to be as open with you as I can be. There were so many people in the castle over the weekend that it's taking us a while to work through all the information we gathered following Duncan's death. Can any of you can think of anything which might have slipped your mind in our earlier discussions? Sometimes, a single detail can be enough to give us the clue we need."

"Did you find a journal in Duncan's room?" I asked him.

"A journal..." He thumbed through the pages of his notebook. "Black leather cover? That the one?"

"Yes. There were some notes inside that may be relevant. I talked with Alistair Ross this morning."

McMahon lifted one eyebrow in query.

"He's a local historian and knows a great deal about the estate. I told him about the notations in Duncan's journal and he said they might possibly have something to do with an old book, a codex."

Eyebrow still raised, McMahon waited.

"I think maybe Lucy and Duncan were looking for the book."

The inspector seemed to suppress a sigh. "When we last talked, you thought they were searching for some kind of egg? One with jewels on it?"

"That's right. And maybe they were. Or this book, or both."

"I see." McMahon's tone of voice made it clear that he didn't see at all. "I'll get one of the team to take a look at the journal," he said. "But the most important task right now is that of eliminating suspects from our list." He stood up and fastened the middle button of his blue suit jacket.

"There's something else you should know," I said. "Even though Mr. Jameson is in custody and probably doesn't have any intention of doing further harm, Fergus is still in danger. His aura is still there."

McMahon glanced at Fergus and then looked away. "There'll be no more deaths on my watch," he said. "If you'll excuse me, I have a lot of work to do.

26

W e'd barely returned to the drawing room after closing the front door behind McMahon when the doorbell rang. It was Fiona, come to check up on Arbroath's eyes and breathing. The castle felt a bit like Piccadilly Circus with all the arrivals and departures, but I was glad to see her. I wanted to ask her more questions about Saturday night and Duncan. First, though, I gave her time to make a fuss over the dog.

She sat on the rug next to him and scrunched his ears in her hands while she inspected his eyes. "Who's my big brave boy, then?" He gave an appreciative bark and thumped his tail on the floor while trying to lick her face.

"He's absolutely fine," she said, getting to her feet. "What about you, Mr. MacKenna? Are you feeling all right?" She paused. "I heard about Nick. That's a terrible thing. Who could possibly want to hurt a nice young man like him?" Tears welled in her eyes and she brushed them away with the back of her hand.

"Do you fancy a cup of tea?" I asked her.

"Okay. Shall we go down to the kitchen?"

I thought quickly. If we were in the kitchen, we might not be able to talk in private. "It'd be fun for me to see something of the village, and get out of the house," I said. "I've heard there's a good cafe? We can go there if you like?"

Fiona's face lit up. "That'd be great. I have to go in anyway, as I have to start work at three."

I turned to Josh. "Is that okay? You'll stay here with Fergus?" I took his arm and led him into the entry hall. "I won't be long, but I want to ask Fiona some questions. And find out if she noticed anything unusual while she was helping Mrs. Dunsmore with getting the guest rooms ready."

"Sounds like a plan. Fergus and I have a boatload of work to do on the contract, and Knox is going to ring us later to talk over a few details." He brushed a wisp of hair away from my face. "It seems odd, to be discussing contracts when Duncan is dead, but I think it's the right thing to do. Fergus has no choice but to sell, so we should keep going. Besides, it's a distraction, to keep his mind off Nick, and Duncan, and the aura and..."

I gave him a hug. "It's exactly right. Look after your uncle, and yourself, until I get back. I love you."

We joined Fergus and Fiona, who were now both on their knees playing with the dog. "May I borrow the car, Fergus?" I asked. "That way Fiona won't have to drive me all the way back out here when we're done."

"I don't mind," she said. "But it would be easier, as I work at the pub."

Fergus gave me his keys. "The locks don't work and the gear shift is a bit sticky. Just give it a hard shove when you go from first to second. Make sure she knows who's boss."

Keys in hand, I grabbed a jacket and followed Fiona out to the drive.

"Parking in town is a right pain," she said, as we reached the cars. "But we can use the pub car park because I work there. Follow behind me."

The drive took fifteen minutes along a windy, narrow road, but I enjoyed being out in the countryside. The moors, amber and bronze, stretched to the horizon under a silvery sky. The gearbox clanked and screeched every time I changed gears. My dad would love the old Land Rover with all its quirks and noises. The heater had just started working when we reached the edge of town, which seemed a rather grand term for the small collection of stone houses that flanked the main road. We passed a Post Office and a small grocery shop, but then the road widened and joined a square flanked by a steepled church on one side and the pub on the other. I saw people out carrying shopping bags, so there had to be a supermarket somewhere close by.

After driving there faster than seemed safe, Fiona took an abrupt left turn up an alley that led to the car park at the rear of the Stag's Head. I followed and, once I'd maneuvered the hulking Land Rover into a tight space, I joined her for a short walk across the square and up a side street to the cafe. Through its steamed-up windows, I saw that it was busy, full of customers sitting at tables spread with flowered cloths. We were greeted by the fragrance of coffee and baking and a rush of warm air, welcome after the chill outside. A glass case held a tantalizing display of pastries and cakes, and an Italian espresso machine hissed behind the bar.

Fiona persuaded me to try a slice of toffee cake. "It's their specialty, and it's delicious," she promised. We carried our plates and cups to a table in a corner.

"The cake's very good," I said, wiping crumbs from my mouth after my first taste.

She laughed. "Most southerners seem to think we Scots live on haggis, but we appreciate the finer things in life too. My mum's teaching me to cook what she calls real food, you know, with vegetables and all. Of course, she's half-Italian, so she has strong opinions on what we should eat."

We chatted for a while about Fiona's family and her studies to become a veterinary assistant. When I'd finished my cake, I pushed my plate away and folded my napkin.

"Fiona, can you tell me more about what happened on Saturday evening? With Duncan?"

"I already told that inspector. He doesn't think I had anything to do with it, does he?"

"No, no of course not. And this isn't official. I'm just trying to understand a few things. Did you know Duncan before this weekend?"

She flipped her dark hair over her shoulder. "I met him a couple of times when he came up to visit. The last time was a year ago, more or less. We had a drink together one evening. He's a big flirt. I'm not stupid and I knew he didn't take me seriously. It was only supposed to be a bit of fun, you know? Some champagne and kissing. I liked listening to his stories of life in London, the private jets and fancy restaurants. It's a world away from here."

"On this visit, did you two discuss the sale of the estate? Or did he mention that he was looking for something in the castle?"

Fiona pushed crumbs around on her plate. "No, I only talked to him for that couple of minutes in the kitchen, just long enough to arrange to meet later." She gave an extravagant shiver. "And now he's dead."

"Do you have any idea who killed him?"

She looked up. "Could have been anyone, couldn't it? There were close to a hundred people in the castle that night, with the guests and the staff brought in specially to help."

"Yes, that's true, but we have to think about motive. *Why* would anyone kill him?"

Fiona tilted her head to one side. "That's a good question. I don't know. I mean, Duncan hardly knew anyone in the castle. Especially none of the blokes hanging out in the kitchen afterwards. Pierre opened a couple of bottles of wine to celebrate that the party had gone well. The inspector asked me who was still in the kitchens at that point. I told him, like half a dozen guys I didn't recognize, and Pierre and his friend."

"Did you talk to his friend?"

"Remy? Yeah, a bit. He was nice enough."

"Remy?" I remembered the name on the business card I'd found under Lucy's dresser. Remy someone. Delacroix. That was it. And his title was something to do with antiques. But why would Lucy be talking to a French antiques dealer?

"He spoke to me in English, which surprised me," Fiona continued. "I wanted to practice my French, but they both teased me about how bad I was at it." She smiled. "Nothing worse than a supercilious Frenchman, *mon Dieu*."

"Did you see Lucy speaking with Remy?"

She raised a neatly plucked eyebrow. "Lucy's the pretty blonde woman?"

"Duncan's girlfriend."

"Really? I thought she was with that rich young American. I can't remember his name. Fox?"

"Stanton Knox."

"Yeah, that's him. The two of them were hanging out in her room when I went up to clean it, that day I did the vacuuming before the party."

"You're sure? You saw the American in Lucy's room?" I felt my cheeks grow warm. "Er, what were they doing?"

"Only talking, as far as I could tell. But they were sitting on the edge of her bed, close together. Maybe closer than friends would, if you know what I mean?"

I sat back in my chair, absorbing that piece of information. Lucy had behaved strangely whenever Knox was around. Usually, she'd disappeared, apart from the night of the party when they'd had a long conversation together. I remembered Friday evening when she said she'd gone outside to get something from Duncan's rental car. Although Knox was in the house with Fergus then, the helicopter had been parked on the lawn. Had she talked to the pilot? Or taken something out there to leave it for Knox?

My thoughts were interrupted by a ping on Fiona's mobile. She bent her head over the screen and typed a response with a dexterity I envied. I grabbed my handbag and retrieved my phone. When I turned it on, three dots in the upper corner confirmed that I had service. Hallelujah. I watched a series of texts scroll past, most of them from co-workers and my boss. My email icon declared that I had 234 unread emails. Finally, I was connected again, away from the thick walls of the castle and the dodgy service on the grounds. I had no intention of reading my email though. That could wait.

Fiona looked up from her phone. "The cafe has free wi-fi," she told me. "I often come in here to avoid using up my data plan." She pushed over a menu that had the wireless access information printed across the bottom.

I logged in and opened the browser to do a search on Stanton Knox. There were hundreds of results, mostly related to his company, its products and share price, but I eventually found a bio of Knox that told me he lived in Palo Alto, California. He'd gone to Stanford University, where he'd earned two degrees, one in History and the other in Computer Science. He'd completed both in record time, while also working on his start-up. I scrolled through more results covering his putative net worth, his private jet, his collection of snowboards, cars and houses, and his extensive library. Huh, I thought. So he did have an interest in books. That might explain his insistence that Fergus include the castle's library contents as part of the estate sale.

"I'm going to use the loo," Fiona said. I glanced up and nodded, still intent on my research. When I entered 'Lucy Cantrell' in the browser, a few results appeared, including her LinkedIn page, and her name on a list of professors in the history department at Kings College London. She'd posted a bio far less verbose than Knox's, but I found the connection I was looking for. She'd spent a year at Stanford while working on her degree in Medieval History. I was certain she must have met Knox while studying in California. But why did they hide the fact that they were acquaintances or friends? They'd avoided each other, as far as I could tell. Had she been surprised when he turned up there, or had they been in touch beforehand? My head was spinning with questions.

"How's it going?" Fiona asked when she came back. "What are you looking for?"

"I'm doing background research on Lucy Cantrell and Stanton Knox. I think they did know each other."

"Like I just told you."

"Yes, you did, thank you. And going back to Remy? You never saw Lucy talk to him?"

"No. He talked to Pierre mostly, although he was very nice to Mrs. Dunsmore. I'm going to get more tea. Do you want another cup?"

I nodded yes, and, while she went to the counter, I returned to considering Knox and Lucy. What were they up to? They'd avoided being seen together for the most part, except for that half-hour at the party and Fiona's accidental sighting of them in Lucy's room. It could be that they'd dated while they were in California and wanted to avoid embarrassing Duncan.

Fiona carried our refilled cups to the table and stirred a sugar cube into hers. "I've been thinking. I can't imagine the same man killed both Nick and Duncan," she said. "Those two had never met, so what connection could there be? I don't get it."

I didn't either. Who could want both Nick and Duncan dead? That lent credence to the unlikely scenario of there being multiple killers involved, a daunting prospect. It would be hard enough to identify and track down one, let alone two.

My tea tasted good, piping hot and not too strong. I savored a few sips before looking up at Fiona again. "Did you ever hear anyone mention a jeweled egg hidden somewhere in the castle? Or an ancient book?"

"Well, it's odd that you should say that. The time I found Lucy and the American in her room, I did overhear a few words. They were talking about an egg, which I thought was strange. I didn't hear much though. I wasn't meaning to eavesdrop, you know."

"Did they say anything specific about the egg? Its location perhaps?"

"No, like I said, I only listened for a couple of seconds. It would have been embarrassing if they'd seen me there." With a glance at her phone, Fiona finished her tea and put the cup down. "It's later than I thought. I should get to work. Thanks for the tea and cake. Let's do it again sometime."

fter Fiona had gone, I stayed for a while, taking advantage of the cafe's wi-fi to do more research. I looked up Pierre's friend, Remy Delacroix. The only result was a listing similar to what was on his business card: his title as Antiquaire and a phone number. There was no website for the business. Remembering the press clipping I'd found in Lucy's room, I took another look through news stories about the Fabergé egg that had been sold in Paris six months earlier. The shop where the sale had taken place was on the Rue des Rosiers, and I was fairly sure that the address was the same one I'd seen written in Duncan's journal. I wished now I'd thought to write it down.

Bemused, I stared at the screen for a while. So, Remy was an antiques dealer in France. A dealer in Paris had sold the Fabergé egg to a Russian collector for only a thousand pounds. Lucy and Duncan had been searching for an egg. It seemed likely that Remy and Lucy had communicated over the weekend, given the presence of his business card in her room. I wanted to talk to Remy and hoped he was still in the area. Pierre would know. And I definitely needed to find out more about the relationship between Stanton Knox and Lucy.

A wash of cold air swept over me when the cafe door opened and a couple rushed in. Laughing, they peeled off their drenched coats, and the girl squeezed water from the tips of her long hair. Rain streamed down the cafe's windows. I closed the browser on my mobile, anxious to get back to the castle before the storm worsened, knowing that Josh would worry.

The sky had turned a threatening bronze color and thunder boomed in the distance. Without an umbrella, I was soaked and shivering by the time I reached the pub car park. Fiona's Mini was still there, diminutive next to the Land Rover. A dozen other cars took up the rest of the space in the cramped lot. I climbed into the car and turned the heater on full blast, but it just blew cold air on my wet legs as I threaded my way out through the narrow alley. The rain had driven people off the streets, which were empty now.

Hoping not to get lost, I set off and soon saw a sign for the road that led me out of the village and south along Loch Awe. Within minutes, the rain had intensified, beating with fury on the vehicle's roof. The old, worn wipers slammed back and forth, barely keeping up with the watery onslaught. Grateful for the Land Rover's four-wheel drive and hefty tires, I nonetheless kept my speed down as I navigated the winding country road.

When headlights came towards me in the gloom, I edged closer to the verge to give the other car room to pass. As it disappeared in my rear-view mirror, the rain came down in buckets. I tapped the brakes lightly, although I was already driving cautiously, and I felt the tires slide on the waterlogged tarmac. My heart rate spiked as I gripped the steering wheel. Panicked, I put my foot down hard on the brake, prepared for a skid, but the forward momentum of the car didn't change. I was on a slight downhill, not an extreme gradient, but enough to pick up speed. With my foot jammed on the pedal, I concentrated on steering through the bends. I tried to downshift to first gear, ignoring the screeching and clattering as the gearbox complained and stayed obstinately in second. Cold shivers ran up my spine as I acknowledged the fact that the car seemed to be accelerating on its own. The bloody brakes weren't working.

My brain didn't seem to be working either, so I forced myself to calm down, to think about what to do. To one side of the road was a metal crash railing. On the other, moorland rolled into the distance. Peering through the windscreen, I saw the road rising ahead. The uphill would slow me enough, I hoped, to guide the vehicle on to the moorland where the thick, springy heather should stop any further motion.

Holding the wheel so tightly it hurt my hands, I concentrated on keeping the car straight as it hurtled towards the low point before the incline. Lights appeared, two yellow disks cutting through the rain as a car crested the top of the hill in front of me.

"Slow down, slow down," I pleaded out loud, but the car kept coming towards me. It would reach me while I was still rolling down-hill, and I was sure the road was too narrow here for us to pass each other safely at speed. As the headlights of the other car grew brighter and larger, its driver leaned on his horn. I yanked the steering wheel to the left, praying there were no rocks lurking under the heather. The vehicle bounced as the wheels left the tarmac and hit the soft muddy verge, propelling me forward, the seatbelt cutting into my shoulder. The Land Rover kept going, bucking like an angry bronco across the uneven ground.

After what felt like an eternity, it juddered to a halt and the engine stalled. I leaned forward, my forehead on the wheel, taking deep swallows of air.

When I raised my head, I peered through the windscreen, but rivers of water obscured my view. Reluctantly, I eased the door open and got out in the pouring rain. I was a hundred meters from the road, and the other vehicle hadn't stopped. There was nothing in sight, no cars, no houses. I reached into the Land Rover for my handbag and fumbled around for my mobile. A single dot indicated I might have service, but maybe not. I called Josh's number even though it was unlikely he'd answer. If he was inside, he'd have no signal at all, and I hadn't thought to memorize the castle's main phone number. My call didn't connect, and I shoved the phone in my pocket as I waded through the wet heather. When I reached the road, I set off towards the castle, hoping to flag down a passing car.

The road remained defiantly empty for almost twenty minutes, and then I heard an engine behind me. A blue van slowed and stopped. "Are you mad?" the driver called, after winding his window down a couple of inches. "Get in."

I did, hauling myself into the passenger seat, thrilled to feel the heater blowing hot air at me. "My car broke down." I kept the explanation simple.

The driver, a middle-aged man in overalls and boots, told me his name was Brian and asked me where I was going.

"Castle Aiten. Do you know where it is?"

"Of course. I've done some work out there, fixing gutters and plumbing. I'll take you there. It's not far out of my way. What happened to the car?"

"I think the brakes failed."

Brian shot me a look of surprise. "Brakes went out? That's unusual. How far back?"

"A mile, maybe a little less."

"I didn't see it when I drove past just now."

"No. It's out in the heather. It kept going for a while after I left the road."

Brian raised an eyebrow but didn't say any more. He reached out to switch on the radio, and we drove to the music of Dire Straits and Steely Dan. In spite of the efficient heater, I was still shivering when we reached the castle. Brian pulled up right at the front door to let me out.

"Can I offer you a cup of tea?" I asked.

He declined, saying he had a job to get to. "Make sure you have that car checked out properly. You'll have to call the towing company in Oban. They're the closest."

I thanked him and climbed the steps, trailing water across the black and white tiles of the entry hall as I shrugged off my jacket. Josh hurried out to meet me. "God, Kate, are you all right? You're soaked." He glanced at his watch. "I was getting worried. You were gone for a long time."

When I told him what had happened with the car and the brake failure, his face blanched and he pulled me close to him. "You're shaking," he said. "You should go take those wet clothes off."

"I'll be all right for a few minutes. We need to tell Fergus."

Looking dubious, Josh led me into the drawing room where Fergus was setting a log on the fire. The bear on the backplate glared out at me with red eyes.

"All okay?" Fergus straightened up. His aura still swirled. "Good grief. You're drenched. Are you all right?"

"No, she's not," Josh said and went on to tell him about the accident.

Fergus looked shocked. "Are you hurt, Kate?"

I assured him I was fine, and that Brian the plumber had given me a lift. "We'll need to call a towing company out to rescue the car. I left it in the middle of the moor." I dug in my bag for the keys and gave them to Fergus.

After I'd done my best to describe where I'd left the car, he hurried to the phone and made the call. While he did that, Josh insisted I go back to our room to change. "You can tell us more later. I'll go make you a hot drink."

I argued but finally gave in. And I did feel better once I'd changed into warm, dry clothes and blotted my hair with a towel. The chill faded, and I stopped shivering. By the time I got back to the drawing room, Josh was waiting with a mug of hot chocolate. I wrapped my hands around it and inhaled the sweet, loamy fragrance.

Fergus had poured himself a scotch. "I don't understand," he said. "The brakes were working perfectly yesterday, weren't they, Josh?"

The two of them exchanged a look I couldn't interpret. "I had to tromp on the brakes on a curve I took a bit too fast," Josh said with a sheepish grin. "Darn near put me through the windscreen."

"Glad you didn't tell me that yesterday," I said drily. "You're supposed to be looking after Fergus, not endangering him."

Josh's grin faded. "You don't think someone tampered with the brakes, do you?"

We all gazed at each other in silence. Finally, Fergus spoke. "If so, was I meant to be driving or was Kate? The mechanic will be able to tell if it was wear and tear or something deliberate. I know the repair shop owner. I'll have a word with him, ask him to put a rush on the inspection."

"While you do that, I'm going to talk to Pierre," I said. "I need to find out where his friend Remy is. Josh, why don't you come with me?" I wanted to tell him about Lucy and Stanton Knox before I mentioned it to Fergus. Anything that involved Knox and the estate sale was a source of stress right now, and I didn't want to add to it.

We walked slowly across the entry hall and paused at the top of the kitchen stairs while I shared what Fiona had told me. "She saw Knox sitting with Lucy on her bed, which makes me think they were acquainted before this weekend," I said. "I did a bit of digging around and found a likely connection. They overlapped at Stanford University for one year, studying history. But they pretended not to know each other."

"Maybe they didn't recognize each other. Their Stanford year must have been some time ago. And they were talking at the party, I seem to remember, so they weren't exactly hiding the fact they knew each other."

"Yes, but that was a big social event," I said. "It's perfectly normal for strangers to strike up a conversation at a party. They probably thought no one would think twice about it."

Josh leaned against the wall and rubbed his cheeks. He looked tired, with dark circles under his eyes.

"Do we tell Fergus?" I asked. "It may be nothing. It might be what you said, that they only recognized each other after a while. Or there's more to it. Knox is buying the estate, and Lucy was here searching for her damned Fabergé egg. Isn't it too much of a coincidence that they both turned up here at the same time?"

"I think we have to tell Fergus, and the police as well," Josh said.

"And if the Land Rover was tampered with, the inspector will need to know," I said. "Let me find Pierre first, and then we'll ring McMahon. I'll bring him up to date on everything. Maybe you should go sit with Fergus. He looks exhausted."

"I don't blame him. I'm knackered and I'm less than half his age and not the one under threat. Come back as soon as you can, okay?"

In the kitchen, Pierre was scrubbing surfaces with Dutch cleanser. "That fingerprint powder got everywhere," he said when he saw me arrive. "*Quel désastre.*"

I looked around. To me, the kitchen appeared pristine. The police had removed the tape and tags they'd put up during their investigation. The gleaming stainless steel door to the meat locker was firmly closed.

"Where's your friend Remy?" I asked. "Is he still here?"

"No, he left yesterday. Why?"

"Nothing important. I wanted to ask him a question concerning antiques. He is an antique dealer, isn't he?"

Pierre stopped cleaning and looked up at me. "Antiques? What kind of antiques?"

"Something my aunt left me. I hoped he might be able to advise me on whether it's valuable or not." It was flimsy, but the best answer I could come up with. "Do you know where he is?"

"He continued on his holiday. He will be hiking in the Hebrides, but I have no idea where. He was going to take the train from Oban yesterday afternoon, I believe."

"That's too bad. I'm sorry to have missed him. So, he has an antique shop in Paris?"

"He does, but you can get advice about your aunt's gift in London, no?"

"Of course. I just thought it would be easy as he was here." I headed towards the stairs and then stopped and turned to look at Pierre again.

He returned my gaze with narrowed eyes. "Is there something else?"

"Had you met Duncan before this weekend? Had he been to the castle since you arrived here?"

"No. I had not seen him before. I am sorry for his death, but I have already told the police I know nothing of it. I closed up the kitchen at 1.30 a.m., and returned to my flat." His eyes lit up. "With one of the young waitresses. I told the police about that too."

"I wasn't accusing you, Pierre. Just asking. We all want to find the killer, don't we?"

"*Bien sur*, Mademoiselle Kate." Pierre resumed his cleaning, and I climbed the stone stairs to rejoin Josh and Fergus in the drawing room. They'd set up a game of backgammon on the coffee table but didn't seem to have made much progress. The counters were still on their home rows.

"Well?" Josh asked. "Did you get any information on Remy?"

"He's gone, apparently. He left on a hiking trip yesterday. I'm not sure it's important, but I'll tell Inspector McMahon that I found Remy's business card in Lucy's room."

"I told Fergus about Knox and Lucy," Josh said, glancing at his uncle.

"A bit odd, I agree," Fergus said. "I'll ask Stanton about it when we talk." He checked the mantelpiece clock. "Four o'clock. That's eight a.m. in California; I'll ring him now. I'll bring him up-to-date on Duncan and the fire, of course, and we have a few contract details to discuss, assuming he still wants to proceed. All the mayhem here might make him nervous. Maybe he'll decide to pull out."

"Do you want us to leave?" I asked.

"Not at all." Fergus stood and walked to the phone where he picked up the receiver and pushed buttons. He got through to Knox after a short wait and began by confirming that the inventories were complete. "There is something, however, that you need to know," he said, and went on to tell Knox about Duncan's murder. Whatever Knox said made Fergus's eyebrows shoot up. "He did? Oh, well you knew already then." He listened quietly for a couple of minutes, interjecting a grunt occasionally. I squeezed Josh's hand. Was Knox pulling out of the deal?

Fergus shook the receiver at one point as though trying to realign the transmission molecules. "Bad connection," he whispered to us. Then he listened again for a while. Josh had told me Knox was voluble in person, and it seemed his phone manner was no different.

"Jolly good," Fergus said finally. "I'll send the lists to you by tomorrow. One more thing before you go. Do you remember Lucy Cantrell? The young lady with the blonde hair who was here with Duncan?"

Again, he listened while Knox talked. "Yes, I can see that," he said. "Well, good to know. We'll be in touch very soon."

He replaced the receiver and came back to his place on the sofa. The call had taken over twenty minutes. "What did he say?" Josh demanded.

"First of all, he'd already heard about Duncan. Inspector McMahon rang him earlier today and, to use Knox's words, interrogated him. McMahon has also spoken to Knox's two colleagues. Apparently, the inspector also mentioned the fire."

"Does Knox still want to go through with the deal?" Josh asked.

"He does. He was as enthusiastic as ever, as far as I could tell, and requested that we send the inventories by tomorrow. It seems that a conflagration and a bloody murder aren't enough to put him off the place."

"What did he tell you about Lucy?" I asked.

"He said they had met at university, briefly. He didn't recognize her when he got here, and she didn't remind him who she was. Then something clicked, and he recalled having met her. Hence the long chat at the party on Saturday night."

"I thought that might be what happened," Josh said.

"What of the little tete-a-tete in her bedroom?" I asked.

Fergus's face turned pink. "I didn't think I could mention that. It seemed rather indelicate."

I pushed a counter around on the backgammon board. "It's too much of a coincidence, don't you think? That they knew each other, what, eight or nine years ago, and then meet up again here?"

"It happens more than you'd imagine," Fergus said. "I walked into a pub in Edinburgh last summer and found myself sitting next to the doctor who set my ankle after I broke it while caving down in the Forest of Dean. We hadn't seen each other for twenty years, but we recognized each other. What do they call it, six degrees of separation?"

"Well, I'm glad that Knox wants to proceed with the purchase. That is good news."

Fergus nodded just as the telephone rang, shrill in the quiet room. He jumped up to answer it. When he placed the receiver in its cradle, he looked troubled. "That was Frank from the repair shop in Oban," he said. "He says the brake cables were punctured, enough for brake fluid to leak out slowly. Could have been general deterioration, but he doesn't believe so. He says it was deliberate."

28

Thirty minutes later, Inspector McMahon rang the doorbell. "There are plenty of spare rooms here," I said when I opened the front door. "You should probably just move in."

His mouth twitched with the faintest hint of a smile, and he followed me into the drawing room. Fergus had phoned him as soon as he'd heard from the repair shop. After I'd described to the inspector what had happened with the Land Rover, Fergus confirmed again that the mechanic thought the damage was deliberate. The crease between McMahon's brows deepened into a crevasse as he scrawled a note in his book.

"Do you think that Mr. Jameson did it while he was on the property before the firebomb attack?" Josh asked. "Sort of a back-up in case the fire didn't work?"

McMahon tapped his pencil on the open page. "Possibly. I'll investigate, but it's likely the brakes would then have failed on the way into the village, not on the way back. My alternative theory is that Kate was the target."

The temperature seemed to plummet. My blood chilled.

"But why target Kate?" Josh asked, grabbing hold of my hand.

"Because she's been asking questions." McMahon looked at me.

"That's not an accusation, merely a statement of fact." He raised his eyes to scan the space over my head. "Would you know if you had one of those aura things?"

Instinctively, I swept my hand above my hair. "No. I've never seen one over myself. I can't see them in mirrors, so I wouldn't know if I had one."

"I'm sure that's not it," Josh said. "It's far more likely that the target was Fergus."

"Well, I'll follow up on the car inspection report and let you know what I find out. Meanwhile, Kate, you should be cautious." McMahon closed his notebook.

Seeing that he was about to leave, I jumped in. "Before you go, I've uncovered a few things you may be interested in." I dug in my pocket and pulled out Remy's business card. "I found this in Lucy's room." I said, passing it over to McMahon. "Remy Delacroix stayed here for a couple of days. He and Pierre knew each other in Paris, Pierre told me, and Remy volunteered to help with the party after Pierre was left short-handed. You know, with Nick being gone."

"Yes, Delacroix was on our list of interviewees, like all of the temporary staff who were here on Saturday." McMahon turned the card over a couple of times, his large hands dwarfing it. "What about him?"

"I found the card yesterday after Lucy left. I didn't pay much attention to it at the time, but then today I found out from Fiona that the Frenchman helping Pierre was this Remy Delacroix and I wondered why Lucy had his business card. I came up with a possible reason. Remember that we think Lucy and Duncan were searching for a Fabergé egg? Well, six months ago, a Paris antiques dealer sold a Fabergé egg to a collector for a thousand pounds, apparently not realizing what it was. Later, the collector discovered it was a genuine Romanov-commissioned Fabergé egg worth millions. Which left the dealer who sold it with egg on his face."

Josh grinned, but McMahon looked blank.

"Remy is an antiques dealer in Paris," I said. "Maybe he sold that egg, or he knows the dealer who did."

McMahon cradled his chin in his hand, eyes narrowed in concentration. "If a collector has the egg, why were Lucy and Duncan looking for it here?"

"I'm confused too," Fergus said.

"They weren't," I said. "They were searching for another of the missing Romanov eggs. It's believed that there are seven missing eggs. Well, six now, with the one that was sold in Paris. The publicity on the newly discovered imperial egg renewed interest and speculation on the whereabouts of the other pieces, motivating collectors and historians all over the world to review everything they knew about the missing Romanov treasures and their possible locations. Remember I told you that Duncan had made some notes in his journal? Were you able to take a look?"

McMahon frowned. "Not yet. I do have other things on my mind, and missing treasure isn't one of them."

"It should be if it's the reason for Duncan's death. And for the ongoing danger to Fergus."

McMahon patted the air in front of him as though trying to calm me. "I'll get to it, I promise. And that brings me to something I want to tell you. The medical examiner has come up with a time of death for Duncan. It proved hard to pin down because of the temperature in the meat locker, but he was most likely killed between two and three a.m."

"That's later than we thought," Josh said. "So where was he between one and two a.m.?"

"Lucy said she went to bed at one after Duncan told her he was tired and wanted to sleep alone," I said. "We were all in our rooms by then." I looked at Josh. "Wasn't it around one when we went to bed?"

"Yes. And Fiona said she waited for Duncan until one-thirty and then drove home. If Duncan was still alive at that time, why didn't he go out to meet her as planned?"

We fell silent for a minute. I reconstructed the evening in my head, but I had no blinding insights. If both Lucy and Fiona were correct about the timing, then there was a period of an hour, possibly two, when Duncan was unaccounted for.

"He must have gone to his room to change," I offered. "He was wearing his tuxedo for the party, and had changed into his casual clothes before he was killed."

"That accounts for some of the time," McMahon agreed.

"And he might have gone to the east wing again," I said.

Fergus lifted his eyebrows. "Duncan in the east wing? Didn't you say Lucy had been up there?"

"She was. And I think it's possible Duncan paid a visit too. He had cobwebs on his jacket when he arrived at the party. Perhaps he went back there after we were all in bed."

"What's in the east wing?" McMahon asked.

Fergus explained how it had been damaged and abandoned in 1941. "The place is a wreck," he said. "I can't see why anyone would want to go in there. And why now? All his life, Duncan's never been in there, and then he decides to poke around on the night of the party? Besides, he could have picked up cobwebs anywhere."

"You'd better not let Mrs. Dunsmore hear you say that." Josh grinned.

"Some people like exploring ruins and old buildings," McMahon said. "There's probably not much more to it. But we can organize a search if you like, to see if there's anything in there that explain Lucy's interest."

"There's one more thing." I glanced at Fergus. "It turns out that Lucy knows Stanton Knox, the American who's going to buy the estate. We didn't think they knew each other, but Fiona told me she saw the two of them in Lucy's room."

"Fiona seems to be a positive fountain of information," McMahon commented drily. He opened his notebook again and flipped pages. "She didn't mention that during my interview with her."

"I'm not sure why she would." I was quick to defend her. "As far as she knew, they were just two house guests. They could have been old friends, or a couple hooking up for the weekend. It wouldn't seem significant."

"Hooking up?" Fergus asked. When Josh leaned over and whispered to him, Fergus chuckled. "Ah. Well, house parties always were

prime territory for illicit affairs amongst the *beau monde*. My ancestors in the Georgian era had quite a reputation for throwing elaborate
entertainments, and there were plenty of guests tiptoeing between
bedrooms in the night."

"And I found some information on the Web," I went on. "Knox
and Lucy were at the same American university for one year."

McMahon made a note in his book. "This has been helpful, thank
you all." He got to his feet. "I'll be back as soon as I have more
information."

Mrs. Dunsmore arrived just then with a tray. McMahon cast a
wistful look at the plate of buttery shortbread biscuits that accompanied the tea. "Take one with you," the housekeeper offered. "You can
eat it in the car."

After accepting the biscuit, McMahon strode out of the room.

Fergus waited until he'd gone. "Not sure what to make of any of
this," he said. "But McMahon seems to be working hard trying to sort
it out."

After pouring tea for everyone, I sipped mine even though it was
hot enough to scald my tongue. McMahon was working hard, no
doubt, but he didn't have the incentive of seeing Fergus's accelerating
aura. Its rapid spinning taunted me. I knew we were running out
of time.

"I need to find a computer," Fergus said, between mouthfuls of
shortbread. "I have to send some papers to Knox." He looked at his
watch. "Five o clock, so it's too late for anything in town to be open.
But I wonder if the hotel might let me use their fax machine. If we
buy a drink in the hotel bar, maybe they'll look on me kindly. What
do you think, Josh? A pint sound good?"

Josh glanced from Fergus to me and back again. "What about
Kate? What if someone is after her too?"

"I'll be fine," I said. "Truly."

"Don't think twice, my lad," Fergus said. "I'll pop over there by
myself and be straight back. You stay with Kate."

"That's not a good idea," I said. "I'll come with you."

We got into our rental car, and Josh drove slowly along the rain-soaked road into the village. "That's where the car landed," I pointed through the dusky evening light when we passed the spot where the Land Rover had left the road. "You'd never know to look at it though."

The heather had bounced back, revealing no sign that it had been flattened by a ton of metal over a one-hundred-meter stretch. But then the Scottish moors were accustomed to hiding evidence of violence and trauma. The spilled blood of centuries of war and the bones of thousands of clansmen lay hidden in the ancient soil. My hectic excursion from the road to the car's resting place was literally only a scratch along the surface, easily mended and quickly forgotten.

Fergus twisted in the passenger seat. "Are you sure you're all right? You must have been shaken up badly this afternoon."

"I'm okay." I flexed my right shoulder, feeling an ache where the seat belt had tightened across it. "Your car is built a like a tank."

Josh pulled into the car park of the hotel, a quaint white-painted building. It had twenty rooms, Fergus told us, and a small restaurant and bar. As we reached the door to the lobby, I heard a shout and turned to see Alistair Ross waving his umbrella at us.

"I'm glad to see you, Kate," he said after he'd crossed the road to join us. "I was on my way to the supermarket but, if you have a minute, I have some information to share with you."

"Why don't you two have a chat while Josh and I wangle some time on the fax machine?" Fergus suggested.

Inside, Alistair and I headed to the bar, where he deposited his umbrella in a stand, and I hung up my jacket, wet from the short walk across the car park. While Alistair chatted with the barman, I admired the beamed ceiling, tanned with centuries of soot and smoke emanating from the large inglenook fireplace. But the tartan carpet was new and plush, and the wood tables gleamed. A faint scent of furniture polish mingled with the smell of beer.

Alistair ordered a half of Scottish ale with a Celtic name I couldn't pronounce, and I opted for a glass of pinot noir. We carried our drinks to a table near the lead-paned windows. Only one other table was occupied, by a young couple in hiking gear.

Alistair took a swallow of his beer and dabbed at his mouth with his handkerchief before taking a piece of paper from his pocket. He unfolded it, smoothing out the creases with the palm of his hand. "I called in some favors with a friend of mine, Ian McPherson, who helped me research the Agnes Fenton story in the past. Ian looked up Cyril Thorpe, the last name on that list of yours. It turns out that Thorpe was actually quite well-known— although notorious might be the better word. He owned an antiques business in London during the late 1930s, and was investigated for fraud several times. He hit the headlines when he tried to sell a Rubens to a Rockefeller who knew enough to recognize a fake when he saw it. Thorpe insisted he was innocent, that he'd bought the painting in the belief that it was authentic, and the charges were eventually dropped." He paused and took another drink of his beer. I sipped my wine, which tasted surprisingly good.

"Anyway," Alistair continued. "Thorpe traveled to Paris in early 1940, hoping to pick up some bargains. People were panicking, and many were selling their valuables before the Nazis could seize them. There's a Customs Office list on record of what he procured in Paris because he was stopped and searched at Dover on his return. I suppose his reputation led the Customs men to assume he might be trying to smuggle in goods without paying duties on them."

Alistair put his glass down, centering it in the middle of a cardboard coaster. "I'll keep it as short as I can. Ian found a list of those receipts for Thorpe's purchases in Paris, which included a collection of books, an extensive assortment of very fine jewelry— and a Fabergé egg."

I leaned forward across the table to look at the paper, a scanned and barely legible copy of the list. "Oh my God," I breathed. "So that note in Duncan's journal listed the egg's owners: Tsarina Alexandra, her lady-in-waiting, and then Cyril Thorpe?"

"Yes." Alistair's eyes gleamed bright. "Do you remember what I told you about the Tsarina's lady-in-waiting? Anna Vyrubova? When everything went pear-shaped in Russia, Alexandra entrusted some of her prized valuables to Anna, who eventually escaped to Finland. In

1939, the Soviets invaded Finland, the start of the Winter War between the two countries. Ian believes that Anna, like many in Helsinki at the time, believed the Russians would overrun the country. She was concerned about the Tsarina's heirlooms. He suspects she must have panicked because she gave the treasures for safe-keeping to a Frenchman who'd been at court with her during the reign of the Tsar. He was supposedly a trusted friend, but he turned out to not be such a good comrade after all— he took the valuables to Paris and sold them for enough money to pay for a ship passage to New York."

"I'd have thought the Tsarina's valuables would have been to enough to pay for his own ship, not just a ticket," I said. "He must have been stupid or desperate."

"Maybe both, but definitely desperate. He, Anna, and many others like them, had suffered terribly during the Russian Revolution and its aftermath. The prospect of another war was undoubtedly terrifying. America was a safe haven."

"So he sold the treasures to Cyril Thorpe?"

"Exactly. The receipts match up with what Vyrubova would have given to her friend."

"And Thorpe brought the items to England?"

"Some of them. It seems he sold them off quickly, probably eager to dump them because of their dubious provenance."

Alistair tapped his finger on an item on the list. "We know that this necklace turned up at auction ten years ago. It's easily recognizable as belonging to the Tsarina because there are photographs of her wearing it. It went for a fortune, as you can imagine. Other items of jewelry have also reappeared over the past couple of decades. Thorpe must have sold Anna Vyrubova's treasure trove to a number of different buyers."

"And the Fabergé egg?"

Alistair shook his head. "Sadly, that we don't know. There's no documentation to show that Thorpe tried to import it to the UK. Either he'd already sold it in France, or he smuggled it in somehow."

"He must have got it into the country, don't you think? And sold it to Gordon MacKenna? Otherwise, how else could it have made its way to the castle?" I tapped my fingers on the table, thinking. "If there is no documentation, how did Duncan and Lucy work out that it's here? There must be something we're missing."

"I agree," Alistair said.

He looked so disappointed that I quickly reassured him. "But what you've discovered so far is brilliant. Now we understand the significance of that list of names in Duncan's journal. It's thrilling to see evidence of the connection between the Tsarina, her lady-in-waiting, and Thorpe. There's just that missing link that would explain Lucy's conviction that the egg is in the castle somewhere."

"There is something that might help," he said. "Anna Vyrubova also gave her untrustworthy French friend a crate of Russian books as part of the consignment of valuables. The Frenchman sold the collection to Thorpe as a single lot for twenty-five pounds." He tapped on the list. "See here? 'Leather-bound novels, quantity 12.' Thorpe then sold the lot in England for fifty pounds."

"And?"

"And Gordon MacKenna bought that case of books. Ian's seen the receipt recording the sale. That one was on record with the customs people."

"Maybe the egg was concealed in that case? That's how Thorpe smuggled it into England. Or maybe he didn't even know it was in there and just sold the case unopened?"

My skin tingled with excitement. This would surely explain how the egg came to be at the castle.

Alistair's eyes gleamed. "Yes, it's possible." He steepled his fingers under his chin. "I'd wondered why Anna Vyrubova thought those books were valuable enough to be worth saving. They weren't even itemized, so we don't know the titles. But if they were a cover for a Fabergé egg then it makes more sense."

"Do you think those books are in Fergus's library? What would we be looking for?"

"Leather-bound books with titles in Russian. That's all we know."

"They shouldn't be hard to find though," I said. "I'll organize a search as soon as we get back."

The thought of searching for books reminded me of Duncan's surreptitious sweep of the library. And Lucy's unexpected offer to help Fergus with his book inventory. Had they actually been looking for these Russian novels? There was something else, another thought swirling through my head, but I couldn't pin it down.

Alistair was watching me, his head angled to one side like a bird. "You've come up with something?"

"What if we've been focusing on the wrong treasure? What if it's not an egg we should be looking for, but something much older?"

Alistair met my gaze and nodded. "Something that has already been killed for. Many centuries ago."

"You and I both saw the vision of Agnes Fenton holding the codex before she was murdered," I said. "There has to be a reason for that."

Alistair nodded. "The Tsarina was the latest known owner of the codex. Let's assume she gave it to Anna for safety, along with her other valuables. Maybe Anna understood the true value of the codex, maybe she didn't, but she did know that her beloved mistress, Alexandra, had treasured it. Anna would have wanted to ensure it survived the coming war. What if she deliberately hid it in a chest full of other old leather-bound books, hoping it wouldn't draw attention to itself if the authorities laid their hands on it? Of course, she couldn't have envisaged her so-called friend selling the entire hoard to an unscrupulous dealer who had no idea what he'd acquired."

"And Gordon MacKenna bought the case of books, which hid the codex and a Fabergé egg." I leaned back in my chair, overwhelmed by the thought that we were close to understanding what had happened nearly eighty years ago.

Josh and Fergus strolled into the bar just then. I jumped up and hurried to join them while they ordered drinks. "Mission accomplished," Josh said. "We were able to fax the lists to Knox."

"Good. And we have some interesting news," I said. "Come and sit. Alistair can tell you himself."

We pulled up two more chairs and gathered around the table.

Keeping his voice low, the historian explained what he'd found out with the help of his friend Ian.

"But where could the items be?" Fergus asked. "Even if my grandfather did purchase the books and the egg, where are they now?"

"We start with looking for the Russian novels," I said. "Maybe that will give us a clue."

"Were there any Russian books on the inventory list?" Josh asked Fergus.

Fergus shrugged. "A few, I think. And some in French and in German, a fair number in Spanish. My father was widely-read and a bit of a polyglot."

"You mean, if we find these books, we find the codex and the egg?" Josh asked Alistair, who lifted his tweed-clad shoulders.

"Not necessarily. We could be wrong about the inclusion of the codex in the original sale to Thorpe, or it's possible he recognized it and removed it from the crate before selling those books to Gordon MacKenna. There are no guarantees. All we know is that it was presumed to be in his possession in 1940 and there have been no reported sightings of it since." Alistair checked his watch. "I must get on before the supermarket closes. Will you ring me if you find anything?"

"Of course," Fergus said. "And thank you for all the work you've done on this. You've discovered a great deal in a very short time."

It was dark when we headed into the hotel car park, and we were quiet as Josh drove home to the castle. Sitting in the back, I watched the landscape roll by, mile after mile of monochromatic moorland, barely lit by a crescent moon that occasionally peeped through heavy clouds.

When we reached the castle, we were surprised to see McMahon's car parked at the top of the drive. The inspector stood at the front door, talking to Mrs. Dunsmore.

"Ah, I'm glad you're here," he said once we'd joined him on the front steps. "Something has come up, and I need a few minutes of your time."

29

Fergus ushered us all into the drawing room, where McMahon produced his mobile. "The video is poor quality because I copied it to my phone for convenience," he said. "But tell me if you recognize this man, Kate?"

The image on the grainy black and white footage was hard to make out, and the man had his back to the camera for much of the video, which only lasted for ten seconds. At the end, however, he turned, and I immediately recognized Remy Delacroix. After asking the inspector to replay it, Josh agreed with me that it was Remy, and Fergus said he recalled seeing the man but hadn't known his name.

"You're sure?" McMahon asked me.

"Absolutely," Josh and I said at the same time.

"Then look at the time stamp." He pointed to white numbers on the bottom of the video clip. "The recording took place at two-fifteen this afternoon." He paused. "The footage is from the CCTV camera in the car park behind the pub in the village."

"But Pierre told me Remy left yesterday for Oban," I said.

"Clearly, he didn't. Maybe he changed his plans."

"Or maybe he lied to Pierre— or Pierre lied to me."

"I requested CCTV coverage of the pub car park," McMahon

explained. "Because you said that's where you parked the Land Rover for an hour or so when you went out with Fiona. The camera only caught images of the entrance, though, so there's no footage of the cars. That means we don't have any hard evidence tying Delacroix to the alleged tampering. However, it is interesting that he was in the vicinity at the time you were in the cafe."

"What now?" Fergus asked.

"We're asking questions in the village. See if anyone noticed Delacroix hanging around the Land Rover, and I've put out an alert for him. Regardless of his reasons for being in the car park this afternoon, there's sufficient justification to bring him in for questioning. Since he was working in the kitchen on the night Duncan was killed, he'll need to explain his actions that night and today. I'm going to talk to Pierre again, given the connection between the two of them."

Once McMahon had left for the kitchen, I gave Fergus a hug. For the first time in four days, a glimmer of optimism lifted the gloom. "The police will catch Remy," I said. "And I believe you'll be safe once he's in custody."

"So, you think Pierre was working with this Remy chappie?" Fergus didn't look as excited as I felt. "I always considered myself a good judge of character, but it seems that I'm wrong about him."

I wasn't sure about Pierre either. His friendship with Remy didn't make him guilty, but something wasn't right, and I couldn't help remembering his dexterity with a knife. "Well, let's give Inspector McMahon time," I said. "Meanwhile, why don't we go search for the books that Alistair told us about?"

Feeling energized by Alistair's revelations and McMahon's pursuit of Remy, I sprinted up the main staircase with Josh and Fergus trailing behind me.

"Shall we inspect the inventory catalogue or look for the actual books on shelves?" Josh asked when we reached the library.

"Let's check the shelves," Fergus said. "Even if we find Russian titles in the catalogue, we'll want to verify that the books are old and leather-bound as Alistair described them."

"Wouldn't you be aware if they were here?" I asked him. "Even if you'd never noticed them before, you'd have found them when you did the inventory, wouldn't you?"

He tapped his cheek, thinking. "Probably. But, remember that Lucy helped me and she did a lot of the physical scanning, clambering up and down that rolling ladder. So, she may have seen them and entered them in the inventory list, as she did with many of the other books."

"I'll check that list," Josh offered. "If you two are happy to start looking for the books themselves."

We were interrupted just then by the arrival of Inspector McMahon. He stood in the doorway of the library, accompanied by Mrs. Dunsmore. "Sorry to intrude," he said. "But I want to let you know I'm taking Pierre Gagnon into custody."

Fergus's shoulders sagged. "Why? Do you think he killed Nick? And Duncan?"

"Following our little chat, I'm finding inconsistencies in his story that I need to investigate further."

"Inconsistencies about what?"

"His relationship to Remy Delacroix, his whereabouts on Saturday night, and what Delacroix told him about his travel plans."

"I know you need to do your job, Inspector." Fergus sighed. "But I'll be glad when this is over."

"We all will," McMahon replied. "I'll wait downstairs until the squad car arrives."

As he turned away, Mrs. Dunsmore threw her hands up in a gesture of despair. I knew she liked Pierre. Then she quickly caught up with the inspector, leaving us in shocked silence.

"McMahon is on it," Josh said. "That's good. Any sort of progress is good, right?"

Fergus sighed again. Then he straightened up and rubbed his hands together. "We may as well get cracking," he said. "Kate, why don't you start over there, and I'll take this side."

I walked slowly along my stretch, scanning the book spines for any sign of the Cyrillic alphabet. When I reached the end with no result, I turned around and repeated the process.

"All done apart from the top. I can't see that high," I told Fergus ten minutes later. The uppermost shelf hung a couple of meters above my head.

"I can solve that," he gestured at the rolling ladder. "You take a break."

I was about to sit on the sofa when lights scrolled across the library windows, and I hurried over to peer outside. Two cars had pulled up at the front door. Both had their headlights on full beam and, although there had been no sirens, blue lights flashed, casting an eerie light on the cypress trees that lined the driveway.

"Police cars," I told Fergus and Josh. I watched from the window while Pierre got into the first car, guided into the back seat. Doors slammed. When the cars slipped away quietly down the drive, I turned around to check on Fergus. His aura still swirled. To me, that indicated the threat had nothing to do with Pierre, but it wasn't definitive. The chef might be released after his interview with the inspector and, once free, could still pose a risk. I hoped that McMahon would keep him in for a while. He'd be one less person to worry about.

While Fergus continued to search the upper shelves, I dropped onto a sofa. "My head's about to explode," I said to Josh when he came to sit next to me, bringing the binder with him. "Alistair Ross seems sure the codex and the egg are here, but where? Why would they go missing if your great-grandfather bought them? Did he sell them?"

I watched Fergus as I spoke. He perched on the ladder, pulling out books and checking the dark spaces behind them, just as I'd seen Duncan do. It seemed like weeks had elapsed since then, but in fact only three days had passed.

Josh continued examining the lists. Suddenly, he slapped a page with the palm of his hand. "They're here. Look."

I peered at the yellowing paper, squinting to read the entries. Whoever had compiled the document wrote in a small, flowery script that I found difficult to read. The books weren't named as individual titles, simply notated as "Assorted Russian books, quantity 12."

"And there are no initials next to the entry, which means Lucy didn't find them when she did the inventory," I said.

It seemed that Fergus hadn't found them either. He stepped down from the ladder and flopped into the armchair opposite us.

"Seems like we've hit a dead end," he said, rubbing his eyes.

The disappointment weighed heavy on my chest. I took a few deep breaths to pull air into my lungs.

"But they must have been here at one time," Josh said. "Because they're on the inventory." He turned a page. "When were these entries made?"

Fergus held his hand out to take the folder and then perused the pages. "The original library register was completed, like the furniture list, around 1920, organized by my grandfather. Then, my father updated all of the inventories in 1952, partly in deference to my grandfather, who'd initiated them, and also to calculate a value for the insurance. As you've seen, many of these books are first editions, or rare copies. Anyway, the later additions are on different paper, see?" He held the file out for us to look at. It was obvious now he'd pointed it out— a distinct difference in the handwriting, on paper that was smoother and less yellowed. "The Russian books appear on the additional pages added in the 1950s." He ran his finger over the words.

"Which is consistent with what Alistair told us," I said. "Your grandfather, Gordon MacKenna, bought the books in November 1940, so they would show up on the later record."

"That's right. But if they were here once, where are they now?"

We'd come to a crashing halt in our search for the Russian books.

"Knock, knock," came a voice from the door, and McMahon stepped inside again. "Pierre has been taken to the station and I'm leaving now. I'll be in touch if anything comes of the interview." He glanced around, and his eyes came to rest on the binder on the coffee table. Fergus must have noticed.

"We're following up a lead from Alistair Ross," he said. "I'm not sure if it's relevant or not, but you might want to hear about it, just in case. Kate can explain it. Can you spare a minute? Come in and sit down."

Aiming to be succinct, I told the inspector the story of the Romanov treasures given to Anna Vyrubova, and how she'd entrusted them to a French friend who'd betrayed her. "He took them to Paris to sell them," I said. "We're hoping to find some books that were part of that consignment. Mr. Ross thinks Fergus's grandfather may have purchased a crate of books which may well have contained an ancient codex and a Fabergé egg from the Romanov collection."

"The egg that you thought Duncan and Miss Cantrell were hunting for?"

"That's right."

McMahon wiped his brow with the back of his hand. "And these items, the codex and the egg. They're both worth a great deal of money?"

"Millions, we believe," I said. "Which would make them worth killing for, don't you think?"

"People have killed for far less," McMahon agreed. He tapped his fingers on the table. "You say this purchase originated in Paris. That's where Delacroix is from. Is there a connection?"

"We're not sure, other than that he's French and an antiques dealer."

"An antiques dealer eighty years after this alleged purchase by Gordon MacKenna." McMahon looked dubious. "I still don't see the connection. It's flimsy at best."

"I know." I sighed. "But will you follow up? Just ask Remy about it when you bring him in? And Pierre?"

McMahon nodded and then stood up. "I should get down to the station. Thank you all for the update. I'll be back in touch very soon. Kate, can I have a word?"

I followed him to the landing outside the door. "I wanted to check up on Fergus," he said. "But I didn't want to ask in front of him. Is there any change there, with that aura thing?"

"No." I shook my head. "Sadly not. But maybe it will go away once you've got Remy in custody too."

30

After McMahon left, Mrs. Dunsmore came up to the library. "Can ye believe he's arrested our Pierre?" she said, her voice shaking with indignation. "Some rubbish about Pierre changing his story and his friendship with that other Frenchman. I think that inspector's a... what's that word? Franco something."

"Francophobe," Fergus said, leading her to the sofa and insisting that she sit down. "I'm sure that Pierre will be home very soon."

"Mind you," she continued. "I dinnae like that man, Remy. Right full of himself, he was." She pressed her hands to her chest. "Do ye think he killed Duncan? Is that why the inspector is looking for him?"

Fergus poured a small amount of whisky into a glass. "Drink this," he said, giving it to her.

Her eyes widened. "It's just a wee dram," he said. "It'll make you feel better."

She knocked it back with more relish than I expected. "And what do we do about dinner, now that Pierre's away with the inspector?" she asked.

"We'll manage," I said. "I'll be happy to help cook. Let's go down and see what there is in the pantry." I looked at Josh. "Okay? You'll stay with Fergus?"

Mrs. Dunsmore led the way to the kitchen where we rummaged around in the fridge and the pantry for likely ingredients. "How about a cottage pie?" she suggested. "We've got potatoes, onions, carrots and beef."

We set to and, forty-five minutes later, filled a casserole dish to the brim with thick stew and creamy mashed potatoes. "It'll need to sit in the oven for half an hour until that cheese on top browns and bubbles," Mrs. Dunsmore said. The smell of the almost-ready pie made me realize how hungry I felt. It seemed that I kept missing meals or turning down food because my stomach was churning with anxiety and stress. Tonight, I intended to eat.

"I'll set the table," Mrs. Dunsmore said. "And I'll ask Master Josh to open a bottle of wine. Will you keep an eye on the pie? Make sure the top doesn't burn."

Alone in the kitchen, I felt the skin on my arms prickling. I glanced at the meat locker, glad to see the door remained firmly closed. Poor Duncan. He was a total jerk, but he hadn't deserved to die, and certainly not in such a callous way, being stabbed in the back like that. He hadn't even had a chance to defend himself. In my strange vision, Agnes Fenton had been stabbed from behind too. From the way she glanced back, she must have been aware of her pursuer. I wondered if Duncan had known someone was there, or had the attacker crept up on him?

Pacing around the empty space, I tried to imagine what had happened here in the early hours of Sunday morning. The kitchen would have been empty apart from the killer and Duncan. Maybe they quarreled, and Duncan turned away. The killer grabbed a knife from the block on the counter and thrust it into Duncan's back. Either dead or seriously injured, Duncan was dragged into the meat locker, and the door slammed closed. What then? The killer would have cleaned up any blood and wiped the surfaces clean of fingerprints. And disposed of the murder weapon somehow.

I opened the oven and checked on the progress of the pie. Personally, I would have eaten it there and then, but I knew it wouldn't yet meet Mrs. Dunsmore's high standards.

In spite of my misgivings about revisiting the crime scene, I walked over and grasped the handle of the meat locker. The door weighed heavy in my hands and took some effort to open. Inside, the hooks hung empty, and the shelves, once laden with cuts of meat and fish, were bare. The interior had obviously been cleaned out, either by the police or Pierre. I stared at the place where I'd seen Duncan lying, spread-eagled on the stone floor. Recreating the scene in my head, I recalled that he'd been wearing tan trousers and a blue shirt. No jacket or sweater, I realized, which made me wonder if he hadn't intended to leave the house. It was raining hard at one in the morning, a precursor to the storm that had blown in later. What about Duncan's prearranged tryst with Fiona? Had he stood her up deliberately? Or had he planned to meet her but something had happened to delay him? Fiona had given up at one-thirty, she said. The medical examiner said time of death was between two and three a.m. What had Duncan been doing until then? I gazed at the floor. A thought poked at my brain, trying to get my attention. I willed myself to focus.

Duncan didn't have any shoes on, I remembered now. Only dark brown socks. Which certainly suggested he hadn't planned to go outside. I couldn't imagine him padding over wet gravel in his socked feet to reach Fiona's car. If that were the case, why had he come down to the kitchen at all? Maybe he'd come to forage for leftovers? Find another bottle of champagne? The more I thought about it, the more confused I felt. He didn't seem like the type to wander around in his socks, and he'd gone to the trouble of changing his clothes, which seemed to imply that he had meant to meet up with Fiona. What had happened to change his mind?

I stepped out and pushed the heavy door closed. The shoes were bothering me. A quick check of the oven assured me I had time to clarify something. I took off, up the kitchen stairs, across the hall and through the picture gallery to the tower. I pushed open Duncan's door and stepped inside. It was as neat and tidy as the last time I visited. Mrs. Dunsmore had told me the police had conducted an extensive examination but there was no sign of their activity now. I opened the wardrobe. On the floor, as I remembered from my earlier search, were two pairs of shoes: his black dress shoes and a pair of oxblood loafers. No suede Guccis. I reached inside the wardrobe, but found nothing, and continued my search under the bed, in the bathroom and under the chest of drawers. No sign of the shoes. That was odd. If he wasn't wearing them, then where were they?

Aware of my responsibilities for dinner that evening, I rushed back down to the kitchen. The tantalizing fragrance of melting cheese filled the room as I peeked in the oven. It was looking good, but still not quite done.

I eyed the phone that hung on the wall and pulled my mobile from my pocket. No service down here of course, but I found Lucy's mobile phone number in my contacts list. I pressed the buttons on the wall phone and heard ringing.

"Lucy Cantrell," she answered.

"It's Kate. Just wondering how you're doing," I said. "There's still no news on the funeral, I'm afraid."

"Has the inspector arrested anyone yet?"

"Actually, yes. Pierre, you know, the chef."

"Pierre, huh? I wondered about him. Sly sort of chap. But why would he want to kill Duncan?"

"I have no idea." I paused. "Lucy, did you already know Remy Delacroix? Before he came to the castle?"

"Remy? No, but I remember talking to him one afternoon. He gave me his business card. He was a bit pushy, trying to interest me in a piece of jewelry or some such thing. He runs an antique shop."

"Right."

"Is that why you called?" she asked. "I'm walking home from work."

At Lucy's end, I heard a faint background hum of traffic and someone else talking as they passed on the street. For a second, I wished I were there in London, surrounded by people and noise and activity, not here in this rambling and isolated castle.

"No, but I have a question. Did Duncan have two pairs of loafers with him? One tan suede. I think they were Gucci. And the others were that oxblood color?"

"Shoes? Good Lord. I don't remember. I wasn't the curator of Duncan's wardrobe as far as I know. Is it important?"

"I don't know. But Duncan wasn't wearing any shoes when he died. I think there's a pair missing."

"That seems odd. Not like Duncan. He was always... so tidy. He..." Lucy gave a little sob and then went quiet.

"I'm sorry, Lucy. Don't worry about it. It's probably nothing."

"Okay. Listen, I have to go. About to get on the Tube. Keep me updated on what's happening there, won't you?"

The line went dead. I hung up the phone and leaned against a cabinet, thinking, and then I dialed Inspector McMahon's mobile. He answered at once.

"It's Kate Benedict," I said. In response, I got silence.

"Has Pierre confessed to anything?" I asked. "Any news on Remy?"

"Not yet. Rest assured we'll tell you the minute we get more information."

"There's something else. I wanted to confirm with you that Duncan wasn't wearing any shoes when you saw him in the meat locker? He only had on socks?"

Greeted by another long silence, I thought I'd lost him. "Inspector?"

"Sorry, my signal keeps dropping out," he said. "You were talking about shoes? I'll need to check my notes but I think you're right. Why do you ask?"

"First of all, why would he be dressed, but not have his shoes on?"

"Maybe he wanted to tiptoe around without being heard," McMahon said. "He didn't have his car keys on him, so I guess he wasn't planning to go out anywhere."

"Not necessarily," I said. "Fiona was waiting for him in her car, don't forget. He wouldn't have needed his keys."

"That's true."

"Plus, one pair of shoes is missing. Tan loafers. I checked his room and can't find them. So, where are they?"

"Tan loafers? I can't imagine how you'd notice a detail like that. I'm not even sure which shoes I've got on today. Hang on. Ah, black lace-ups. But then I always wear black lace-ups."

I smiled at McMahon's stab at humor. "I don't have a shoe fetish or anything weird," I said. "It's just that I noticed he was wearing them when he arrived on Thursday night, because they were so, you know, sort of ostentatious. Gucci, very expensive. And you have to be a certain kind of person to wear that sort of thing. Anyway, I thought I'd mention it. It might be relevant."

"It's appreciated, Kate," he said. "Look after yourself. I'll be in touch soon."

31

"**M**cMahon has released Pierre. He should be home soon." Fergus said, coming back to the table after taking McMahon's phone call. We'd finished dinner and had eaten every scrap of the cottage pie. For the first time in three days, I didn't feel hungry. It wasn't that I was feeling any less anxious, but hunger had to overcome all other states of being at some point.

"I'd like to have a word with Pierre myself," Fergus continued. "Although McMahon took a statement, he isn't willing to share it with us yet. But I can't see any reason not to ask our own questions." He took a sip of the wine we'd opened. "I've had just about enough of all the secrets and cloak-and-dagger stuff."

When the doorbell rang, Fergus met the chef at the front door and ushered him into the dining room.

Pierre's eyes widened when he saw the empty plates. "You cooked your own dinner?"

"Yes, Kate and Mrs. Dunsmore did, and it was delicious," Josh told him.

The Frenchman pursed his lips in disapproval. His youthful good looks were frayed at the edges, I thought. The skin around his mouth was drawn tight, and his eyes were dull. I supposed that spending a few hours in police custody would do that.

"Come in." Fergus spoke in a firm tone that made it clear this was no social invitation. "Take a seat and tell us everything that happened. Bring us all up to date."

Pierre was nervous. He clasped and unclasped his hands, crossed his legs and then uncrossed them again. "I told the inspector everything."

Fergus waved his hand in the air. "Yes, of course you did, but we'd also like to hear it from you."

"I did not kill anyone."

"Then who did kill Nick and Duncan?"

Pierre blinked rapidly. "I don't know anything."

"What about Remy?" I was impatient to get him talking. "You said he was leaving for his hiking trip, but it appears that he was still in the village yesterday, and that he's suspected of messing with the Land Rover in order to cause an accident. Were you aware of his real plans?"

"He never told me the truth, not from the first day."

"And when was that?"

"Four or five months ago, when he persuaded me to come to Scotland."

I did my best to hide my surprise, but Fergus had shot forward in his chair and was glaring at him. "What do you mean, he persuaded you?"

Pierre sighed. "I already told the police all this. But I will explain again. Remy wanted me to work here, so I could look for something for him."

"A book and a Fabergé egg," I said.

He frowned. "He wanted me to find a book. The egg, he had already sold. Six months ago."

"No, a different egg. Not the one he sold. But he asked you to look for just a book?"

"As I said. But I did not find the book. So Remy came this weekend to check up on me, to hurry things along, he said."

"How do you know Remy?" I asked.

"We were friends in Paris, ever since we were kids." Pierre shrugged. "We did different things. My career was successful, his not so much. But we remained in touch."

"Why wasn't he successful?"

"In my opinion, Remy is lazy. He inherited an antiques business from his father and he ran it badly. He declined to learn what was necessary in order to be good at it. And then he sold that Fabergé egg for a very small fraction of what it was worth. He was careless."

So, it *was* Remy who had sold the Romanov egg described in Lucy's press clipping. I'd wondered about that and was glad to have it confirmed. A good start, but that one detail was like a single drop in a raging waterfall of misinformation and confusion. There was still so much I didn't understand. What had made Remy believe the codex was in Britain, on this Scottish estate?

"Try this." Fergus poured a glass of wine for Pierre. "You look as though you could do with a drink."

Pierre smiled and took a sip. "A St. Emilion Grand Cru. Very good," he commented.

"So back to Remy," I said. "Why did he send you here? And why did you come?"

"Before I say anything, I want to emphasize that I have committed no crime. That is why Inspector McMahon released me."

"We understand," Fergus said. "We're merely trying to understand what's been going on here."

Pierre sipped his wine and set the glass down carefully. "Remy told me the codex was worth millions and he would share the proceeds with me. If I had that sort of money, I would open my own restaurant, which is my dream. As to why here?" He gave an exaggerated shrug. "When news of the egg sale leaked out, someone went to his shop, enquiring about a book. They told Remy that the egg had once belonged to a Russian who also owned a valuable codex. Remy turned his shop inside out, but there was no sign of it. Then, he told me, he found a *billet*?" He frowned.

"A ticket? I asked. He shook his head.

"A receipt?"

"Yes, a receipt showing that his grandfather bought the egg and some jewelry from an Englishman in 1940. Then the war came and the shop closed for several years. His grandfather reopened it and ran it for some time until passing it on to his son, who then left it to Remy about three years ago." Pierre's nose wrinkled. "The place was a mess. Shelves loaded with junk, old cabinets full of paper. Remy had no idea what he owned or how much it was worth."

Given that Pierre had just declared his true opinion of his old friend, it surprised me that he'd gone along with this scheme. But I supposed the money was a big motivator.

"What led Remy to believe the codex would be in this castle, of all places?"

Pierre picked at a piece of lint on his trousers. "Remy never told me the name of the visitor who explained the connection between the Fabergé egg and the old book. But that person must have provided enough information for him to follow the lead to the English dealer. You'd have to ask Remy."

"We would, if we knew where he was." Fergus slitted his eyes at Pierre. "You really don't know?"

"I swear, I don't. He lied to me. He said he was taking a bus to Oban to start his hiking trip. That's the last time I saw him."

"Remy doesn't look like the hiking type," Josh said. "You can't have believed that's really what he planned to do?"

Pierre shrugged again. I wanted to go over and put my hands on his shoulders to keep them in place.

"So, did Remy kill Duncan?" Fergus moved his upper body closer to the Frenchman, like a lion moving in for the kill.

"Why would he? He had never heard of Duncan before he arrived at the castle."

That might be true, I reflected, but it didn't mean their paths hadn't crossed at some point over the weekend.

"Did Remy know Lucy Cantrell?" I asked.

"Lucy? The blonde woman? No, I think not. Her name was not mentioned at any time." He finished his wine and stood. "May I leave now? I have cooperated with the police. I have answered your questions. And now I am tired and wish to sleep."

"You searched for the codex for four months and didn't find it?" I said. "How hard did you try?"

Pierre looked indignant. "I hunted through the whole house, or most of it anyway. The book is not here, of that I am sure."

"Good to hear you were so thorough," Fergus said drily.

Finally, the chef showed a brief sign of contrition. He lowered his eyes. "I am sorry for lying to you." He looked up. "But you must admit my dinners were a success, no?"

"They were, but you won't be doing them anymore." Fergus leaned back in his chair and crossed his arms.

"You're letting me go?"

"What did you expect? You've been snooping around my house and digging through my things. You may be a great chef, but your actions have left a bitter taste in my mouth. We're done here."

"You might think we are. But this is not the end of it." Pierre stood and stalked out of the room.

"Was that a threat?" I asked. "We should advise McMahon to keep an eye on him."

"We can do that, but I'll be happy never to see Pierre again." Fergus glared at the doorway as though daring the Frenchman to return.

I didn't blame him. Learning that Pierre had been planted in the castle specifically to search for the codex had really ticked me off, too.

After a long silence, Josh spoke. "Shall we carry on looking for the Russian novels?"

"I'm not sure I see the point, to be honest," Fergus said. "I've had more than enough of old books for one night. Besides, our gallant Frenchman searched for the elusive codex for four months with no success, which makes me wonder if it really exists."

Trying to not let Fergus's doubts dent my optimism, I stood up and collected the dinner plates. At least I would save Mrs. Dunsmore a trek up from the kitchen. As I gathered up the silverware, Josh got to his feet and began pacing between the table and the window, back and forth several times. Arbroath seemed to find that interesting and lifted his shaggy head to track Josh's movements, thumping his tail against the floor in time with Josh's footsteps.

"What are you doing, laddie?" Fergus asked.

"If it weren't dark, I'd go for a run." Josh paused briefly in his perambulations. He cricked his neck from side to side. "I hate to complain, but I'm not used to going so long without exercise. I brought my running gear with me but haven't had much chance to use it."

"What a load of tosh," his uncle said. "Are you scared of the dark? Go out and run up and down the driveway. It's two hundred meters long, more or less."

"I'll come with you," I offered. I'd been feeling the same way, cooped up and out of shape.

"What if Remy's out there?" Josh asked. "I mean, I don't care for myself, but we don't want to give him another chance to have a bash at Kate."

"Take Arbroath. And I'll call Lachlan in and he can sit with me, so you don't worry about my being alone in the house."

Josh grinned. "Okay. You coming, Kate?"

Fifteen minutes later, dressed in sweats and running shoes, we stepped outside with Arbroath loping along beside us. The rain had diminished to a light drizzle, and it felt good to be out in the cool night air. The crescent moon peeked between scudding clouds, lining their outer edges with silver and throwing just enough light for us to see the path. Arbroath was excited, running ahead and then back to us as though encouraging us to run faster.

After twenty or so laps, I was out of breath and turned towards the house. The building loomed ahead, its lit windows throwing polygons of light onto the ground below. On the west side, the crenellated ramparts of the tower were silhouetted against a moon-lit cloud. To the left, the east wing appeared as a solid black rectangle. From the outside, in the dark, it looked intact with no hint that the interior lay in ruins.

I turned to check on Josh. He was jogging up the drive towards me. I pointed to the front door, indicating that I was going in, and he waved in acknowledgement.

Turning around, I took a few steps towards the house and then stopped, perplexed. I swiveled my head to gaze up at the moon. It was still half-shrouded in cloud, emitting only a pale glow that bleached the color from the grass and trees. And yet I was sure I'd seen light reflecting on the damaged roof of the east wing. I walked closer and stopped when something glinted again, high up on the tiles.

Josh arrived next to me, breathing hard. "What are you looking at?"

I pointed. "Do you see lights up there?"

We both stared for a full minute, but the roof remained dark. "It must have been the moon shining on the slate." Josh shivered. "I'm getting cold. Let's go in."

After one last examination, I followed him inside, and we pulled on the sweatshirts we'd left on the hall bench. Lachlan strode from the drawing room, accompanied by Fergus, who fussed over Arbroath as though he'd been gone for days. The dog shook himself wildly, spreading droplets of water all over the tiles.

"G'night," Lachlan said. "I'll be on my way."

"See you around lunchtime tomorrow," Fergus said.

"Aye, bright and early." The groundskeeper nodded goodnight and left through the front door, closing it behind him. He was an odd one; so aloof and withdrawn, he was almost sinister. I still thought he deserved to be on my suspect list, in spite of Fergus's objections.

"Good run?" Fergus asked us.

"Yep." Josh rubbed a calf muscle, which sometimes spasmed after he'd been exercising.

"Are you all right, Kate?" Fergus gazed at me. "You're looking pensive."

"I thought I saw a light up on the roof on the east wing."

Fergus exchanged glances with Josh. "It was moonlight," Josh said. "What else could it be?"

"Can we check inside? Just to be sure?" An idea had struck me. "It could have been light from a torch shining out through the gaps in the tiles."

Only Arbroath's exuberant shaking broke the ensuing quiet.

"Let's take a gander," Fergus said, somewhat to my surprise. Until now, he'd seemed so averse to talking about the east wing, baffled that anyone would have thought to enter it.

After grabbing a couple of torches from the hall cupboard, we climbed the stairs, pausing briefly while Fergus told Arbroath to stay. The big dog wagged his tail hopefully until his master repeated the instruction. With a sigh, Arbroath slumped to the black and white tiled floor, head resting on his front paws.

When we reached the east wing door, Fergus went in first. The door creaked as he eased it open, letting in light from the corridor. Beyond the first few meters though, the space was black, the darkness impenetrable. I looked up through the ruined ceiling to the rafters and the underside of the roof. In several places, thin slivers of grey light revealed spaces between the boards.

"There." I pointed upwards. "There are gaps. If someone were in here with a torch, the light would be visible from outside."

"But there's no one," Josh pointed out. Fergus clicked on his torch and gave the other to Josh. I blinked in the sudden brightness. Apart from the blighted furniture, the salon was empty. There couldn't have been anyone inside. In a way that was a relief. We didn't need any intruders to add to the chaos, but it left me wondering what I'd seen from the driveway.

"Bloody hell," Fergus murmured, surveying the ravaged room. "I haven't been in here for years. It's worse than I remember. I never liked coming in here. Too many bad associations, I suppose, of the war and the bomb that killed my great-aunt."

Skirting the hole in the floor, Josh toured the once-grand salon, stopping occasionally to examine the mildewed furniture and damaged artwork. "I seem to remember that roll-top desk was on the inventory list," he said. "We never found it in the main house."

Fergus joined him in front of the desk. "My father said this was my grandfather's favorite piece of furniture." He patted the ornate inlaid top. "He sat at it to write letters and pay his bills. Maybe I should have moved it and had it renovated."

"You still could, and we could try to find that Queen Anne tallboy too," I suggested. "It might be downstairs. Shall we go look?"

"I'm not sure we should be rambling about in the darkness," Fergus said. "We can come back in the morning."

"It won't make any difference. It's perma-dark in here with all the windows boarded up."

"All right, but be very careful. Kate, you lead the way and I'll bring up the rear."

I picked my way around the room to the green-painted door that led to the landing and the stairs to the lower story.

"The staircase is in bad shape, so hang on to the banisters, or what's left of them anyway," I warned the others. As I turned the old-fashioned porcelain knob and eased the door open, I heard a noise. It seemed to come from downstairs. "Did you hear that?"

Josh nodded. "It sounded like a door slamming."

"Opening this one probably caused a draft," Fergus suggested. "Let's go check it out."

Cautiously, staying close to the wall, we descended the shattered staircase to the hall below.

"They reversed the layout in this wing," Fergus said. "The salon took up the entire top floor to take advantage of the views. There were windows on three sides, and lots of natural light, rather like the Great Hall in the main building."

"So these are bedrooms?" Josh poked his head around a plank of wood that dangled from one hinge, and pointed the torch inside.

"Five of them, if I remember rightly, two bathrooms, and a dining room," Fergus said, as we followed Josh into the first bedroom.

"Is the door upstairs the only access point to the main house?" I asked.

"No. There's a passageway from the scullery here to the big kitchen in the main building. The servants used the big kitchen to do most of the food preparation and then brought them through here to the dining room. There's a wine cellar on this side. I'll show you before we leave. But take a look around first, if you like."

I followed Josh into one of the bedrooms, which was dominated by a four-poster bed with carved newels. Remnants of red silk hung in tatters from the wooden panel overhead, and the quilt on the bed was ripped, leaking its feather stuffing in grey mounds. A nice place for a mouse to nest, or perhaps a whole colony of mice.

Josh seemed to be enjoying himself, sweeping the torchlight along the walls, exclaiming at the damage. Sidestepping a massive cobweb that joined a crystal chandelier to the back of a faded floral wingback chair, I wondered how big the web's architect was and tried not to dwell on it. I didn't mind spiders, just not very large ones.

Josh led the way into another bedroom where the floor boards were splintered and the ceiling, ten feet above our heads, had a gaping hole in it. He held the torch up, highlighting the jagged edges of the salon floor. "That must be where the bomb crashed through. Can you imagine if it had actually gone off?"

We wandered back into the hall. "Which door could have slammed?" I asked. Three of the rooms still had functional doors and two of them were closed.

"Let's take a look," Josh said. Fergus stayed in the hall, examining some pictures that hung askew on the walls.

We examined the last bedroom and the dining room where two silver candelabra festooned with cobwebs stood on a broad wooden table. It was creepy, but here was no sign of anyone or anything untoward. When we rejoined Fergus, he was looking at a painting of two horses. He unhooked it and tucked it under his arm, sneezing as dust flew up from the gilded frame. "I suppose it would be a good idea to come through and rescue what I can," he said.

Josh agreed. "I saw a jewelry box on a dresser in the bedroom that I think my mum would like, if that's all right?"

"Of course. Anything you want."

"Great. I'll come back tomorrow with a bag and gather up a few things."

Fergus led us to a narrow door at the end of the hall. "This is the entrance to the scullery and wine cellar." We passed through two small rooms with stone walls and wooden shelving, and through an arched opening into a corridor. "We'll go out this way instead of risking those stairs again," Fergus said. "They're a deathtrap."

"Funny," Josh said. "I knew about this passageway when I was a kid, but my mum was adamant that I never come to the east wing. She was terrified I'd fall through a hole or that the remains of the roof would collapse."

The corridor was narrow, with a flagstone floor. A series of gas lamps hung on the green-painted walls.

"No electricity?" I asked.

"The castle didn't get electricity until the mid-1940s," Fergus explained. "And even then it was limited to the main part of the house. The tower wasn't wired until the '60s, and of course the east wing never was. When I was a boy, I used to help change the mantles in the gas lamps in the bedrooms. I liked the light those lamps gave out, and that faint hissing noise of the gas in the pipes."

We continued walking until a sudden skittering noise made me jump. I grabbed hold of Josh's arm. "Only a mouse," he said, directing the torch at the flagstones. As he lifted the light, I put my hand on it to lower it again. "Look at that." I pointed to something that gleamed against the stone, then leaned over to pick it up. "It's a button."

Josh nodded. "So it is."

"But it's not old." I ran my finger over the silvered surface. "It's shiny. It must have been lost very recently."

"Well, you said that Lucy and Duncan had been in here. It could be one of theirs," Fergus said.

"But that would mean they knew about this passage."

"Duncan knew about it," Josh said. "One summer when were both staying here, he stole a bottle of cooking wine from the kitchen and sneaked in here to drink it. Then he boasted about it to me for days afterwards."

I examined the button more closely, trying to match it to anything I'd seen either of them wearing, but nothing came to mind. I slid it into my jeans pocket and caught up with Fergus, our footsteps echoing on the stone floors.

Rounding a curve in the corridor, we came to another door. Fergus pushed it open and I looked past him, expecting to see the kitchen but, instead, we walked into a narrow room lined with shelves that were piled with pots and pans.

"What is this?" I asked.

"We're in the old scullery. It's not been used for years." He crossed the room to a pine door, which he opened to reveal a larger space where there was an old-fashioned, coal-fired range, a farmhouse sink and a stone counter. "This is the servants' kitchen."

We continued on. Just around a corner was the butler's pantry and, beyond it, the kitchen, modern, clean and empty. Fergus turned on all the lights. In spite of myself, my eyes were drawn to the meat locker, and my mind rushed to finding Duncan in there.

I turned to look at Fergus. Under the bright halogen lights, his aura was moving so fast it made me nauseous. My skin chilled as the blood rushed to my feet, and I bent over, hands on my knees.

Josh hurried over and crouched in front of me. "Are you ill? What can I do?"

I shook my head. "I'm fine. It's Fergus. We're running out of time."

32

When daylight broke on Tuesday, I stumbled out of bed after a short and mostly sleepless night. Fearing that Fergus had little time left, I didn't want to waste any minutes at all. Josh had already gone, his side of the bed cold, so I threw on some clothes and hurried downstairs. Through the wide-open front door, I saw DCI McMahon talking to Fergus and Josh, with Arbroath keeping them company. I joined them on the front steps. The sky glowed pink, threaded with purple and gold, but a stiff breeze bent the bare branches on the trees and whispered in the gables.

McMahon was huddled in a navy blue waxed jacket with a red tartan scarf knotted at his neck. I shivered in my woolen cardigan.

"So Knox isn't a suspect?" Josh asked, clearly continuing a conversation that had already started.

McMahon shook his head. "He was on the suspect list, of course, but he told us that he and his two colleagues worked in his room after they left the party at midnight— through until about three-thirty a.m. All three swear to the other two being present the entire time. And Knox emailed me a copy of his phone record, showing a steady flow of calls to and from the head office in Palo Alto for those hours."

"He makes his employees work on weekends?" I said.

McMahon sighed. "A lot of us work on weekends."

"That's true, I'm sorry." Then something struck me about what he'd said. "He gave you his phone records, but there's no mobile service in the castle. I can't use my phone at all here. There's no signal."

McMahon smiled. "Knox brought a satellite phone with him. He told me he knew the service here was almost non-existent and so he came prepared. I got the impression he regards Scotland as still being in the dark ages when it comes to technology."

"You mean he's in the clear?"

"I believe so."

Fergus nodded. "Well, I for one am glad to hear it. I'm trusting that Knox only has the best possible intentions with regard to the estate purchase."

I put my hand on Fergus's arm, averting my eyes from the aura that rotated in the soft morning light like an eddy in a clear pool.

"And the other piece of news I wanted to share with you is that I reviewed the CCTV footage from the pub car park again." The wind tugged at McMahon's scarf. He pulled it more tightly around his neck. "It's my opinion that Remy was after Kate." He looked directly at me. "We can place him at the car park when you left the Land Rover and crossed the road to go to the cafe. So, he certainly knew it was you driving the vehicle, not Fergus."

"How would he have known I was there?" I asked. "It's the first time I've left the castle."

"I wondered that too," McMahon said. "I assume he must have been watching the place. He saw you leave and followed you to the village."

"Charming." My skin prickled at the thought of Remy stalking me.

"Why would Remy want to kill Kate?" Josh asked.

"I don't think he intended to kill her. Messing with brake cables is a highly unreliable way of getting rid of someone. It's more likely he just intended to scare her. He must have known Kate was conducting her own enquiries and he was, presumably, nervous she would soon be able to identify him as a killer."

"You think that Remy killed Duncan?" Josh asked.

McMahon took a deep breath. "I can't confirm that yet. But I do believe Remy killed Nick."

I gasped. I'd almost forgotten about poor Nick.

"What brings you to that conclusion?" Fergus asked. He hadn't shaved, and grey stubble dotted his chin and cheeks.

"I'm not at liberty to say quite yet," McMahon said, "I have a lot of questions for him. Oh, and I understand Nick's funeral is this after-noon? Are you going?"

Fergus nodded. "Of course. Mr. Jameson called to ask me."

I exchanged glances with Josh. I hadn't realized the service had been scheduled already.

"I'll be there as well," McMahon said. "Sometimes murderers can't help but turn up to watch their victim's funeral. It's sick, but it happens."

"Shall we go inside?" Fergus asked, rubbing his hands together to warm them.

"You go ahead," McMahon said. "I'll be off. Lots to do."

"One thing," I said to him, digging in my cardigan pocket. "Last night, we found this button in a passageway that leads from the kitchen to the old east wing." I held it out. "It looks new. Could it be important? I think it means someone used that passage recently."

"It's not in regular use," Fergus explained to the inspector. "Most people don't even know it's there."

McMahon turned the button over in his hand. "Could be from a blazer or a jacket of some kind. Leave it with me. I'll run it by my team."

When he'd driven away, we went inside.

"I'd like to finish my breakfast," Fergus said. I followed him and Josh, and we served ourselves from the sideboard. I stuck to my now usual diet of tea and toast and marmalade.

"McMahon said Duncan's autopsy should be finished this morn-ing." Fergus said once we were all seated. "Then we'll be able to finalize plans for the funeral. Perhaps when Nick's service is over later today, I'll have chance to talk with the vicar and the funeral director." He ran his hands through his grey hair. "Two young men, two funer-als. Who would have thought?"

"Kate and I will do whatever we can to help," Josh said. "I've already heard back from most of the family that they'll come up for Duncan's service, and so will Duncan's boss, who'll also tell his work colleagues."

"What about Lucy?" Fergus asked. "Will she come back up?"

"I can ask her," I said. "She was still very upset when I talked to her last night. But I'm sure she'll come."

"You talked to Lucy?" Fergus asked, holding his fork in mid-air.

"Only briefly. I wanted to ask her about... never mind. It's not important. I'll ring her once you have the date and time and let you know what she says."

"I don't have a tie with me," Josh said after a pause. "Fergus, can you loan me one for the service this afternoon?"

"Yes, we'll get that sorted out. But first, I have a meeting with the solicitor about the sale. He should be here any minute."

"Do you want me to help?" Josh asked.

"It won't be that interesting," Fergus said. "We're going to finalize the wording on the contract. Why don't you spend some time with Kate? I'm feeling guilty. You two haven't exactly had a holiday here."

"*Dinnae fash yersel,*" I told him, proud of my one Scottish phrase. I'd been waiting for a good time to say it.

Fergus chuckled. "Very well, lassie, I won't worry about it."

"Maybe Kate and I can go back to the east wing to collect that jewelry box," Josh said. "And look for any other little bits and pieces we might want to rescue, if that's all right."

"Take anything you want. Just be careful," Fergus begged as he handed over the key. "No falling through holes or down the stairs, please."

As we stood up, Mrs. Dunsmore made one of her miraculously timed appearances to take away our plates. Josh and I loitered in the entry hall until Mr. Dunne arrived. Then, satisfied that Fergus had someone with him, we each took a torch from the hall cupboard and went upstairs. Josh unlocked the door, and we stepped into the east wing salon.

"Where do you want to start?" I asked.

"Might as well begin up here," Josh said. While he gathered mementoes, I planned to keep searching for clues as to what had drawn Lucy and Duncan here. We separated, Josh circling the hole in the floor to reach the built-in cupboards at the far end. I decided to check the roll-top desk. It was striking, with marquetry inlays and brass drawer pulls that gleamed in the light of the torch. The light also exposed several deep scratches along the front of the roll-top cover, almost as though someone had tried to lever the top open. When I tried to raise the lid, it gave an inch or two and then stuck. I put the torch on the floor and pointed it at the desk, then, using two hands, pulled on the top. This time it moved about ten inches, partially exposing the writing surface inside before snagging again. My best effort only produced a squeal of recalcitrant wood.

Bending down, I shone the torch inside to see the surface partly covered by a mildewed green blotter, which held an antique ink pen with a bone handle. At the back was an array of small drawers and compartments. I reached my hand in as far as I could, but couldn't open any of the drawers. Disappointed, I moved on. I could come back later with some lubricant, or maybe a pry bar, that would release the top and open up the interior.

Josh had been exploring the cupboards that flanked the fireplace. "Found these," he said, holding up a pair of silver candlesticks. "I'd like to look around downstairs. Are you ready?"

I edged around the hole and followed him down the ramshackle stairway. When he disappeared into the bedroom where he'd seen the jewelry box he wanted for his mother, I stayed in the middle of the spacious hall, swinging my torch around to examine the space.

On my previous visits, I hadn't noticed many of the finer details, like the crystal doorknobs and silk wall coverings. The floor's octagonal green and white tiles, though chipped in places and coated with dust, appeared to be well-preserved. I directed the light of the torch at the domed ceiling, where the painted flowers still bloomed and cherubs with pink cheeks fluttered on candy floss wings.

Choosing a bedroom at random, I stepped inside. Motes of dust danced in the light as I swung the torch around, looking for anything that might interest Josh. But the dresser surface was clear, and the door hung open on an empty armoire. About to leave, I noticed tracks on the dusty floor, leading from the door to the bed. I hadn't walked in that far, so it wasn't me who'd disturbed the dust. Slowly, I followed the trail of faint footprints to the end of the bed where the mattress sagged under a decaying yellow quilt. I doubted anyone would have come in here for a nap, so there had to be another reason. Bending down, I peeked under the bed, holding my breath, praying that a rat wouldn't come hurtling out from under there. Instead, by the light of the torch, I saw a plastic bag. Grabbing a corner, I pulled it towards me. It was heavy and it took a couple of heaves to bring it out into the open.

The white dustbin bag was the only thing in the east wing that wasn't covered in dust, which made me think it had been placed under the bed recently. I loosened the tie at the top and pulled the bag open. Inside was a stack of books. The title on the top one was embossed in flaking gold leaf. I couldn't read it but the Cyrillic alphabet was unmistakable. With a yelp of excitement, I called Josh's name.

He came running. "What's wrong?"

"Nothing. But look what I found."

Josh smiled when he saw the book and then he sneezed three times in a row. "Let's get out of here," he said, lifting the bag easily. "We'll take this over to the library, and I'll find Fergus to see if his meeting is over."

Fifteen minutes later, we were all seated around the library coffee table, with Arbroath at Fergus's feet. Josh lifted out the first book. It was thick, its tan leather cover water-spotted and darkened at the edges. With great care, he raised the cover. The frontispiece bore an engraving of a woman in an embroidered dress, with pearls around her neck and her hair piled high. Underneath was an inscription written in Russian with an ink pen.

"Can't understand a word," Josh commented, closing the book. He took another from the box and then another. By the time he'd finished, the table was covered with eleven leather-bound books, all with Russian titles embossed in peeling gold leaf.

"Is one of these the codex?" Fergus asked, leaning forward, running his fingers along the covers.

"I doubt it," I said. "For one thing, these are what I'd think of as normal size, quite a bit larger than the small volume I saw in the vision. And there should be twelve books in total. We only have eleven. But we should check each one, to be sure."

I turned the pages of the first book, which released a potent fragrance of dust and tobacco. The paper was fine, almost transparent, and filled with indecipherable type. As I expected, there were no drawings or diagrams. We gently leafed through each book. They were all similar, filled with dense text.

"So, who put the books under the bed?" Fergus asked. "And why?"

"Duncan," I said.

"Remy," Josh said at the same time. Fergus raised his brows.

"Duncan was searching the library, don't forget," I said. "If he knew about Anna's crate of books, he'd recognize their significance—so he hid them."

"But why? Why bother to move them?" Josh asked.

"Perhaps to confuse anyone else who might be looking for the codex or the egg or whatever he was really looking for." Something struck me. "Perhaps he was trying to hide the evidence from Lucy. You know they seemed to have an odd relationship. A little combative. Maybe he'd decided to work alone, cut Lucy out of the deal. We know he needed money. If he'd worked out that the codex was originally hidden with a collection of Russian novels, then he would assume that Lucy, or perhaps Remy, would be able to figure it out too. By concealing the books, he'd muddy the trail."

"That might have been what he was doing before he came to the party on Saturday," Josh said. "Or it could have been Remy who hid them, for much the same reason, to hinder anyone else who was looking."

"That's true," I agreed.

Arbroath snored softly. I wished I could sleep as easily as he did. My cumulative lack of sleep over the last five nights had fried my brain. Giving myself time to think, I stood and examined the bookshelves. "They were probably up there." I pointed to the top shelf in the furthest corner, where gaps were visible between the books, as though someone had spread them out to hide the missing volumes. A few lay horizontally, taking up more space. The absence of books wouldn't have been noticeable to a casual observer.

"Should we tell McMahon?" Josh asked.

Fergus grunted. "So someone moved a few books. That's not a crime. I doubt Inspector McMahon would be particularly excited about it."

"I think McMahon will be interested in everything that happened here this weekend," Josh said.

I pushed the ladder to the place where it seemed the books had been rearranged. From a high rung, I was able to look down on the surface of the shelf. Even the fastidious Mrs. Dunsmore didn't come up here very often. There was a fine layer of dust on the shelf, dotted with fingerprints and streaks where books had been moved around.

"We should get the police to check for prints," I said. "That would at least tell us who found the books and hid them."

"Do we assume that whoever discovered them also found the codex?" Fergus asked. "Isn't it likely that all twelve books were stored together?"

I came back down the ladder and went back to my seat. "If Duncan found the codex, then where is it?"

"It can't have been in his room because the police have searched there already," Josh pointed out. "If they'd found it, we'd know about it. If he put it somewhere unexpected, we may never find it."

My temples throbbed, and I massaged them with my fingers. "That's a depressing scenario."

"And if Remy found the book, why didn't he head for the hills with it instead of hanging around puncturing brake cables?" Fergus asked.

I picked a dog hair off my cardigan. "That's a good point. The fact he stayed local makes me think he can't be the one who discovered it. He's probably hoping for another chance to poke around."

Josh stood and wandered over to the drinks table to pour himself a glass of water. "Remy's still my number one suspect for killing Duncan," he said, coming back to his seat. "He had the most vested interest in finding the book. Think about it. He inadvertently sold that Fabergé egg for a pittance, then someone visits his shop and tells him about its connection to this priceless codex. Pierre told us Remy's not very savvy or very motivated, but he was smart enough to plant Pierre in the castle, months before Duncan or Lucy got here. For him, it's about more than the money. He wants to salvage his reputation as an antiques dealer too."

"You have a point, but why would he kill Duncan?" Fergus asked.

"Maybe Duncan worked out who Remy really was and threatened to tell the police. Or Duncan found the book, and Remy tried to force him to disclose where he'd hidden it. They quarreled, and Duncan ended up dead. Remy had access, don't forget. He was working in the kitchen until late that night."

Fergus cradled his head in his hands for a moment. When he looked up, his face was creased with worry.

Josh leaned over to put his hand on his uncle's shoulder. "I'm sorry. We should take a break from talking about all this. Anyway, I need to take a shower before we leave for the funeral."

At the reminder of Nick's funeral, Fergus got to his feet, grimacing as though his back hurt. "Me too. We can talk about this later."

"DCI McMahon will work it out," Josh said. "Try not to worry.

He'll catch Remy and stop him from doing whatever he intends to do next."

"I'm not worried about Remy coming after me," Fergus said. "I just wish to God I could have done something to save Duncan."

Fergus might not be concerned about Remy, but I was. Fergus's aura was moving fast. I prayed that Josh was right, that McMahon would find Remy Delacroix soon, before it was too late.

33

"The dog will be fine by himself for a few hours," Josh told me, knotting his borrowed tie with a practiced hand.

"Yes, but Fergus is fretting. It's only right that Mrs. Dunsmore and Lachlan want to go to Nick's funeral to pay their respects. I'll hang out with Arbroath and make some sandwiches for when you all get back." I smoothed the lapels on his jacket. "It's not really about the dog, although I'm happy to stay with him. Selfishly, I'd rather not go. You know funerals always remind me of Mum..."

The shock and grief of my mother's death still lingered, and mentions of funerals always reminded me of those awful days when we struggled to come to terms with the loss.

"I don't mind at all that you don't want to come. I understand," Josh said. "But I am worried about leaving you here alone."

"It's a castle. I'll lock the doors, lower the portcullis, and prepare the vats of boiling oil. Even Attila the Hun wouldn't stand a chance of getting in."

Josh smiled and gave me a kiss. "We'll come back the minute it's over. Fergus won't want to linger long."

A few minutes later, I stood on the doorstep with Arbroath, watching the four of them drive off in Josh's rental car. Fergus's eyes had lit up when we'd told him I'd stay with the dog. "Thank you," he said. "The old mutt's not used to being alone. There's always someone home with him. He needs to be let out frequently so he can tinkle."

When the car turned out of the gate, I beckoned the dog inside, contemplating what to do next. First, I wanted to ring Alistair Ross to tell him about the Russian novels. I was very happy we'd found them, but it was all very frustrating. We'd come so close, but we still had no idea where the codex or the egg were. All we really had were theories — and perhaps we were all wrong. Maybe the story of the chest of books concealing the codex was a myth. Maybe the codex had never left Finland.

And yet, I mused, perhaps it had. The Russian books were here, in the castle. There was every reason to believe that the codex had been part of that chest of valuables entrusted by Anna Vyrubova to her friend. He'd sold that chest, or at least some of its contents, to Cyril Thorpe, a dealer with a dodgy reputation who was hanging around in Paris looking for bargains. After that, what happened? Lucy had told us Thorpe had sold a crate of books to Gordon MacKenna. Had the egg and the codex been in that crate? Strangely, Remy had only told Pierre about the codex, not the egg. I sat on the hall bench to think things through, leaning against the wood panel-ing. Arbroath settled in front of me, resting his huge, shaggy head on my knee.

After Gordon MacKenna had purchased the books from Thorpe in 1940, had he then carefully chosen a place in Castle Aiten to keep his new acquisitions? A place high on the library shelves, not notice-able to a casual observer, but obvious to himself? Or had he randomly assigned the books to storage on the only shelf that still had space? Did he realize the significance of the codex or had he regarded it as simply another book?

Arbroath moved his head, tapping his nose against my hand, asking to be petted. When I obediently stroked his ears, he closed his eyes in doggy bliss. I felt faintly envious. Any version of bliss seemed far away for me right now. Turning my mind back to the question of the books, I recalled Fergus saying that his grandfather had been an avid and knowledgeable collector. Even if he didn't realize he had bought a famous codex, wouldn't he have figured out that he'd acquired something very unusual?

Arbroath's ears pricked and he shot towards the front door. Nervous, I followed him and checked that the door was locked, which it was. I hurried into the drawing room and peeked out of the window that had a line of sight to the entry steps. There was no one there.

"Silly Arbroath," I told him. He blinked at me and lay down. Within seconds he was snoring. I perched on the arm of a sofa, and picked at a loose thread on my cardigan. Unraveling the history of the books might be very interesting, but not helpful in getting me any closer to saving Fergus. Much as I hated to admit it, it seemed likely that only the police could do that. They had the resources and the manpower. I trusted Inspector McMahon.

Wondering if there was any news yet on the hunt for Remy Delacroix, I moved to the phone to call McMahon. But then I remembered he planned to attend Nick's funeral; I would just have to be patient for news from him. Instead, I rang Alistair Ross. When I told him there was no sign of the codex, he sounded as disappointed as we were, but asked if he could come over to look at the Russian books.

"Come whenever you like," I said. "I'm here all afternoon. Oh, and come to the tradesman's entrance at the back. I'll be down in the kitchen."

"I'll pop by soon. I'm finishing a late lunch."

Putting down the phone, I stood, gazing at Arbroath. "Want to help me make sandwiches?" I asked him.

We clattered down the back stairs into the kitchen, where I wandered around collecting ingredients. It was strange to be down there without Pierre or Mrs. Dunsmore. Or the police. Arbroath padded over to the back door and whined, reminding me of what Fergus had said about the dog needing regular loo breaks. I let him out, and he ambled off towards a cluster of bushes at the edge of the parking area. I was rummaging around in the butler's pantry for bread when I heard Arbroath barking outside, probably demanding to be let back in.

"I'm coming," I called, making note of the fact that I was talking to the dog out loud again, and headed back into the kitchen to let him in. Instead, at the door, stood Remy Delacroix. In shock, I dropped the bread and backed up towards the kitchen island. "What are you doing here?" I tried to keep my voice steady. Arbroath had stopped barking and was now sniffing Remy's shoes.

Ignoring the dog, Remy took two steps inside, leaving the kitchen door open. Was it my imagination, or did he appear as shocked to see me as I was to see him?

"I thought you'd be at the funeral with everyone else," he said.

"Funny, I thought you would be too." I remembered what Inspector McMahon had said about killers sometimes turning up to their victims' funerals.

Remy took another step towards me. Although not very muscular, he was tall. Clad head to toe in black, with dark, lank hair, he cut a menacing figure. I backed up again, sidling around the edge of the island.

"What do you want?" I asked.

I glanced towards the phone on the wall. It hung out of reach. I'd never get to it if Remy made a move. But he stayed where he was and held up both hands. "I'm not going to hurt you," he said. "But, as you're here, you can help me. Then I'll be on my way."

"Why should I help you? You nearly killed me."

Arbroath padded in, stopping once more to sniff at Remy's black jeans and sneakers and was rewarded with a pat on the head.

"You've got nothing to lose," Remy told me. "Give me thirty minutes without raising the alarm, and I'll leave you in peace."

"And if I don't?"

He put his hand inside his leather jacket. I tensed. Did he have a gun? A knife? But he pulled out a slim silver case. He opened it and took out a cigarette.

I took another step closer to the range, where the knife block sat, loaded with sharpened steel, apart from the one empty space. He watched me but stayed where he was. He looked exhausted, I saw now. The bright halogen lights over the kitchen island highlighted the dark stubble on his chin and purple circles around his eyes. The initial fear that had jolted me on seeing him ebbed away. It struck me that he might know where the book was hidden.

"Pierre said you were looking for the codex. Is there anywhere you didn't look?"

"Fergus's office. That was the hardest room to search. Pierre had no reason to be in that area of the castle, so he never went up there for fear of being caught. And I never had the opportunity to examine it myself."

My knees felt weak, and I put my hand on the counter to steady myself. I hadn't really considered Fergus's office as a potential hiding place. "You didn't hear about the fire?"

"Fire?" Remy's head jerked up.

"Let's just say that if the codex was in the office, it's now a pile of ashes."

"*Mon Dieu.*"

Exactly. For a moment, I actually found myself hoping that Duncan had hidden the book somewhere safe. Better that than it be lost forever. "Was it Duncan or Lucy who came to your shop in Paris to talk about the codex?" I asked.

Remy's dark eyebrows rose. "How did you hear about that?"

"Pierre said someone came, after you inadvertently sold a Romanov egg to a collector."

He crushed the cigarette, obviously unhappy to be reminded of his blunder. "It was Lucy," he said.

"She came to you, asking about items from the Romanov collection, right?" When he nodded in confirmation, I went on. "I think she had a theory that, as the Fabergé egg had gone unnoticed in your shop for nearly eight decades, it was possible the codex also lay neglected on a shelf somewhere, waiting to be found. What did she suggest? That you work together to find it?"

"Yes." He frowned. "She said that if we cooperated, she and Duncan would share the profits with me. A three-way split. That was an attractive offer, so I agreed. First of all, we examined every inch of the shop." He paused to extract another cigarette from the case. I remembered Pierre saying that the antique shop was a mess, that Remy had never organized it and had no idea what was on the shelves.

"We didn't find the codex, of course," Remy continued. "However, we uncovered a stack of old receipts in a box in the back. One of them was for the Romanov egg, purchased by my grandfather for a trivial amount. He bought it from a man called Louis Deauville. Lucy investigated him and discovered he was the friend of Anna Vyrubova, the Tsarina's lady-in-waiting."

"Not much of a friend," I said. "This man, Deauville, betrayed her. He took her treasures, hawked them for a few thousand dollars, and ran away to America."

Remy shrugged. "Apparently so."

"And the rest of Anna's treasure trove? The books and the codex? Did your grandfather buy those too?"

"It appears he did. The receipt showed the purchase of a box of twelve old books. He paid very little for them. But he made a small profit when he sold them to an English collector just a few weeks later."

"The Englishman was Cyril Thorpe."

"Yes. His name was on the receipt."

"And Thorpe sold the box of books to Fergus's grandfather."

"That's what Lucy thought, yes."

"Let me see if I have this straight. You enlisted Pierre to infiltrate the castle and search for the codex. But did Lucy and Duncan know you planned to do that?"

"No. By that time, we'd had...had a falling out. They didn't want to involve anyone else."

Remy moved towards me. I took another step back. We had the butcher block island between us now, and I intended to keep things that way. But, to my surprise, he didn't come any closer. Instead, he pulled out a stool and sat down. Arbroath, not showing much good judgment, stretched out at his feet as though they were the best of friends.

"Is that why you killed Duncan?" I asked.

"I didn't kill Duncan."

"You didn't kill Nick either, right?"

"Nick's death was an accident. He was threatening Pierre. He'd found him snooping around and guessed he was planning a robbery. He said he'd tell Fergus and have him fired. When I got here, I could see at once the bad feelings between them. I followed Nick out to the lochan on Friday and told him to mind his own business. We had a fight."

"You hit him with a rock and then left him there to die."

Remy covered his eyes with one hand. "It was an accident. I panicked."

"That doesn't sound like an accident to me."

"He'd been drinking and was irrational." He straightened up. "You weren't there to see how deranged he was. He tried to hit me with his whisky bottle."

My legs felt like jelly. For all of his pathetic excuses, Remy had just confessed to murdering Nick. I glanced again at the phone on the wall, wishing I could reach it to call the police. Remy must have noticed. "Don't even think about it," he said. The timbre of his voice had changed. It was lower, more threatening.

I contemplated my options. Could I bolt for the door and outrun him? Unlikely. He was closer to the door than I was, and I'd have to get past him.

"Okay," I said finally. "You didn't mean to kill Nick. But what made you decide to mess with the brakes on the Land Rover?"

"I'd been watching you. You were asking questions, poking around."

"Oh right. So naturally you tried to kill me."

"I didn't try to kill you. The idea was to scare you off, to stop you snooping."

That was what McMahon had thought. Not that it was much consolation for the hair-raising ride in the disabled Land Rover.

Remy's dark eyes stared unfocused at the unlit cigarette in his hand. "Nick's death was bad enough, but then Duncan showed up dead. The police were all over the place. It made it impossible to search where we wanted to. I decided to disappear for a while."

"You didn't do a very good job. The police caught you on CCTV at the pub car park. They're well aware you didn't leave the area. Listen," I said. "Why don't you turn yourself in? If you cooperate with the police, maybe they'll reduce the charges against you. Manslaughter instead of murder, something like that." I knew it was unlikely to be that easy, and I also believed Remy had killed Duncan. He could deny that to me all he liked, but the police would uncover the truth.

Arbroath stirred. He lifted his head and growled, looking towards the back door. Hauling himself to his feet, he barked as Alistair Ross poked his head around the door. "Can I come in?" he asked.

Remy shot to his feet. He looked like a scared rabbit. And he ran like one, sprinting to the door, where he shoved Alistair out of his way, throwing him to the floor. I wanted to run after him, but Alistair lay on his back, not moving. Fighting down my panic, I felt his wrist for a pulse. His eyelids fluttered open. "I'm all right. He just knocked the breath out of me," he gasped. "Go on, see if you can find the blighter."

At the door, I caught a glimpse of Remy disappearing into the undergrowth beyond the parking area. I had no intention of following him out on to the moors and I had to be sure Alistair wasn't hurt. When I went back to him, he insisted he was fine and suggested I call the police, so I hurried to the phone and rang 999. The operator listened while I explained the situation and asked her to track down Inspector McMahon. By the time I'd finished the call, Alistair had taken a seat on the stool Remy had just vacated, and Arbroath had gone back to sleep as though nothing had happened.

"What was that all about?" Alistair asked. He said again that he wasn't hurt, simply a bit shaken up, so I put the kettle on and put tea in a pot while I explained about Remy and his connection to the codex.

"Are you comfortable enough here?" I asked as I handed Alistair a mug of tea. "Do you want to lie down?"

"I most certainly do not want to lie down. I've survived far worse, young lady, far worse."

"All right." I kept an eye on him, worried that he was just being brave. "I'm supposed to be making sandwiches for when the others get back from Nick's funeral, and I haven't even started. But I can take you up and show you the Russian books if you like?"

"No, you do your sandwiches, and I'll enjoy my tea. We can go up later. I'm glad to hear you found the books. No codex, though. Any ideas?"

"Remy suggested the codex could have been hidden in Fergus's office," I said, as I sliced cheese and opened a jar of Branston pickle.

"That's a terrible thought," Alistair said. "The book would have been destroyed."

"But I think it's more likely Duncan has hidden it."

Alistair's eyes widened. "Can you elaborate?"

I thought about what we knew so far. Everything pointed to Lucy and Duncan collaborating on the search and trying to cut Remy out. They must have been furious when he turned up at the castle. I quickly filled Ross in on the details of Lucy's visit to Remy's shop in Paris and their agreement to look for the codex together. "I think Lucy found evidence of the Russian books while she was helping Fergus with an inventory of the contents of the library. Duncan moved them the night of the party. It was only after we found the books under the bed that we examined the library shelves and noticed an empty space on a top shelf that Fergus couldn't recall seeing before."

"Yes," Alistair said. "It's easy to ignore the obvious when you're not looking for it." His brows met over his nose as he frowned in concentration. "But why move them? No one else knew their significance."

I stopped spreading butter on the bread. "Remy did. If he'd seen them, he'd conclude that the codex had been brought here with them. But if there are no novels, there's no proof that the chest of books had ever been here. Lucy and Duncan were just trying to close off his search and give themselves more time to find the codex themselves. Ever since they got here on Thursday night, they've been foraging through the castle. The book inventory project provided the perfect excuse for Lucy to sift through the library."

I dropped the knife and retrieved it, sticking it in the sink before finding a clean one. Something struck me. "The inventory, of course. That's where Knox comes in."

"Stanton Knox? The buyer?"

"I'm quite certain that Knox and Lucy knew each other. Fiona saw them together in Lucy's room."

Alistair's cheeks bloomed red.

"Nothing like that," I said. "At least I don't think so. But I'm fairly sure they were collaborating."

"You've put butter on that slice of bread three times," Alistair pointed out. I contemplated the goopy mess I'd made and began scraping some of it off.

"Does Knox know about the codex as well?" he asked. "All three of them were in on it? But if Knox were after the codex, why bother with all the clandestine sneaking around? He could simply wait until he owned the estate and take all the time he needed to find it."

"Not if he thought Lucy and Duncan would find it before the sale was concluded. Perhaps he was worried they were going to cut him out of the deal. So he comes up with the idea of buying the estate, gives himself the leverage he needs. All along, he's been hurrying the sale through. Once the estate is his, the codex is too, as long as his former collaborators don't beat him to it."

"Well, that's not going to happen now," Ross said. "Duncan's dead and Lucy's out of the picture."

"So we have to find it before Knox signs on the dotted line," I said as I pressed the last slice of bread on top of the cheese and pickle filling. "We can persuade Fergus to slow things down a bit. He's got plenty of good excuses to miss a deadline or two."

34

The blare of sirens jolted Arbroath from his sleep, and he jumped up, his paws sliding on the tile floor. Seconds later, several uniformed police officers barged into the kitchen, followed by Inspector McMahon. "Where is he?" he asked.

"Gone," I said. "He ran off when Mr. Ross arrived. I think he was cutting through the garden towards the moors. I'm sorry I couldn't keep him here."

"Well, as long as you're safe," McMahon said. "Don't worry. We'll catch him."

He gave instructions to the officers. "Use the car radio to put out an APB for Remy Delacroix. Check the bus stop and get people out to the train station in Oban."

Once the officers had jumped into their cars and driven off, McMahon asked me a few questions about my unexpected visitor. He took notes in his battered notebook and then told us to be cautious and to secure the place in case Remy returned.

From the door, I watched him cross the gravel parking area, his sturdy shoes crunching on the stones. When he reached his car, I turned back into the kitchen and refreshed Alistair's tea. He still looked a bit pale. We both jumped when we heard a door slam upstairs and footsteps on the back stairs. My heart rate shot up as Arbroath sprinted off, but I relaxed when I heard Fergus greeting him.

"Kate?" Josh called.

"I'm here. Everything's okay."

The second Fergus appeared at the bottom of the staircase, I saw that his aura still swirled over his head. Why? Surely the danger was over? Remy wouldn't risk coming back to the castle, not now. The police were right behind him. He'd be lucky to get to Oban before they caught him.

A nasty cold sensation coiled in my stomach. Remy seemed to be out of commission, effectively prevented from doing harm. Lucy was in London and the police were about to pay her a visit. Who was left? Who or what threatened Fergus? Perhaps I'd been wrong all along. Maybe he was going to have that heart attack I'd been worrying about, or fall down the stairs, or bang his head on the bathtub. Something I had almost no chance of preventing. Disheartened, I blinked away the tears that blurred my vision.

Mrs. Dunsmore followed Fergus into the kitchen, removed her coat and hat and began arranging my sandwiches on a platter. "Thank you for doing this, Kate. We're all in sore need of some sustenance, I think."

Lachlan, who'd trailed down after her, declined to join us and said he had some work to do. When he'd gone, Mrs. Dunsmore smiled ruefully. "He should eat, but he's had enough of people for one day. A couple of hours of enforced company is about his limit. I doubt we'll see him again before dinner."

Fergus looked at me, then at Alistair. "Has something happened? Alistair, you're looking a bit peaky."

"Remy paid us a visit," I said. "When Alistair arrived, he ran away. DCI McMahon was here, briefly, and the police are out looking for Remy now."

"Bloody hell. Well, sit down, sit down. Tell us all about it."

We all settled round the big island, drinking tea and eating the sandwiches, which weren't bad considering my lack of concentration when I'd made them. I brought everyone up to date on what Remy had told me.

"Good God, Kate. You were alone here with a murderer," Josh said, his cheeks almost as pale as Alistair's.

"He never threatened me. And he claims he didn't intend to kill Nick."

"Good try, but I don't believe that for a minute," Josh said. "So, what do we do next?"

"We stay busy," his uncle replied. "We let the police do their jobs, and we'll get on with planning Duncan's service and cleaning the place up ready for the handover to Knox."

"That will still be a month or two, won't it?" I asked. "You've got plenty of time." If Alistair and I were right, then Knox was highly motivated to keep things moving at a fast clip. We needed more time to search for the codex ourselves.

"Aye, but consider how much there is to do with clearing out my personal things, my papers, and the furniture I want to keep."

Fergus finished chewing on his sandwich while Mrs. Dunsmore described Nick's funeral service and praised the vicar's heart-warming sermon. She and Alistair talked about a few people who'd attended the service and then drifted into a discussion about her scone recipe.

"I've been thinking," Fergus said to Josh and me. "You two should get yourselves back to London. I'm sure your boss isn't too happy about all the days you're missing, and I will manage quite well here with Lachlan and Mrs. D. You can come back up for Duncan's funeral, whenever that will be."

"We'll leave when everything is resolved," Josh said.

"You mean when this aura disappears— or whatever is going to happen to me actually happens?"

"Nothing will happen to you."

Fergus didn't answer. He took another sandwich from the platter.

"I promised I would show Alistair the Russian books," I said, to change the subject. "And he wants to peek inside the east wing, if that's okay?"

Fergus waved his sandwich at me, which I took as a yes. I quickly conferred with Josh, who said he would stay with his uncle. While I carried our dirty plates to the sink, the wall phone rang, and Fergus answered it. He was silent during the short call, apart from a 'thank you' at the end.

"That was Inspector McMahon. They've picked up Remy Delacroix; he's in custody. He was on his way to Pierre's flat. And they're bringing Pierre in again and will hold him as a possible accessory to murder."

"Pierre's still here?" Josh asked. "I assumed he'd have rushed straight back to Paris."

"Pierre's convinced he did nothing wrong," Fergus reminded him. "He had no reason to run."

Perhaps not, but Fergus's aura was still moving rapidly over his head, even though the police now had Remy in custody. They didn't have Pierre yet. Was he the threat? But if so, why? I felt like banging my head against a wall. There was something I was missing. Leaning against the sink, I ran through the possibilities. My eyes rested on Mrs. Dunsmore, but I rejected that idea immediately. What would she do? Feed Fergus poisoned lemon shortbread? Lachlan was a mystery. He was going out of his way to avoid spending any time with us, but that wasn't necessarily a sign of a man plotting to kill his employer.

I found myself eyeing kind, gentlemanly Alistair Ross. He wasn't on my suspect list, but was that an omission I should correct? He knew more about the codex than any of us. Perhaps our request for assistance had come like manna from heaven, giving him unfettered access to the castle and to information he might not have otherwise had.

The idea seemed ridiculous. "Shall we start with the east wing?" I asked him. When he stood up, I eyed his neat tweed suit and clean white shirt. "But I have to warn you, the place is a mess. Cobwebs, dust. Are you sure you want to see it?"

"Absolutely sure."

"If you're going into the east wing, you'll need the torches," Josh said. He got up, opened a kitchen drawer and pulled out two Maglites.

Each holding one, Alistair and I set off through the old scullery and through the pine door into the passageway that ran under the house. As we passed the place where I'd seen the button, I stopped. I had a memory of a cardigan with silver buttons that Lucy had worn. Still pondering it, I continued walking until we reached the small east wing scullery and then out into the hall with the painted ceiling.

Alistair was fascinated, poking around, murmuring to himself. I let him take his time, but I was jumpy and stayed close to him, unsure whether I needed the comfort of his presence or the reassurance that he could get up to no mischief if I watched him closely.

Inside the first bedroom, he examined the rotting furniture, swinging his torch around and commenting on the damage. A curtain stirred at the boarded-up window. A floorboard creaked. Was someone there, lurking among the shadows in the corners? As the torchlight meandered along the perimeter of the room, I was sure I heard a footstep in the hall. My heart sped up.

"Did you hear that?" I asked Alistair.

He looked over at me blankly, shielding his eyes from the light I was pointing at him. "What?"

I shook my head. "Nothing. Never mind." I pointed the Maglite at the bed. "See here, this is where the books were hidden."

Alistair bent down to look under the bed frame and then straightened up, sneezing. We moved on to examine another couple of bedrooms, tableaux frozen in time from the moment the bomb came crashing through the roof.

Finally, we crossed the green and white tiled floor of the central hall and arrived at the base of the rotting staircase.

"Perhaps we should go around the other way and come in through the upstairs," I suggested.

"Young lady, I may look old to you, but I still ramble ten miles on Saturdays and I recently completed the Hadrian's Wall hike. I can manage a few stairs. You lead on."

We reached the top without mishap and crossed the sloping landing to the door that led to the salon.

"Marvelous," Alistair said when we were inside. He was gazing at the limestone fireplace as I held my torch up high to illuminate the space as much as possible. After a circuit of the room, he came to a halt in front of the roll-top desk. "This is a fabulous piece." He ran his hand over the walnut inlays.

"The lid is stuck. I tried to open it but could only get it halfway. That's as far as it goes."

"Too bad." His voice was muffled as he bent down to peer inside as I had done earlier in the day. "You should convince Mr. MacKenna to have this renovated. In good condition, it'd be worth a lot." He ran his fingers over some scratches on the front panel. "It appears that someone tried brute force to open it at some point."

The door rattled just then, and we both jumped. It was silly to imagine an intruder, but I still blew out a breath when Fergus stepped in. "Just checking on how you're doing," he said.

"I was admiring this wonderful desk." Alistair patted the surface. "It's really quite beautiful. I hope you might consider rescuing it and restoring it to its former glory."

"Yes, I intend to. I've been thinking about it since Kate told me it was here."

"The lid is sticking," I said. "I tried to look inside."

"I'll have a go with a bit of oil later on then."

"And I saw the Queen Anne tallboy downstairs in one of the bedrooms," I went on. "Remember, it was on the list, but we didn't find it in the main house? It's in decent condition, considering. Imagine it all refurbished and shiny. It has fan-shaped insets on each of the drawers."

"We'll salvage it," Fergus said. "At least I'll bring some of my grandparents' belongings with me, wherever I end up." He gazed around the room for a second. "It's very sad that the place was abandoned. I feel a bit guilty that I haven't paid it any attention for the last ten years. I should have made more of an effort to reclaim what I could."

"Well, it was abandoned a long time before you got here. Besides, it happens a lot with these old houses, doesn't it?" I said, trying to cheer him up. "To save money, whole wings are closed off, even when they're in good shape. And this one would have cost a fortune to repair. I don't think you should feel bad about it."

"Maybe not." He rubbed his hands together. "It's chilly in here."

"Have you seen enough?" I asked Alistair, who was examining the fireplace. "If so, we can sit in the drawing room to look at the books."

"Yes, of course. Whenever you're ready."

Once we were all back out in the corridor, Fergus paused to pull the door closed and then caught up with us. As we passed the library, he stopped. "I left Josh reading over some paperwork, so you two go ahead. We'll join you once we're finished up here."

After the chill and damp of the east wing, I was happy to see the fire lit in the drawing room. Alistair and I sat on the sofa in front of the coffee table where the Russian novels were stacked. With great reverence, he lifted up the first book and examined the title. "Fascinating."

"None of us speak Russian," I said.

"Me neither." He turned the tissue-thin pages. "They are lovely to look at, though."

He worked his way through the pile of books, examining each one while I looked over his shoulder.

"I wonder what this is?" He pointed at the title page of the book he'd just opened. Under the printed Cyrillic title was a handwritten number. '51088.' The script was cursive and neat, penned in black ink that had rusted with time. Around the numbers was a hand-drawn rectangle, half an inch high and about two inches wide.

Alistair adjusted his glasses and peered at the figures for a few seconds before closing the cover. He put it aside and opened the next one. The indecipherable black type blurred as my mind wandered, contemplating Fergus's uncertain future. The uneasy feeling I'd had in the east wing had dissipated while we examined the books, but now returned in full force. I felt my heart rate spike and my palms grow damp. I needed to see Fergus.

"Wait here for me," I said. Alistair looked startled, but he nodded. I ran out of the drawing room and up the stairs. When I reached the library, the doors were open, but the room was empty. That made me feel a little better. At least Josh was with his uncle somewhere. I wondered if they had gone to the east wing to look at the roll-top desk and decided to try there first. As I rounded the corner, I breathed a sigh of relief when I saw that the door was ajar. I was right, then, that they'd come here. When I reached the door, I pushed it further open and peeked in. The salon was filled with white light from a battery-operated hurricane lamp placed on the floor close to the desk. Next to it, Fergus stood with a spray can in his hand, obviously trying to free up the broken roll-top.

I stepped inside, glad to see Fergus working on the beautiful desk. *The desk.* I thought about the scratches on the front panel, as though someone had tried to force their way in. Someone looking for the codex?

"Fergus..." I stopped when I heard a noise, a creak in a floorboard in the hallway outside. Before I had time to turn around, something slammed into me from behind, and I stumbled and fell to my knees.

Fergus turned. "What the..." He didn't get any further before a figure dressed in jeans and a hoodie flew towards him, hand raised. Glimpsing a strand of blond hair, I realized it was Lucy. And she had a knife in her hand, the eight-inch carving knife that was missing from the kitchen.

35

"Get out, Fergus," I yelled, but Lucy had already grabbed his arm, sliding the blade under his chin.

"Shut up, Kate," she said. "Any more shouting and I'll kill him, understood?"

I clambered to my feet, a shooting pain burning my left knee. "What do you want?"

"The codex, of course. Nice of Fergus to be making it easier for me."

"I'm not making anything easy for you." Fergus dropped the can and watched it roll away. It teetered for a second on the splintered edge of the hole in the floor and then fell in, landing with a tinny clatter in the room below.

Keeping the point at his neck, Lucy motioned me closer. "Come and make yourself useful. And don't even think of trying any heroics."

I walked to the desk, taking the opportunity to squeeze Fergus's hand for a second. He squeezed back. I wondered where Josh could be.

Lucy nodded towards the curtains that hung at the boarded-up window. "Secure Fergus's hands behind his back. Use the tiebacks."

"No."

"I would cooperate if I were you." Lucy pushed the point of the blade into Fergus's neck, drawing a single drop of blood.

"Just do it," Fergus said. Reluctantly, I unhooked the braided rope ties. Once crimson, they'd faded to dirty pink. I hoped they'd fall apart in my hands, but they felt surprisingly sturdy. I took them and wrapped them around Fergus's wrists, knotting them loosely.

"Pull them tight, Kate. And get a move on. We don't have all day. Now, roll the lid all the way up."

I heaved on the pulls with both hands. Although the lid squealed in protest, I persevered and managed to get it to the open position. Then I tugged open the first drawer, which yielded a handful of mold-splotched papers. When I held the pages out to Lucy, she shook her head.

"You look at them. Tell me what they are."

She shifted the grip on her knife, holding it more firmly against Fergus's neck, her other hand grasping his upper arm.

As I leafed through the papers, dust and mold spores flew up, making my nose itch. "They're bills," I said. "Mostly from food merchants. And this one seems to be an invoice from a gardener. It's dated November 1939."

"Throw them on the floor. Check the next drawer."

I did, retrieving more stacks of bills, all dated between late 1939 and May 1941. At Lucy's insistence, I went through each drawer, removing piles of paper: invoices, bank statements and letters addressed to Gordon MacKenna or his wife, Helen. Although historically interesting, their presence seemed to infuriate Lucy.

"Enough with the drawers. Lift the blotter out of the way," she instructed.

I paused, considering my options, but they were very limited. I raised my eyes to look at Fergus, trying to communicate with him. If we both moved at the same time, surely we could overpower Lucy, even with his hands tied. It seemed that she read my mind though. She pressed the edge of the blade into the soft flesh under Fergus's chin until a thin red line appeared, leaking blood.

"Stop it," I said, holding both hands up in the air. "Don't hurt him."

"Then do what I say. Raise the blotter." I did, revealing the desk's surface, gleaming and unscathed by time. An inlay of light-colored wood formed a decorative geometric pattern in the center.

"Push on that." She pointed to a small circle of pearly white wood right in the middle of the inlay. When I pressed it, I heard a click. At the back of the desk a panel cantilevered open, revealing a shallow box.

"That's it," she said. "I knew it. Look inside." She wiggled the blade against Fergus's neck.

I peered at it. "There's nothing."

"You're not trying hard enough." Lucy raised her voice.

I picked up the hurricane lamp, surprised at how heavy it was, and held it closer to the desk. "Okay, I can see better now. There's a thin metal strip with some marks on it."

"A combination lock maybe," Fergus said. I was glad to hear his voice, as strong and firm as ever. "I've heard of these old desks being fitted with secret compartments, where people could hide valuables or papers."

"Or a book," Lucy said.

"But we don't have the combination," I pointed out.

"Fergus knows it." Lucy said.

"I don't. How would I? It's been years since I even saw the desk."

"Think," she said. "This was your grandfather's. What would he have used?"

"I have no idea."

"Then I have no choice." Lucy pulled the knife back as though preparing to plunge it into his neck.

"For God's sake, Lucy." I straightened up. "This is ridiculous. It's over. You may have found what you were looking for, but we can't get at it. Just walk away. Go home. Fergus won't press charges." My voice caught. "I can't believe you're behind all this. Did you kill Duncan?"

"Do me a favor and shut up. I intend to take the codex and disappear. So just cooperate and no one will be hurt."

I glanced at the door, praying for Josh to appear. Fergus followed my gaze and then shook his head. "He's working in the library."

I hadn't seen him there when I passed by. Maybe he'd been in the drinks cupboard or had gone to use the loo.

"Who?" Lucy demanded.

"Josh. He'll soon realize Fergus is missing and will come looking for him."

"Then we'd better crack on," she said. "Check that metal strip again. And please don't underestimate me, Kate. I will use this weapon quite happily."

I shone the light right on the metal band and saw five tiny dials, each one set to zero. Five numbers. I closed my eyes for a moment, trying to see it. The handwriting on the title page of the Russian book, the number Alistair had pointed out.

It might not be that number, but I would bet money it was. Fergus's grandfather had bought those Russian books and stored them in the library. Anyone could have written in them, I knew that, but the clue was the thin box drawn around the numbers. It was almost identical in size and shape to the metal strip that held the five dials. But now what? If I gave Lucy the number, would she release Fergus? It was unlikely. If we discovered the codex, would she grab it and run? Or keep Fergus with her for protection? And if it weren't there, I dreaded to think of what her reaction would be.

"Kate, what the hell...?" she demanded. "You look as though you're meditating. Wake up and tell Fergus to give me the number. Then I'll let him go. If not..."

Fergus thrust his hands backwards, catching her in the ribs. As he pivoted away from her, she jerked the blade, cutting deeper into his neck. He sank to his knees, blood dripping to the floorboards. Lucy pounced, the knife raised high, aiming at the point between his shoulder blades, exactly where Duncan had been stabbed.

Screaming, I dropped the lamp and threw myself at her, pushing her away. She staggered and recovered, holding the knife out in front of her.

"Put down the knife, Lucy," I said.

She backed up. "Stay right there."

Next to me, Fergus tried to rise to his feet and failed. He collapsed back on the floor. Ignoring Lucy, I bent over him. "I'm going to get you some help," I said. "Hang in there."

"Not until he tells us the combination, you're not," Lucy said, moving closer to us. Fergus needed urgent attention, and I'd had more than enough of Lucy. I grabbed the lamp, jumped up and faced her and then I charged, swinging the lamp at her. She took a step back and then another.

"Watch out!" I yelled, but it was too late. With a scream, she disappeared through the jagged hole in the floor and a sickening thump preceded the clatter of the knife hitting the floorboards in the room below us.

36

Fergus lifted his head. "Jesus," he groaned. "Is she dead?"

"I don't know. Right now, we need to get you some medical attention."

I rolled him on to his side, and put my hand against the cut in his neck. Blood leaked between my fingers, making my heart rate spike. Just as I opened my mouth to shout for help, Josh and Alistair burst in, Josh holding a torch. Its beam blinded me for a second until he clicked it off.

"Thank God you're here," I cried. "Call for an ambulance and the police."

"I'll do it." Alistair rushed back out while Josh came to help his uncle, propping him up against the desk and untying the ropes from around his wrists.

"What the hell happened?" Josh asked, as he ripped off his shirt and pressed it against Fergus's neck. Blood soaked through the cotton, but Fergus was still conscious.

"I'll explain later," I said. "Let's take a look at the wound."

Josh slowly lifted the shirt away while I hoisted the lamp so we could examine Fergus's neck. The flow of blood had slowed. "It's not bad as I feared," I said. "We just need to keep pressure on it until the medics get here."

"One of you should check on Lucy," Fergus said.

"I will," I said. But there was something I had to do first. While Josh reapplied the wadded-up shirt to Fergus's neck, I lifted the lamp higher.

"What are you smiling at?" Fergus demanded after a few seconds.

"Your aura has gone."

"Whatever you say," he replied, but he and Josh high-fived each other, both grinning like mad people.

Satisfied that Fergus was safe, I clambered to my feet. Josh gave me his torch, and I picked my way around the room and down the derelict stairs. In the hall, I turned towards the bedroom where Lucy had fallen. My heart pounded. She was a first-class liar and a thief, and quite probably a killer, but I didn't want her to be dead.

That fear was quickly dispelled when I pushed open the door. "What the hell kept you?" she demanded. "I could have been dying down here."

In the darkness, she was leaning against the foot of the bed, her legs stuck out in front of her. "My right leg's broken," she said calmly.

I scanned the floor for the knife and kicked it, sending it sliding across the floorboards into the hall, out of reach. Then I carefully rolled up her jeans an inch or two and removed her tennis shoe. "You've got a bad sprain," I told her, after feeling the swelling around her ankle. Earlier in the year, my doctor friend Anita had insisted I take a first aid course because, she said, I so often found myself in the midst of shootings, stabbings and drownings while investigating auras.

Lucy was skeptical of my diagnosis, however. "It's broken," she insisted. "What would you know?"

"It might be," I said, although I knew it wasn't. "So it's best that you don't move at all." I took off my cardigan and folded it into a small pillow. "Rest your leg on this. Someone has called for an ambulance. And the police, of course."

"The police? I don't see why," Lucy said. "I'm the only one who was injured, and I don't intend to press charges."

I stared at her in disbelief. She was either in a state of denial or she seriously underestimated Inspector McMahon. "I may as well tell you," I said. "The police have been looking for you."

"Why? I haven't done anything wrong."

"Apart from stabbing Fergus in the neck?"

I was certain now that Lucy had killed Duncan. I had seen how she'd held the knife over Fergus, fully intending to thrust it into his back.

"Don't stand there looming over me, for God's sake." She patted the floor beside her. "Sit down."

I hesitated, still in shock at the violence of her attack on Fergus. But I wanted to find out if she'd killed Duncan. I leaned against the door jamb, a comfortable distance away from her. I could sprint for the stairs if I needed to, but I doubted she could move far with that ankle injury.

"Did you set the police after me?" she demanded.

"You know I didn't. But you're a suspect for Duncan's murder."

"I didn't kill Duncan." Her voice caught. "All I wanted was the codex."

"Well, you worked out where it is. That was quite an achievement."

"It was, actually."

How did you know it was in the desk?"

"It was a guess."

I doubted that. There were scores of desks, cupboards and armoires, and thousands of nooks and crannies in the castle. The book could have been anywhere. I liked to believe I would eventually have pinpointed the roll-top desk, after Fergus had told me it was his grandfather's favorite piece of furniture. But Lucy couldn't have known that. So what made her identify a forgotten piece of furniture in a derelict, closed-off wing of the castle?

"A guess?"

"Well, not exactly. I found a note in the furniture register, a scrap of paper folded up between the pages."

"When did you see the furniture inventory?" I asked, confused. "We only worked on that after you left."

She leaned forward to rub her ankle. "I examined everything," she said. "All the inventory registers, every shelf in the library, even behind the portraits in the gallery. I'm very thorough in my work."

"What did the note say?"

"Not much. Just 'EW salon' and the word 'folio' with the initials GM. A message, maybe, to Gordon MacKenna's successors, or a memory aid for himself, I'm not sure. It wouldn't have meant much to most people. But that focused my search in the salon, and the desk was obviously a good hiding place. The problem was that I only found the note on Sunday morning, while everyone was running around looking for Duncan, so I had no time to investigate properly before the police arrived."

"But you left the castle voluntarily that afternoon," I reminded her. "Why didn't you stay on, to give yourself more time to examine the desk?"

"I was worried about being arrested after Duncan's death," she replied after a long pause. "As you say, McMahon seemed to consider me a prime suspect. It's always the spouse or the girlfriend, isn't it, on the TV programmes? Such a cliché."

And probably true in this case, I thought. But I'd leave that to the police to determine. For now, I was more interested in the story of the codex.

"We argued, but I didn't murder him," Lucy said again.

"What did you argue about?"

"He threatened to expose me, to tell Fergus what I was up to."

"So? We all knew you were looking for something. I doubt Fergus would have been shocked to learn you were after the book."

"No, but he would have been shocked to learn that Stanton Knox was paying me to find it for him."

Ah yes, Knox. He'd had been out to screw Fergus all along.

"After that Romanov egg was discovered in Paris earlier this year, Stanton contacted me. We hadn't spoken for a while but he had this whole theory about the egg and the codex being part of a collection of Romanov treasures. He said he'd pay me to research it and, if I found the codex, he'd give me a million pounds, and, even better, he'd let me take all the credit for the discovery." Lucy shifted her leg. "God, that hurts."

"It looks painful," I said. "Keep talking. It'll take your mind off it."

"My academic career was going nowhere. There were rumors I might even be let go. Retrieving the book would change everything. In academia, I'd be a superstar. Ever since I was a child, I've dreamed of being famous."

Or infamous, I thought. "Then you've achieved your goal. You certainly contributed to finding the codex. Its discovery will be one of the greatest scholarly feats of modern times." In fact, I doubted she'd ever achieve any academic recognition. She'd committed a string of crimes, from breaking and entering to assault and, for all I knew, murder.

"Do you really think so? I'm afraid that my part will be overlooked, forgotten. I need to tell my side of the story."

"I should think an interview with a well-placed journalist might be helpful."

Lucy brightened. "Do you know anyone? Reputable, of course."

I did have a journalist friend, a serious and conscientious reporter. He'd helped me with some background research the year before, and we stayed in touch, meeting occasionally at his local pub for a drink and a chat. "I have a contact who might be interested, but I'd have to know more about what happened and how you came to learn about the codex in the first place."

Lucy twisted to look at me. "All right then. What else do you want to know?" She seemed genuinely eager to tell all, to brag maybe about how she'd completely misled me, and the others.

"When did Duncan figure out you and Stanton were collaborating? He didn't know before the weekend?"

"No, he'd never heard of Stanton Knox until we arrived at the castle, but he saw Stanton come to my room on Friday afternoon. Duncan knew it couldn't be anything romantic. I would never stoop so low as to take an American lover. He realized that Stanton and I must be plotting something. It didn't take him long to connect the dots. He confronted us later that day, became rather ugly, in fact. That's why Stanton left on Friday night, just to let things cool a bit. Duncan had worked himself up into a lather about it all and decided he needed to find the book before anyone else did."

I contemplated that for a few seconds. I could imagine how outraged Duncan would have felt when he discovered Lucy and Knox's cozy little scheme. But, with Duncan's anger issues, I thought that might have made him a killer, not a victim.

"How did you meet Duncan in the first place? Was that luck?"

"No, I don't believe in luck. I made it happen." Lucy's voice was stronger now, more confident. "After I found out that Gordon MacKenna had purchased the books, I dug into the family records and realized that Duncan was a great-grandson and that he worked in London. I tracked him down and trailed him for a few weeks to learn more about him. I stage-managed a meeting in a bar close to his office, and we started dating."

I guessed that it would take more than silky blonde hair and high cheekbones to attract and keep someone like Duncan. There were plenty of young women trying to land a wealthy City banker. Lucy must have played a very convincing role, probably sucking up to him and stroking his ego. She certainly was a master manipulator as well as an accomplished liar.

"I was optimistic at first. Duncan kept making plans to visit his uncle. But then at the last minute, he'd cancel because of work. This was the first time we'd been able to come and, by then, Stanton had taken another tack. He'd decided to buy the estate, which would give him all the time he needed to locate the book. That would leave me out of the picture, so the weekend of Fergus's birthday party was it. My only chance to find the codex and get the money."

She shifted her leg and winced.

"Why Knox?" I was confused. "Stanton has all the money in the world. Why did he want the codex so much?"

"For the same reason a French king or a Russian Tsarina wanted it. It's unique, the masterpiece of an extraordinary intellect, with an incredible history. Stanton is an avid collector, from houses to art and musical instruments." She gave a dry laugh. "He imagines himself to be a connoisseur of fine things and he certainly measures his own worth by the value of his possessions."

"Did he intend to cancel the sale if you did find the codex? He was never really interested in the estate?"

"Oh, he intends to continue with the purchase," Lucy said without hesitation. "To him, honestly, the cost is insignificant. I think he genuinely fell in love with the place— or he just thinks it's cool to have a Scottish estate. The problem is mine. Without the codex, I have nothing. But you can help me get something back— recognition. You have to promise to contact your journalist friend for me."

"I will," I said. "But tell me about the Russian books you found. It was you, wasn't it? Not Duncan."

"You know about those books? Of course you do. It took me a while to locate them because it seemed you were always watching me. At first, I was bitterly disappointed not to find the codex with them. I'd been so sure it was part of the consignment from Anna Vyrubova. But then I realized the presence of the Russian books was actually good news. They gave me renewed hope that the codex was indeed somewhere in the castle. I moved them so Duncan wouldn't find them— or you wouldn't, for that matter. Without them, he wouldn't have the certainty I had that the codex was here."

"How much did Duncan know?"

"He wasn't stupid. After we started dating, he realized quickly that I was looking for something valuable— especially after I flew to Helsinki. I wanted to see if there were any traces there of Anna Vyrubova, but she died in the 1960s, and it was a dead end. Duncan kept after me, always demanding information, until finally I decided to give him a few hints about the codex. By that time, I was desperate to gain entry to the castle, and only he could arrange it. It was a gamble, but it paid off. Rather than dump me, Duncan suggested we cooperate. He had some sizeable debts, and half a million pounds would have come in handy. But, once we arrived here, I did my own thing. I'm not exactly the collaborative type. And of course, Duncan said all that stuff about taking over the estate but he never intended to do it. He was just trying to buy some more time to keep looking for the book."

"What about Remy Delacroix? You offered him a three-way split?"

"Remy?" She scoffed. "He's such a loser. He certainly muddled things here, though, just by turning up. He threatened me too, but I convinced him we'd share the proceeds once we found the codex."

Lucy leaned forward and examined her ankle, which was continuing to swell. "Kate, you seem to have Inspector McMahon's respect. Has he told you who he thinks killed Duncan?"

Tired of standing, I slid down the door jamb to the floor, where I shifted around to get comfortable while I thought about what to tell Lucy. If I gave too much away, she could use that to her advantage and I didn't want to mess up McMahon's investigation.

"The inspector keeps his cards close to his chest," I said finally. "I don't know what he's thinking. But he's smart, Lucy. If you were involved in Duncan's death in any way, he'll work it out."

I heard footsteps and voices overhead. A light shone down into the bedroom.

"Are you all right down there?" It was Josh. "The ambulance is here. They're checking on Fergus and then they'll come down to help Lucy. The police will be here any minute, as well."

Damn. I really wanted to hear the end of the story before the authorities took her away.

"McMahon won't find any proof," Lucy said. Her voice wavered and she held the palm of her hand over her eyes. Was she crying? She sat up suddenly and tried to stand. That didn't go well. With a yelp of pain, she sank back to the floor.

"Did you kill Duncan?" I asked when she'd stopped fidgeting.

"I told you already. I didn't murder him." She twisted her upper body to look at me. "I need your help, Kate. McMahon will listen to you. Fergus will too."

I took a deep breath. Lucy had lied to me all along. She'd put on a great act of being sweet and shy and scared of Duncan's temper. And I'd fallen for it. "I'll do what I can," I said. "But only if I understand what really happened and what was going on with you and Duncan? Starting with the night of Fergus's party."

She nodded. "I thought that Duncan and I had patched things up after he'd seen me with Stanton on Friday. On Saturday morning, we enjoyed riding our horses together— until you found Nick's body, at least." How did she manage to make that sound as though I'd done something wrong? "But by the evening," Lucy continued, "Duncan was back to being mad with me. I tried. I went to his room to ask him to help me zip up my gown before the party, but he was too distracted to pay me any attention. Kept pacing around and complaining that we'd run out of time. We were due to fly back to London on Sunday afternoon. I was equally frustrated. Our attempt to find the codex seemed doomed to fail." She fell silent.

"He got rather drunk at the party," I prompted. "What happened afterwards?"

"We went back to my room. He was, as you say, plastered, and I assumed he'd just pass out on the bed, but he began ranting about Stanton Knox and how he was out to screw Fergus and seize the estate. The way he described it, you'd think Stanton was trying to storm the bloody castle, not pay good money for it. Anyway, Duncan got more and more worked up. His anger actually seemed to sober him a bit. He said he planned to go to Fergus first thing in the morning to tell him what Stanton was really up to, and reveal my part in it. Then he said maybe he'd go tell Fergus right then." Lucy sighed. "I kept him talking for as long as I could, hoping he'd change his mind about waking his uncle in the middle of the night. At about one forty-five, he left my room to go to bed, he said. But I heard him leave again soon afterwards."

Remembering that night, when I had listened to footsteps in the corridor, I wondered if things would be different if I'd investigated more thoroughly, instead of retreating back to bed. Maybe Duncan would still be alive.

"I couldn't trust him not to go to Fergus," Lucy said. "So I followed him. He went down to the kitchen, which was dark and empty. Everyone had left. He unlocked the back door and looked outside, but he didn't go out."

I knew that Fiona had given up by then. She'd left at one-thirty, she said.

"As he turned around," Lucy continued, "I hid on the kitchen stairs so he wouldn't see me. He grabbed a torch from a drawer and headed towards the butler's pantry and then a scullery I didn't even know existed. I followed as he went through a door to a narrow hallway. It leads here, to the east wing."

"I know," I said.

She ignored me. "He must have realized I was following him, because he turned around and shone the torch in my eyes. We argued. He told me he'd been planning to meet that young woman, Fiona, but she'd gone, which was all my fault for keeping him so long. He frog-marched me back to the kitchen and pointed at the stairs. He said I should leave the castle immediately and go home, that he was going to wake his uncle and tell him that I'd deceived him and planned to steal the codex. If I stayed in the castle, they'd have me arrested.

"Naturally, I went on the offensive. I threatened to tell Fergus about Duncan's debts and all his shady deals. I said that Fergus would certainly disinherit him and leave his estate to Josh. That made Duncan furious. He shoved me against the wall so hard it scared me. He'd kill me, he said, if I breathed a word. There was a block of knives on the counter, and he pulled one out. One word, he said, and he'd slit my throat."

Lucy was obviously adept at lying, but I believed her in this instance. Duncan certainly seemed to me to have anger management issues.

"I was terrified," Lucy went on. "I grabbed another knife from the block. He laughed at me. Said I didn't have the nerve to kill him. He headed towards the stairway, intent on waking Fergus. I raised the knife and yelled at him to stop, but he carried on walking, and I ran after him. When he reached the first step, I stabbed at him. I was aiming for his arm, but he moved. I never intended to kill him, only to stop him. I had to protect myself." She paused. "It's clear I acted in self-defense, isn't it?"

"You can certainly make your case," I said, although I doubted a jury would see a stab in the back as self-defense.

"I dragged his body to the meat locker and dumped it in there." Lucy's voice fell. Perhaps she was capable of feeling remorse after all. "I never imagined there'd be so much blood," she continued. "It was everywhere."

"The kitchen was spotless when I got there," I said.

"That's because I mopped and cleaned. And I took the knife with me. As I said, I'm thorough in my work."

"And his shoes?"

"Ah yes, you asked me about that on the phone, didn't you? One of his shoes came off when I was dragging him. I tried to put it back on, then realized I'd put bloody fingerprints on the calf leather. So I took off his other shoe and threw them both away."

"Where did you put them?"

She laughed. "You're a good little sleuth, Kate. Maybe you'll figure it out." She exhaled loudly. "It sounds callous, I can see that. But it wasn't premeditated. You believe me, don't you?"

It didn't matter what I believed. Lucy was going to have to face Inspector McMahon very shortly. Over our heads came a volley of shouts and what sounded like a cattle stampede. A minute later, I heard a crash and someone swearing on the decrepit stairway. Seconds later, two policemen burst into the room, waving torches. As one of them helped me up from the floor, pins and needles pricked my feet and legs. He kept his hand under my elbow and led me towards the door while the other officer crouched down next to Lucy.

"Don't forget to call that reporter," Lucy called. I turned around. In the glare of the torchlight, she stared at me intently as though willing me to do her bidding. "I'm counting on you."

The policeman exerted gentle pressure on my arm and I started back towards the door. "Sergeant Piper," he said, introducing himself as we picked our way up the broken stairs. "I'll stay with you, miss, until Inspector McMahon arrives."

When we reached the salon, I was still wondering if he was there to provide support or to keep an eye on me. We arrived just in time to see Fergus being carried off on a stretcher. My chest tightened.

"He's fine," Josh assured me. "It's what they do, just a check-up to make certain he's all right." He took me in his arms and squeezed so hard I couldn't breathe.

Sergeant Piper stayed close as Josh, Alistair, and I followed the paramedics down to the entry hall, listening to Fergus insist the whole time that he was perfectly well. Outside, in the watery sunlight, I checked again to be sure. The aura had disappeared. Fergus needed medical care, but he wasn't going to die. Joined by Lachlan and Mrs. Dunsmore on the front steps, we watched while he was loaded into an ambulance.

"I'll be back," Josh said. "I'm going to the hospital. I want to be there for Fergus." He dashed to his rental car and started down the driveway behind the ambulance. Halfway to the gate, he pulled over as Inspector McMahon's green Renault drove in. They both lowered their windows and talked for a minute or two. As the ambulance continued on and turned out of sight, Mrs. Dunsmore started to cry.

"Why don't you make everyone some tea," I suggested to her. "I'll wait for the inspector, and we'll come down to the kitchen."

The housekeeper patted the tears from her cheeks. "Good idea. Would you like one, officer?"

"Aye," Piper said, smiling for the first time. "I never refuse a cuppa."

Mrs. Dunsmore's way inside was momentarily blocked by the medics bringing Lucy out on a gurney. She raised herself on her elbows when she saw me and told the crew to stop. "One more thing, Kate. You have to rescue the codex," she said. "Don't let Stanton Knox lay his grubby hands on it. You need to find the combination to the desk."

"I know the combination," I said.

Her eyes narrowed. "You had it all along?"

"Did you ever look inside the Russian books? The ones you took from the library?"

"Briefly. I didn't have much time to examine them."

"Thanks to Mr. Ross," I said, "I did."

37

The ambulance crew were sliding Lucy's stretcher into the ambulance when Inspector McMahon drove the last hundred meters up the drive and parked his car close to the entry steps. He got out, slammed the door shut and strode towards us, his tartan scarf flapping in the breeze. With dark circles under his grey eyes, and the suspicion of a five o'clock shadow on his usually well-shaven jaw, he looked exhausted.

"I'm sorry we weren't able to find Lucy before she got to Fergus. Things could have ended badly if not for you, Kate."

"Well, all that matters is Fergus is safe. His aura has gone."

McMahon shot a look at Alistair, as if wondering what he'd make of the mention of an aura, but Alistair's expression didn't change. I'd already shared the good news with him. He'd done a sweet little victory jig and had planted an unexpected kiss on my cheek.

"We'll know more in the next twenty-four hours," McMahon continued. "After I have the opportunity to interview Lucy in depth. Our initial findings show she never did return to London. She kept the car that Duncan had rented and hid out in Oban."

I thought back to the phone call when we'd talked about Duncan's shoes. I had assumed she was in London, of course, as she'd intended me to. Just another thread in her web of lies and untruths. Alternative facts, as they'd say in the States.

"Someone called in a report of a car abandoned by the side of the road a mile from here," McMahon said. "It had been there for several hours. Turned out to be Duncan's rental car, which means Lucy dumped it and walked the rest of the way."

"And she must have sneaked into the castle sometime earlier today." I remembered the creaking floorboards in the east wing when I visited it with Alistair. "She was waiting for a final opportunity to have another look for the codex before Knox took possession of the estate and didn't need her any longer."

McMahon raised an eyebrow, so I explained what Lucy had told me about Stanton Knox paying her to find the ancient book. "What else did she tell you?" he asked.

I looked down, examining the specks of glittering mica in the grey stone of the steps. Noticed my boots needed polishing after all that traipsing around in the dust.

"Kate?"

When I looked up again, the inspector's eyes were the color of granite. "I'm aware of her attack on Fergus," he said. "But did she confess to killing Duncan?"

My stomach cramped. My father had been a barrister in London before he retired, and I'd picked up a rudimentary understanding of certain aspects of the legal system. Dad was a stickler for rules. If he were here, he would warn me to be very careful about what I said next. Anything I told McMahon would almost certainly make its way into the legal record. Lucy had shared her story with me in the expectation that I would argue her innocence with the inspector. The problem was that I didn't believe she was innocent. I had no intention of blocking McMahon's investigation, but, even so, it was hard to get the words out. "More or less," I said finally. "However, she claimed it was self-defense."

"But he was stabbed in the back," Alistair blurted out. "How can that be self-defense?" His cheeks burned red. "I'm so sorry. It's not my place to comment."

"Duncan was threatening to go to Fergus, to reveal the arrangement she had with Knox to find the codex," I continued. "They argued, and it became violent."

McMahon remained silent, his eyes on my face.

"Remember our conversation about the missing shoes?" I asked him. "Duncan's tan loafers? It would help if you could find them." I didn't specify why. That Lucy had admitted her bloody fingerprints were all over them.

McMahon nodded, as though accepting I'd said all I could at this point. After a long pause, he pulled his scarf more tightly around his neck, glancing up at the sky. "It might rain. You should get inside. I'll be back with more questions soon. Come with me, sergeant."

Sergeant Piper's face fell. He'd probably been looking forward to a nice cup of tea in the warm kitchen. I watched as the two men strode off, and then McMahon stopped and turned. "I'm very glad about Fergus," he said. The corners of his mouth twitched with a faint hint of a smile.

I was glad too. I smiled back at him. The grey damp blanket of anxiety that had been smothering me for the past five days lifted. I felt almost euphoric, a feeling I'd experienced after other auras had disappeared. For now, I intended to put Lucy out of my mind, confident that McMahon would deal with her, and that the oiled wheels of justice would carry her case to a resolution. All I wanted was for Josh and Fergus to come home, for one more check to be sure Fergus's aura had truly disappeared, and a chance to hug Josh and tell him how much I loved him.

And there were things to be done. I needed to bring Fergus up to date on Knox's role in the nefarious quest for the codex. Knox may not have broken the law, as Lucy had, but his actions were despicable. More importantly, we had to search the desk. I hoped with every fiber of my being that the book was inside. It was a challenge not to run up and play with those dials myself, but it was only fair to wait for Josh and Fergus. I followed Alistair inside and down to the kitchen where we passed the time drinking tea with Mrs. Dunsmore and rehashing the events of the last few days.

When Josh and his uncle arrived an hour later, Fergus had a bandage on his neck, but the color had come back to his cheeks, and he wore a broad grin. The air over his unkempt silver hair was clear and still. Josh had stopped clenching his jaw, and his light green eyes sparkled for the first time since I'd told him Fergus had an aura.

Fergus enveloped me in a hug. "Thank you for what you did, lass. You saved my life."

My voice caught in my throat, so I squeezed his arm instead.

"I think we should bring this little adventure to a close," he said. "Shall we examine the desk?"

"I thought you'd never ask," I replied. "Let's go."

Alistair put his cup in its saucer and looked up, his eyes shining. "Do you mind if I come along?"

"You're more than welcome, if you don't mind cobwebs and rotten floors," Fergus replied. "Mrs. D.? Would you like to join us?"

Mrs. Dunsmore was at the sink, rinsing out the teapot. "I'll be fine here, thank you. I've scones in the oven to wait for."

Stopping at the hall cupboard to collect a torch, the four of us tramped upstairs and along the corridor. Fergus paused for a second at the east wing door, no doubt thinking of Lucy leaping at him with a knife. Inside, he gave the torch to Josh.

"You know the combination number?" Fergus asked me.

Glancing at Alistair, I recited it. "51088." Alistair nodded his head in agreement.

Fergus repeated it. "That's my grandfather's birthdate," he said. "The fifth of October, 1888. He was only 53 when he died, a few months before my dad's nineteenth birthday."

He cracked his knuckles before leaning into the desk. One by one, he turned the five tiny dials until they showed the correct number. I heard a faint click, and a previously invisible panel in the left pedestal swung open to reveal a narrow cubbyhole. A single book nestled inside.

"Wait." Alistair pulled a clean white handkerchief from his pocket and gave it to Fergus. "Better not touch the cover."

With the cotton fabric wrapped around his fingers, Fergus

released the book from its hiding place. I gasped at the same time as Alistair. Small with a tan leather cover, it was exactly the same book that I'd seen in the vision of the murder at the priory.

"Let's get out of the dust and gloom," Fergus suggested.

We followed him downstairs to the drawing room where he laid the codex on the coffee table, and we gazed at it, absorbing the fact that it had lain hidden and abandoned in the east wing for nearly eighty years. Fergus carefully raised the leather cover. On the title page was a short paragraph of looped writing, the initial letter of the first word beautifully illuminated in red, blue and gold. At the bottom was an elaborate signature.

"Is this it? The codex?" Fergus asked.

"Yes," Alistair answered. "See this?" He pointed, his finger hovering an inch above the smooth vellum. "This is Aethelwin's signature." He clasped his hands together as though in prayer.

"I can't understand a word," Fergus commented after we'd stared at the page for a minute.

"It's Old English," Alistair explained. "A Germanic language brought to Britain by the Anglo-Saxon raiders in the fifth century. *Beowulf* is probably the most famous work written in that language. More specifically, this codex was written to the Winchester standard, a classical form of Old English established by Aethelwold, Bishop of Winchester. However, following the Norman Conquest of Britain in 1066, there was a gradual evolution into Middle English, the language of Chaucer. Relatively few Old English manuscripts have survived the passage of the centuries, as you can imagine."

"I'm at a bit of a loss for words." Fergus looked dazed, which was hardly surprising given Lucy's attack and the incredible discovery of the book. Just then, Arbroath bounded in, tongue hanging out, panting with excitement at seeing his master again. Fergus grabbed the codex from the table, enveloping it in the white cotton. "We don't want dog slobber on it." He patted Arbroath. "Sit, boy, sit."

Cradling the book on his lap, Fergus leaned back against the cushions. "What do we do next?"

"I have a friend at the British Museum," Alistair offered. "Perhaps we can ask him how best to proceed? You can keep it, of course, or perhaps you want to sell it?"

"Is it mine to sell?"

"Of course it is," Josh said. "Your grandfather bought it. It's part of the estate and your inheritance. And you haven't signed the sale documents yet."

The sale documents. I doubted the American would go through with the estate purchase now the codex had been found. It might be bad news for Fergus, but I had to tell him what Knox's real objective had been.

"There's something you need to know." I leaned forward towards him. "Stanton Knox knew all about the codex and believed it was hidden here in the castle. He hired Lucy to find it. Then, when she wasn't making the progress he wanted, he ran out of patience and decided to buy the castle so he could search for it himself. If he'd found the book after the sale, it would have been his property, legally purchased with the rest of the estate. But he never got that far."

"Why go to the trouble of buying a rundown pile of stones just to get hold of an old book?" Fergus ran a hand through his already disheveled hair, leaving it sticking up in spikes.

"Because," Alistair said. "It is worth a great deal of money. I don't know how much you're selling the property for..." He shook his head as Fergus started to speak. "You don't need to tell me. It's none of my business. But I'd take a bet it's far less than the codex would bring at auction."

Josh and I exchanged looks. If Alistair was right, and I trusted his opinion, then money would never again be a problem for Fergus. He could keep the castle if he wanted to. And, one day, I realized with a jolt, Josh would inherit it.

Fergus didn't seem to have absorbed the information Alistair had just shared. Instead, his face was creased in confusion. "So Knox was after this all along? How did he know Lucy? Where did she come into it?"

It took a while to explain everything, by which time Mrs. Dunsmore had found us and delivered a tray of tea and scones still warm from the oven. When Fergus explained that we'd found an ancient book in the east wing, she sat on the edge of a chair, fanning herself with her a napkin. "My goodness. Have you told Lachlan?"

"Why would Lachlan be interested?" The lines on Fergus's forehead deepened.

"If I'm not mistaken, he knew about that book," Mrs. Dunsmore answered. "Saw a vision, he did, out on the moor, of a young woman holding it in her hand before she was murdered."

Fergus gaped. "Lachlan saw a vision?"

"Aye," Alistair said. "He did, the same one that Kate saw. And I did as well. It's what set me off delving into the history of the codex and what had happened here in the 1500s. But it wasn't until Kate arrived that I had any faith the book might once again be in the castle."

"I'll be damned." Fergus took a swallow of tea. "Lachlan, eh?"

"Can we examine more pages?" Alistair ventured. "If the rumors are true, Aethelwin wasn't able to complete his opus, so the final few pages were left blank. Many of the book's owners wrote notes or signed their names on those pages, creating a historical record— incomplete, but nonetheless fascinating— which considerably enhances the worth of an already priceless volume."

Using the handkerchief, Fergus placed the book on the table and gently opened the vellum pages. We saw mathematical formulae, paragraphs of hand-written text, and drawings of clock gears and other mechanisms. In the margins were random images resembling the doodlings of a bored student. Then came a page bearing a single line of script in French and a signature.

"What does it say?" Fergus asked.

Alistair adjusted his glasses and peered closely. "The signature is Napoleon Bonaparte's," he said. "And the sentence says something like 'Glory is fleeting, but obscurity is forever.' It's remarkable." He sat back and patted his forehead.

I thought about Lucy and her quest for glory. She wanted to be a superstar amongst her peers, she'd told me. Her fear of obscurity must have been heightened by her renewed contact with Knox, who had achieved the fame and fortune she craved. But even Stanton

Knox was only a comma in the annals of history. Would he be remembered in two hundred years' time? Or fifty years or even ten?

I turned my attention back to the book as Fergus leafed through the pages. There were other notes in different hands, in English, French, and Russian. We identified the signatures of Charles I, signed as Charles R., and of the first Duke of Marlborough, the revered ancestor of Sir Winston Churchill, but most were hard to read. It would take experts to decipher the full record of ownership over the last five hundred years. Still, my heart beat faster to see this evidence of the book's migrations, remembering Alistair's account of the crimes and deaths that had occurred in its pursuit.

Finally, Fergus closed the codex and wrapped it in the handkerchief. "I'd be grateful if you'd talk to your contact at the British Museum as soon as possible," he said to Alistair. "I won't sleep easily until this is in a safe place, with people who know how to care for it."

"More than happy to." Alistair jumped to his feet. "I'll get to work on that at once, if you'll excuse me?"

"I think we should tell Inspector McMahon that we've found the codex," I suggested when Alistair had gone. "It's probably relevant to his murder investigation."

Fergus nodded. "Aye, it will be. Poor Duncan."

"What about Stanton Knox?" Josh asked. "Even if he wants to proceed, we won't sell the castle to him, knowing what we do now."

"Absolutely not," Fergus agreed, hugging the book to his chest. "That scheming Yank probably intended to put his own sorry little signature on one of these blank pages."

With his other hand, he patted the dog's massive head. "Not on my watch, he won't. Arbroath and I will see to that."

38

Six weeks later, Josh and I sat with Fergus and Alistair Ross on a flat-topped rock overlooking the lochan. It was our second trip back to Scotland, this one a month after Duncan's funeral, which had taken place on a cold, rainy day with a blustery wind that blew our black umbrellas inside out.

Today, the rock was warm under my legs, and the lochan sparkled in the sunlight, even though it was late October and winter could roll in at any time. It had been Fergus's idea to eat lunch by the water. We'd brought a rustic picnic of cheese sandwiches and apples, with bottles of locally brewed beer. A bird sang overhead, a light trilling that reminded me of summer.

Fergus raised his beer in a toast. "To Duncan and to Nick," he said. As he lifted his bottle to his lips, I saw the white scar on his neck, a reminder of Lucy's assault with the carving knife. Memories of that attack, the fire, and the loss of Duncan and Nick flooded back, chilling my skin. But we were here today to try and put some of it behind us. Earlier, we'd stopped at the spot where Nick had died, and Fergus recited a lyrical Celtic poem that I had to admit I didn't understand.

"Is there any update on the investigations?" Alistair asked.

Fergus took a swallow of his drink. "DCI McMahon told me that the preliminary hearings are scheduled for next month. Lucy's still insisting she's been wrongfully charged with murder, although of course she can't deny the charge of assault." He ran his fingers over the scar. "There were too many witnesses for her to get away with that one."

Although Lucy had told me, the day she fell through the east wing floor, that she'd killed Duncan, so far she was refusing to confess to McMahon, insisting that I was making it up and that she'd been in bed when Duncan was killed. Fortunately, McMahon had followed up on my observation about Duncan's missing shoes. His men had searched every inch of the castle and had found them in a dusty cabinet in the old scullery in the east wing. Complete with bloody fingerprints, they were wrapped up in the cardigan she'd been wearing that night. The cardigan had blood stains on it and one button was missing. McMahon believed the prints were enough to convict her, despite her claims of innocence. Meanwhile, she was being held in a prison cell from which she'd sent me several letters, accusing me of betraying her, claiming that my recounting of the events of that Saturday night was pure fantasy.

Josh had made me tear the letters up. "Don't dwell on it," he'd said. "You spoke to McMahon on her behalf and gave him her side of the story. You did what she asked you to do, but self-defense isn't going to stand up in court, and she knows it."

Fergus shifted his weight on the rock. "Remy Delacroix, on the other hand, has agreed to plead guilty to Nick's murder," he continued. "He wants to serve his time in a French prison. It's complicated, but McMahon is working on it."

"It's too bad that McMahon can't charge Knox with anything," I said. "If it weren't for him, Lucy might never have got involved. But he seems to be getting off scot-free, if you'll forgive the Scot pun."

"His intentions were all bad," Fergus agreed. "McMahon talked briefly about charging him with conspiracy to commit murder. But, while Lucy initially claimed Knox told her to get rid of Duncan, she keeps changing her testimony. It's unlikely any charges against Knox will stick."

For a few minutes, we all sat in silence, finishing our sandwiches. I closed my eyes and turned my face up to the sun, feeling its warmth on my cheeks. I felt sad for Lucy and angry that Stanton Knox had dangled the twin stars of money and fame over her head. In all likelihood, she would be convicted and spend time in prison.

A cloud passed over the sun, leaching the warmth from my skin. I sat up straight and packed the rubbish from our picnic into a small rucksack. Josh slid the straps on to his shoulders before jumping down from the rock, and we all walked together to the head of the lochan. When we passed the Brynjarr Stone, I paused to trail my fingers along the smooth black rock. I noticed that Alistair didn't touch it. In fact, he gave the magical spire a wide berth. I thought I felt a faint vibration under my fingertips, but perhaps I imagined it.

A light breeze ruffled the heather, carrying a scent of damp grass, as we walked the narrow trail that led to the remains of the former priory. I stepped off the path and led the way into the center of the rectangle of broken walls and scattered stones. There, I braced myself, waiting for the vision to appear. Alistair came to stand next to me and grasped my hand. "Anything?" he whispered.

"Nothing." No swirling mist, no monk in black robes, no blade glinting in the thin light. I was relieved not to have to endure the sight of the murder again, but disappointed too. For weeks, the vision had haunted my dreams as I replayed the images of the knife wielded by the monk, and like a grim parody, Lucy brandishing her knife and threatening Fergus.

Today, the ruins were quiet.

I crouched and ran my hand over the ground that had once been drenched with Agnes Fenton's blood. From my bag, I lifted out a small posy of white carnations, a token of recognition for her courage, and laid it on the pristine grass. We could never know the whole truth of the story, but Alistair's research strongly suggested that Agnes had died while trying to protect the codex from Hubert, the Frenchman who'd masqueraded as a monk with the objective of stealing the codex. No one knew how Agnes had discovered his intent, but when she attempted to rescue the book, he killed her. He was never caught and charged. He ran away, probably back to France, where the codex reappeared three years later. From there, the strange book had journeyed thousands of miles over hundreds of years.

And now it was back home. I thought of the twist of fate that left it undiscovered in a secret drawer, lost when Fergus's grandfather died suddenly without revealing its existence to anyone. If not for Lucy, it might have remained there for another eighty years. Or maybe Knox would have taken the castle apart, one piece of furniture at a time, until he found it.

Alistair held out his hand to help me to my feet. "Agnes Fenton can rest in peace now," he said. "The codex is in safe hands. Her part is done."

FOR THE REST of the day, Mrs. Dunsmore and I cooked and baked, producing a feast worthy of a gathering of clan chiefs. Josh and I would fly home in the morning, so this was our last night at the castle for a while. At eight that evening, we gathered in the formal dining room. Alistair and Mrs. Dunsmore joined us, but Lachlan had requested a reprieve, saying he'd rather eat alone and read a book. Fergus poured champagne for everyone.

"I have received a signed letter of intent for the purchase of the codex," he said with a wide smile. We all knew that there had been something of a bidding war for the codex. Following an evaluation by the British Museum, Fergus had worked with Christie's in London to catalogue and promote the book. There had been a huge response and, within a very short amount of time, a number of collectors, both individual and institutional, had submitted bids.

"One of the bidders, an American, turned out to be representing Stanton Knox," Fergus told us, as we sipped our champagne. "It seemed that even though Knox failed to buy the whole estate and the codex for just under four million pounds, he was determined enough to get the book that he put in a bid for thirteen million. That's a million more than the bid I accepted. I just couldn't bring myself to let the codex end up with Knox. The buyer is an English collector, and the good news is that he has agreed to loan the book to the British Museum for one year. The museum is planning a special exhibition, but first they'll carry out an extensive analysis of the contents. They have access to advanced scanning and digitization technology, which preserves the integrity of the book. That's what they told me anyway. I don't really understand most of it. But the important thing is that the codex will be well looked after, and shared for a while with the public. After the special exhibit, the collector will be free to do with it whatever he wishes."

"To the codex," Alistair toasted. We all clinked our glasses together.

"Of course, that money means I can keep the estate and make all the necessary repairs."

Fergus was looking far younger than his sixty-five years, I thought. The prospect of saving his beloved castle had given him new energy.

"I've already chosen a contractor to work with. It will take time but the old place will one day be restored to its former glory. We're going to remodel the east wing too, and set it up as a small museum showcasing the history of the castle. Alistair has agreed to train the docents."

"It's so exciting," I said. "You can bring school groups through."

He nodded. "And, as long as Josh doesn't mind my spending some of his inheritance, I'm planning to set up a foundation to provide scholarships for needy students in the area. Aethelwin possessed a prodigious mind, and he shared his knowledge by creating the codex. It seems right to honor him by encouraging learning and providing education opportunities for kids. What do you think of naming the foundation after Duncan?"

We were silent for a moment, acknowledging that, in spite of the happy discovery of the codex, Nick and Duncan had been killed in its pursuit.

"That's a great idea," Josh said finally.

I squashed the first thought that popped into my head. Duncan wasn't exactly the role model I'd choose for any child of my own. But I kept my mouth shut.

"And I still want to talk to you two about that thing we discussed on the phone." Fergus put down his fork. Earlier in the week, he'd rung Josh to say he wanted us to have some of the money from the codex sale. We'd refused, of course. The proceeds would save the estate, and that was sufficient reward for us.

"Nothing to discuss," Josh said.

His uncle shook his head, picked up his fork and speared a piece of salmon. I guessed we hadn't heard the last of it. Josh, I knew, still hadn't come to terms with the fact that he was now next in line to inherit the estate, but we all hoped that would be far in the future. Fergus would live for many more years yet.

Mrs. Dunsmore took a sip of her champagne, coughing when the bubbles tickled her mouth. "First time I've ever tasted the stuff. I think I'd like a drop of sherry better." She put the flute down on the table. "I'm confused by one thing, though. Whatever happened to the Fabergé egg that Lucy was looking for?"

"There never was an egg," I explained. "That was Lucy's smoke screen, intended to conceal her real search for the codex, and throw us off the scent. She almost succeeded. I was so distracted by the egg story that I really didn't pay enough attention to the vision on the moor and the book."

She leaned over and patted my hand. "Well, it all worked out for the best. And that horrible Knox chappie doesn't get to take away our lovely castle. That's the important thing."

THE FOLLOWING MORNING, I lifted my bag into the boot of the car and hurried around to get in the passenger seat. We were running a little late, and I was anxious not to miss our plane back to London. Our boss had approved a half-day off on Friday, and I had no intention of pushing my luck by inadvertently extending our trip. I shivered in the chilly mist that had gathered overnight and hoped it wouldn't affect our flight.

"Miss Kate!" Lachlan strode across the driveway, rifle in his arm. I was still amazed by the revelation that the dour and taciturn groundskeeper had seen the vision of Agnes Fenton being killed and was even more surprised that he was addressing me directly. I'd had the feeling he was going out of his way to avoid me this past weekend.

Standing by the open car door, I waited for him to reach me. "Is something wrong?" I asked.

Eyes on his feet, he dug the point of his boot into the gravel, pushing the stones around to reveal the bare earth underneath. It seemed he couldn't bring himself to look at me.

"Lachlan?"

He raised his eyes then, which were dark green, I noticed, matching the olive-colored field jacket he always wore.

"I just want to thank ye, for saving the master's life."

"Thank you, Lachlan," I said, making an effort to hide my surprise that he was talking to me. "Did you ever, you know, see any sign that Fergus was in danger? Mr. Ross said you have the second sight."

Lachlan shook his head slowly. "Alistair's imagination runs wild on occasion. I saw that vision of the murder at the priory, it's true. And don't ye go blethering about that to anyone. But predicting the future, seeing when someone's going to die. That's..."

"Weird?"

"Aye. Now get along. Ye'll not be wanting to miss your flight to *London*." He made it sound as though we were traveling direct to the underworld.

Before I could answer, he turned on his heel and stalked off around the side of the house, disappearing into the swirling mist. After watching him go, I slid into the passenger seat, glad that Josh had the heat turned up.

"Everything all right?" he asked.

"Yes. Lachlan was just saying goodbye."

Josh cast me a skeptical look. Lachlan rarely engaged in such mundane niceties of life. "And making it clear that he doesn't hold with auras and all that."

Josh grinned as he pushed the gearstick into first. He paused, peering through the windscreen at the castle. "I, for one, am very happy you can see auras. Fergus might not be here—"

When I put my hand on his, he stopped talking and turned his head to look at me.

"Drive on, Macduff," I teased. "We don't want to miss our plane."

THE END

Acknowledgments

With many thanks to my Scottish expert, Paul Mitchell, for all your help with geography and single malts.

I am deeply grateful, as always, to Susan Garzon, Maryvonne Fent, Diana Corbett and Gillian Hobbs for reading and improving this book. Your insights and comments are invaluable. And I am especially grateful for the expert guidance of Julie Smith and Mittie Staininger. It's such a pleasure working with you, thank you.

**Want to start at the beginning with
Kate's very first aura?**

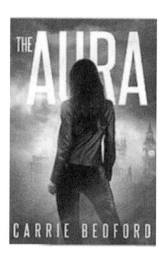

http://amzn.to/1TZGb7Q

What they said about THE AURA:

Carrie Bedford is a real find... a fine writer, an accomplished novelist, and a terrific storyteller whose characters ring true and pull us deep into the mystery." — *Shelley Singer, author of the Jake Samson-Rosie Vicente mystery series*

"... a terrific book with a likable protagonist, skilled plotting, and a supernatural spin. This gripping mystery had me hooked from the first chapter." — *Janet Dawson, author of the Jeri Howard series*

Also by Carrie Bedford

NOBILISSIMA: A Novel of Imperial Rome

The Kate Benedict Paranormal Mystery Series
THE AURA
DOUBLE BLIND
THE FLORENTINE CYPHER

A Respectful Request

We hope you enjoyed *The Scottish Connection* and wonder if you'd consider reviewing it on Goodreads, Amazon (http://amzn.to/1stEtAz), or wherever you purchased it. The author would be most grateful.

ABOUT THE AUTHOR

Born and raised in England, Carrie Bedford is the author of the award-winning *Aura* series of mysteries, along with the *Nobilissima* historical novels set in Ancient Rome. After a long career in Silicon Valley in California, she is now fully dedicated to writing fiction. She lives in Italy with her husband and their aging yellow Labrador.

Made in the USA
Monee, IL
15 September 2021